"I wouldn't choose a different path…"

Adel's voice was quiet. "It's more fulfilling than I ever dreamed to be a part of things this way. I don't want to take on another husband or his children. You're right. I don't want it. I want to see what *Gott* has on this path He set me on."

"Maybe you'll end up being Redemption's official matchmaker," Jake said.

"Maybe. But I'm not a snob."

"You're not a snob," he said quietly. "I'm sorry I said it."

"Thank you."

"But this isn't going to be a one-way street, either," he said with a smile touching his lips. "You'll be digging into my life, but I'm going to figure you out, too, Adel."

Adel rolled her eyes. "You can try, but we're better off keeping to our mission."

The grin he shot her suggested that he'd just accepted a challenge, and somehow she doubted it was only about finding his wife.

Were all bachelors this difficult?

If her goal was to become the matchmaker around here, she might be taking on more trouble than she ever imagined…

Patricia Johns is a *Publishers Weekly* bestselling author who writes from Alberta, Canada, where she lives with her husband and son. She writes Amish romances that will leave you yearning for a simpler life. You can find her at patriciajohns.com and on social media, where she loves to connect with her readers. Drop by her website and you might find your next read!

Vannetta Chapman has published over one hundred articles in Christian family magazines and received over two dozen awards from Romance Writers of America chapter groups. She discovered her love for the Amish while researching her grandfather's birthplace of Albion, Pennsylvania. Her first novel, *A Simple Amish Christmas,* quickly became a bestseller. Chapman lives in Texas Hill Country with her husband.

PATRICIA JOHNS

&

USA TODAY Bestselling Author

VANNETTA CHAPMAN

The Perfect Amish Match

2 Uplifting Stories

The Amish Matchmaker's Choice and
The Amish Twins Next Door

LOVE INSPIRED
INSPIRATIONAL ROMANCE

LOVE INSPIRED®
INSPIRATIONAL ROMANCE

Recycling programs
for this product may
not exist in your area.

ISBN-13: 978-1-335-50833-1

The Perfect Amish Match

Copyright © 2023 by Harlequin Enterprises ULC

The Amish Matchmaker's Choice
First published in 2022. This edition published in 2023.
Copyright © 2022 by Patricia Johns

The Amish Twins Next Door
First published in 2022. This edition published in 2023.
Copyright © 2022 by Vannetta Chapman

For questions and comments about the quality of this book, please contact us at CustomerService@Harlequin.com.

Harlequin Enterprises ULC
22 Adelaide St. West, 41st Floor
Toronto, Ontario M5H 4E3, Canada
www.LoveInspired.com

Printed in U.S.A.

CONTENTS

THE AMISH MATCHMAKER'S CHOICE   7
Patricia Johns

THE AMISH TWINS NEXT DOOR   219
Vannetta Chapman

THE AMISH MATCHMAKER'S CHOICE

Patricia Johns

To my husband and our son.
Thank you for your support as I write.
I love you both more than anything!

I have taught thee in the way of wisdom;
I have led thee in right paths.
—*Proverbs* 4:11

Chapter One

Jake Knussli sat on the couch next to Bishop Glick, his palms damp. The windows were cranked open, letting in a whisper of breeze, and Jake adjusted his suspenders over his shoulders. It wasn't just the hot July day that brought sweat to his brow. The bishop had an ulterior motive to suggesting the Draschel Bed and Breakfast for him to stay in while his uncle's farmhouse was fumigated.

"So you need a wife," Adel Draschel said. She looked as cool and neat as a spring day, and she regarded him with a distanced, thoughtful expression as if he were some unknown entity instead of someone she'd grown up with.

Adel was exactly his age, thirty-seven—they'd gone to school together in that one-room schoolhouse as *kinner*. The years had been kinder to her than they had been to him, he thought. With her soft figure and creamy skin, set off by auburn hair, tucked under a silky white *kapp*. There were a few lines around her eyes, but she looked more youthful than he did with the gray working its way into the stubble on his chin. Adel bent over a tray, pouring tea, one finger on the teapot's lid to keep it in place.

"*Yah*, I do need a wife," Jake replied.

"If Jacob is going to inherit that farm, then we have to find someone quickly," Bishop Glick added, stroking his wiry salt-and-pepper beard with one hand.

"You mentioned it was rushed," Adel said, passing a teacup to the bishop. "Why now? He's been back for a few months now."

"I needed to come back properly," Jake said. "I had other things to worry about, like getting baptized."

"How much time do we have now before the will runs out?" she asked.

"Two weeks," the bishop replied.

Adel blew out a breath. "Two weeks!"

She turned that skeptical stare back onto Jake, and he suppressed the urge to squirm. He wasn't asking *her* to marry him. The bishop thought she could act as matchmaker. Granted, it was a short period of time to secure a marriage match, but she didn't need to look at him like it was quite that impossible, either.

Jake fiddled with one side of his suspenders across his shoulder where his shirt was getting damp from sweat. He was still wearing his straw hat, and he pulled it off his head and scrubbed a hand through his hair, which was still growing out that last bit from an *Englisher* style.

"What did the will say exactly?" Adel asked, politely and rather pointedly ignoring his attempt to smooth out his appearance.

"It said that if I was to inherit the family farm from

Uncle Johannes," Jake said, dropping his hat onto his knee, "then I needed to be both Amish again and married within six months of his death."

"But why did Johannes do that?" she asked, shaking her head. "Do we know? He didn't have any *kinner* of his own, and Jake, you are the logical one to inherit that land. I can understand asking that you be Amish again to inherit, but married, too? Why make it difficult?"

Jake exchanged a look with the bishop. He and Bishop Glick had discussed this for a couple of hours the night before. Why would Johannes have made those stipulations in his will? Because it felt like his uncle was being obstinate, even in death.

"I think he wanted to bring Jacob home," Bishop Glick said. "And a home grows roots with marriage. I didn't know the specifics of his will until after his death, but I did pray with him before his passing. Johannes knew his time was close, and he wanted to be right with *Gott*. He spoke about wanting to make up for past wrongs. Maybe this was an attempt to do just that."

"If he wanted to make up for some wrongs, this setup seems to be creating a few new ones," Adel said, and Jake smiled in response to her wry perspective.

The bishop took a sip of his tea but didn't say anything.

"So if you aren't legally married in two weeks, then what happens to the land?" Adel asked.

"It goes to my cousin Alphie," Jake replied.

Adel leaned back in her chair, then she turned to the bishop. "And if we don't find anyone for him to marry? What then?"

"Jacob?" the bishop said, turning toward him.

What choice would Jake have? He'd been quietly looking around ever since he returned, hoping to find someone the natural way, but it was harder than he thought. If his cousin Alphie was very kind, he might let Jake run the farm with him, since it would go to him if Jake's quest to find a wife by the will's deadline failed. But it would only ever be a job, not his own property in that case. Their family dynamic had been a difficult one—nowhere near the Amish ideals.

"If we can't find me a wife, then I will thank you for trying and for the time you put into it, and I will accept that *Gott* has other plans," Jake said.

Adel nodded somberly, exhaling slowly. "And what do you have to offer a wife, Jacob?"

Jake met her gaze, and he felt a smile tickling the corners of his lips.

"You're acting like I'm a stranger, Adel. I used to pull your *kapp* strings when we were *kinner*. You know me."

"I knew a boy," Adel said, her cheeks pinking. "This is a grown man in front of me. And a little tease who used to pester us girls isn't exactly going to recommend you to the marriageable women in our area."

"Point taken," he replied, sobering. "I'm a hard worker. I have a nice little nest egg in the bank, and if I'm married in time, you can add a paid-off farm to that. I'm in relatively good condition for my age, but you'd have to be judge of that."

Adel looked away, annoyance flashing in her blue eyes, but he couldn't help himself. He wasn't the stranger she was pretending he was.

"And I don't drink, smoke or gamble," he added.

"That's a relief," she replied wryly. "But for my own

conscience, I need to ask a few questions. I hope you don't mind." Her gaze flickered toward the bishop.

"Go ahead," Bishop Glick said.

Just for a moment, Adel's perfect poise cracked, and he saw a flicker of the girl he used to know all those years ago—opinionated, fiery—and he felt a rush of satisfaction at finally getting through that prim-and-proper reserve of hers.

"Jacob, *why* are you back? Before, it seemed like you were ready to come home again." Her cheeks flushed slightly. "But now I find out that there is a will involved that was pushing you to it. Are you back just for the land?"

Jake smiled faintly. "You think that's the only reason I'm here?"

"Are you?" she asked.

"No, I'm not. I'd been thinking about coming home for a long time, but when my *daet* passed away, Uncle Johannes and I weren't exactly on good terms. There were hard words between us, and there was always some reason or other to put it off another year."

Alphie, who was actually a second cousin once removed, had filled him in on the continuing bitterness here at home whenever he got together with his cousin for a coffee. He'd known what was waiting for him.

"Will you stay Amish now?" she asked.

"*Yah.* I will stay living the Amish way. If I marry an Amish woman, I'm not going to leave the Amish life and I will stay on the farm I inherit, if that's what you're asking."

"That's exactly what I'm asking." She pressed her lips together and put her teacup down next to her. "If

I set you up with someone, I need to be able to tell her that she can trust you to be a good and Amish husband."

"I understand," he said.

"That is a very big thing for me to tell a woman," Adel said. "She would be taking my word that your character is marriageable within that short of a period of time. That is a lot to ask of me. She'd be well and truly married within a week upon my say-so."

"It's a big step," he said seriously. "It's a lot to ask of any woman. I do understand that."

Adel sighed. "The bishop speaks for you, and that should be enough." Somehow he got the sense that it wasn't, though. "And I won't be setting you up with anyone under twenty-five, for the record," she added, giving him a pointed look.

"I'm not looking to marry someone that young," Jake countered. "I'd much rather be with a woman closer to my own age."

"Good, because a woman any younger than that has other prospects still," Adel replied.

He felt the sting of those words. "Ouch."

"Sorry." Adel winced. "But asking someone to marry that quickly, she'd have to have good reason to be willing to take the risk. This is the rest of her life we're talking about, and I'm afraid that a very young woman wouldn't be able to fully understand what she was getting herself into. That would be…cruel."

"I have to agree with that." He met her gaze. Did she think he wanted some young eighteen-year-old? Because he didn't. "And I'm not marrying just anyone, either. I have a few requirements on my list, too. But for a chance to have the family farm again, I'm willing to try to find a match."

"Good. I'm glad you've been thinking about it," she said. "What are you looking for?"

"We have to find each other mutually attractive," he said. "Marriage is for life, and I want to wake up to a woman I find beautiful in spirit. And I want her to see something attractive in me, too."

"A good point," she said. "What else?"

"Like we agreed—no one too young, or too old, for that matter. I'd like a woman who is age appropriate for me. I'll trust your opinion with that."

"That's fair. What else?"

"She has to be real," he said.

Adel frowned.

"Authentic," he clarified. "She has to be open and comfortable."

"Okay." Adel nodded. "Anything else? Are you looking for a good cook? Does it matter if she has children?"

"Uh—" He exhaled slowly. "I think it would depend on the woman."

"Good." Adel nodded. "It's good that you're staying here at my bed-and-breakfast, since it will make it easier for us to save time. My sister and I sleep here in the house, and the *dawdie* house is set up for our guests. You'll be very comfortable."

"I'm sure I will be," he agreed.

"I'm going to pray on this," Adel said. "And I'll do my best."

The bishop spread his hands. "The Lord works in mysterious ways, Adel. Perhaps He has something to achieve here. The Good Book does tell us that it isn't good for a man to be alone. I think that we can extrapolate that it is the same for women. I do enjoy seeing people married for that very reason. Two are stronger than one."

The bishop looked at Adel meaningfully, and her cheeks colored again. This conversation seemed to be expressly between the two of them. Obviously, it was a subject that had come up before.

"I have my sister here, Bishop," she said with a good-humored smile. "I'm not alone, and I have no interest in getting married again. I haven't changed my mind."

"Of course." The older man pushed himself back to his feet. "Call me sentimental, but I keep on trying to find you a match, Adel. I'll consider myself a success when I finally do. Well, I will leave you to get your guest settled in. Thank you for helping, Adel. I trust your insight."

Adel nodded. "As Mark used to say, some things take a man's leadership, and others take a woman's intuition."

"He was a wise man." The bishop and Adel both nodded soberly. Then the bishop headed for the door. "Jacob, I will leave you to Adel's care. Let's see what *Gott* provides. I'll be praying, too."

Everyone would be praying, it seemed, including Jake. While the main concern seemed to be for the poor woman who was stuck with him, Jake had the most at stake here. And they'd need all the blessing and guidance they could get. Jake rose to his feet and went to the door to grab his duffel bag that he'd left on the porch, waving to Bishop Glick as he headed back out to his buggy.

Then he turned back to Adel, who was still eyeing him with an uncertain look on her face, her cup of tea balanced on a saucer in front of her.

"Now that it's just the two of us, you can be brutally honest with me," he said. "What are my chances of finding a wife?"

"I have a few ideas." A smile lifted the corners of her lips. "We'll see what we can do."

Adel heard the sound of the bishop's buggy rolling back down the drive. Bishop Glick had been a good, personal friend of her late husband's. The two men had discussed various community issues together, late into the night, and there were times that they'd called her in from the kitchen to get her perspective, as well.

"My wife is a discerning woman," Mark used to say. "And she's discreet. I'd like to hear what she thinks."

After her husband's death, the bishop still came to her from time to time, asking her opinion on issues that might relate to the women of their community, or the young people. Adel had married Mark when she was eighteen, and she hadn't been a frivolous young woman at all. She'd prayed that *Gott* would use her, and His answer had been in her deacon husband. *Gott* hadn't blessed them with *kinner* of their own, but Adel still felt needed and valued. The fact that Bishop Glick came to her for sensitive community issues like this one meant more to her than most people realized.

Adel gathered up the tea things to bring them back into the kitchen.

"Let me show you to your room, Jacob."

"My friends call me Jake," he said.

His friends...the *Englisher* ones? They'd never called him anything but Jacob here in Redemption. She stole another look at Jacob. He was tall, muscular, fit. His face was shaven, as was proper for a single Amish man, but she could make out the gray in the faint stubble on his chin. His face was tanned, and there were lines around his dark eyes that still held a certain playfulness that he'd retained since his youth. He was handsome— there, she'd just admitted it. But she wasn't crossing any lines with him. She wouldn't be calling him Jake.

"Your friends can call you anything they like, but your matchmaker calls you Jacob," Adel replied.

Jacob laughed, the sound low and warm, and she felt goose bumps rise up on her arms at the sound of it. She cast him a faint smile and led the way into the kitchen with the platter. He followed her, his bag in one hand and his hat in the other, and when she placed the platter on the counter, she turned back toward him.

"This is the kitchen, obviously. I always keep some pie, muffins and a few other snacking foods on the counter. No need to ask, just eat what you like. My sister and I have meals ready for a seven o'clock breakfast, twelve noon lunch and a six o'clock dinner."

"Thanks." Jacob glanced around. "This will be very comfortable. I appreciate it."

"Okay, well, let me take you through to your room, then."

The *dawdie* house was actually an extension that had been built onto this home a few decades ago for Mark's elderly parents, who lived there until their passing. It allowed the older people to maintain a little bit of privacy while letting the younger generation take over the main house. The Amish loved to keep family together, but they were also pragmatic about giving couples their own space. Turning the no-longer-used *dawdie* house into a room to rent had been Adel's idea.

The *dawdie* house was connected to the main house on the other end of the kitchen, which was a convenient layout giving her and Naomi privacy upstairs, but also giving their guests full access to food when they were hungry. The kitchen was the center of any home.

She led him into the guest quarters, which included a small bedroom with wide windows that let in plenty of light, and a sitting room with its own stove for heat, not needed this time of year. Instead, she had the windows wide open to let in some fresh air. Naomi had left a few brochures on the bedside table for local activities that would be of interest to tourists, and Jacob picked them up, leafed through them, then quirked an eyebrow at her.

"I'm not exactly a tourist," he said.

"We put them out for all our guests," she replied. "That must have been Naomi. She wasn't thinking."

Adel ran the bed-and-breakfast with her unmarried sister, and they'd grown much closer over the last few years.

"I am sorry about your uncle," she added. "He would have been like a father to you after your own *daet* died."

"He would have been if he cared to be," Jacob replied. "He and *Daet* never did get along. Nothing like you and Naomi do, it seems."

"Oh, Naomi and I disagree sometimes, too," Adel said. In fact, she and her sister were very different. Naomi was a plump, smiling woman who thought that

Adel was far too serious. If Naomi were left to her own devices, she'd have turned them into New Order Amish within a year, just by concessions and bright new ideas.

"So why do you refuse to get married again?" Jacob asked.

Adel shot him a wry smile. "I am not on your list of potential wives, you know."

"I would never ask you to lower yourself," he said with a teasing grin in return. "I'm curious, though."

"I've already been married," she replied.

"That's all?" he asked.

"That's all." That was all she was willing to tell him, at least. When a woman married, she took on her husband's station in life. She was his helpmeet, and through her marriage to Mark, she'd found her place in this community, and she was deeply satisfied with it. Besides, well-respected widowers weren't in such common supply as many a single woman might wish.

"Why didn't Naomi marry?" he asked.

"She's one of the Good Apples." It was the kind way of saying that she'd been passed over in the marriage market. She was too high on the tree, and while she was wonderful, no one had been able to reach her. That was how they put it delicately.

"Hmm." Jacob nodded.

"And you?" she asked. "You're not a young man anymore, and you're not married, either."

Jacob shrugged. "I was far from home. I wasn't going to marry a girl without a *kapp* and apron, was I?"

"I don't know," she replied. "You didn't come back… You might have wanted to settle down in your *Englisher* life."

Jacob grew more serious. "I might have, too, if I'd met the right woman. But I never did. It's hard to find someone who truly understands you when you're Amish born and they're…not."

"*Yah*, I could see that," she agreed.

But he had stayed far from home for a very long time, and that was worrisome. At any point, he could have come back. *Would* a marriage be enough to keep him here?

Outside, Adel heard the clop of horses' hooves, and she leaned to look out the window. Naomi was back with the groceries, and her curly red hair was coming loose from her *kapp* like it always seemed to do.

"That's my sister," Adel said. "I'll let you settle in. Come into the kitchen when you're ready for something to eat."

"Thank you."

Adel headed out of his room and closed the door behind her. She let out a little shaky breath, and then headed across the kitchen to the side door to go out and help her sister unhitch the horses. There were no specific men's jobs here—there were no men around to do them.

"How was shopping?" Adel asked as she met Naomi at the horse's side.

"The price of flour went up again," Naomi said. "And the price of sugar."

"It never seems to stop," Adel said. She remembered when Mark used to take care of the money, and Adel hadn't ever worried about the rising prices. What a burden he'd carried all that time, and she'd never known.

"Is he here?" Naomi asked, looking toward the house. She didn't need to specify whom she meant.

"*Yah*, the bishop just left," Adel replied. "Jacob is settling in." She cast her sister a look. "Why did you leave brochures in his room? He's not here as a tourist."

"I don't know," Naomi said with a twinkle in her eye. "He almost feels like one, he's been gone so long."

Adel chuckled. "Well, he's here now, and I've agreed to help find him a wife."

They worked quickly together unhitching the horses, unbuckling straps and easing the horses out of their tack to send them loose into the field to graze. The sun shone off their glossy backs, and the animals tossed their heads in enjoyment of their freedom.

Naomi opened the gate, and Adel patted their sides to encourage them to head through. They didn't need the encouragement.

Naomi pushed the gate shut again. "I'm just as single as the rest, and a paid-off farm is rather enticing."

"You aren't actually considering marrying Jacob!" Adel said.

"He's a nice-looking man…" Naomi glanced toward the house again and Adel rolled her eyes. "What?"

"Jacob is a risk!" Adel said, lowering her voice. "A big one. He went to the city to work, and just never came back. He wouldn't have come back, either, if it weren't for this inheritance. He'd still be living English. He isn't here because he believes that the Amish life is the best one, because actions speak louder than words. He's back for the land—a personal connection to it or not, that's why he's here."

"Did he say that in so many words?" Naomi asked.

"Not in so many, but…" Adel sighed. "I admit, I do think he's got good intentions. Don't get me wrong.

If he marries an Amish woman, he knows what that means, but will an Amish life ultimately make him happy? What happens if he gets bored of farm life and decides to go back to the city? Would you go with him? Or would you stay on your own and run a farm without him? He might be back, but I'm not so sure that he'll even stay. Good intentions only go so far."

Naomi nodded. "I know, I know. How long do you have to find him a wife?"

"Two weeks."

"Two weeks?" Naomi shook her head.

They headed around to the back of the buggy to get their groceries, and stopped in the shade that it cast.

"You don't sound like you think he's worth marrying," Naomi said.

Adel was silent for a moment. "The bishop thinks he's back for good."

"But what do *you* think?" Naomi pressed. "Because if you're going to sit down with one of our friends and neighbors and tell her that she should take lifelong vows to Jacob Knussli, then you'd better believe he's worth the rest of her life, because I know you. You're honest to a fault, Adel. *To a fault.*"

"I don't take the trust of our community lightly," Adel said. "People look to me to give them the honest truth, and I don't play with that."

Her position in the community wasn't one of a widow looking for a husband. Mark had left her enough money to continue supporting herself, so she didn't have that kind of desperation. And while her husband had passed, people still looked to her for the same insight and advice that she'd provided while he was alive. Their trust was sacred.

"Which is all fine and good," Naomi replied, "but you're not going to succeed in finding him a wife unless you can find something redeemable in him yourself."

Adel let out a slow breath. Her sister was right. She couldn't warn Naomi off him and then foist him on some other unsuspecting woman in their community. The bishop thought that Jacob would stay, but men didn't always have the same insight that women did. Sometimes they were downright blind to the true state of things.

"What do I do?" Adel asked.

Naomi picked up a bag of white sugar and eased it into Adel's arms. "You'll have to spend some time with him."

That was the logical conclusion, of course.

Adel waited while Naomi picked up the bag of flour, and together they headed toward the side door. Adel had her work cut out for her.

Chapter Two

Jake didn't have many items of clothing. He took his two shirts out of the bag and opened a closet, where he spotted a few wooden hangers. After shaking out his shirts, he hung them up along with his second pair of pants. When he'd returned to Redemption, the first thing he had to do was get some new clothes, and the bishop's wife had set to sewing immediately along with a couple of the older women in the community and he was set the very next day.

He was grateful—that kind of selfless giving wasn't common out there with the *Englishers*. They saw things differently—they believed in the virtue of self-suffi-ciency. It made sense, except at the end of the day when a man had provided everything for himself without the help of anyone else, he could pat himself on the back and make some comment about bootstraps, but he had no one to feel grateful toward. It closed doors between people. It didn't open them.

He looked around the little guest room. There was a clock hanging on one white wall and a calendar hanging on the other. The bed had crisp white sheets that smelled ever so faintly of bleach, a thin, faded quilt on top and a foiled chocolate resting on the center of a plump pillow. He smiled, unwrapped it and popped it into his mouth.

A somewhat springy cushioned chair was angled toward the window, outside of which he could see the stable and the chicken coop. Adel had opened the corral door and the horse plodded cooperatively inside. His own horse—or his uncle's, to be completely factual— was already in the corral. His uncle's buggy that he'd been using since his arrival sat empty, its shafts resting on two blocks of wood. A couple of minutes later, he heard the door open and shut, and from the kitchen, he could hear the murmur of women's voices, although he couldn't make out the words. Cupboards clicking closed resonated clearly through the walls.

This was a much nicer room than the one he'd been sleeping in at his uncle's farmhouse. It still felt strange. He'd thought about returning home to Redemption time and time again, and he'd never felt quite ready to let go of everything he'd learned to enjoy in the *Englisher* world. Even now after nearly six months of living Amish again, his fingers itched for a cell phone. He had this undeniable urge to scroll through social media feeds and let his mind go blank, or just turn on a TV and listen to the jangle of a rerun in the background. He was praying for *Gott* to take that away. But here with the Amish, he had nothing but quiet, community and no distraction from facing the reality of his own choices.

All the same, he was hungry.

Jake opened the door and stepped out into a short hallway that led into the kitchen. Adel and Naomi had their backs to him as they put some bags of dried goods up into a cupboard. Adel was slimmer than Naomi, but he'd recognize Naomi's wild curls anywhere.

"Hi, Naomi," Jake said.

Both women turned, and Adel's cheeks were pink. Naomi shot him a grin.

"Hi, Jacob." Naomi put her hands on her hips. "I hear there's a wedding coming up."

If only it were that easy. It seemed less complicated when he'd gotten the call from the lawyer six months ago than it did now.

"Well, we'll see," he replied. "I'm trusting my future to the hands of Adel."

Jake caught Adel's eye, and she picked up a towel and wiped her hands, avoiding his look. Was it possible that he was able to discomfit the perfectly prim Adel? Some primal part of him enjoyed that thought. She had a rather ageless look about her—her skin smooth and creamy, but her eyes holding more experience than she should for her years. And she was distractingly beautiful.

"*Yah*, my sister the matchmaker," Naomi said, shaking her head. "I suppose she does have a lot of experience in marriage, and in working with the community. Still, if she's going to be a matchmaker now, maybe she can find me a nice single man who likes to eat."

"I'm only his matchmaker at the moment," Adel said with a chuckle. "Although it might be a nice new occupation—helping young people find love."

"Young people." Naomi mouthed the words at Jake and rolled her eyes. Naomi was five years younger than Jake and Adel were, making her thirty-two, he realized. None of them as young as they used to be.

"We aren't that old, Adel," he said jokingly. "*I'm* not that old."

"I've buried a husband already," she replied and this time she met his gaze evenly. His humor evaporated.

"Right." He cleared his throat. "I'm sorry."

Adel had gone through more than the rest of them had, and it would have changed her. It certainly explained those eyes that seemed to be brimming with more life experience than anyone else he knew. And maybe she didn't want any reassurances that she was just the same, because she wasn't.

"Naomi and I were talking before we came in," Adel said. "And she had a good point."

Jake glanced toward Naomi, but this time she wasn't joking around.

"We don't really know you anymore," Naomi said.

"And I should know you a lot better if I'm going to introduce you as a potential husband for a woman in this community," Adel added.

"That's fair," he agreed. "What did you have in mind?"

"Well, we are rather stuck for time," Adel said. "We're hosting an Amish tour that is coming through this evening, but Naomi can take care of that, I think. Why don't we have an early supper, and then you and I can go take a look at your family's farm? The more information I have, the better."

"I don't make sense to you, do I?" he asked.

"No, you don't," she agreed.

He nodded, and a smile toyed at his lips. "The feeling is mutual."

Adel was beautiful, soft, intelligent and running her own bed-and-breakfast. She was trusted with sensitive situations by the bishop. But she was choosing a single life, not a choice that many Amish women made voluntarily. She was a tangle of contradictions.

"Well…" Adel turned toward the cupboards. "Let's get something to eat, and then we can head out."

The horse, a ten-year-old Clydesdale named Samson, pulled the buggy easily without even seeming to notice the extra weight behind him. He plodded along, his tail swishing in the evening breeze, and Jake leaned back, the reins loose in his hands.

Adel was here to size him up. It was her job to judge him, figure him out, decide if he was worthy enough for one of their local women. This shouldn't annoy him, but it did just a little bit.

"Is there anyone you're interested in?" Adel asked. "You've been back for a few months. Are there any single women who have caught your eye?"

"I've talked to some," he said. He rattled off a few names. "But if there wasn't a spark without a farm, it's a little insulting to try again with one, you know?"

She nodded. "That's understandable. Does this scare you at all, having to choose a woman this quickly—vow to love and take care of her for the rest of your life after knowing her a matter of days?"

He cast her a wry smile. "Yes. Very much."

"Then why are you doing it?" she asked.

Jake let out a slow breath. "I grew up on that farm. I was born there. I've worked the last few months to put it back together again, and it's been a huge amount of work."

He thought back to his childhood after his mother

passed away. It had been just the three of them—*Daet*, Uncle Johannes and Jake. They'd worked the farm together, and kept house together, too. Their house had started to get cluttered right away without a woman living with them. Women didn't like clutter—they picked things up, put them away, set them aside to be brought to someone else who could use them. But without *Mamm*, Jake, his father and his uncle used to sit by the wood-stove during cold evenings, and Uncle Johannes would read aloud from the *Budget* newspaper, updating them on all the goings-on in the surrounding communities. Something had obviously gone very wrong, however, because a cluttered farmhouse had turned into a farm-house that was alarmingly full of things—old copies of the *Budget,* stacks of milk bottle crates, worn-out shoes that were piled up in pairs, empty bailing twine spools…from floorboards to rafters, the house was simply full.

"I couldn't wait to get out of Redemption when I was a teenager," he went on. "The tension between my *daet* and uncle was unbearable. I took that factory job in the city knowing full well it wasn't the kind of place a good Amish man lived, but it got me off that farm and gave me a chance to build something of my own." Jake batted a swarm of tiny flies away from his face. "But it's funny—you can't start over as easily as you think. That land is Knussli land. It belonged to my great-grandfather, my grandfather, my uncle… I never knew how to come home, but my uncle's frustrating will gave me a reason to try. If I don't get that land back, I'm losing a bigger part of myself than I ever realized. I'm Amish. I might be disillusioned, and I might have some tough memories, but it's who I am. That land is part of my heritage."

"Didn't you at least try to talk to your *daet* or your uncle?" Adel asked.

His mind went back to those difficult years. "I used to meet up with Alphie for a coffee in town, and he'd fill me in on the family drama."

"What kind of drama?" she asked.

"Oh, just how they felt about me after I left, things they were saying when they saw Alphie—that kind of thing."

"So you didn't talk to your *daet*?" she asked.

"My *daet* was telling everyone else that he was so deeply disappointed in me that he didn't want to see me unless I was fully penitent," he replied.

"I honestly never heard him say anything like that," Adel said. "All I ever heard your *daet* say was how he missed you."

Jake's gaze flickered in her direction. "Really?"

"Yah." She eyed him. "Are you telling me that you stayed away because of what Alphie was telling you?"

Jake swung his attention out the other side of the buggy, shielding his face from view. "He was sympathetic to my situation. He understood better than anyone else did."

"I'm sorry to say this, Jake, but if he was so sympathetic to what you were going through, he should have helped you to fix your relationship with your *daet* while you still had time."

"That did occur to me a few times," Jake said. "After the funeral, I tried to talk to my uncle, but it was no use. Alphie had been right about his attitude, so I figured he had probably been right about my *daet*'s, too."

"And now?" she asked. "Johannes left you the farm. I mean, he didn't make it easy, but he could just as easily have left it to Alphie."

"Yah..." He sighed. "I shouldn't have been listening to my cousin instead of talking to people directly. I was being a coward. I didn't want to face their anger. And that was both wrong of me and cowardly."

"Was Alphie talking to Johannes and your father on your behalf, too?" she asked.

"Not that I asked him to, but I suppose that's how it works when someone is in the middle, isn't it?" He shot her a forlorn look. "I made a mistake. I should have come back sooner and faced my own father. I should have."

"Are you close with Alphie now?" she asked.

"We talked a bit over the last few month, but—" He sighed. "I'm not foolish enough to empty my heart to him again. Besides, we're now in competition for that land, aren't we? If I can't get married, he gets it." He was silent for a moment. "But you know, I don't think Alphie was trying to do any damage. I think my leaving was the most interesting thing going on here in Redemption, and he got the inside scoop on it. He didn't mean harm..."

"But he also wasn't trying to fix it," she countered. "He wasn't making peace."

"True." He pressed his lips together grimly. "I'll have to sort things out with my cousin one of these days. Eventually. I haven't gotten there yet."

"I think you should," she said.

"The thing is, I stayed away because I didn't want to face all the judgment and anger that I was sure was waiting for me, and the longer you stay away, the more you slide into a completely different way of life. I mean, I started out using electricity for the stove and fridge— because it was a rental, and anything else wouldn't be allowed. And after a year, I had a cell phone, a TV, a laptop computer… And every single one of them had come with a very sincere excuse, you know?"

"I suppose that's how it works," she said.

"I never meant to slide that far. But when you're out there, it makes sense. It's just…life."

"It didn't feel empty? Wrong?" she asked.

"No. It was just how people lived. It was how they worked in their community. People communicated with phones and internet. They got to each other's homes in cars and buses. It didn't feel wrong."

"Does it feel wrong now?" she asked softly.

He wouldn't lie. "No. I mean, it isn't part of the Amish life that I'm choosing, but *wrong* is a strong word. Let's say it isn't something I'm choosing."

He was talking too much. He hadn't actually intended to say so much, but besides the bishop, Adel was the first person he'd encountered in years who'd asked, or who understood how different his life had become.

"That was all rather personal," he added, and he glanced over at her to find her softened gaze locked on him. "I'm not trying to put you into the middle here, either. I—"

"I'm used to keeping confidences," she said quietly.

That's right—she had been the deacon's wife, and there was something of that role that had stuck to her.

"I have to admit," he said. "My family problems aside, what I want most is to find a woman I fall in love with—hat over boot nails. That's why I waited so long to tell anyone about that part of the will. I wanted a woman to fall for me without the money as incentive. But I'm running out of time, so maybe it'll happen, like Isaac and Rebecca did in the Bible—with an introduction."

"You think *Gott* is working in mysterious ways?" she asked.

"Well, I'm back in Redemption, aren't I?" Jake shrugged. "And after everything that's happened, if that isn't *Gott* working, I don't know what is."

They came up over a hill, and tumbling across the landscape was the familiar patchwork of the Knussli family farm. There was a field of oats flanked by another field of wheat, and the pasture for what used to be a rather large herd, but now was only about thirty head of cattle. The red barn was worn, and even from this distance he could see the gray smudges against the red paint. The sun was lowering, the rays were long and golden, warming up the entire scene below them, and Jake's heart gave a squeeze.

Home. For better or for worse, this farm was the place that held his childhood memories, his adolescent hopes, and those dreams he used to have when lying in the bedroom of that apartment in the city, the ones where he could smell the country air and it was more real than even being there. He'd hated this place at some points in his life, and he'd loved it in equal measure, but it was home.

Adel waited as Jacob unhitched the horse and she surveyed the front yard. It needed work—a flower garden seemed to have been abandoned years ago, because she could see some ornamental onion and catmint flowers scattered around the grass that hadn't been mown in some time. Once upon a time, those perennial flowers would have been corralled in a little garden instead of traveling across the yard. There had been a woman here—Jacob's mother. But that was long ago, and if all went according to the bishop's plans, at least, there would be a woman here again soon. It only seemed right. This place was badly in need of a wife's touch.

The house was covered in a yellow tent—the work of the fumigators—but beyond, she could see the stable, the barn, a chicken house and even a covered area for storing hay farther on. It was a decent farm.

Adel looked back toward Jacob. His Amish clothes fit him well with his broad shoulders, and he had an easy way of standing with all his weight on one leg that made her recognize just how handsome he was. That was something she'd noticed repeatedly over the last few months since his return. Jacob was handsome in a way that tugged at her. This last decade seemed to have hardened Jake, though, solidified him into a more powerful version of himself. He wasn't a safe Amish man, but he was attractive. She shouldn't be noticing that—not the way she was, at least. If he was an attractive option for another woman, that was good. But not for her.

Jacob had finished with the horse, and he had both thumbs in his suspenders, looking out across the fields. As if he could feel her scrutiny, he suddenly turned toward her, his dark gaze catching hers. She felt her cheeks heat, and she smoothed her apron down—a nervous gesture. He jutted his chin toward the fields in a silent invitation, and a smile quirked up one side of his mouth.

Adel headed in his direction, and she fell into step beside him as he led the way. They went out a side gate that he secured behind them after Adel had passed through. She could see him relaxing as he walked.

"The barn needs a lot of work," Jacob said. "More than just a paint job. The roof needs to be redone."

"Hmm." Adel nodded. "But you could take care of that easily enough."

"*Yah*, I can replace a roof. I decided to wait until it's mine, though. I've invested enough of my own money into making this place more livable, but I don't want to put in too much if it's not going to be mine, you know? Alphie can deal with new roofs if he's going to inherit it." He slowed to a stop, his gaze locked on the barn. "Do you want to see inside?"

"I suppose," she replied.

Adel followed his lead, and they headed in that direction.

"A wife will be spending most of her time in the house, though," she said.

"*Yah*, but I can't show you inside there right now. Besides, I think a woman could appreciate a farm that can support itself, too," Jacob replied. "Can't she?"

"Of course."

"The house needs a lot of work, though. I've cleaned up some of it. My uncle never did fix it up inside, and he filled it up with all sorts of trash. I don't know what happened, because when it was the three of us, we kept things in pretty good repair. I mean, it was cluttered, but it wasn't as bad as I found it."

"Your cousin didn't warn you about that?" she asked.

"Not a word." He pressed his lips together in a look of frustration. "I don't suppose a woman looks forward to coming to a run-down house, an unstocked kitchen and rooms that are still filled with garbage."

"You didn't manage to clean it out?" she asked.

"I was running the farm on my own." He sighed. "I managed to clean out some of it. Not enough."

He dropped his gaze, and she could see the shame shining in his eyes. But it wasn't his fault. He'd come home to this mess—he hadn't created it himself.

"A good woman will take it as a challenge and make a home out of it," Adel said with more certainty than she felt.

"But if a woman is accepting a rushed marriage proposal, the very least she could expect is a decent kitchen," Jacob said.

They arrived at the barn, and he pulled the door wide and stepped inside first, holding it open for her behind him. He strode inside, turned in a full circle, then pulled off his hat and looked upward. His not-quite-Amish haircut was still disconcerting for her.

"The struts are still good," Jacob said. "See?"

She looked up, mostly out of a cooperative instinct, but apparently she wasn't looking in the right place because he sighed audibly and came up beside her. He put warm hands on her shoulders, pivoting her, and directed her attention upward.

"There—" He pointed at the beams that braced the roof. "Still strong."

He didn't move his hands right away, and she found herself enjoying the warm gentleness of his touch. Then his hands fell away from her shoulders, and she let out a cautious breath.

"When I was about ten, I climbed up there from the hayloft," Jake said. "I used to like to read up there, so high above everything. I fell one evening and broke my collarbone. That was after my mom died."

"Ouch," she murmured, then paused before asking, "How old were you when your mother died?"

"Eight." He glanced toward her, then shrugged. "And you're probably thinking that if I had a mother at home, she wouldn't have let me do that. And you'd be right."

"What was she like?" Adel asked.

"I don't remember much." He glanced over at her, his expression thoughtful. "The *Englishers* have photos. I know we don't do that, but what I wouldn't give for a picture of my *mamm* right about now…"

"You must remember something, though," she said.

"I do. I remember the kitchen being brighter, and everything being cleaner. I remember sunlight feeling warmer, and birdsong being sweeter… There was just something about those years when we had *mamm* that made everything better." He licked his lips, then shrugged. "I have a couple of concrete memories. One of them, I must have been pretty young, because I remember playing with her apron strings and her mixing something in this white bowl with a red stripe around it. She used that bowl for everything. I remember her hands, too. Her fingers were always cool, and that felt nice on my head when I was sick… I remember lying in my bed upstairs, and listening to my mother sing while she worked."

"That's beautiful."

"She was a terrible singer." Jacob chuckled. "It's a nice memory now, but she was so off-key, and she never seemed to know."

"Maybe she didn't care," Adel replied.

Jacob shrugged in acceptance. "When *Mamm* died, things changed right away. I had some aunts who would come by and keep the garden, do some cooking, do our laundry… But that couldn't last forever. We figured out how to keep things running, but we did it in a man's way."

"What's a man's way?" she asked.

"The cooking is quicker, I'll tell you that," he said. "Lots of stews and pots of soup. As for laundry, I don't think we ever got our whites all the way white again. And my *daet* and uncle didn't much care if I climbed up to the rafters in the barn, so long as I got my chores done."

"It sounds very lonely."

"You don't see too many Amish only-child families, do you?" The joking was back in his eyes. He was backing away from the personal memories. "I had no siblings to tell on me."

A younger sibling was an early warning system for all sorts of shenanigans. Being the fourth of eight children in her family, she'd been both the tattler and the annoyed older sibling in that arrangement. But Jacob's childhood had been exceptionally solitary.

"Come on," he said. "I'm just getting a feel for the state of the place. If it's going to be mine, I'll need to get to work on getting it back into shape."

She saw the way his eyes lit up as he said it, and she

had to wonder what would happen if this farm didn't come to him. How much would that hurt?

"Will you stay in Redemption if you don't get the farm?" she asked.

Jacob rubbed a hand over his chin, his gaze still moving over the inside of the barn. "That's something to think about, isn't it? I'd have to face Alphie having the land that should have been mine…"

But he didn't finish the thought.

"The answer to that matters," she said quietly. She needed a clear understanding of where he stood.

Jacob glanced down at her. "I don't like this balance between us, Adel."

"What balance?" she asked. "I'm your matchmaker."

"You were my schoolmate," he replied.

"We're a long way from school days, Jacob."

"I'm Jake!" He shook his head. "Adel, I'm Jake… Say it."

"Jake," she conceded.

"Thank you." He scrubbed a hand through his hair and replaced his hat. "And while you're perfectly comfortable there trying to figure me out, I don't like this. You're just as much of a puzzle to me, you know."

"Me?" Adel put her hands on her hips. "There's nothing to sort out. I'm widowed, and I've been asked to help you find a wife. That's all that matters."

"Widowed—" He waggled a finger at her. "You use that as a very convenient shield. You can cut off any conversation that gets uncomfortable for you by pulling that up. You lost your husband—discussion over."

"What discussion, Jacob?" She winced. "I mean, Jake…"

"Maybe I want a few answers from you, as well," he said.

"Like what?"

"Like why *you're* still single," he said.

Her heart skipped a beat, and she forced what she hoped was an easy smile. "I told you. I've already been married."

This was her well-thought-out answer. It had sufficed for everyone else...

"But that doesn't add up. You're still young. Your life is over?" He shook his head. "One wedding, you tragically lose your husband, and you shut down for the rest of your life?"

"I haven't shut down!" Her anger was rising now, too. "I have a life here! I'm respected! I'm a part of things!"

"And you wouldn't be if you got married again?" He crossed his arms, watching her face a little too closely for her liking. "We're Amish. Life centers on family— marriages, kids..."

"I gained something with my marriage to Mark," she said, and she pressed her lips together. She didn't want to talk to him about that.

"Respect," he said.

So he'd noticed? She let out a slow breath. "Yes."

"And you think you'd lose that if you married someone else."

"I wouldn't be the deacon's wife anymore, would I?" she said. "Or the deacon's widow. I'd be someone else's wife."

"Is that such a bad thing?" he asked. He waited a beat, then he nodded. "I see."

"You see what?" she asked.

"Adel." He leaned closer. "You're a snob."

"What?" She felt the blood rush from her face. "I am no such thing!"

"Yes, you are," he said. "You don't want to be some humble farmer's wife, or the wife of a shopkeeper. You don't want to be a stepmother, either, I imagine. You like being the woman that the community looks to for wisdom and insight into things. You'd rather be the woman who lives alone with the community's awe than one who pours all that energy into her own home. You like the *position*."

"That is not the Amish way," she said tartly. "You may have forgotten."

"We may be Amish and live by our ideals, but we're human, too, Adel."

"You've been away a long time," she countered. "Maybe that's the *Englisher* way of seeing things seeping in."

"*You're* human, Adel." His voice dropped, and he didn't look cowed, or derailed. He took a step closer to her, and she felt her breath catch in her throat. He didn't scare her, but she was rather struck by the size of him.

"I'm not arguing about whether or not I'm human," she said. "I'm flesh and blood like you are, but that doesn't mean I'm a snob, either! I have the right to choose who I marry, if I marry, and whether or not I want to dedicate my life to any particular man!" Her voice shook. "It is not my duty to keep house and raise the children of any man who needs a wife. It is my duty, however, to live the life *Gott* gave me with as much faith, hope and charity that I can!"

Jake nodded. "Agreed."

"Really?" She was prepared for more argument than that, and she halfway wished he'd put up more of a fight, because she was ready to give him one.

"You don't have to take on any man as your duty in life," he said. "I fully agree with that. But you also don't have to hide behind your widowhood, either."

"It isn't hiding," she said simply. "You're right—my marriage to Mark did change things. But it isn't snobbery. When Mark and I weren't able to have *kinner*, I prayed that *Gott* would use me in a different way. And He did! Without babies of my own to care for, I was available to help others in their times of need. I could be there for women when they were struggling with their own difficulties. I was able to be there for children who needed to talk things out, or teenagers who were frustrated with our rules. Do you know how they say that if we could see the path *Gott* planned for us, we'd never choose a different one?"

"Yah." Jake's dark gaze was still locked on her face.

"I wouldn't choose a different one, Jake," she said quietly. "It's more fulfilling than I ever dreamed to be a part of things this way. I don't want to take on another husband or his children. You're right. I don't want it. I want to see what *Gott* has on this path He set me on."

"Maybe you'll end up being Redemption's official matchmaker," he said.

"Maybe. But I'm not a snob."

It mattered to Adel that he know that. She didn't think she was better than anyone, but sometimes *Gott* put people on the outside of the circle for a reason.

"You're not a snob," he said quietly. "I'm sorry I said it."

"Thank you."

"But this isn't going to be a one-way street, either," he said with a smile touching his lips. "You'll be digging into my life, but I'm going to figure you out, too, Adel."

Adel rolled her eyes. "You can try, but we don't have much time to find you a legal wife. We're better off keeping to our mission."

The grin he shot her suggested that he'd just accepted a challenge, and somehow she doubted it was only about finding his wife.

Were all bachelors this difficult? If her goal was to become the matchmaker around here, she might be taking on more trouble than she ever imagined.

Chapter Three

Jake took one more look up at the barn roof. He could see the sections that were weak and would leak like a colander again during the next big rainstorm. He'd already stretched big, blue tarps over the hay and supplies that lay beneath them, and he felt a wave of frustration toward his late uncle.

Or had Johannes's health been failing for longer than anyone knew? He couldn't help the nagging sense of guilt that if Jake had at least visited, he would have known if his uncle needed more help than he'd been able to hire. Uncle Johannes hadn't been an easy man to deal with, but he'd been family. Jake could have come to his aid.

But he couldn't change that now. Jake nodded toward the barn door.

"So, more about you—" Jake said, holding the barn door open for her as they went back outside into the summer sunlight.

"You're serious about trying to figure me out?" she asked.

The sun felt good on his shoulders, and he led the way up to the fence that separated pasture from the barnyard. He gave the rails a shake, and a few were loose. Jake looked down the line of fencing. He'd already fixed some broken sections, and now it was sturdy.

"Who tried to court you after your husband died?" he asked, turning back toward her.

She blinked at him, then swallowed. By her reaction, he'd hit on it, it seemed.

"What do you mean?" she asked.

As if he didn't know anything about how men thought. The single men would have taken notice when Adel became a widow.

"It was someone," Jake said, and when she looked ready to protest, he added, "I'm looking at you, Adel, and you're gorgeous. Forgive me for saying it so bluntly—that's admittedly very English of me to do— but you are not a woman who'd just melt into the background. You never were. So knowing how men work, I know that there would have been men who tried to court you. There's no question about that. I'm just curious who it was."

She smiled faintly. "You flatter me."

"Not at all," he replied soberly. "I tell the truth. And I'm right, aren't I?"

She gave him one of those sidelong looks he was growing to associate with her. "Two men, actually. First, there was Duncan Huyard, who's five years younger than me and couldn't hold down a job to save his life."

"Ouch." Jake cast her a sympathetic look. "Not any woman's ideal. Was there pressure for you to accept him?"

Adel shook her head. "No, everyone knew why I didn't want to marry him. But it was the second one who tried courting me, Abner Graber, that everyone thought I should accept."

Abner... An image rose in his mind of a meaty, tall man with a round, unfriendly face. He was older than they were, and very stern. That was all that Jake remembered of him.

"Didn't he marry that young woman—"

"Susanna, *yah*," Adel said. "They had six *kinner* in five years—two sets of twins. She died in childbirth with the last baby—it was born prematurely six months after her last birth."

Jake's heart stopped in his chest. "What?"

That math was...cruel. What husband didn't think about those things?

"*Yah*... Abner wanted a houseful of *kinner*, and I don't think he cared one bit about the health of that poor girl he married. Anyway, regardless of those circumstances, he was in want of a wife, and he thought I would do nicely to take care of those six *kinner* for him."

He could see the flutter of her pulse at the base of her neck and the way her cheeks paled—that marriage proposal had scared her, and he could understand why.

"He wouldn't have been a good husband," Jake confirmed.

"Not everyone agreed with that, though. He works hard," she said. "He has a well-kept farm. His wife never lacked for material for sewing or food in her pantry."

But he was a bully.

"No one else saw the warning signs in Abner?" he asked.

"Maybe they didn't think I had any reason to complain," she replied. "I was widowed and in need of a husband. He was a widower in need of a wife. He was a hard worker, and so was I. They saw no problem."

"Maybe they thought you'd improve him," he said.

"If they thought that, they were being very foolish, indeed." Adel paused. "Did no one try to get *you* married?"

"Oh, my *daet* asked me to come home and meet a nice girl a couple of times," he replied. He remembered the letters—the pleading between the lines. But he couldn't do it. Taking a wife was a huge responsibility both financially and emotionally. He couldn't just choose a nice girl and decide to love her.

But that was what he was doing now, wasn't it?

"You never did come back and look for a girl, though," Adel said. "Not that I saw."

"I wasn't ready," he replied.

"Are you now?" she asked.

Jake sobered. That was a good question. Because the responsibility hadn't changed. He'd need to provide for a wife, and for their *kinner*. He'd need to be there for her emotionally, too, and make her happy on a heart level. That was harder to guarantee.

But all the same, when he thought about this farm, it wasn't from the days of just the three men running things. It was a whisper from the past that tugged at him, a time when the house was filled with baking and a woman's laughter. It was from a time when brilliantly white laundry fluttered out on the line.

"I'm ready to have a bright kitchen again," he said quietly. "I'm ready to have a woman's touch in my home, and her cooking on the table. I'm ready to hear singing when she doesn't know I'm listening…"

He cleared his throat. That was too much—why did he keep doing that? When he looked over at Adel, he saw sympathy in her eyes.

"A woman is the heart of a home," he said. "I'm no fool."

And whether he was ready to be the husband and father a family needed no longer mattered. There was a beautiful life waiting for a man who was willing to step up and take it, but it did require a step up. A man couldn't drag a woman down to his level. He had to accept the responsibilities that came with a family and become the stable provider they needed.

With this farm, he could do it.

Without the farm? He felt a dark cloud at the prospect of losing this land, and he knew that was dangerous. But if he didn't have the family farm, he'd be back at the beginning again, with the best-paying job he could get being in the city. So *yah*, he was ready for a wife and family, but he was afraid to want it too badly. The longing began in a place that was too deep. That disappointment would hurt if it didn't work out.

Jake looked down to see Adel leaning against the fence next to him. The sun shone off the bit of hair that was visible, and she smelled sweet, but what made women smell that way, he didn't know. It was like they were from a different world, almost.

"I'm going to tell you the truth," he said quietly. "The house is in bad shape. There's a whole bedroom filled up with junk, and most of the dishes are broken and thrown out, so I think there's about four plates all together that are left, and some big pots that have been burned too often. My uncle repaired some cushions on the couch with duct tape…" He looked down at Adel thoughtfully. "I was glad that the fumigation wasn't done yet, because I didn't want to show you that."

There were a lot of painful, tender places in his memory that he didn't want to show her, too. He wasn't the most polished-up man, either. He'd run away from the family *Gott* gave him, and backslid down to living like a common *Englisher*. Whoever married him was going to get the sad reality, in both house and husband.

"It's probably best to be up-front about the state of the house," Adel said.

"I suppose so," he agreed. "But it won't endear her to me, I'm sure."

"You said you wanted love," she said. "If a woman loves you, she'll roll up her sleeves."

Jake looked down at her. *"Yah?"*

"Yah." She nodded. "But love… That's not something I can guarantee, is it? I can work to find you a wife, but it'll be up to you to secure her heart."

Jake looked back out at the cows, his thoughts in tangles. He could see the reason why this community saw Adel as a wise woman. She had more answers than he did.

"All the same, I'd like to clean out the kitchen, at least," he said. "I haven't done that yet. I'm more comfortable fixing fences and tending cattle."

"Fixing the kitchen would be nice," she said.

"Even if I'm cleaning it out for Alphie," he said ruefully. "There will be a woman in that kitchen eventually, and leaving it in the state it's in feels wrong."

"You're a decent man," she said.

"Decent enough to put your conscience at ease about recommending me as a husband to some local woman?" he asked.

"Yah." Her eyes crinkled as she smiled, and she shaded her eyes to look up at him. "I think you'll do nicely. It's a matter of picking the right woman now."

Adel seemed a little gentler, less reserved. Was that because she'd decided he wasn't quite the danger she had suspected? Or was she just feeling sorry for him?

"Thank you," he said.

And here was hoping that *Gott* was using this for His own purposes, because a marriage was for life, and this decision would be a fast one. It would be awful to marry a woman and find himself in an unhappy union for the rest of his life for the sake of this land.

This farm might be his home, but a woman would be its beating heart.

Back at the house, Adel checked the chicken legs in the oven. Naomi made a delicious homemade barbecue sauce, and the meat was roasting gently, the aroma making Adel's stomach grumble. The tour group had already come and left, and Naomi stood at the kitchen sink washing plates from their visit.

Jake's words had stuck with her, though, about the things he was ready for in his life. He wanted the beauty back—the feminine touch about a home—and that had stabbed at her heart. How much had Jake suffered when the community didn't see? There were times when privacy covered up pain, like in the case of Abner's young wife. Adel needed to learn from this, and be more vigilant.

"I sold about fifteen jars of jam," Naomi said, pulling Adel's attention back. "So that, added to the fee from the tour group, made it a successful day."

"Did you write it all out in our ledger?" Adel asked.

Naomi cast her a long-suffering look. "*Yah*, Adel."

Adel chuckled. "Sorry. Of course you did."

"What has you stressed?" Naomi asked. "You only start trying to control every detail when you're upset about something."

"I'm not upset, but I am realizing just how big of a job this is to find a wife for Jake," Adel said. "He's been through a lot, and he'll need a wife who will understand him on a heart level."

"He needs a legal wife who will get him that farm," Naomi countered. "That's what this is about."

"It's more than that," Adel replied. "He wants…a real marriage."

"In two weeks?" Naomi shook her head. "That's asking a lot."

"All the same, those vows are for life. It's best to enter into a marriage soberly," she replied.

The women exchanged a silent look, and Naomi turned back to washing the dishes.

"If I recall, you didn't know Mark very well when you married him," Naomi said. She rinsed a dish and put it in the rack.

Adel thought back to when she'd met Mark. It had all been very proper. He was fifteen years older than she was, and he'd been introduced to her at a wedding.

They'd talked for a few minutes, and he'd asked if he could see her again. He'd called on her a few times, visits with her parents in the room, and then he'd asked her out for a buggy ride where he'd proposed. Somehow, none of it had seemed frightening. He'd always been respectful of her feelings and listening attentively when she talked. He'd had a dry sense of humor, and he'd never treated her as if she wouldn't understand his jokes. Adel had liked Mark from the start—he was funny, thoughtful and gentle. There was nothing to be scared of in a husband like that.

Would other women feel the same way about Jake, though? He was physically much bigger than Mark had been, and his personality was stronger. He had a way of looking at Adel that locked her to the spot. There was nothing gentle and unassuming about Jake. He was all testosterone and longing.

"Mark was different," Adel said. "He was very gentle by nature, and very thoughtful and bookish. If he wasn't out with the horses, he was reading."

"Well, what is a woman looking for in a husband?" Naomi pulled the plug in the sink and turned around to face Adel as she dried her hands. "She needs a man who will provide, and that farm will do the trick."

"She'll be looking for a good father for her children, too," Adel added.

"*Yah*, that's important. And a man who will be faithfully Amish." They exchanged another look. "Will he stay in the community?"

Adel lifted a lid on a pot on the stove, looking down into a bubbling pot of potatoes. "I think so, but he's got his own views on things. He'll be Amish, but he won't be staunch, if you know what I mean."

"What views?" Naomi asked.

"He's lived with the *Englishers* for a long time," Adel said. "He doesn't have the aversion to *Englisher* ways that might feel a little safer."

"He is a good-looking man, though," Naomi said. "Very good-looking."

Adel felt her cheeks warm. He was—there was no denying it. "Looks aren't everything, Naomi."

"Perhaps not, but I happen to think that marriage is about more than raising *kinner*," Naomi replied. "It's about the time together as a husband and wife, too."

Adel let out a slow breath. "Before I told you that you shouldn't consider Jake for yourself, and I think I was wrong. If you're interested in him, I could see what he thinks about you."

"Me?" Naomi laughed and shook her head. "No, not me."

"You've changed your mind?" she asked.

"Yes, I have."

"Because he's a risk," Adel agreed.

"No, not because of that." Naomi took some dinner plates out of the cupboard and headed toward their thick, wooden kitchen table. "I'd be stupid indeed to even consider a man who looked at another woman the way he does."

Adel frowned. "He ogles women? I didn't see that."

This might change things. Had she missed out on some glaring character flaws, blinded by her own softening feelings for the man?

"Adel, he doesn't look at other women in the plural," Naomi said, casting her a smile. "He looks at you."

"Me?" Adel shook her head. "I drive him crazy, and he doesn't like that I'm the one set up as judge over him in finding him a wife."

"All of that might be true," Naomi replied. "But he looks at you like… He looks at you the way a man working in the sun all day looks at a tall glass of water."

A smile turned up her sister's lips, and Naomi's eyes sparkled with repressed laughter.

Adel blinked at her sister. "That's not true."

"You think I'd pass up on a hand-delivered husband complete with a paid-off farm for nothing?" Naomi shook her head. "You might not be interested in him, Adel, but I'm not tying myself for life to a man who looks at my sister like *that*."

"I'm sorry, if I——" Adel started.

"Adel, I'm not upset," Naomi said. "I honestly think you should consider him for yourself."

That was easy enough for her sister to say. But Adel had no interest in tying herself to a new husband right now, either. She'd gone five years in this new path of hers that fulfilled her in this strange, unexpected way, and simply giving it up because a man came along who was handsome and in need of a wife didn't change anything.

"Not me," Adel replied. "But I will find him a good woman. He deserves that much."

Naomi nodded. "Do you have anyone in mind?"

"Verna Kauffman is about the right age, and she's never been married," Adel said.

Naomi was silent.

"Delia Swarey needs a *daet* for her four boys," Adel went on. "They've been taking care of things on their own, but they'll be grown and getting married soon enough. She needs a husband of her own again."

"And the younger women?" Naomi asked.

Adel firmly shook her head. "The thing with the young women is that they have every opportunity to find a boy they know well, and do things the old-fashioned way. They should have that chance to get to know someone, and be courted... Because marriage isn't easy, and going from a first meeting to man and wife in a matter of a week will not be easy on anyone. That isn't fair to a girl with her whole life ahead of her."

The thought of a girl of eighteen walking into a run-down mess of a house was heartbreaking to even consider. Adel had gotten married that young, but Mark had been prepared. There had been a lovely kitchen waiting for her, all clean and organized by her mother-in-law.

But nothing was going to be properly ready for this wife, and while a community would pitch in to help get things spruced back up if they found out Jake needed it, that would take time. And it would take a special kind of strength from the woman who stepped into marriage that way.

Strength, or foolhardiness, Adel wasn't sure which. It would be a risk, that much she was sure of.

Adel went back to the stove to check the potatoes, and on her way past the window, she looked outside to see Jake walking back down the drive toward the house. He moved with the easy grace of a man who worked with his hands, and he fiddled with one side of his suspenders as if they weren't quite comfortable.

Jacob Knussli was certainly a good-looking man, but he would be a hard one to match if Adel wanted to do the job properly. And she did want to find him the right match. He deserved to be understood, appreciated and loved.

Just then, Jake lifted his gaze, and he spotted her. She had the urge to jump out of his line of sight, but she stopped herself. She wasn't some girl watching cute boys. She was his matchmaker, and she'd best act the part, even when she felt least qualified. He didn't smile, but his expression softened, and he reached up and touched the edge of his hat in a hello.

Adel felt Naomi's arm brush against hers as she looked out the window over her shoulder.

"*Yah*, that's the look," Naomi said with a low laugh, and she carried on to the oven, pulling on oven mitts. "I'd be foolish indeed, Adel."

Chapter Four

A del and Naomi served the meal—mashed potatoes, chicken legs, coleslaw and brown buttered noodles. She had put a little extra effort into this meal, if she was forced to admit it, but it felt worth the work seeing Jake polish off three full platefuls of food.

Adel scooped up the last of the mashed potatoes into the spoon and held them invitingly toward Jake.

"Will you eat the last of them?" she asked.

"No, no, I couldn't eat another bite. But I might come finish them up tonight sometime."

Adel smiled. "Feel free."

"You two really put on a spread," Jake said. "Your bed-and-breakfast must be popular around here."

"We have a steady flow of guests," Naomi said. "We had some guests cancel at the last minute, though, which meant there was space for you."

"So who comes?" he asked.

"Englishers," Adel replied. "Mostly. They stay here and see the sights."

"Couples?" he asked. "Families?"

"Some families," Naomi said, and she took another spoon of coleslaw for herself. "But mostly couples. We're considered quite a romantic spot."

"Are you?" Jake shot Adel a teasing smile. "Should I be surprised? I suppose you are a matchmaker now."

Adel stood up and collected the plates. "I run a business. I'm glad if my guests enjoy themselves."

"What about the couple who got engaged here?" Naomi said. "Last summer, a young man brought his sweetheart here for a dinner, and right here in this room, he got down on one knee and pulled out a ring. Adel got all teary."

"Well, engagements are a beautiful thing," Adel said.

"You're in the right business, Adel," Jake said with a grin. "Love follows wherever you go. I'm in good hands."

Adel carried the plates to the sink. "I do my best."

"I've been telling Adel we should advertise ourselves as a romantic spot," Naomi said. "But she won't do it."

"It isn't proper," Adel replied. She turned in time to see Naomi mouthing her words back at Jake.

"Naomi, you aren't helping," Adel said, annoyed. "I run a proper Amish place. We serve meals, and we have overnight guests, and we give people a glimpse into our way of life. And we Amish don't advertise our romance."

Jake leaned his elbows on the table and met her gaze. "Well, unless we're trying to match a couple up. And then, there's a certain amount of advertising…"

Adel sighed. He wanted to banter, and this wasn't helping! He was handsome, and funny, and interesting to talk to, and that was all well and good for the woman he'd marry to enjoy, but Adel didn't want his direct, warm attention.

"I think it's my turn to take care of the horses," Adel said.

"*Yah*, it is," Naomi replied. "I'll take care of the kitchen."

"Have some pie," Adel said, casting Jake a smile. "Naomi makes a wonderful peach pie. I think we have some left."

Outside, the evening was cooling off, and a grass-scented breeze came in over the field. Adel let herself into the stable and left the door open to let the breeze come inside. She exhaled a sigh. What was it about Jake Knussli that left her feeling so scattered? She didn't get this way with anyone else. And it wasn't that Jake was being inappropriate, really. He was just being charming.

"Why does that bother me so much?" she muttered aloud.

It threw her off-balance, somehow, that was why. And it wasn't even his fault!

The horses were out in the back field. There was grass out there, but she liked to make sure they had extra feed, especially now that Jake's horse was grazing, too. This was an acreage, not a full farm, so the actual grazing field wasn't as large as it could be for three horses.

Adel lifted a bale into a wheelbarrow, and it took her a few attempts to get it inside. A compressed bale of alfalfa hay was incredibly heavy, but she had a few tricks of her own to make the job easier. She started pushing the wheelbarrow toward the door, and the alfalfa tipped heavily to one side.

"Oh, no," she muttered, and she stopped, then grabbed the twine to readjust it.

"You want help?"

Adel looked up to see Jake standing in the doorway. He looked more impressive, somehow, backlit against the open entry. He was a tall, strong man... When she didn't immediately answer, he strode over, hoisted the bale up to get it balanced, then lifted the wheelbarrow by the handles.

"It's okay," Adel said, her voice suddenly coming back to her. "I can do it. We've been doing the work ourselves for years now."

"Come on, Adel," Jake said with a half smile. "What kind of man would I be watching a woman do the outdoor work while I ate peach pie inside?" He met her gaze, and didn't release the handles. "A lazy one, that's what. You can tell prospective matches that I at least know how to take care of men's work."

"I think your farm proves that," she replied, but she stepped back as he wheeled the hay out the door and toward the gate.

Adel jogged ahead and opened it, and he carried on through toward the big, iron feeder. This job always took most of Adel's strength, but he worked easily enough. He hoisted the bale up and over the side of the feeder, then pulled a pocketknife off a loop on his suspender. He popped the twine and the hay sprung free. The horses came ambling over to the new hay, and Jake walked back to the fence next to Adel, and leaned against the wooden rungs.

Adel looked over her shoulder toward the house. She

could see her sister in the kitchen window, washing dishes.

"Jake, I think we need to talk about boundaries," Adel said.

"What kind?" he asked.

"The kind between a matchmaker and her client," she replied.

"Ah." He raised an eyebrow and waited.

"It's just that—" She swallowed. "I'm not your friend, or your schoolmate anymore. Things have changed. A lot has changed since you left. And you seem to be wanting to relate to me as a friend, and I can't be that right now."

"You can't be my friend." His tone was low, and he met her gaze easily enough.

"No." She straightened her shoulders. "I'm supposed to be your matchmaker, and in that role, I'm not the one you should be chatting with."

"So I should be chatting with Naomi?" he asked. He looked back toward the house and waved. Naomi, in the window, waved back.

"If you want to," she replied.

"But not with you."

This wasn't going the way she intended, and she sighed. "Jake, I have limited time to find you a wife, and you're not cooperating."

"I'm being stubbornly personable and helpful come chore time," he said with a teasing little smile.

"Jake, cut it out! You know what I'm talking about, and you're purposefully misunderstanding me!"

"Maybe I am," he replied. "But you're being silly. I've known you since we were tiny. We used to stomp in puddles together in grade school. We had fun."

"I got into trouble for that," she said. "It was less fun for me. I'd go home with a filthy dress and my *mamm* would give me extra chores for being so careless."

"But while we were stomping, it was great!" He shot her a grin. "And there was that time we had to memorize that Christmas poem together."

"You didn't do it properly," she said. "You made us both look bad. I really cared about that Christmas presentation."

"I did try." Jake softened his tone. "I memorized and studied that poem for weeks. But I got nervous in front of people, and I forgot it all."

"You should have said that instead of making farm animal noises," she said. "You were a rebel from childhood, Jake."

Jake's joking disappeared. "I was ten. Ten-year-olds don't always deal with embarrassment gracefully. I could have run off in humiliation, or I could play it off like I meant to do it. I chose the latter."

His expression was serious now, and she felt her own cheeks warm.

"I didn't know you were embarrassed," she said.

"I'm not so bad in front of people now," he said. "But I still get a little nervous sometimes. And when I'm nervous, I...act like it's all part of the plan."

"Are you nervous now?" she asked.

"Yah."

"Well...don't be," she said. "I intend to find you a good wife. I want the best for you. I want to see you happy."

"You talk like you're some matronly aunt, or something, like you have no mutual history with me," he said.

"We're the same age, Adel. I'm not some young man looking to you for your wisdom. I'm your equal."

Adel sighed. "You're saying we have memories together. And you're right, but you're wasting your time using up your charm on *me*."

"Who else should I chat with?" He spread his arms and looked around. "And while I'm here, I'm supposed to act like a tourist or something? Eat your food and sit in my room? Eat the pie and watch you work? Would that make you more comfortable? I thought this was your idea—us getting to know each other so you'd be able to recommend me honestly. But I'm not going to pretend you're some old lady when you aren't!"

"I didn't say I was an old lady!" she shot back.

"Well, you're acting like one," he said.

Old? She was acting *old*? Annoyance surged up inside her.

"I'm acting like a respected member of this community who has been given the task of finding you a wife!"

"I think you're being fake," he replied.

"Me?" She tried to tamp down her rising anger. "How would you even know, Jake? You've been back for a few months, and I've chatted with you a few times. That's it. What do you know about who I am on a heart level? What do you know about what I've been through, and how I've contributed to this community?"

"Because you're scared of a human connection!" he retorted.

"I am not."

"This—" He waggled a finger between them. "This is a human connection. Seeing me as a man, as a whole and complete person, as your equal. That's a human connection. And it's freaking you out."

He caught her gaze and held it. Her heartbeat sped up and she broke off the eye contact and looked away. Yes, she was noticing the man in him, more than she should.

"This is too casual for a single man and woman to be together," she said. "You might recall that we do things differently here."

"We were friends once," he said.

"We were schoolmates. Not friends." It sounded harsh, but the distinction mattered. She felt bad all the same. "I don't mean for that to sound cruel, but we don't know each other as adults, Jake. We knew each other as *kinner*. It's different."

"Yah," he agreed, but he didn't look daunted, either. "Very different. We're both all grown up now."

More than grown. She'd already buried a husband. And that wasn't an excuse—it was a fact. That love and loss had molded and changed her.

"But being grown and good-looking isn't everything, Jake," she said.

"Who are you calling good-looking?" he asked with a slow smile. "You or me?"

She'd said too much, and she felt her cheeks heat. "I'm not a vain woman—"

"So it's me?" He was teasing now, and she turned away.

"I normally have a little more poise than this."

"Then I take that as a compliment," he replied.

"You've been with the *Englishers* for too long," she said curtly.

He chuckled. "You're more human than you think,

Adel." He was silent for a moment. "And for the record, you have matured into a beautiful woman."

And maybe Jake had been with *Englishers* too long, but there was something about Adel that he liked so much more on this side of thirty. She was serious, sure, but he sensed a softness under all that bravado. The things that enticed him in his younger years were no longer the same things he was looking for in a wife. And while he knew that Adel had zero interest in marriage right now, he did see what she had to offer—maturity, insight, grace, dignity. And it didn't hurt that she was also incredibly beautiful.

So yes, that last shred of immaturity in him was enjoying getting a reaction out of her. She might not want marriage, but she had noticed him, and he liked that.

"You shouldn't be flirting with me," Adel said.

"I know. I'm sorry. I didn't really mean to flirt. I was just being honest," he replied.

She cast him an unimpressed look. "You're supposed to be building a life. And a choice in wife is a very important one. You can't play with this."

"Who says I'm playing?" he countered. Then he sighed. "I'm sorry. I'm not going to tease you. You're right."

"This is serious," she said. "Because you have to build it from the ground up, and a marriage is part of the foundation. A life doesn't happen by accident. It is built one choice at a time. Every goal comes with a price. If you want to be a farmer, you have to buy the land. If you want to be a woodworker, you have to be able to open a shop. And you can't do more than one thing, most times, because there is only so much time and so much money you can invest into it. When you marry, that choice is for a lifetime—the length of which, only *Gott* knows. So knowing what you want and walking purposefully in that direction is incredibly important."

Jake nodded. "Did you do that—with your first marriage?"

"No." She smiled faintly. "I stumbled into a wonderful first marriage, and I can't take any credit for having done anything more than simply being a well-behaved girl who listened to her father about a man's character. But I've seen a lot since then, and I won't be simply stumbling into another marriage again."

Would any man live up to her ideals? he wondered.

"What if you stumbled into love?" he asked.

"That's an *Englisher* problem," she said. "Falling in love with the wrong person, I mean. For example, if a man is wonderful in many ways, but married to someone else, is it difficult for me to stop any inappropriate feelings for him? No. Not at all. It's the same with a man who isn't a good fit for my future. You don't stumble into love, Jake."

She was so serious, and she sounded so convincing that he was tempted to accept her word as unwavering truth, and yet he'd seen evidence to the contrary.

He smiled faintly. "I've heard of several people who have. Not with inappropriate people, but with someone they didn't expect."

"Then they weren't watching where they were walking," she replied.

That almost sounded like a challenge, but Adel wasn't looking to get married again, and she might very well get her wish if she was focused enough on keeping her single life. Sometimes people got what they prayed for, even if they later regretted it.

"*Englishers* wait for that experience—the tumbling into love," he said.

"And look at the success rate of those relationships!" she shot back. "I read in a paper a few years ago that their marriages fail at a tremendous rate. There isn't enough planning or serious thought put into it. There is a reason why we pursue marriages the way we do. Our young people get to have that experience...within boundaries. If they associate with appropriate friends, then they can trip into love wherever they like, as long as they behave appropriately in the process and get married. But when people come to a matchmaker, it is normally because that tactic didn't work, and they're ready to be more practical."

She raised her eyebrows at him, and he rolled his eyes.

"You have a point," he said. "We're no spring chickens, you and me."

Maybe he wouldn't be able to experience that falling into love after all.

"*You're* no spring chicken," she retorted. "I'm not available, so it doesn't matter."

Jake met her gaze, and they both laughed. Adel's face relaxed into a stunning smile. Some women grew more beautiful the older they got, and Adel was one of them. She really had no idea, did she?

"And speaking of choosing the right person to love, tomorrow morning, I'm going to bring you to visit a prospective wife," Adel said.

"Oh." Jake blinked. "Good. Who?"

"Lydia Speicher."

Jake combed his memory for some recollection of the woman, but he came up empty.

"She's in her late twenties right now," Adel said. "So she was a few years younger than us."

"Ah. I don't remember her at all."

"Then it will be a nice introduction," she replied. "We should get back."

As Jake walked next to Adel, he had to wonder how this was going to work. Would he feel anything special when he met the right woman? Or would it be completely practical—a choice based on age, relative good looks, cooking ability and a compatible personality?

Could he promise himself to a woman on those criteria alone?

Adel didn't like the idea of falling in love, but without some sort of tumble, what would a lifetime be like with the woman? Was learning to love a good woman enough?

That evening, Jake sat in the kitchen with a glass of lemonade in front of him. Adel had gone up to bed, and the kitchen was spotlessly clean. His mind was still running along similar lines as earlier that day—wondering if it would even be possible to choose a wife this quickly.

He'd heard some stories about some local marriages. Ben Hochstetler had married an ex-Amish social worker who came to his farm to pick up an abandoned baby. He'd been stunned to hear that story! And then there was Thomas Weibe, who'd married Patience, the Amish schoolteacher who helped him out with his daughter.

More shocking still, Thomas's brother Noah married the pregnant girl who was going to give her baby up for adoption to Thomas and Patience. How the family had sorted that one out, he still wasn't sure, but he'd been told the family stayed close. It would seem that the community of Redemption had seen its fair share of surprising and quick weddings...and all of them working out very nicely.

Maybe his wedding would join the ranks of the others, and he'd get both his farm and a woman he loved, too. The chances were very slim, but wasn't that where Gott worked best—when it seemed impossible?

The side door opened, and he looked up to see Naomi come inside with a flat of eggs balanced on one hand. She shot him a friendly smile.

"You're up still?" she said.

"So are you," he pointed out.

"I was just getting the egg order from the neighbor," she said. "We get them weekly."

Jake nodded. He wasn't sure what to say to that. Naomi brought the eggs to the counter and put them down, then glanced up the staircase.

"She's got her back up, hasn't she?" Naomi said.

"Well, she's staying very serious," he replied. "I have a feeling she sees me as a little boy sometimes."

"Oh, she comes across that way, but it's how she is when she's scared," Naomi replied.

"Of what?" he asked. "Me?"

"No..." Naomi poured herself a glass of lemonade and joined him at the table. "It's not you, exactly. The bishop gave her an incredibly tough job, you know."

"*Yah*, I know," he replied. "Marrying me off in two weeks. That's not easy."

"And if this task was given to anyone else, they'd do their best and their conscience would be clear," she said. "But for my sister, letting the bishop down isn't even an option."

"Why not?" he asked.

"Because the bishop is offering her a way forward that is hard to refuse. She's got a chance at being something more in this community—a leader of sorts. She's been through a lot, and she has advice she can give to others. She's respected, loved, and women go to her with their problems. You're a bit of a trial run for her."

"Oh…" He hadn't realized that. Was she having to prove herself with him?

"Adel and I are very different," Naomi said quietly. "What I wouldn't give for someone to need me."

She smiled wistfully, and Jake's stomach tightened. Was Naomi suggesting what he thought she was? She met his gaze, and then shook her head, laughing.

"You can relax, Jake. I'm not proposing marriage."

"You wouldn't be a bad choice," he said.

"I'd be a terrible choice," she replied. "I've seen the way you look at my sister."

Jake felt his face heat. "What do you mean?"

"You've noticed how gorgeous she is," Naomi said. "She's the only one who hasn't. She just gets prettier as the years go by. In fact, I think the two of you would be rather well matched."

"She doesn't want marriage again," Jake said. "And if I'm to get that farm in my name, I need a legal marriage right quick."

"Yes, there is that..." Naomi shrugged. "But you have a spark between you."

"I irritate her," he said with a low laugh.

"A little bit," Naomi admitted, and they both chuckled. "So are you really going to do this—scoop up a wife that fast?"

"Yah," he said, then hesitated. "I'll try. But I'm going to listen to my gut. Maybe I'll meet someone truly wonderful and know right away. Some men say that about their wives—they knew the moment they saw them."

"And what did you think the moment you saw Adel?" she asked with a grin.

"Naomi, you should be the matchmaker," he chuckled, waggling a finger at her.

"You can't take Adel so seriously," Naomi said. "She's a planner. When she and Mark couldn't have *kinner*, she was heartbroken, but she took solace in the idea that *Gott* had something else in mind that would make it all make sense. And then Mark died..." Naomi sighed. "My sister might have married Mark because he was kind and gentle and respected, and she wanted very badly to be a wife. But she fell deeply in love with him after the marriage. Without *kinner*, she was able to see the beauty in her life as his wife, even without babies. That's how much she loved him. So when he died, it was like all the beauty in her world winked out. You see her now—fresh, pretty, and eyes that sparkle? Well, she was a shell of herself. She was pale, thin, gaunt. She looked like she might die of heartbreak."

Jake leaned back in his chair, his gaze moving toward the staircase. How much had she endured that he hadn't given her credit for? He wished she'd been the one to tell him this, instead of her sister.

"She found a way to embrace all that loss," Naomi went on, "and it was by holding on to Mark's memory. She's the deacon's widow, and there is still a role for her in this community in that capacity. It not only gives her a future where she can contribute in a meaningful way, but it means that everything she lost came together into something good."

"And if she married, it would negate it all...in a way. For her, at least," he concluded.

"Yah." Naomi nodded. "Exactly."

"I should stop teasing her," he said softly.

"No!" Naomi shook her head. "Not at all! She laughs with you. You get a rise out of her. You're reminding her that she's not the old woman she wishes she was! She has a whole life ahead of her, and I think it's good if you jostle her out of her comfortable rut."

"But you said—" he started.

"Compassion is a good thing," Naomi said. "But my sister needs to live, too. Not just grieve all the time. Sometimes, we go through hard times and there is no explanation why. It's a different kind of faith that keeps on believing *Gott* is good and life is good, too, in the face of that."

Why was Naomi telling him all of this? It was very personal information, and with the way he'd been joking with Adel and teasing her, he thought her sister might want him to let up. So why was she divulging this if she wasn't wanting him to leave Adel alone?

"You want to see her married again," Jake guessed.

"I truly do." Naomi smiled. "And you'd do nicely as a brother-in-law."

He laughed and shook his head. "I think it'll take some time to get your sister married again, especially after all you've told me. And time is not on my side."

Naomi nodded. "Very likely." She rose to her feet and drained the glass of lemonade. "I'd better turn in. I have a busy day tomorrow. We have two tourist groups coming through."

"Good night," he said. "And thank you for the explanation."

Even if he didn't really deserve all that information, it was nice to know. It made Adel make a little more sense to him.

"I'm praying you find a wonderful wife, Jake," Naomi said.

"Thank you." He smiled. "I appreciate that."

Naomi headed up the stairs, and Jake stayed where he was, the clock on the wall ticking comfortingly in the background. Adel was beautiful, interesting, and she'd definitely caught his attention. But she wasn't ready for marriage again, and with her sister's explanation, he could fully understand why. If only he weren't on this unfair time constraint, and he could take his time and get to know her better.

But that wasn't the way things were. If he was going to keep this farm, he needed a wife in a matter of days. And perhaps that was *Gott*'s intention, forcing him to move on and look further for a wife. Maybe this Lydia Speicher would be the one for him. Who knew? *Gott* could move very quickly when He wanted to.

Gott, *show me the woman for me,* Jake prayed. *And*

when You do, make it very clear. Because I don't think my head is on straight right now.

It couldn't be if he was feeling this way about his matchmaker!

Chapter Five

Adel had chosen Lydia Speicher for a reason. Lydia was a kind woman, but she was strong, too. Redemption had a good number of strong, self-sufficient women. To run an Amish home took a great deal of skill and fortitude, and the woman who married Jake would need every last ounce just to put that home back together again.

Lydia was twenty-eight, and somehow, she'd just never been courted. It happened sometimes—a girl would have too much competition, or just not enough boys her age, and she'd end up left behind when everyone else was getting married and setting up their own homes.

Adel had suggested that Lydia go visit some friends in another community, and she hadn't had any luck there, either. So when Adel said she might have someone for her, Lydia had enthusiastically agreed to meet him.

Jake held the reins loosely in his hands, and he leaned forward to check traffic before he flicked them and the buggy started forward. A car whipped past them, and

Adel reached out and grabbed Jake's sleeve. He cast her an amused smile.

"I'm fine," he said. "I've driven both cars and buggies."

She let out a breath. "*Yah*, I know."

His gaze flickered toward her again. "You're used to being the one holding the reins. That's what this is."

Adel felt her cheeks heat. "I might be used to it, *yah*."

It had been five years of fending for herself, and she'd started to even enjoy taking care of things herself. It drove Naomi crazy. She said Adel had gotten bossy.

"Do you want to drive?" he asked.

"No! It would look very bad for me to drive you to see a woman about marriage. You'd look—" She saw the twinkle in his eye. "You were joking."

"I was joking." He chuckled. "Lean back and stop mentally driving this buggy, Adel. I can get us to the Speichers' farm."

Adel let out a breath. He was right, of course. She was trying to do everything herself again. No doubt, Naomi would be able to joke with Jake endlessly about Adel's tendency to do that.

"I never did ask, does Lydia remember me?" Jake asked.

"She does, actually," Adel replied. She repressed the urge to point out that the next intersection ahead was where Jake needed to take a right-hand turn.

"Is that a good thing or a bad thing?" he asked.

"She remembers you being a rather rebellious older boy," Adel said. "But she thought you were handsome back then, and if you've gotten over the rebellious bit, she'd be very happy to meet you again."

"What did you tell her?" he asked.

"That you've chosen an Amish life," she said.

"That's it?"

"And that I think you'll stay Amish," she said. "You might always be a little rebellious, though."

"That's fair." He reined in the horse at the next intersection, and flicked the battery-operated turn signal. "If she'll still see me after that explanation, then we might have a chance."

Adel tried to tamp down the twinge of discomfort she felt. It wasn't that she thought the two wouldn't be a good match. She wouldn't have suggested it otherwise. It was something else…the tiniest swell of jealousy. What was wrong with her?

"You do know the way," Adel said as he brought the buggy around the corner.

"Of course," he replied with a chuckle. "I've been back for months, Adel."

The Speicher drive was half a mile down the road and their name was on the mailbox. As they pulled in, Adel felt a flutter in her stomach. This was it—her first matchmaker introduction. She'd have to stop this foolishness she was feeling for Jake, and make sure she presented herself properly. This very well might be the beginning of an important role in this community.

The side door opened as they pulled up next to the house, and Bonita Speicher, Lydia's mother, appeared on the step.

"Hello!" Adel called cheerily.

Bonita waved and smiled. Jake led the horse up to a water bucket, let him drink and then strapped on a feed bag. They walked together up to the house, and Bonita stood back to let them inside.

For the first few minutes, there were the general introductions. Bonita said that she remembered Jake from boyhood, and she'd actually had a pleasant memory of him—cutting the lawn here when her husband had a broken leg. Lydia stood by the sink looking bashful, and then she came forward and shook his hand.

"Hello," Lydia said.

There was an assortment of baked goods on plates on the table—very likely all made by Lydia's hand. Lydia invited Jake to sit down, and Adel and Bonita retreated to the other side of the kitchen.

"What do you think of him?" Bonita asked, her voice low. "Honestly?"

"He's a good man," Adel replied. "I wouldn't have brought him by otherwise."

"He never did like the rules," Bonita said. "And now we find out he came back because of the will."

"He always did want to return," Adel said. "He just didn't know how. It isn't my story to tell, but... It was more complicated."

Bonita nodded. "My daughter likes him. You can tell by the way she's feeding him."

Adel looked over to see Bonita pushing a plate of cookies in Jake's direction. Jake took one and gave her a polite nod. They watched the couple in silence for a couple of beats.

"This is where I make the case for my daughter," Bonita said. "She's smart, she's a wonderful cook and she takes after my mother, who is still doing her own laundry and gardening at eighty-seven. She's got a good heart, and she'd given up on finding a husband. I'd love to see her married."

"You don't have to make your case to me," Adel said. "Lydia is wonderful."

"She's a little stubborn, too…" Bonita blushed.

"A good thing in this situation," Adel said. "If they hit it off, there will be a lot of learning between the two of them. He'll need a strong woman."

Bonita exhaled. "*Yah…* Well, let's go join them now."

Bonita led the way, and Adel followed. They pulled up some chairs, and Adel met Jake's gaze. He pressed his lips together.

"So what work did you do when you were…over the fence?" Lydia asked.

"I worked at a factory," he replied. "It was pretty good pay, and I liked my coworkers a lot."

"Oh…" Lydia glanced over at Adel, looking mildly panicked. Had they run out of things to talk about already?

"Jake is working to put his uncle's farm back together again," Adel supplied. "He's quite passionate about the barn roof."

"Are you?" Lydia asked.

"Uh—" Jake nodded. "Maybe not passionate so much as wanting to replace it. The barn is in pretty good shape. It's a strong building, but it won't stay that way with all the leaking going on. The supports will rot."

"True," Lydia said. "When will you do it?"

"When it's mine," he said. "I've put a lot of time and effort into fixing things up, but I can't put any more personal money into it if it won't be mine. Whoever owns that land will replace the roof. I'm just hoping it's me."

"And the house?" Lydia asked. "How is it?"

Jake's cheeks reddened a little bit. "It's…in need of work."

"Hmm." Lydia wouldn't ask too much about it, or it would look like all she cared about was the farm.

"Lydia won a quilting contest at the fair," Adel said. "She's very skilled with a needle."

"Nice!" Jake smiled. "Congratulations. You must like quilting, then?"

"I like crocheting more," she said.

Jake fell silent. This was getting very awkward. Adel reached out with her foot under the table and gave Jake's boot a nudge. He looked over at her, surprise on his face, then he smiled.

"Do you want to show me something you've crocheted? Honestly, I've never learned much about it. My *mamm*—" He swallowed. "She didn't crochet much. She did more sewing. That I can remember, at least."

"Of course I'll show you." Lydia pushed back her chair. "You don't seem hungry."

"I'm kind of nervous," he replied.

"The spare room upstairs has become a sewing room," Lydia said. "Come up with me, and I'll show you what I've been doing."

Bonita cast Adel a questioning look and Adel shrugged.

"They're both adults," Adel said softly as the two disappeared up the stairs. "And well-behaved adults, too. Trust me, Jake is looking for a wife. Listen."

The soft murmur of their voices came down the staircase, and then through the ceiling from above. Adel found herself straining to make out words, but she couldn't.

"How is it that you're acting as matchmaker for Jacob Knussli?" Bonita asked. She nudged a plate of cookies toward Adel, and she took one. It was a buttery short-bread, and she chewed and swallowed before answering.

"The bishop asked me," she said. "I was surprised, too, but honestly, Bonita? I'd love to do more of this."

"You should be finding yourself a match," Bonita said with a wink. "You're very young, you know."

"Oh…" Adel shrugged. "I don't know about that. I'm not looking for a husband."

"Well, I'm glad you're thinking about getting our young people married. Definitely keep my daughter in mind, even if this match doesn't work."

There was something in Bonita's voice that made Adel give her a questioning look.

"You think it won't work?" Adel said. "Give them some time. They have to break the ice."

"The most relaxed that man ever looked was when he was looking at you," Bonita said. That was similar to what her sister had told her about the way Jake gazed at her. She might need to warn him that he'd best stop that, or he'd come across as interested in the wrong woman.

"He's nervous," Adel said. "This is a big step—getting to know a woman in hopes of marrying her that quickly. Of course, he's not at his best. In fact, he's normally quite charming. He chats for hours. I think it's a good sign if he's a bit nervous with her."

Bonita gave her a funny look, but didn't say anything.

The floorboards overhead squeaked, and Jake's boots could be heard on the staircase coming down.

"It was so nice to meet you," Jake was saying. "Properly, I mean. Thank you for the tour."

Jake and Lydia came back down into the kitchen, and Lydia was looking at Jake uncertainly. Jake looked over at Adel and met her gaze meaningfully. He was ready to go, it would seem.

"Well—" Adel forced a smile. "We'll be in touch, and everyone can talk and see how they feel..." Adel shot Lydia a smile. "Your baking is amazing, Lydia. I know if I ask for the recipe, I'll never be able to repeat it."

"Oh, you're too kind," Lydia said with a blush, but she did grab a paper bag from a drawer, and she filled it with baked goods. "For the drive home." She handed it to Jake.

"Thank you. I do appreciate it." He held the bag in both hands. "Goodbye. So nice to see you, too." He gave Bonita a smile.

After a few more cordial farewells, Adel followed Jake out to the buggy. He walked faster than her, and while she boosted herself up into the seat, he saw to the horse's feed bag. When he joined her, he dropped the paper bag between them. Adel leaned forward and waved to Bonita and Lydia, who both stood on the step side by side.

Jake flicked the reins and turned the buggy around. He exhaled a slow breath as they rattled up the drive toward the road.

"So..." Adel felt a little tightening in her chest. "What did you think of Lydia?"

Jake leaned back as the buggy rattled up onto the main road, and he let out a slow breath. It was a relief to be driving away, and every yard the buggy moved, the better he felt. There was absolutely nothing wrong with that family. They were good Amish people, and the home had been immaculately kept. The baked goods in the bag next to him were going to be absolutely delicious if he could relax enough to actually eat them. He was looking for a wife, and Lydia was painfully appropriate.

He looked over to find Adel's gaze locked on his face.

"Uh—" He swallowed. "She's a lovely person."

"She is," Adel agreed. "I wouldn't have brought you otherwise."

He nodded. "And she's very nice."

"Oh, Jake, now is not the time for politeness!" Adel said. "I won't give a word-for-word report back to anyone. As your matchmaker, I need to know your honest thoughts. Could you make a life with her?"

Could he? He tried to imagine coming back to his farmhouse and finding Lydia inside. There would be delicious cooking, he was absolutely sure. The house would be clean like the one they'd just left. And Lydia would be there waiting for him in her neat cape dress and crisp white apron. Lydia. A very nice woman.

"I probably could…" Jake sighed. "She's a good cook. She's moderately attractive. She seems to be good with crochet and quilting. If she got her hands onto a house, it would be put in order in no time."

Adel nodded. "Yes, a very good point. She'd be good with needlework and she knits some really beautiful blankets, too."

As if he cared about the intricacy of her needlework, or the quality of the lap blankets. Maybe he should care about those things a bit more, but he didn't. Jake needed to be reasonable here. He was looking for a good woman to marry in a ridiculously short amount of time. And Lydia checked all the boxes but one.

"Her mother remembered you from when you helped cut their grass when her husband was injured," Adel said. "And they'd accept a quick marriage for their daughter. They're a very nice family, if you recall."

"Their son is Mordecai Speicher, right?" he said.

"*Yah*—he was in our grade."

"I didn't like him much..."

He could almost hear Adel rolling her eyes beside him. And he knew he was grasping at excuses here.

"What's wrong with her brother?" Adel asked. "He owns a trinket shop in town. He does quite well, actually."

"He was always kind of pompous," he replied. "I don't know. I didn't like him. That's all."

"Are you telling me that he's an obstacle for you?" Adel asked. "Would you like to see him again and see if you could manage being related to him? I'm sure I could set up a visit."

"No, no," he said with a shake of his head. "That's not necessary."

"Do you want to know what I think?" Adel asked.

He looked over at her, a sense of relief flooding through him. If this was left to his feelings, he wasn't going to know the right step. But someone with some perspective would be incredibly helpful. That was what matchmakers were for, wasn't it?

"Yes," he said. "I really do."

"I think she's strong enough to keep you in line," she said.

Jake met her gaze, and then laughed. "Are you serious?"

"Deadly," she replied. "She's very strong in the faith, and she knows right from wrong. She also doesn't take any guff. I think she'd be good for you."

"So... You think I need that?" he asked. "Is that a real worry here?"

Adel cast him a wry smile. "You're a rebel, Jake. Rebels need someone who stands up to them. Lydia would do that."

"I think you stand up to me just fine," he said.

"I do," she said. "Because I'm not cowed by your charm or good looks. But I'm not going to be around day in and day out to keep you in line, am I?"

Jake chuckled. "Okay... So opposites can be good for each other."

They rode in silence for a few minutes, and Jake wondered if he was being too picky. Lydia was a very nice woman, and besides one obnoxious brother, she came from a very nice family. He was the one looking for a wife, so what was his problem here?

"So what's the matter?" Adel asked, mirroring his thoughts.

Jake reined the horse in at the four-way stop, then proceeded around the corner, a little faster than usual, Adel was jostled against him as the wheel hit a rock in the road, and her warm arm pressed into his side. He put a hand out instinctively and caught her fingers in his.

His heartbeat sped up, and for one eternal moment, her hand clasped in his, he felt a tug toward her so strong that it shocked him. No! This wasn't the woman who was available. Was this just some way of sabotaging himself?

He let go of her hand and when he allowed himself to glance at her face, the stern stare was gone, and she was looking at him questioningly. Great. He'd seem foolish if she knew what he'd just been thinking.

"We need to nail this down so I know how to proceed," Adel said.

With Lydia. Right.

"I don't think she's the one for me," he said. "I mean, she's perfectly pleasant, talented, nice-looking…"

He glanced over at Adel. But Lydia wasn't as beautiful as this woman beside him. And he couldn't bring himself to open up with Lydia—not naturally. He'd felt quite open with Adel from their first meeting—even with Adel doing her best to keep him at arm's length. And that ability seemed rather important in a marriage.

"What?" Adel asked.

"I think Lydia deserves a man who thinks she's wonderful," Jake said. "She deserves a man who wants to steal a kiss with her."

"The kisses would come in time," Adel said.

"You think?" He wasn't convinced of that.

"I've been married," Adel said gently.

"And I haven't, so you're the expert here," he admitted.

"At first, I was shy and uncertain, and then one day, about a week after our wedding, things just relaxed with us. It does take a little bit of time, Jake. No one goes from modest discretion to marriage without a little bit of transition."

"Don't they?" he asked.

She shook her head. "Nope. The first year of marriage is all about adjusting. And that adjustment looks different for every couple."

But he was assuming that the grooms in these marriages at least wanted to kiss their wives. As nice as Lydia was, he couldn't imagine kissing her.

"It's just that I don't feel any kind of spark with her," he confessed. "Like…any spark at all. I don't think anything would suddenly ignite a week after the wedding like it did for you. You fell deeply in love, Adel. It took you some time, but that was real, honest love."

She froze, and he realized his mistake the moment it was out of his mouth. Adel hadn't told him that. Her sister had. He looked over at her and winced.

"Naomi told me that," he said.

Adel sighed. "Did she, now."

He could hear the annoyance in her tone, and he couldn't help but grin at her.

"Your sister knows you, Adel. Be glad of that."

"She doesn't need to make sure you know me just as well as she does," Adel retorted. "I'm your matchmaker, not your match!"

True. If Adel was his match, it might be easier. He could imagine kissing Adel, and he could imagine enjoying it very much. He felt his face heat, and he pulled his mind away from the brink.

"The point remains," Jake said, "there was something really special between you and Mark. And I don't feel that with Lydia. I don't even feel the beginning of that…"

Adel nodded. "That's fine. It's good to know that there isn't something specific that's wrong. If it's a matter of a spark, maybe my next introduction will be more successful. Do you want to go meet her now?"

"Not really," he said with a faint smile. "I think I just need to unwind a while before I meet the next one."

"That's fair," Adel said, and she suddenly broke into a stunning smile. "You look downright terrified, Jake."

"That's amusing?" he muttered.

"It's a relief," she said. "I hope you're scared—at least a little bit. It means you're finally seeing how serious this choice is."

He saw the sign for the bed-and-breakfast approaching. If only he had more time, or the days could stretch just a little bit longer as he got his balance.

Wife hunting was turning out to be the most stressful thing he'd done in his life.

Chapter Six

When Adel got back into the house, the kitchen was clean, and it still smelled of vegetable soup from the tourist groups who came through. They always served a delicious soup with crusty bread and butter from the Petersheim Creamery that made the most delicious butter blends in Pennsylvania. A note lay on the counter in her sister's familiar handwriting.

Both tourist groups have come and gone. They went well! Dishes are done—as you can see. Ha, ha! I'm going to help Maria with her garden for a couple of hours, and I'll stop by the creamery for our butter order. You don't mind starting dinner, do you?

There was no signature at the bottom, and there didn't need to be. It was just as well that her sister had gone out. Adel's mind was still on the introduction with Lydia. It would seem that Jake was truly not interested in pursuing more with Lydia, but maybe she should hold off on telling Lydia that for a few days. Perhaps he'd circle back around later, after some time to think.

Being a matchmaker sounded lovely when it came

to finding marriage matches for people, but she wasn't looking forward to telling the ones who weren't chosen the bad news. What could she tell Lydia—that Jake simply didn't feel a connection? Granted, it could go the other direction, and a woman who did interest Jake might not be interested in return. The path to love was fraught with disappointment, and she would be not only the bearer of good news, but of bad, as well.

And then there was the unsettling fact that she was actually feeling relieved that this introduction hadn't worked. What did this say about her? She'd been so certain that she was ready to step into the role of matchmaker, and when faced with a handsome man in want of a wife, she was feeling jealous of the women who might interest him?

Gott, wash my heart out, she prayed. *I want You to use me, and I'm being petty! Help me to stop feeling this way. It isn't about me, and I know that.*

She pulled a chicken out of the icebox and deposited it into a roasting pan just as the side door opened. Jake came into the kitchen and he glanced around.

"I gave the horses the extra feed a bit early. I hope you don't mind."

"No, I appreciate it. Thank you." He didn't have to do that, but it was sweet of him to insist. She went to the windowsill where she grew some herbs and plucked some twigs of thyme and parsley.

"Chicken dinner tonight?" Jake asked.

"Yah." She cast him a smile. "I thought we could all use a comforting meal."

"Do I seem a little shaken?" he asked, but she heard humor in his tone.

"A little bit," she admitted. "Tomorrow morning, we have another appointment. This one is with Delia Swarey."

"Delia... She was married to Zeke Swarey for years," he said.

"He passed away," she replied. "Two years ago. He got lung cancer."

"I didn't hear about that." He sighed. "That's too bad. And she's looking for a new husband?"

"She's ready to consider it, *yah*," Adel replied.

"She's older than us, though," he said.

"By two years. At this point in life, it doesn't matter as much. She's got the four boys to raise on her own, and they need a *daet*."

"How old are they?" he asked.

"Between twelve and seventeen." They were good boys, but they were strong-willed, and Delia had been struggling with raising them alone. Parenting was one part of life that Adel couldn't give advice on, but she knew that the bishop had visited Delia's home to talk to the boys about some infraction or other.

"And you thought I'd be a good father?" Jake asked.

"I thought you could grow into the role," she replied. "Like every man does."

"I wouldn't be starting with babies," he said. "That's how most fathers start, and they learn as they go. They aren't starting with teens."

Adel regarded him for a moment, and he was right. She knew exactly what she was suggesting when she put Delia's name on her list. Jake was a strong man who'd seen the world already. His experiences could be valuable to some equally rebellious stepsons who might be saved some hard lessons of their own. Besides, it was good to be needed—and challenged—in a relationship.

"Perhaps I have faith in you," she said.

Jake's expression changed to something more self-conscious, and he lifted his shoulders. "Thank you. You really think I could handle it?"

"I do," she replied. "You can handle a lot more than you think. We don't grow into our true full potential comfortably, you know."

"You're probably right." He nodded toward the bag of potatoes on the counter. "Why don't I give you a hand?"

He didn't wait for her to answer, and he pulled open a couple of drawers at random, and pulled out a peeler. Adel watched him in mute surprise. Help in the kitchen? *Why?*

"Do you have a bucket to peel into?" he asked. "Oh, here it is."

He grabbed an old ice cream pail used for food bits that would be sent out to compost.

"What are you doing?" she asked. "You're my guest here, and helping with the animals is more than enough. I provide meals. You don't need to—"

"I'm a good cook," he said, one side of his mouth turning up in a half smile.

Was this a comment about her cooking? She wasn't entirely sure. She'd never seen a man volunteer to help in the kitchen over the age of twelve. *Kinner* helped their *mamms*, but grown men sat themselves down and waited. Their work was payment enough, and they knew it.

"This isn't a man's job," she said pointedly. "Go sit down. I'll take care of this."

"You know, the *Englisher* men cook," he said. "And in my time away, I've learned. It was either that, or starve. And I like tasty food. I'm pretty sure my mashed potatoes would rival even yours."

Adel laughed uncomfortably. "You can't be serious, Jake."

Her mashed potatoes were a fluffy, buttery delight. Guests Amish and English alike always complimented her on her perfect mashed potatoes.

"I'm completely serious," he replied. "I need butter, some cream cheese, black pepper and maybe a bit of cheddar, if you have it."

She glanced toward the icebox. "I actually have all of that…"

"Excellent. Prepare to be impressed."

"Amish men leave the cooking to the women," Adel said. "You know that."

Jake ignored her and started peeling potatoes. He worked quickly, his hands seeming to know the work as the peels curled and dropped into the bucket. His hands were strong and work-worn, and she found her eyes drawn to his strong forearms as he peeled.

"This will not impress the women I set you up with," she said. "They're looking for an Amish husband. Whatever you picked up with the English is best left there, you know."

"I'm not trying to impress them," he said, looking up for the first time. His dark gaze locked onto hers meaningfully, and her breath caught. He didn't drop his gaze, either, and she felt her pulse speeding up. "This is about me just being me. And tonight, I want to cook with you."

He dropped his gaze then and turned back to his work. She exhaled a pent-up a breath, and her face felt hot. Was she blushing? She put her fingers against her cheeks. If Jake had used a bit of that smolder on Lydia, today's introduction might have gone better...

"So you like cooking?" she asked, her voice sounding strange in her own ears.

"*Yah*. It's relaxing. I enjoy it. I get to make food the way I like it."

"Oh..."

"I don't mean that as an insult to your good cooking, Adel," he said, his voice softening. "I could grow plenty fat just eating what you put out, I assure you."

"Thank you... I think." She chuckled.

"I've obviously got a lot on my mind, and sitting there watching you cook isn't going to help," he said. "I'm antsy. And I'll go back to my own farm and get to work soon enough, but until I do, I'd rather have your company than not."

Adel felt the compliment in his words, and she turned back to trimming the chicken. "It's nice to have the company...other than my sister. Although this does feel strange to be cooking with a man."

"If it isn't strange to do dishes with a man, why would it be strange to cook with one?" he asked. "Where are your knives?"

"You're standing in front of the drawer."

"Thanks." He pulled out a paring knife and cut the few potatoes he'd already peeled, then picked up a fresh potato and the peeler once more. "You tell me when to stop peeling. I'm used to cooking for one."

She looked over his arm at the potatoes in the pot. "Keep going."

She added the fresh herbs and a few dried ones to the chicken, then poured some water into the pan. A roasted chicken almost cooked itself, she always said. She grabbed an onion out of a bowl on the counter and reached for a cutting board.

"Who taught you to cook?" she asked.

"TV." He shrugged. "They have these cooking shows where you watch people make meals, and I figured out the basics that way."

"Wow… That's so different," she said. "I honestly thought you'd say a woman taught you."

"Well, she was a woman, but she was on TV." He shot her a teasing smile.

"And you weren't trying to impress an *Englisher* with all this?" she asked.

"No, I just wanted to eat," he replied. "Now, tonight, there is the smallest chance I'm trying to impress you."

Adel rolled her eyes. "I told you that Amish women aren't impressed by this."

"Most Amish women probably aren't." He leaned over and nudged her arm with his elbow. "But you are…just a bit. You can admit it."

Adel laughed, and when she looked up at him, his eyes glittered with humor.

"A little bit," she admitted. "But you'd shock every available woman in Redemption."

"Then by all means, keep this to yourself," he replied with a grin.

Adel continued to chop onions and celery, dumped them into the pan with the water and the chicken, drizzled some oil over the whole lot, and then went to the big, black wood-burning stove and squatted down to add some wood to the fire.

"Would you mind cranking open that window a little farther?" she asked.

Jake did as she asked, and she put another couple of logs into the fire, then closed the door. Jake put his pot onto the stove, and he held out his hand as she started to rise. Without thinking, she accepted, and he boosted her easily to her feet. But once standing, she found herself so close to him that her dress brushed the front of his pants.

Jake didn't release her hand, and she didn't move. It was like the room melted away, and it was just this man, the musky scent of him, his strong fingers holding her up.

It had been a very long time since Adel had been in a room alone with a man, let alone one as handsome as Jake was. It had been even longer since a man had held her hand like this... Because this was something different than a hand shake or simple assistance. This made her breath come quick and her knees feel weak. She licked her lips and pulled back her hand.

"I should get started on the salad," she said, just a little bit louder than she needed to. It felt like she'd almost shouted into his face, and she felt her face heat with embarrassment again. She really did have more decorum than this with other people!

"*Yah.* Sure." He hesitated for a beat, and then he stepped back. "Maybe I'll just get a drink of water."

They parted ways, and Adel couldn't help but steal a look over her shoulder as he filled a water glass from the tap. He was tall, and so well built. It was a scandalous thing to even notice, but there was something about Jake that kept tapping on a door inside her heart that she'd closed very firmly at her husband's death. And the embarrassing part was, he seemed to do it without even noticing, or trying. What did that say about her? Why on earth did the good bishop choose her to find Jake Knussli a wife? The bishop should have chosen an older woman with wisdom, and wrinkles, one who wouldn't be swayed by this man's charm.

But then, how could the bishop have possibly known that the likes of Jake Knussli would sway her? This was her own humbling truth to bear.

Jake drained a glass of water at the sink, and his heart was beating just a bit faster than it should be. Adel was a truly beautiful woman, and standing next to her at the stove had brought some heat to his face that had nothing to do with the stove next to them. She was more than beautiful—she was interesting, and deep, and wise, and… Was there a word to describe the way he felt himself pulled toward her, like he was caught in a current?

Jake watched as she rinsed lettuce at the sink, refusing to look at him as she worked. Had he made things weird between them now? Maybe there was a rebellious streak in him still, because he knew he was knocking her off her balance by offering to cook. He knew this wasn't the traditional Amish way, and yet he was doing it. Why? To be true to his own way of doing things? That shouldn't matter with his matchmaker, should it?

If he had to be completely honest with himself, he

liked getting a reaction out of *her*. It wasn't that he wanted to prove he was so different, so much as he wanted to show her who he really was deep down. This was going to prove a problem.

"Are you sure you want to be Amish?" Adel asked, and it pulled Jake out of his thoughts.

"What?" he asked.

"You haven't come back all the way," she said.

"I'm here," he replied. "That counts."

"You haven't left behind all of your *Englisher* ways, either," she countered.

Jake met her gaze for a moment. "Life changes a person. My life certainly formed me, and that isn't a bad thing. I can't strip away fifteen years of maturing in order to come back to an Amish core. And I don't think you'd really want that. I grew in a lot of ways out there. I learned to cook. I also learned to appreciate everything I'd left behind. I'm going to be a combination of all of it—my Amish upbringing and my English experiences. It's the choice to live Amish that should matter."

She didn't answer, and he wondered if she disagreed.

"If a young married couple is living alone, and the wife is pregnant," Jake said, "and let's say that she gets sick and can't cook for a few days, would the Amish husband cook?"

"Of course," she replied.

"And if an Amish wife got sick with a flu, the husband would prepare the meals for the *kinner*," he said.

"Those are emergencies," she said.

"Those are expressions of love." She froze, and as the words came out, he knew how it sounded. "What I mean is, it doesn't have to be a dire emergency for a man to cook. He might be doing it because he cares. Or because he enjoys it. Or because he enjoys a woman's company..."

He was being too honest. What was he doing?

"Do you—" She didn't look up from the cutting board, her fingers working quickly as she chopped. "Do you really like my company?"

The chopping stopped then, and she didn't turn. She cared about his answer—he could tell. He swallowed.

"*Yah*, I... I do like your company. Better than anyone else I've met so far."

His heartbeat hammered in his throat. Adel looked at him over her shoulder, and she smiled.

"You're just saying that," she said.

"Adel, I'm not asking for anything," he said. "I know where you stand. I'm just saying that I'm more comfortable with you somehow. I can be myself, and you can chide me for it, and you're still someone I like to be with."

"You should try harder to like the available women," she said.

"I am trying," he replied. "I know exactly what's on the line here. But it's fully possible for us to be friends, you know."

"Friends?" She smiled faintly. "You'll be a married man, if all goes according to plan."

"Well, until I'm a married man, then," he said.

"And how is that fair to me?" she retorted. "We spend time together, we get to know each other, to enjoy each other's company, and then you whisk off to married life. Just as you should! But it's not very fair to the friend left behind who can't continue being your friend in that way, is it?"

"Maybe not," he agreed. "Are you saying you'll miss me?"

Her cheeks colored. "I'm your matchmaker."

"And you *like* me." He shot her a grin. "I'm fun. I cook. Just wait until you taste those mashed potatoes."

Teasing her was easier somehow. When he was joking around, he could say what he meant, and what he felt, and he didn't feel foolish. Because if he dropped the joking, he'd just have to say what he felt, and that couldn't end well.

The potatoes were boiling on the stove, and he went over to check them. He used an oven mitt to lift the lid on the pot, and stabbed them with a fork. They were soft enough now. The kitchen had begun to smell pleasantly of roasting chicken.

Jake drained the potatoes into the sink, then he headed to the icebox and pulled out butter, cream cheese and a little block of cheddar.

"I just need a—" he started, and she held out a potato masher. "Thanks."

They exchanged an amused smile, and she crossed her arms and leaned against the counter, watching him. He didn't normally cook with this much direct attention, but with her, he didn't mind.

"Now, it's all about the cream-cheese-to-chive balance," he said.

"I'll mince some chives for you. How much?"

"About…" He didn't normally measure. "Oh, a handful, I suppose."

Adel chuckled. "You're that kind of cook, are you?"

"Hey, my skill is all about instinct," he joked. "Not recipes."

As he mashed potatoes and added ingredients, he listened to the soft tap of Adel's knife chopping chives. Then she appeared at his elbow with a small bowl of the minced herbs.

"Enough?" she asked.

"Perfect." He dumped the chives into the potatoes and continued to mash. Then he added the cream cheese, then the cheddar, a lump of butter, a dash of salt... When he was satisfied with the consistency, he picked up the fork from the counter and lifted a bite to her lips. "Taste it for me."

Adel looked surprised, and she parted her lips and he slid the bite of mashed potatoes into her mouth. She took the fork from his fingers and pulled it slowly out from between her lips.

"Jake, this is amazing," she said, swallowing.

He felt a little surge of pride. "Thanks."

"No, I mean, really, really good." She looked into the pot and inhaled deeply.

"So you're impressed?" He met her gaze teasingly, but deep down, he wanted to know.

"I'm impressed, Jacob. You can cook."

He grinned. "That's what I needed to hear."

Why he'd needed that confirmation from her, he wasn't quite sure. But he did care about her opinion, even if he never got to cook at home with whatever woman he married. And the thought of marriage to some faceless woman suddenly felt heavy and uncomfortable. This state was easier—single, looking and with plenty of reason to spend time with Adel.

He heard footsteps on the stairs outside, and then the side door opened. Naomi came inside, her curls erupting from her *kapp* like a ginger explosion. She was carrying a plastic bag in one hand, and her cheeks were reddened from the heat.

"Hello," Naomi said hesitantly.

Suddenly, Jake was very aware of how close he and Adel were standing to each other. Her arm brushed against his, and if he just reached out, he could have easily slid his hand around her waist. Naomi's gaze flickered quickly between them.

"You're back." Adel took a step away from him, and her voice sounded slightly breathy. "Jake here made the mashed potatoes."

"Why?" Naomi asked.

"Because I wanted to!" he replied with a short laugh. "And they're good."

He looked down at Adel and she glanced up at the same time. She smiled—a sweet smile, just for him—and said, "They really are good."

"Did you tell Lydia that you like kitchen work?" Naomi asked.

Both women looked at him then, and Jake rolled his eyes. "No, I didn't. Naomi, is this really so shocking?"

"It's…unusual," Naomi said. "Nothing I'd brag about, Jake."

"So it's going to be a problem finding a woman who'll let me make my mashed potatoes?" he asked with a laugh.

"It'll be a challenge finding a woman who lets you anywhere near her kitchen if she thinks you're going to meddle with the meal," Naomi said with a chuckle. "Let me try those potatoes."

She got a fork from the drawer and Jake stepped back as both women leaned over the pot. Naomi took a bite, exchanged a wide-eyed look with her sister and then looked back at Jake.

"Jacob Knussli, these are better than Adel's."

"Better than mine?" Adel said.

"Well, aren't they?" Naomi asked her sister. "These are amazing. We need the recipe."

"I know how he made them."

"And from now on, we'll have to call them Jacob's Superior Mashed Potatoes," Naomi said, and she burst out laughing when Adel swatted her arm.

"Superior, my foot!" Adel laughed. "Okay, they're very, very good. I will concede that they are equally as good as my own."

Jake chuckled. "I'll take it. I'm hungry, by the way."

"I'll check the chicken," Adel said, and headed toward the stove.

Naomi came over to where Jake stood and eyed him with a little smile on her face. "So you've spent your precious afternoon cooking with my sister instead of getting to know an available woman?"

"I did meet an available woman," he said, feeling just a little defensive. "Lydia is very nice."

"Is it set? Will you marry her?"

"No—" He shrugged. "I don't think she's quite right for me. Or me for her."

"Hmm." She nodded slowly. "You have what, two weeks to arrange this? No sense of urgency here?"

"Naomi, you're as bad as your sister. You two could be a matchmaking sister duo."

"We could be, because I see what my sister can't," Naomi said with a meaningful smile. "I still think your perfect match is right under your nose. And she seems very pleased with your cooking. That's a rare quality around here."

He looked up to see Adel pulling the roasted chicken from the oven. Her face was pink from the heat of the stove, and when she closed the oven door, she pulled off the oven mitts and fanned herself with one of them.

The thought of cooking with Adel, talking with Adel...just spending time with her, was all very pleasant.

"Your sister doesn't want a husband," he said. "Besides, trying to convince my matchmaker to match with me would get me a very bad reputation around here. I'd never get a wife that way."

Naomi shrugged. "Suit yourself, Jake."

But Naomi's smile looked a little too smug for his liking. Maybe she had a point, though, and he was spending just a little too much time with his matchmaker instead of finding that match which would give him the farm.

Chapter Seven

That evening, Jake went to his uncle's farm to do the chores. The house was still locked up, covered in a yellow plastic tent, and it would be another two days before it was opened and he could go inside again. He'd be permanently locked out of this place if he didn't find a wife, though, and standing in front of the barn, looking out across the farmyard, he felt the depth of everything he would lose.

Gott, is it Your will that I get this farm in my name? he prayed silently. *Or do You have other plans for me? Should I be trying to let go of this farm instead of struggling to keep it?*

He wished at times like this that *Gott* would just give him a clear answer, but all he got in response was the chattering call of a blue jay in a nearby tree.

The cattle were out grazing in a far field, and Jake had tagged the ear of two new calves. The herd was growing. Since he'd come back, ten new calves had been born. But this wasn't just about bringing a rundown farm back from the brink. Jake had grown, too.

Living English, he'd forgotten the feeling of tired muscles mingled with the awe of watching a sunset over the fields. He'd forgotten the panic of a calf born limp and lifeless, and then watching it lift its head for the first time and feeling like that one weak bawl from a newborn held all the hope in the entire world. He'd matured into a man out there with the English, but he was deepening into the man he was born to be back home with the Amish.

Who would he be if he lost the family farm now? And would he have to find out?

He didn't know why he was feeling so fatalistic after meeting one woman, but he'd been looking at the available women in Redemption ever since he returned, and the only woman to spark his interest was his matchmaker—the one with reasons to keep herself single. Up until this point, he'd assumed that he'd meet someone. He'd certainly prayed that he would, and he'd truly believed that *Gott* would put a woman in his path who would fill his heart and give him the ability to be married in time to keep the farm. So having to use a matchmaker with the deadline steadily approaching was starting to feel desperate.

Jake headed back in the direction of the chicken coop. His shoulders were sore, but it did feel good to be out in the open air, working a job where he could see the results and feel the good he was doing on a heart-deep level. If nothing else, he was learning where he belonged, and it wasn't back with the English.

"Jacob!"

He shaded his eyes to see his neighbor, Corny Moser,

at the fence. Corny was a man nearing fifty with a house-ful of *kinner* and a plump, serious wife.

"How are you?" Jake called as he headed in the man's direction.

"Good, good." Corny leaned against the rail. "How's the fumigation going?"

"Two more days, and then they'll let me back inside," he said.

"Yah, yah…" Corny chewed the side of his cheek. "I heard some rumors about your inheritance being in question?"

"It's not final unless I'm married," Jake replied.

Corny pulled off his hat and inspected it. *"Yah,* I heard that. I have a younger sister coming to visit me next month. She's thirty-five, has three *kinner* from her first marriage, and she's a good cook. She's also good with cattle—which is something you don't think of right off when looking for a wife, but it's real useful. There are times you need a woman to do more than open and close gates for you, you know? Like when the calving is going strong, or when you're getting ready for mar-ket. So a woman who can pitch in is real helpful when you're starting out and don't have a pile of nephews or cousins to pitch in, you know?"

Corny looked up then and met Jake's gaze seriously.

"That's something to think about," Jake replied.

"Yah. It's something to consider. I didn't think about it when I married Ruth, but it turns out she's good with cattle. They like her. She's got the touch, you know? She can stand at the fence and sing and she'll get a whole audience of cattle who come to just listen."

"I didn't know that," Jake said, and he thought fondly

back to his own *mamm*'s singing—not quite the kind that would call up cattle from the field, though.

"I can introduce you when she comes," Corny said. "You could come for dinner at our place, and maybe take her for a stroll."

"Honestly, Corny, I need a wife in a week and a half," he replied.

"That soon?" Corny shot him a look of surprise. "Why'd you put it off so long?"

"I didn't!" Jake insisted. "I was looking, talking to available women, saying hello…"

"Not saying you wanted a wife," Corny replied. "That's a different message altogether."

"Maybe so, but I was hoping for love," Jake replied.

"Right. Right." He nodded a couple of times.

"How did you meet Ruth?" Jake asked.

"She was in the youth group. I asked her home from singing."

Jake's youth group days were behind him, nor did he want a wife half his age. But he could see how he'd missed out on that prime time for pairing off when young couples took the plunge. It was how Alphie had met his wife, too. It wasn't quite so easy at his age.

"But you fell in love with her, right?" Jake asked.

"*Yah*. That's how it works in a buggy in the moonlight," Corny said with a chuckle. "You should try it. And if you're still single when my sister gets here, we'll have that dinner."

"If I'm still single when your sister gets here, I won't have a farm," he replied seriously.

Corny pressed his lips together and didn't answer that. Perhaps he was rethinking his offer of introduction.

Because without a farm, what could Jake actually offer a woman? Just his heart? At eighteen, a girl would accept that from a boy she loved. Now? He'd better have more.

"Do you have a backup plan?" Corny asked after some silence.

"I have some money tucked away, and I would find some work of some sort—farmwork, hopefully," he replied.

"You should have come home sooner," Corny said. "Coming back now is like starting from scratch where a twenty-year-old kid starts."

"I know it." Jake clenched his teeth together, trying to push back his own rising frustration.

"That's like fifteen years lost..." Corny seemed to be talking more to himself. "Fifteen years of building a career around here, a reputation. *Englisher* work is different."

"I know, I know," Jake said. There was no turning back time. "But if I get married in time, I've got the family land back, and when I have *kinner*, I'll have something to leave them."

Corny nodded. "That would be best. I sympathize, Jacob. I really do."

Corny Moser hadn't wasted his time, and neither had most of the community. Starting life was important to the Amish, and Jake had missed out.

"I need to finish up chores tonight," Jake said. "If you're so inclined, send up a prayer for me that I'll find the right woman in time."

"I'll certainly do that," Corny replied. "Remember what I said about buggies in the moonlight. I'm a firm believer that they aid the process very nicely."

Jake chuckled. "Thanks. I'll keep it in mind."

Jake tapped the fence in farewell and he headed back in the direction of the chicken coop. Corny's sister wouldn't arrive soon enough for Jake to inherit this land, and wherever he looked, he was faced with memories. Corny was right, though, he'd come home too late. If he'd returned sooner, his uncle might have put him in the will without this silly requirement that he be married.

Alphie was married now. He'd found a wife, and they had three little ones. Alphie had the Amish life that Jake had missed out on. And Alphie had been so full of gossip to pass along, the stories that kept Jake from coming home.

Jake couldn't really blame anyone but himself, but he had a few residual feelings left for Alphie, too. He'd visited him a few times since his return, and looking around Alphie's Amish sitting room, with a plump wife in the kitchen and little ones playing overhead, he'd felt a wash of jealousy. That and his growing sense that perhaps he'd listened too much to his cousin's family tales that kept him away from Alphie now.

He had no one to blame but himself, but he'd also trusted the wrong source of information about what was happening at home. Not everyone's interest in his life was selfless. Some people saw entertainment in someone else's difficulty—not intentionally, but it was what it boiled down to—and Jake was the one who had to live with the fallout.

The sun had just set, leaving a crimson glow along the horizon. Adel sat on the porch with a kerosene lamp to illumine her knitting. She was making a scarf. In the later months of the year, the tourists who visited their bed-and-breakfast liked having some handmade items to purchase, and Adel was working on her stash of them that would be for sale.

She heard the plod of hooves as Jake sent his horse into the pasture, and then the click of the gate locking shut again. Sounds seemed to carry farther in the night air with nothing to compete with but the hum of insects and the creak of her porch swing as she gently rocked back and forth.

She put her knitting aside for a moment, and inspected a burn on her wrist. She'd gotten it when cleaning the coals out of the oven that evening. They hadn't been as cool as she'd thought. She picked up her knitting again; the familiar looping of yarn and clicking of needles was soothing. She didn't have to think when she knitted—her hands knew the work.

"Are you waiting up for me?" Jake's deep voice broke through the stillness, and she looked over her shoulder to see him coming up to the house.

"Sort of," she replied. "I like to sit out here and think. It's soothing."

"Where's your sister?" he asked.

"She's in bed."

"You want company?" he asked.

She should say no. She should send him in and use the opportunity to smooth down her own feelings, but when she found his gentle gaze locked on her face, she didn't have the heart to turn him away.

She lifted the skein of yarn. "You can hold my wool, if you like. Don't tell me you knit, too."

Jake laughed, and he took a seat on the swing next to her, dutifully holding the skein of yarn in one palm. "No, I don't knit. You're safe from having to explain *that*."

His arm was warm against hers, and he smelled faintly of hay and sunshine. He took over rocking the swing, his long legs pushing them farther than she'd been able to, and she enjoyed the sensation of just letting go.

"So what are you thinking about out here?" he asked.

"You." She felt her face heat, and she dropped a stitch. "I mean...getting you a match."

"Of course." He slowed the rocking while she picked free her mistake and got it back on the needle. "What are my chances here?"

"I don't know," she admitted. "It's in *Gott*'s hands, as is every marriage. I'm going to do my best to find you a good and virtuous woman. The decision you two make will be up to you."

"My neighbor suggested I meet his sister," he said. "She's a little older than me, has three *kinner*. But she won't be in Redemption in time, and when he realized that it would be past the date for getting the farm in the mix, I think he cooled to the idea."

"Hmm." She continued knitting. "He wanted two family farms right next to each other. It's understandable."

"Yah," he said quietly. "But it made me think... Who am I without a farm, Adel?"

She glanced up at him. "You're Jacob Knussli."

"Yah, but what do I have to offer if I have no paid-off farm?" he said. "I realized that I've wasted fifteen years."

"You have yourself, Jake," she said. "And that's the difference between a marriage of convenience and a marriage for love. If you marry for love, you're both willing to sacrifice a lot to be together."

"The farm won't matter?" he asked.

"For the right woman."

"Will I find that kind of love, though?"

Adel put down her knitting. "I'm going to tell you a story that Mark told over and over again to young people looking for love."

"All right."

"When you want a barn, you don't look around yourself for one that has simply dropped from the sky ready-made, do you?"

Jake chuckled. "No."

"That's right. You look for the spot. You look for a piece of farmland close to the house, but far enough away to give you some space to live. You need a place that is a little higher so it won't flood during storms. You need a spot that is level and that is just the right distance from the fields. And then, you build it."

Jake was silent, and her mind went back to when her husband would tell that story to some young man thinking about marriage.

"I hated that story," she said softly.

"What?"

"I did," she confessed. "It's very wise, but what he was saying was that you find a woman who has good characteristics, and then you build a life with her. It's what he did with me."

"That's not a good thing?" he asked.

"It is a good thing. It's the very advice I'm giving

you," she replied. "But for me... It sounded like he hadn't really loved me, but he'd learned to. Or he knew he could, if he just tried. I was young and I didn't like to hear that I was just a good collection of characteristics he could learn to love."

She was probably saying too much, but there was something about a cool evening, the velvet darkness and the warm pool of kerosene light around them that softened the moment.

"I'm sure you were much more than that," Jake said, and his voice was firm. "I'm serious, Adel. From what you've told me about him, he respected you deeply. He went to you for your insight into situations. He loved you."

"He did love me." She knew it. "But that story rankled me all the same."

Jake smiled faintly. "I'm glad you told me that."

"Does it help?" she asked.

He shook his head. "It means you trust me. You haven't told anyone else that, have you?"

Adel dropped her gaze. He'd guessed right. "No, I haven't."

"A wife is more than a collection of good character traits," he said quietly. "She's not just a woman in the kitchen, or a woman hanging your laundry. She's the one you come home to, both physically and emotionally. She's the one who will build you up when you feel weak, make you feel like you can face life's challenges again. She's the one who will brighten your home and make it sunny during rainy days. And she's the one you work every backbreaking hour to provide for, because you want her to have everything she could ever need. And

I think if a man is really blessed, that wife will open up to him and show him the tender parts inside of her, too."

Adel's breath caught. It was beautiful… His gaze dropped down to her wrist and he frowned.

"What happened?" He caught her hand in his and turned it over to expose the burn on the inside of her wrist.

"I was cleaning the stove," she whispered.

"Ouch," he said in sympathy, and he ran his thumb over the tender flesh beside the burn. He didn't let go of her hand, either, as if he'd forgotten he was holding it, and while she knew she should pull back, the moment to do so gracefully had passed.

"I don't want to tell a woman that she simply had potential, and so I married her," he said quietly. "I want to be able to tell her that I fell in love with her. If I'm to build a life, choose a spot and start nailing together a life with a woman, then what better foundation than love?"

"Do you have time for that?" she breathed.

He ran his fingers in a tingling line down her palm, and then released her hand.

"If I'm building a life, and the foundation is a piece of land and a woman who'd like the financial security of living there, I'm not sure that I'll feel secure. Not on a heart level. And yet, I have to offer a woman something more than this battered heart of mine."

"You want to be loved," she said softly, and the realization brought tears to her eyes. He'd been talking all this time about finding a woman he felt a spark with, but it went deeper than that. Jacob wanted a woman to love him back… It was the only thing that brought any kind of security in a relationship.

"Yah." He leaned back, his arm pressed against hers. "I'd very much like to be loved."

For a couple of minutes they swung gently together in silence, her knitting forgotten.

"For what it's worth," she said quietly, "I do think that a true and honest heart is the most important thing a man can offer."

But there was no time for him to fully explore that with any of the women she was introducing to him. Unless *Gott* moved and showed Jake beyond a shadow of a doubt that the woman he chose was *Gott*'s will for him.

"But the farm is what will draw them in," he said, his voice low. "A man's heart is important, but so is his ability to provide."

If only Jake had come to her a few months sooner, she might have had more time to help him find a love match. It was heartbreaking now to think of a man with such a longing for love settling for less. Because even though he was a rebel, and even though he was formed by his *Englisher* years spent away, Jacob Knussli deserved that.

Chapter Eight

Dear Gott, Adel prayed while she lay in bed that night. *Guide Jacob to the woman You have for him. Show him Your will. Give him the love he longs for...*

A cool breeze came in the open bedroom window, ruffling the curtain and cooling her bare arms. She lay with the blanket and sheet flung back, too hot for covers.

And when You do provide that wife for him, help me to be happy for him—truly and sincerely. Help me to let go.

Because as much as she hated to admit it, Adel was getting attached to her very first client. She had started out more protective of the women in Redemption, not wanting them to be taken advantage of or have their hearts broken, but somehow her emotional investment had changed. Now, she was seeing Jake's sensitive heart, his deeper longings, and she was feeling more than she should be.

Perhaps this was a chance for her to grow, too. It was time for her to learn how to draw a line between herself and others, to keep her emotions in check. She no longer had a husband to help with that. When a woman was married, her heart belonged to her husband, and everyone understood when she took an emotional step back from the men in the community. It was right and good.

But she was no longer married. There was no husband to offend…there was no husband to turn her emotions toward. She had to learn how to be more selfless, and to work for the good of others without anything in return. And to keep her heart secure in the process.

And yet, she would get something in return—a position in this community, respect from the other men and women and the knowledge that her presence here in Redemption truly did make a difference. It was the kind of return that took time, and self-control, and maturity. She'd been praying for this exact thing in her life for the last few years, and *Gott* was giving it to her! But like anything, getting what she wanted felt different from how she'd imagined it would, and it would take more strength than she'd ever dreamed.

Adel fell asleep that night, the sheet and blanket flung back so that she could feel the cool breeze on her feet and her arms, and she had the sense that she was changing, too. Growth was rarely comfortable— Mark said that often. And *Gott* was giving her a chance at the life she'd prayed for.

It was time for her to step up and accept the challenge.

The next morning, Adel and Jake arrived at the Swarey Flower Farm. Delia Swarey sold flowers to local florists, as well as to vendors looking for blooms for weddings and the like. She had massive gardens that she and her four sons tended, as well as greenhouses that extended her growing season well into the fall with a few specialized plants that she tended through the winter, as well.

As Jake unhitched the horse, Adel sank into a chair in Delia's kitchen.

"Jake is younger than me," Delia said.

"By two years," Adel said. "That's not such a big deal this side of thirty, is it?"

"Not as much," Delia agreed. "It's the maturity that matters. You think he's...mature enough for this family?"

Adel nodded. "I wouldn't have brought him here if I didn't think so. I've seen a side to him that he keeps hidden from most people, and he's a wonderful man. He's kind, considerate, a deep thinker. And he's glad to be home in the Amish world again."

"Did he come for the inheritance?" Delia asked. "That's something that worries me. You said that he only gets the farm if he's married. I don't need a farm. I have the flower farm here, and I'm managing all right. This wouldn't be about money for me."

"I wouldn't be so crass as to suggest it," Adel said earnestly. "It isn't about money for him, either."

"How do you know?" Delia asked. "He would say that, wouldn't he?"

She knew because she'd spent some time with him, listening to him, reading his expressions when he shared his deeper feelings. Jake was a special man, and while he came across as charming and handsome without much else to him, that couldn't be further from the truth. Yet, how could she explain that to Delia?

"At first I worried about that, too," Adel said. "Coming home to Redemption was a complicated experience for him. His uncle Johannes wasn't exactly welcoming, so it wouldn't have been an easy return, especially after his *daet*'s death. But Jacob is back now because he truly wants to be here."

"What did he say?" Delia pressed. "What convinced you?"

But those conversations felt precious, somehow, and she'd assured him that she could be discreet.

"You'll have to ask him about it, and see what I mean," Adel said.

Jake had deepened more than anyone might realize, and she'd seen such a tender core to him that it made her feel a strange urge to protect him, to encourage him. It gave her a glimpse into the depth of emotional intimacy he had to offer a woman he trusted with his heart.

"Are you ready to get married again?" Adel asked softly.

"I miss Zeke a lot," Delia said. "You understand, I know, because you lost Mark."

"I do." Adel nodded. "It's hard."

"Very hard." Delia sucked in a deep breath. "But my boys are running wild on me, and I could use some help in raising them. Jacob isn't a *daet*, though. He might not understand how I love my boys."

"There also isn't the complication of blending a family of stepsiblings," Adel pointed out.

Delia nodded. "Good point. What does he think of me?"

"He's here, isn't he?" Adel asked. "He's a bit overwhelmed with this process of finding a wife this quickly."

She felt a little twinge at sharing that personal detail about Jake. Did he want her to tell that to his prospective matches? Or was Adel just feeling protective of her deeper discussions with Jake? Delia was a good woman, and she had a big heart. Of anyone, Adel was sure she could love her second husband dearly, and Jake needed that.

"I talked to my boys this morning about the possibility of me getting married again, and them having a new *daet*," Delia said.

"What did they think?" Adel asked.

"They thought it was too soon," she said. "They miss their *daet* a lot. They did everything with him. They talk about the things he said, and the way he did things all the time. When I told them that you wanted to introduce me to a man looking for a wife, they said they wanted to meet him before I do." Delia shrugged and laughed softly. "They're such protective boys."

Adel looked out the window. Jake was standing with Delia's oldest son, Ezekiel.

"They look like they're getting along," Adel said.

Delia leaned forward to look, too. "*Yah*, they do…"

"They don't want a new father in their lives?" Adel asked.

"I don't think they know what they want," Delia said. "They miss Zeke, but he's not coming back. And we do need a man around here to give them an example. They can't only work with a memory."

"They want to take care of you themselves?" Adel asked.

"They do." Delia nudged a plate of pastries closer to Adel. "But that won't work when they have sweethearts of their own, will it? Of course, they're boys, and they don't see that." She sighed. "I miss having someone to lean on."

"I think you're doing a great job with them," Adel said. "But I know what you mean about missing that support."

Adel missed it, too. There was something about the strength of a husband that no other relationship could replace.

"I wouldn't say this to anyone else, but I know you understand, Adel," Delia said, lowering her voice. "I miss being kissed. Zeke used to kiss my forehead on his way past, and it was just such a little thing, but I miss that. I miss being hugged—not by a son, but by a man I'll go to sleep with, and wake up next to."

Adel swallowed. Yes, she missed all of that, too.

"I feel guilty for missing it so much," Delia said.

"Don't," Adel said. "It's normal. And I do believe that *Gott* gives us that longing for connection for a reason. He places the lonely in families, remember? There is nothing wrong with yearning for the very thing that *Gott* provides!"

"But you've gone much longer on your own," Delia said. "And you seem fine."

"*Gott* has different paths for all of us," Adel said. And she'd truly believed these last five years that *Gott* was not leading her toward another marriage. But now, at the least opportune time, she was yearning for all those things that Delia yearned for. Adel wasn't as "fine" as she seemed.

Adel looked out the window again, and this time she saw that the other three boys had materialized from somewhere. The boys were standing around, one digging his boot into the gravel, another with his thumbs stuck in his suspenders. Ezekiel's arms were crossed over his chest and he straightened up to his full height, just a few inches shorter than Jake was. Delia had promised her boys that they could talk to Jake first, and Adel couldn't help but wonder what tests they were putting him through.

Jake looked toward the house, and he met Adel's gaze with a look of perplexed panic. She couldn't help but chuckle.

"I wonder what the boys are saying," Adel said.

"I wonder..." Delia murmured.

Jake could see Adel in the window, and Delia standing behind her. But it was Adel's serious, clear gaze that met his. What he wouldn't give for Adel at his side right now, because the four teenagers weren't responding to any of his attempts to be friendly.

"How come you lived English?" the oldest, Ezekiel, asked. "You were English for a really long time, too. We know an older boy who went English during his *Rumspringa*, but only for a few months. He was back before spring."

"I'm glad he came back so quickly," Jake said. "That was wise of him."

"Why didn't you?" Thomas pressed. He was younger than Ezekiel, but stood an inch taller, just about as tall as Jake was. "You're avoiding the question."

"You're speaking to your elder," Jake said.

"I'm only asking what my mother will ask you,"

Ezekiel replied. "She said we could ask you the questions that mattered most to us. And this one matters."

"There were other pressures," Jake said. "My father and I didn't get along, and when he passed away, I didn't think my uncle would be glad to see me."

"We lost our father," Thomas said. "And nothing would chase us away from our responsibilities right here at home."

"Are you old enough for your *Rumspringa*?" Jake asked.

"He's not, but I'm old enough." Ezekiel met his gaze like an equal. "I'm skipping mine. I don't need to go wild to find out what's important."

"I'm glad to hear you have the maturity," Jake said. "Your *mamm* raised you well."

"My *daet* raised us all well." There was some defiance in that gaze.

"We heard you've got a farm," one of the younger boys said. This was Aaron, and he looked to be about fifteen.

"*Yah*. I *will* have a farm…" How much was he supposed to say to teenagers? This was a conversation that should be happening between adults. He looked toward the house again. The women weren't in the window. The boys had been permitted to question him, and they were perceptive, and not inclined to trust him, it seemed. Should he just walk away from them? This was where he needed Adel's advice.

"You'll only have the farm if you marry our *mamm*." That was from the youngest boy—Moses. "We know that."

"You want our *mamm* to marry you for the inheritance," Ezekiel said. "She'd be useful to you."

That sparked anger, and Jake sent the boy an annoyed look.

"Women are not tools to be used. I haven't even discussed this with your mother," Jake said. "And I won't discuss it with the four of you."

"Our *mamm* said you *have* to talk to us first," Moses said, squaring his not-quite-grown shoulders. "We're the men here."

Jake sighed. "You're boys."

"She didn't exactly say that," Thomas said to his brother.

"But she won't marry him if we tell her we won't accept him," Aaron retorted.

Jake rubbed a hand over his eyes.

"What do you want in a wife?" Ezekiel asked.

Jake shut his eyes for a moment, praying for patience. "I want a good woman who loves *Gott*."

"That's very broad," Ezekiel said dryly. "That's all that matters to you? So she'll be the one who cooks your meal, cleans your home…and that's all that matters to you? What about her happiness? I doubt picking up after you is all that fun. We want our *mamm* to be happy."

Ezekiel was old enough now at seventeen to have a few opinions of his own, and if Jake were on the outside of this, he'd be impressed with the boy's strength of resolve.

"All right. You want to talk like men?" Jake's patience was spent. "I want more than just a good woman. You're right. Marriage isn't just about a man who works outdoors and a woman who takes care of the house.

There's a whole lot more to a happy home than shared work. And that is why discussing the finer details with the four of you doesn't help anything." Jake looked at the glowering faces before him. "You don't like me, do you?"

"Not a lot," Moses said. Jake smiled grimly at the youngest boy, and he shuffled uncomfortably, stepping back.

"Don't let him intimidate you," Ezekiel said to his brother, then turned back to Jake. "If we don't like you, how do you expect to be our *daet*?"

"It wouldn't be easy," Jake said soberly. "This would have to work for the whole family, and it's not just about the adults."

"You better believe that," Aaron muttered.

"So with the understanding that you all can't stand me," Jake said with a small smile, "will you at least let me talk with your mother? If you have as much sway as you say, then I don't have a hope, anyway. But I can't even leave until your mother and I have spoken. They're waiting for me in there."

The boys exchanged a look among them. They could obviously see the reasoning there. They were the *kinner* in this home, after all, and their mother was the final say.

"*Yah*, all right," Ezekiel said.

Jake eyed them for a moment, but they stared back at him in silence. There was nothing reassuring he could say to them. He was here to discuss the possibility of marriage with their mother, and they'd rather see the back of him. So he sighed and headed toward the house without another word.

Jake tapped on the door and opened it. They were expecting him, after all. He found the women in the kitchen. He caught Adel's eye first, wondering what the tone was in here. If the boys were that antagonistic toward him, was Delia going to even want to entertain this? Should they just leave now?

"Jacob Knussli, you remember Delia Swarey," Adel said. "We saw you chatting with the boys."

"Yah." He smiled faintly. "They...are a protective bunch."

"Oh, they are that," Delia said with a fond smile. "They figured that you should talk to them first, man to man. I didn't see the harm. They're sweet boys."

Downright adorable, he thought wryly.

"Have a seat?" Adel prompted.

"Yes, do sit down," Delia said. "Would you like a pastry?"

Delia had a nice smile, and an easy way about her. She was older than Lydia, and she had some lines around her eyes, but she still looked youthful enough. But he could feel the same thing he'd felt with Lydia already. They were both perfectly nice women with so much to offer...and just not for him.

"Thank you," he said, accepting an apple pastry, flaky and delicate. "This looks delicious..."

"Delia makes the best apple strudel," Adel said. "I've bought some of her strudel to serve at the bed-and-breakfast. No one can bake it flakier here in Redemption. That's a guarantee."

Jake took a bite—he had to taste it now—and he chewed slowly. Adel was right. He'd never eaten a better strudel. Now they'd make small talk about strudel and gardening, or whatever it was they decided to talk about that wasn't the real reason why he was here. Because when they did discuss what they wanted in life, it wouldn't be so terribly different. They'd both want an Amish home with peace and happiness inside those walls. But the boys needed someone they could respect and accept, and that wasn't going to happen in a matter of days.

Those boys loved their *mamm*, and they wanted to keep her safe. If he did manage to win them over, it would happen with persistence and time—the one luxury he didn't have. And plowing forward to marry their *mamm* would ruin any attempts at a relationship with them in the future. This wasn't about marrying a woman. For the Swarey home, it was about building a family. That was too precious to rush.

Finding a wife wasn't turning out to be a very simple thing. The Bible said, "House and riches are the inheritance of fathers: and a prudent wife is from the Lord." The more he thought about it, the truer those words rang. A wife was a gift from above.

Gott, guide me, he prayed.

An hour later, Jake sat in the buggy, fiddling with the reins. Adel was still in the house—she'd stayed to talk to Delia alone with him safely out of earshot. The boys, who'd helped him hitch his horse back up in record time, had retreated to the stable, but when Jake leaned over to look in their direction, he found all four of them eyeing his buggy uncomfortably, and when they saw that he'd spotted them, they sauntered off toward the house with exaggerated nonchalance.

He turned forward again. The side door opened and Adel came out of the house. The boys headed up the steps, looking over their shoulders in his direction.

"Ezekiel, you've grown again," Adel said with a smile. "And Moses, Thomas, Aaron—every time I see you you're bigger! What does your mother feed you?"

The boys all seemed to soften toward Adel, and shy smiles broke over their faces. They murmured replies, and Adel turned and said something to Delia, who stood in the doorway. Delia gave him a friendly look, but nothing more.

When Adel pulled herself up into the buggy, the door closed firmly behind the boys, and the horse started forward. Jake licked his lips and glanced down at Adel.

"They are really nice boys," Adel said.

Jake gave her a wry look. "Are they?"

"*Yah.* Very good *kinner.* They work hard for their *mamm.* That flower farm flourishes because of their hard work."

He nodded. "They don't like me much."

"Their *daet* only died two years ago, and I really did think they'd be more ready to accept a new *daet,*" Adel said, casting him an apologetic look. "I had a good talk with Delia, and she said that she can't rush anything without her boys' cooperation."

"That's understandable," he said.

"She likes you," Adel said. "She said she thinks you'll make someone a very good husband, but unfortunately, she can't look any further into a marriage."

"She's a very nice person, too," he said, and he felt an unexpected wave of relief.

"I'm really sorry," Adel said. "It's my fault. I really

thought she'd be more eager to get a man back into her home, but... I didn't think far enough ahead. And I should have."

"Hey, it's fine—" He reached out instinctively and squeezed her hand. He hadn't thought before he did it, but her soft fingers felt good in his. She was a comfort.

"You have so much to offer a wife," Adel said. "I know this is rushed, but I truly do believe you have so much to give. I just need to be able to show people what I see, and I feel like I failed there with Delia."

He looked over at her. Her hand was still in his, and she looked so full of remorse, he could have hugged her right there. Instead, he let go of her hand.

"You didn't fail," he said. "It wasn't the right match. That's all."

Jake reined the horse in where the drive met the road.

Adel thought he had a lot to offer... Somehow that warmed him in a way nothing else could. She saw the man in him, and even if it was entirely unhelpful right now, he saw the woman in her.

"Do you have to get back?" he asked, glancing over at her.

"Not really," she replied. "Why?"

"Because I want ice cream." He flicked the reins and guided the horse onto the paved road. "Some days, after being particularly humbled, a man just needs some caramel ripple."

Chapter Nine

Somehow, Adel had been preparing herself to let Delia down, not the other way around. And she wasn't sure why Jake being rejected by a potential match had pricked her heart quite this way, but it had. At first, she might have thought that a rejection would bother him, but she had misjudged Jake, too. She'd discovered a softer center to the man than she ever guessed existed. Not only did he have good intentions in what he wanted to offer a wife, but Jacob wanted to be loved, too.

And yet, there was this one, selfish, wicked part of her that was happy that Delia had pulled back—not because she wanted to see Jake hurt, but because it meant she had a little more time getting to know this complicated man. It was an unlikely friendship, but one that was sinking under all her defenses.

"Ice cream does improve a day," Adel said.

"*Yah.* It does." He flicked the reins, and her gaze was drawn to his strong, broad hands.

"Have you been going to the Aberdeen Dairy often?" she asked, recognizing the route.

"No." He glanced down at her, and a playful smile tickled the corner of his lips. "But I've driven by the place often enough, and I kept telling myself I'd stop in when I had more time."

"At least you're taking the time now," she said. "That's a very *Englisher* way of looking at things—not having time."

"Maybe." He smiled faintly, and he fell silent. His expression turned cloudy and he kept his gaze locked on the road.

"I didn't mean to offend," she said after a moment.

"What?" He looked over at her. "It's not you. Sorry. Not you at all. It's something I had on my mind last night and can't get rid of. I've been thinking that it's probably time I hashed a few things out with my cousin, but I wanted to wait until I knew whether the farm was mine or not before I did."

"You said you've visited him," she said.

"Yah," he replied. "But I've never said my piece. The thing is, I believed him. I listened to him and I took his perspective seriously. And he was so eager to gather up these stories that kept me distanced from my family and pass them along to me, so supportive of me not coming home…"

"Do you think he wanted the land?" she asked.

He shook his head slowly. "No. He was plenty surprised when he found out he'd get it if I didn't get married. And he didn't think he had any hope of that farm coming to him because he was convinced I'd find a wife. I believe him about that. No, he passed along stories to me because he enjoyed telling them. And he passed stories back to my father and uncle for the same reason. He liked being involved. He liked being the bearer of news."

"A gossip," she murmured.

"Is that what it is?" He sighed, then shook his head. "He was married, had *kinner*, and he was so supportive of me living my life on my own terms. He would never judge, he said. Well, I wish he'd judged a little bit. Because me staying away benefited him more than any of us anticipated."

"Have you told the bishop about this?" Adel asked.

He shook his head. "And I won't. It's my personal business. I'll talk to my cousin myself. I don't need church leadership involved. This is a family issue."

The short, brightly painted ice cream shop was ahead with a sign that read Aberdeen Dairy. It was set back from the road a little way, nestled next to a treed area, and beyond it was the actual dairy farm. It was modern and spread out, bright new buildings shining in the sunlight with a generous parking lot that made use of the shade from the trees. Some families occupied a few picnic tables in amid the trees, as well. One *Englisher* couple sat on the lowered tailgate of a big red pickup truck as they ate ice cream sundaes, and they looked up in idle curiosity as Adel and Jake parked the buggy next to a horse rail. This was an *Englisher*-owned-and-operated shop that many Amish people frequented, but this morning, there were mostly cars and pickup trucks in the parking lot.

Jake held the door for Adel, and they went into the comforting blast of air-conditioning. Adel shivered in pleasure and scanned the menu board.

"Whatever you want," Jake said. "It's my treat."

Adel went over to look into the freezer where the buckets of ice cream sat, rows of creamy, colorful swirls. There were a few people ahead of them in line, so there was time. Jake stood next to her for a moment, his arm just a whisper from hers, and she could feel the warmth of him next to her.

"You deserve some payoff for all the work you're putting in with me," he said.

"It's not all misery," she said jokingly.

"Good." She glanced up and he was closer to her than she'd thought he'd be, and his gaze dragged over her face, then he took a step back. "I'm just going to check the corkboard for job listings."

Adel surveyed her favorite ice cream choices—peach, raspberry, mint chocolate chip... When she looked up again, she saw Jake tearing a phone number off a posting.

"Next!" the cashier called, and Jake came over to join her at the counter.

"Hi," Jake said. "Can we get two large cones, please? One caramel ripple and one—" He looked at her.

"Peach, please."

Generous scoops of ice cream were loaded into sugar cones, and Jake pulled out his wallet to pay. Then they headed back to a free booth. Adel took a lick of ice cream as she sat down, but her gaze was on that little slip of paper he ripped from the board.

"You have a farm," she said quietly.

Jake laid the piece of paper on the tabletop next to his napkin. "Alphie might very well have that farm. I'm trying to be prepared."

"But what about faith?"

"I'm praying, Adel," he said quietly. "I pray constantly. But *Gott* doesn't always give us exactly what we pray for. He gives us what is good for us—and we don't always see the bigger picture."

"There is the kind of faith that accepts what *Gott* gives and chooses not to question," she said quietly. "And then there is the kind of faith, like the children of Israel at the Jordan River. Nothing happened until their toes touched the water."

"I think I'm already fully invested," he said. "If that's what you mean."

"Are you?" She looked down at the slip of paper with telephone number and address. "I think we need to put our feet into the Jordan, Jake. This isn't done yet. You're still meeting prospective matches."

He sighed. "I'm doing my best, Adel."

He was—she could see that. But Adel hadn't given up yet.

"When is your house open again after fumigation?" she asked.

"Today, actually. I swept it out this morning after I did chores. The opened it up for me a day early."

"Excellent timing." She took another bite of ice cream. "Let's get to work on your kitchen. You want to be prepared in case everything falls apart around you. But I think you should be prepared for *Gott* to answer your prayer and give you a wife."

He smiled faintly. "What are my chances here, Adel?"

"With just me and our best intentions?" she said. "That's anyone's guess. But with *Gott* working? Your chances suddenly turn into certainties. Have some faith, Jake."

His gaze softened. "I'm a little bit embarrassed to have you see it."

"I won't judge your home," she said softly. "I've already gotten to know you again, and I know how hard you've worked. But let's get it straightened up so there is less to explain to a wife."

"You're a treasure, Adel," he said quietly.

The word was the same one Mark used to use, and her breath caught. A treasure... And something inside her yearned to hear it again from his mouth. To be truly treasured by a man was a unique and wonderful experience...

She had to stop this. She was helping find a wife. She wasn't the one he'd treasure going forward. She was here for the transition, and then she'd have to step back.

It was best not to forget that when his voice was low and his warm gaze locked on hers. Because Jacob Knussli was turning out to be very, very easy to fall for.

When they arrived at the farm, Jake reined in the horse and eyed the farmhouse warily. That old house, the place that held so many memories, was also one he was ashamed of. He'd worked much harder on the farm than he had on the house, and he wasn't even sure why.

"I can start on the kitchen while you do chores," Adel said.

"You could, but—" He swallowed. "I mean, if you felt like coming with me to do the chores, we could—"

"Jake, putting this off won't make it any easier," she said. "I've seen many kitchens before. I've helped families clean out a dead relative's house before, too. I've helped clean out bedrooms from the bedridden. I understand how big a mess can get. There is no shame in needing help."

Did she know how big the emotional mess was for him, too? Because that was probably the bigger problem right now.

"Jake, you go do the work you need to do," she said. "And trust that I'll hold all judgment."

Trust her... He didn't have much choice, did he?

Jake unlocked the door and pushed it open. The kitchen was dim, the curtains all pulled shut, and there was the musty smell of old house to greet them. He scanned the familiar kitchen. He had one side of the table he kept clean for eating, but the rest of it was covered in junk from piles of old *Budget* newspapers to bottles of boot black, an old roasting pan, some baskets in a wobbling pile, two old spools from bailing twine. He should have thrown all of it away—just filled a wagon and made a trip to the dump—but it seemed like every day he dedicated to cleaning out this house left him facing a whole new mess underneath the last one.

"It's better than it was," he said, his face heating with embarrassment. "I had to throw out all sorts of rotting food when I got here. And I just emptied everything into the garbage. The rest is just clutter. My uncle didn't throw anything away. Believe it or not, I've actually cleared out a lot, but I started upstairs."

He hadn't been able to face sleeping in the clutter, and he'd completely emptied his old bedroom. Then he'd moved on to his late uncle's bedroom and hauled out a full wagonload of garbage. He'd burned it all one night, and watching it all go up in flames had been strangely therapeutic. He'd had the urge to do the same thing to the house—just burn it down to the foundation, but, of course, he wasn't crazy. The second floor was almost done now, but the downstairs had been more than he could tackle yet.

"It's okay." Adel picked up a dusty container of vinegar from the tabletop. "This is a great place to start. You'll see a big difference when you get back."

Jake turned to leave, then stopped. He marched back into the kitchen and flung back the curtains, letting rays of warm sunlight into the room. He went to the window over the sink and did the same thing. It was time to empty this old house of all the mustiness and garbage.

Then he shot Adel a wobbly smile. "I'll hurry up."

Jake put his back into his chores. He didn't want to leave Adel alone with that mess any longer than necessary. One of the reasons he hadn't asked for help was because he hadn't wanted to open that door to the women of the community. Then they'd see, and there was still a part of him that wanted to protect his family image, even though he'd run from it all himself.

When he finished the chores, his muscles ached and he was sweaty from work. He headed back toward the house just as the door opened and a rug was flung over the banister. Adel looked up and gave him a cheerful wave.

How could she be happy working on something like this? She'd maintained her own neat, organized home, and now to be faced with this mess? He noticed a pile of garbage she'd started off to the side.

"That can all be burned," Adel said when she noticed where his attention went.

"Okay," he said.

"Come and see how much I've gotten done already," she said, leading the way inside. "I did peek upstairs—I hope you don't mind—and you did an incredible job up there, if down here is any indication of what you had to start with. So really, Jake, don't feel bad."

As he stepped into the kitchen, his heart skipped a beat. The kitchen table was completely clear, washed and even polished with some wood oil. The counters were covered in neat piles of dishes, and a cardboard box sat in the center of the room, where he could see some cracked and broken dishes inside. The whole room smelled of a mixture of mild bleach and vinegar.

"I'm cleaning every last surface," she said. "We have to get any residue off from the fumigation. It wouldn't be safe for you, otherwise."

"Yah." He smiled faintly. "Well, let me get scrubbing, too. What can I be working on?"

"Why don't you wipe out the cupboards while I wash all the dishes," she said.

Somehow, the mess seemed much more manageable with Adel by his side. He climbed a stepladder to reach better and accepted a rag that Adel handed to him. There was a bucket of soapy water sitting on the counter beneath him, and he got to work.

"I hope you don't mind, but I'm tossing anything that's broken," she said as she turned on the water at the sink.

"That makes sense," he said. A woman didn't want to be saddled with broken dishes. He looked down at Adel as she reached for a mismatched pile of bowls, and he spotted one on the top—ceramic with a red stripe around the side of it. It had a crack that started at a chip at the lip, and he suddenly froze.

Adel lifted the bowl, surveyed it for a moment and started in the direction of that cardboard box of discarded junk, and his heart nearly beat out of his chest.

"No!" he said suddenly.

Adel turned back. "What?"

"That bowl." He came down the ladder and took it from her hands. "It was my *mamm*'s favorite."

"Oh…" Adel nodded. "I'm sorry, I didn't know."

"How could you?" He felt his chin quiver. "Look, maybe this is a bad idea."

Adel was silent, and he looked around at the mess of a kitchen. It was coming together, and he knew that most of this was junk, but it was junk that was attached to his heart in the strangest of ways. He couldn't blame Alphie for keeping him away—he'd been running from more than Alphie ever realized.

"Jake?" Adel put a hand on his arm.

"I, uh—" He licked his lips. "Somehow burning this whole house down would be easier than going through it piece by piece."

"The bowl stays," she said softly. "We'll glue it. It'll last for years, if you're careful. The bowl stays."

Jake let out a slow breath. His mother had been the heart of this home, even when his grumpy uncle lived with them. She'd been the source of pleasant aromas, of comforting routine and of a list of rules as long as his arm. He missed those rules after her death, because no one told him to brush his teeth before coming downstairs, or to hang up his clothes neatly in the closet. No one made him eat vegetables, either, unless he felt like it. Or insisted upon pleases and thank-yous, or saying something nice even when he wanted to grumble. When *Mamm* died, they lost all the sunshine and civilization in the home. But a bowl wasn't going to bring her back.

"A wife isn't going to want some chipped, cracked bowl," he said. "Toss it."

"What?" Adel frowned.

"Throw it out. It's fine," he said, and he started to turn.

"No, it's not fine." She caught the front of his shirt to stop him. "Jake, these are your memories. This is your home."

"Is it? It won't be my kitchen once I'm married," he said. "I'm supposed to be getting ready for a wife, remember? This will be her domain, not mine."

"Any woman who wouldn't care about the bowl your late mother used when you were a boy isn't worthy of you!" Her voice shook, and she still didn't let go of him. "You don't have to sacrifice everything you care about for a wife."

"But that's not true, is it?" he said, his voice low and rough. "I'm hopefully getting married to *someone* in a week's time. I'm sacrificing a whole lot."

"The right woman—" she started.

"The truly right woman would be someone I spent time with," he said, and he ran a finger down her cheek. Her skin was soft, and she tipped her face toward his touch, and if it weren't for the bowl in her hands between them, he would do more. "She'd be someone who'd gotten to know me, gotten to understand me. She'd be someone I wanted to pull into my arms—"

She'd be someone a whole lot like Adel. She looked

up at him, her lips parted, and the rest of his thought just seemed to seep away. Because he wanted a wife who made him feel like this.

Adel licked her lips and dropped her gaze. "I'm doing my best for you..."

"I'm not blaming you, Adel," he said. "This whole situation is stupid. My uncle didn't need to make this difficult, but he did. And I tried to do this the old-fashioned way and meet a woman, fall in love... It didn't work. But I'm starting to realize what I'm giving up for this farm. I've got a few ideals of my own, you know, and I have half a mind to just let Alphie take it."

Adel lifted her gaze to meet his. "Then keep this bowl—wherever you end up. Because even though you're upset right now, and this is a huge emotional tangle, you're going to be glad you did. I'm going to put it on the table where it's safe. But you keep it."

Jake gave her a weak smile. "You insist on taking care of me."

"Someone has to do it," she said softly. "And until there is...someone...to take over, I'm happy for it to be me."

It was the most selfless thing anyone had done for him, and he felt a surge of tenderness toward her.

"Is it part of the job of being matchmaker?" he asked, a catch in his voice.

She shook her head. "No. It's part of being your friend."

He wished she hadn't said that, because the word *friend* put a fence between them, and right now he longed to be so much more to her than a friend.

"I appreciate it," he said. She met his gaze for a moment longer, then she turned and put the bowl in the center of the kitchen table.

"You'll see," she said. "We'll get this place cleaned up. And tomorrow there's a hymn sing and a game night going on at the Hochstetler farm. Who knows? Maybe with less pressure you'll see someone who interests you, and I can talk to her on your behalf."

Jake was looking at someone who interested him right now...and he realized in a rush that his growing feelings for Adel were a big part of his problem. He should think more clearly before he gave up this farm to his cousin.

Adel wasn't available, and he'd better figure out his life without her.

Chapter Ten

Late the next afternoon, Jake parked the buggy and un-hitched the horse at Hannes Hochstetler's farm where a scattering of peach trees surrounded a generous garden. Hannes's daughter, Iris, and her new husband, Caleb, were living with Hannes for the first year of their marriage while Caleb saved for a place of their own, and the farm was thriving as a result.

A lot of the neighbors had come to the evening of fun, and Adel scanned the familiar faces. The teenagers had set up some volleyball on the lawn and were diving after the ball with shrieks of fun. Some young mothers had their babies on quilts, and they sat chatting together as the babies crawled, kicked and played. There was a group of older people already singing hymns together, several groups of men chatting and three long tables of food set out.

"Adel!" Adel's friend Bernice, a mother of three school-aged children, came up beside her and tweaked her arm. "I heard that you're acting as matchmaker these days."

"I am," Adel said with a smile.

"Any luck matching up Jacob Knussli?" she asked.

"Not yet," Adel replied.

"Why not match him with your sister?" Bernice asked. "She'd be perfect for him. And what a cook! I know you're glad to have her at the bed-and-breakfast, but Adel, she's just wasted there. She needs a family."

"My sister isn't interested," Adel replied. "I did try that already. And it isn't like I haven't tried to get her married, but I'm her sister, and what I think is good for her she thinks is boring."

"Sisters." Bernice chuckled. "I heard that Delia's boys weren't so keen on Jacob, either."

"That's already gotten around?" Adel winced.

"Well, Delia hasn't said a word, but her boys told my boys, and that's how word gets out. If there was more time, I think Delia would be a good match, too. She's been lonely since Zeke died."

"Yah," Adel said. "But *kinner* make it more complicated. Especially teens. I feel a little foolish even thinking that match would work now."

"It was worth the try," Bernice replied. "What about Sarai Peachy? She's twenty-five, single and very sweet."

"Maybe too young," Adel said quietly. "Only twenty-five. Twelve years younger than him."

"You were fifteen years younger than Mark," Bernice reminded her.

But Mark was different. Still, time was getting short for finding Jake a wife, and while Sarai was younger than Adel had hoped, she'd had a decent amount of time of being single to grow and mature...

"She's a sweet young woman," Bernice said. "And

he does come with a paid-off farm. That's worth something. Or there's Verna Kauffman. She's about to head east to see if she can find someone marriageable out that way. We could save her the time."

Verna was closer to Jake's age, but she'd never been married. She was slim, a wonderful cook and full of energy. But somehow, she didn't strike Adel as the sort of woman who would interest Jake. Maybe she was wrong, though—it wouldn't be the first time.

Adel nodded. "She's a possibility, too. I'll introduce him around tonight. You never know what might stick."

But her heart sank just a little at the thought. Tonight, she might see Jake's eyes light up for another woman, and that would mean that she'd succeeded. Because he was handsome, kind and truly decent. If he found someone who interested him, barring some unruly teenagers to get in the way, Adel could open a woman's eyes to Jake's virtues.

Bernice looked in the direction of the buggies. "Well, he's coming back. I'll let you get to work. See you later, Adel."

As her friend left, Jake arrived at her side. He nudged her arm with his own and gave her a small smile.

"We're going to make the most of this evening," Adel said. "You are going to meet every available woman here who is at least twenty-five or older. So remember names of the women who interest you, and don't be shy about chatting with them. This is going to save us a great deal of time."

"You seem very confident," he said.

"Why wouldn't I be?" she asked. "You clean up nicely, Jacob Knussli."

He chuckled. "Thank you. I think."

"I have a couple of women to introduce you to," Adel said, shooting him a smile. "In fact, they're both over there playing lawn darts."

"With Naomi?"

"Yah." Naomi, Verna and Sarai were all playing the game together. Sarai looked particularly pretty this evening, and Adel heard the ripple of her laughter as she did a bad throw.

"Who is the one in pink?" he asked.

Yah. He'd already spotted her. Adel tried to put more enthusiasm in her voice. "That's Sarai Peachy. She's twenty-five now, and a very nice woman."

"Hmm." He looked down at Adel, and for a moment he just met her gaze. Then he sighed. "Should we get this over with?"

Was that for her benefit? It would be even worse if he was pitying her now. She was his matchmaker, not someone who would feel jealous…or at the very least, not someone he should know might feel some jealousy. Her emotional upheaval was not his problem.

"You'd better have a more positive attitude than that," Adel said, tapping his arm. "Come on. Let's go say hello. Just be your charming self, and you'll be fine."

That sounded confident, didn't it? She was actually quite pleased with her own deportment today. She was getting better at acting the part of a confident matchmaker. They started off in the direction of the lawn dart game.

"I'm not sure I'm usually very charming," he said, leaning down so that his words stayed for her alone.

"Hogwash," she said. "You're perfectly charming with me."

More than charming. He could make her breath stop in her chest with one of his drilling looks. He'd managed it last night in the kitchen.

"That's different," he murmured.

She looked up at him. "Is it?"

"Entirely." He met her gaze, but he didn't say anything else. They were too close to other people now anyway to keep their conversation private, and Adel let out a shaky breath. Was he toying with her? Or was she just too susceptible to every little flirtatious thing he said?

He *was* charming. And if this was the way he could make his own matchmaker feel, if he decided to, he could sweep any woman he wanted off her feet.

"You don't have a lot of time left, Jake," she said quietly. "Don't forget that."

"I know." He sounded irritable.

"Then use some of the charm you've laid on me, and find yourself a wife," she said. "There's only so much I can do unless you put in some effort, too."

Naomi smiled and waved when they approached, and both Verna and Sarai looked up, too. Verna suddenly smoothed her dress and her fingers fluttered up to her hair and her *kapp*, so it would seem that she'd already knew why Adel would be bringing Jake around. Sarai just smiled in a friendly way and put her hands on her hips.

"Hello," Adel said. "I wanted to properly introduce you to Jacob Knussli."

"Hello." Verna put her hand out and he shook it.

"We don't actually need an introduction. We've talked a few times."

Jake looked mildly confused.

"I'm Verna. I make the lemon meringue pie you liked," she said.

"I thought you were Abram's wife—"

"No, that's Amanda." Verna's cheeks reddened.

Jake gave her an apologetic smile. "I'm sorry about that. I had just filed you away as married. You'll have to forgive me."

"Oh…" Verna's smile was back. "It's nice to see you again, Jacob."

"Call me Jake."

"Jake." Verna smiled, then she turned toward the younger woman next to her. "This is Sarai."

"Hi." Sarai didn't offer her hand to shake, but she did smile. "You're the subject of a lot of gossip, Jacob Knussli."

"Am I?" Jake turned and shot Adel a pretend look of alarm. "I should fix that."

Adel rolled her eyes and gave him a rueful smile. Yes, he'd be just fine here.

Sarai nodded toward the lawn darts. "Are you any good at this game?"

"Probably not," he said.

"Well, you can't be any worse than me," Sarai said, and she eyed him for a moment. "Besides, I like winning, Jacob Knussli."

"You should call me Jake, too," he said. "It's what everyone calls me."

"No, I'll call you Jacob," she said. "If everyone

calls you Jake, I want to be different. How old are you, Jacob?"

Adel felt her own face heat, then. She'd insisted upon calling him Jacob for quite some time, too, but for different reasons. It felt almost like treading upon her turf.

"I'm thirty-seven," Jake said.

"You look younger than that." Sarai smiled sweetly.

When Adel's gaze flickered toward her sister, Naomi handed her lawn dart to Jake.

"Take over for me," Naomi said. "And don't hurt yourself."

Jake laughed and waggled a finger at Naomi. Then Adel and Naomi moved a little ways away to give the group more privacy.

"Sarai is downright flirting!" Naomi said. "And I've never seen Verna quite that forward with any man before. Did you plan that?"

"I couldn't have planned that if I tried," Adel said. "But I think having something social to do while talking is at least an easier way to start things. The formal sit-downs have a way of squashing Jake's more relaxed nature. He flirts better when he's relaxed."

"You'd know about that." Naomi nudged her arm.

"No, I'm being serious. Look at him! He's downright charming."

"And you're…okay with this?" Naomi asked softly.

"I'd better be. If this works, he'll have his wife and his farm. That's the plan."

"You're better for him than either Verna or Sarai would be," Naomi said.

Adel watched as Sarai took her turn tossing the lawn dart. It was Jake's turn next, and his landed right in the middle of the hula hoop. But instead of looking toward Sarai, who was groaning because he'd virtually just won, Jake's gaze turned toward Adel, and he mouthed the word *wow*.

Adel chuckled and gave him a thumbs-up.

"See?" Naomi said. "He's not trying to impress either of them. He's doing this for you."

Was he? Even with the beautiful, young Sarai right there, his gaze moved toward her. The thought made her stomach tickle. But no—she couldn't toy with this! This was Jake's future, and the farm that held his memories. He needed to make a choice, and she was only getting in the way.

"We should move farther away," Adel said. "Come on, let's get some food. I don't want to get in the way of him actually talking to them."

Naomi sighed, and they headed for the food table.

"How do you like being a matchmaker?" Naomi asked.

"I thought I'd like it," Adel said. "I'm not sure I do."

"Because you have to set Jacob Knussli up with another woman?" Naomi asked.

"Because meddling in anyone's love life is a bigger responsibility than I had previously appreciated," she replied. "Someone always gets hurt."

Her sister put her arm through hers. "I'm sorry, Adel…"

Adel hadn't meant herself when she talked about getting hurt, but maybe it applied, too. She sighed. They arrived at the food tables. Adel took some cut vegetables and dip, and for a moment, she just swirled a broccoli floret in the puddle of ranch dressing. She refused to look in Jake's direction.

"Are you okay?" her sister asked.

"It'll be fine," Adel said. "Let's just give Jake some space so he can apply that charm to the right woman."

"*You* might be the right woman," Naomi said.

"Not me!" Adel said irritably. Why would no one listen to her when she said that?

Jake finished the game of lawn darts and when he looked around for Adel, he didn't see her. He chatted with some friends from his boyhood, and listened to them talk about family life. Noah and Thomas Wiebe were both married now, and Thomas was talking about a little girl from Haiti. He already had a daughter from a relationship with an *Englisher* woman, and he and his Amish wife had adopted a little boy named Cruise, who followed Thomas around like a shadow.

Thomas scooped up the boy into his arms.

"We're praying about adopting another child," Thomas said. "The child we're praying to bring home is a little girl who was born in Haiti, but she's in America now. She's four years old, so she's very close in age to Cruise. They'll make good playmates. We've seen pictures of her, and she's really cute. Patience and I are looking forward to meeting her soon. Her name is Fabienne."

"From Haiti?" Jake asked in surprise.

"*Yah.* It's a different culture, but she's still a little girl in need of a loving home." Thomas looked a little defensive. "The adoption workers are quite impressed with our determination to raise our *kinner* with the memory and pride of the family they were born to while still giving them an Amish life."

"I didn't mean to offend," Jake said quickly. "I lived English for a long time, so I can appreciate diversity. Truly."

"These adoptions between very different cultures might not happen often, but it does happen," Thomas said. "Plus, there was Micah Graber down in Indiana who married an Amish convert originally born in the Philippines. She speaks perfect Pennsylvania Dutch now, as well as a few other languages. And I've met some men who had adopted *kinner* from different cultural backgrounds. Love is what makes all the difference. *Gott* is calling us Amish to grow in new and deeper ways. I'm sure of it."

"Amen," Jake said quietly.

"If she comes to us, Fabienne will be raised Amish," Thomas went on. "But we will never take her heritage from her. Ever. *Gott* created her as a full person, and we'd never take a piece of her away."

"That's amazing," Jake said. "I have heard of that happening…but no one I knew personally."

"Well, you haven't met Patience," Noah interjected. "She's the heart of their home, in every way."

"That's the truth," Thomas said quietly. "Patience already wants to learn how to do her hair in braids, she's so certain that *Gott* will bring Fabienne to us."

"If her heart is in it, I'm inclined to believe it, too," Noah said with a somber nod. "*Gott* seems to tell a woman things he doesn't tell a man. So it's a wise husband who listens to her."

"That's some marriage advice for you," Thomas said.

Cruise wriggled to be let down and Thomas set him on the grass. The boy headed off in the direction of the women who were chatting under a peach tree.

"Noah's wife is expecting their second baby," Thomas added.

"Yah." Noah nodded proudly and pointed in the direction of a largely pregnant dark-haired woman sitting on a blanket. A toddler boy was playing with some sticks in the grass next to her, and Cruise joined his cousin and aunt. "We're having another boy. Samuel will be a big brother."

Thomas shaded his eyes and looked over at a pretty blonde who was also looking at him. Thomas pointed to where Cruise had gone with Noah's wife, and the woman smiled and nodded. She had a little girl at her side wearing an exact replica of her own dress and apron.

"That's Patience," Thomas said. "And that's our daughter, Rue, with her."

Their connection, even across the yard, as they parented in unison, was impressive to witness.

"So listen to your wife...any other advice?" Jake asked.

"Choose the right woman," Noah said quietly. "Even if she seems like the least appropriate choice. If she's the right one, it makes all the difference. I would know. Eve wasn't the appropriate choice for me, but I just knew on a bone-deep level, you know? And so did she. There was really no keeping us apart. At every turn, *Gott* seemed to be tugging us together."

Jake nodded slowly. "It's what I'm looking for."

But would he find it in time? Because the one woman

who'd caught his attention like no other was in no way interested in him. She saw him as her client, nothing more.

The rest of the afternoon slipped away with a lengthy hymn sing, and the sun sank below the horizon. A bonfire crackled from a firepit on the far edge of the yard where the older kids and teenagers were roasting marshmallows. Jake had seen Adel around, but she'd kept a bit of a distance from him, giving him nothing more than an encouraging smile when he stopped to talk with any woman who happened to be single. Word was out, it seemed. Jake was in want of a wife, and there was a farm in it for the woman who took him on.

But Jake was tired now. Deeply tired. He didn't have it in him to make nice with any more women this evening. He was ready to head back to the bed-and-breakfast, but he'd driven Adel and her sister out to the hymn sing, and he'd have to drive them back.

He spotted Naomi over with Verna and Sarai, and he didn't dare go back over there. Sarai had developed a keen interest in him, and while she was incredibly pretty, she was too young for him. That was it, wasn't it? That was why he just couldn't summon up the determination to talk to her more seriously... He needed a woman more like Adel—his age, with some life experience, and beautiful. He needed to find what Thomas and Noah had found.

He headed away from the people and toward the farmhouse. He just wanted some space for a few minutes. He had a lot to think about. The sound of some men singing together surfed the breeze, and he strolled out toward the house, meaning to head toward the buggies.

But as he passed the side door, it suddenly opened and Adel stepped out. It took her a moment to see him in the shadows where he stood, and she startled.

"Oh, Jake!" She laughed breathily, and there was something about the way she said his name that warmed him from the inside.

"Sorry to scare you," he said. "I was just...taking a walk."

She hesitated on the step.

"You've been avoiding me," he added.

"I've been giving you space," she said. "You needed to talk to women on your own."

"Well, I've done that," he said. "Do you want to walk a bit?"

He'd missed her this evening—knowing she was around somewhere, but never able to get close enough to her to talk or just take a rest by her side.

"Sure," Adel said, coming down the steps. "You can let me know how it went."

He looked down at her. He didn't *want* to talk about other women... That wasn't helpful with his match-maker, was it? They strolled together in the direction of the buggies, away from the murmur of voices, the laughter of children, the singing of those men who'd taken up a new hymn... The evening was warm, and he felt the reassuring brush of her sleeve against his arm.

"Well?" she prodded. "Tell me."

"Uh—" He looked toward the fire flickering in the distance. "Verna is very nice, again, but no spark."

"Okay," Adel said. "I expected that, after watching you a bit. But what about Sarai? You liked her."

"She's...great. I mean, she's pretty, she's fun, she

certainly seems to like me—" He looked down at Adel and she quickly looked away. "But no."

"No?" She looked back. "Really?"

"She's too young."

"She's twenty-five."

"*Yah*, but she's very perky," he said.

"She's happy. She's upbeat." Adel shook her head.

"She's not right," he said. "I want someone older—our age. I want someone who's experienced some life, who could understand me a little better."

"You didn't have a list when we started, and now you're getting a whole lot harder to please, Jake." She sounded annoyed, and he smiled in the darkness.

"Adel, I want her to be more like you." He wouldn't have dared to say it in the light of day, but he felt Adel freeze. Was she holding her breath? "Adel?"

"Like me?" she whispered.

He caught her hand. "You're quite wonderful, you know."

Adel looked down, and he stepped closer to see her better in the darkness that was illuminated by a sliver of moon and a splash of stars.

"You're smart," he whispered. "And you've seen things—you know that life is hard. You're funny, too. You're fun to be around, and—" He swallowed. "You're beautiful."

She looked up then, and her face was so close to his that he could feel her breath tickle his chin. He ran his hands lightly down her arms.

"You're supposed to choose one of them," she whispered back.

"Adel, you understand me," he said quietly. "You

see me as…as a man. As a person. Well, I see you the same way."

"As a man?" Her lips turned up into a teasing smile.

"Hardly." He chuckled. "But I understand you."

"Prove it." She lifted her chin in a sort of challenge.

"All right." He caught her hand in his. "You got married young, and you didn't marry for love. You married for respect, and the love came later. You trusted our Amish way of life to deliver you a beautiful future, and it did deliver. So our ways are a safe haven for you. Am I right so far?"

"Surprisingly accurate," she said softly.

"Okay," he said, encouraged. "Well, you're also scared. Because when you got married, you trusted your *daet* to steer you right, and you don't have that anymore now that he's passed. I think you've been looking to the bishop to provide you with that kind of insight these days. So you're widowed, and you appreciate all that your marriage provided for you, and you're digging your heels in. You don't want to risk what you've already gotten."

Adel's breath quickened. "You're right. I don't want to risk it."

"I think I understand you pretty well, given a short amount of time," he said.

"*Yah*, but I'm the one who's supposed to understand you," she said. "And you won't just do things the normal way, Jake."

"I like my way better." He squeezed her hand. "Besides, it's only fair."

She dropped her gaze.

"You were a puzzle to me before," he went on. "But I get you now."

"Not many people do," she said, and he felt a rush of satisfaction at that. She wasn't the typical Amish person, either. And maybe that was why he felt so drawn to her.

"But you've never experienced *this* before," he whispered.

"Experienced what?" She looked up. She really hadn't put it all together yet?

"Attraction," he said softly. "The natural kind that just pops up between a man and woman sometimes when they're both free and single. You haven't had this."

"I was married," she said with a dismissive little laugh.

"Yah." He nodded. "You were, but it didn't start like this. That's what I'm saying. You aren't in control of these feelings between us."

"I'm not *supposed* to be feeling this," she said softly.

"Maybe not." He touched her cheek. "But I'm glad you do. It's not just me, then. There's something here that we both feel..." he licked his lips "...and I'm thinking about kissing you."

She didn't answer, but her eyes glistened in the moonlight, and he thought he could make out a soft blush on her cheeks. Her lips were so close, and when he touched her chin, tipping her face up just a little bit, she leaned toward him ever so subtly, and he threw all his reserves to the wind and lowered his lips over hers. Her lips were soft, and her hands pressed gently against his chest, his own heartbeat thudding against her touch. She sighed and leaned into his arms. She was warm, and soft, and she smelled ever so faintly of baking. She felt like happiness and moonlight all wrapped up together. This kiss was exactly what his poor, battered heart needed.

Adel suddenly pulled back, and she pushed against his chest. He released her, taking a surprised step back.

"We can't do that," she breathed.

"Oh…" He'd offended her. He didn't mean to. "We're both single," he added.

"That might be reason enough in the *Englisher* world, but you should know better here!" She touched her lips with the tips of her fingers. "What if someone saw us?"

Jake looked around. There was no sign of anyone around. Over by the bonfire, there was an eruption of laughter with the teenagers as two boys tussled over something they were too far away to make out.

"Adel…" She turned to look at him. "There *is* something between us."

"Maybe so," she whispered. "But this isn't part of my plan. This isn't how it's supposed to work."

"Sometimes things go differently than you planned," he said.

"We need to snap back into reality. You don't have time for this!" She met his gaze earnestly. "You have a matter of days now to find a wife. *You don't have time.*"

And she was right, of course. This would be a waste of time if what he felt for her wasn't so overwhelming. But he couldn't seem to look at another woman seriously now that he'd had some time with Adel…and now that he'd kissed her?

"We have to stick to the plan," she said, and he could

hear a note of pleading in her voice. "We'll be glad we did when this is over. I'm sure of it."

Was she really so sure? Because he wasn't. Of all the women he'd met today, the only one to stick in his heart was his matchmaker, and she resisted every effort to get closer to her.

Chapter Eleven

The buggy rattled over a dip in the road as they headed back toward the bed-and-breakfast. Jake had the reins, and Adel sat between him and her sister, Jake's solid bulk on one side of her, and her sister's softer figure on the other. Jake moved his leg so that his knee touched hers, and she was sure it wasn't intentional. They didn't have much room with three adults squeezed into the front of one buggy, but all the same it reminded her of the feelings she shouldn't be feeling for him.

What would people say if they saw her kissing the single man she was supposed to be matching up with another woman? Her reputation would be crushed, and there would be no coming back from that. She couldn't take chances like that... This wasn't the kind of woman she was!

But we're both single... His words replayed in her mind. She wasn't doing anything sinful or wrong if she explored a future with another equally single man. Still, she wanted to be a respected woman who could provide wisdom, insight and possibly even arrange a marriage match for people. People with responsible positions in the community had to be more careful than others. They had more to lose and further to fall. Women would look to her for guidance and for a good example.

"Sarai seemed very interested in you, Jake," Naomi said, looking over Adel toward Jake.

"Yah," Jake said. "I know."

"She's a nice young woman," Naomi said. "She's got a good reputation around here, too. She's living with her grandmother right now to help her out with the garden and the house. She's been taken driving by a few hopeful young men, but she isn't courting anyone right now."

"Yah?" Jake's voice sounded tight.

"She cooks well, too," Naomi went on brightly. "And she's very pretty, isn't she— Ouch!" Naomi wriggled. "What was that elbow for, Adel?"

The buggy went over a bump and Adel pitched to the side.

"Sorry," Adel said meekly. "That was an accident."

At least it was...mostly.

Naomi shot her a mildly annoyed look. "She asked me to speak for her. I'm doing that."

"Verna is also a nice option," Adel said. Did they have to lean on Sarai quite so much?

"She's a nice option for someone else," Naomi replied. "Right, Jake? You said you wanted someone you had some spark with, and I didn't see anything between you and Verna. Unless I'm wrong there."

"No, there was no spark," Jake said, his voice low.

"Are you two having any luck finding that spark?" Naomi asked. Adel nearly choked, and her sister looked at her with exaggerated innocence for a couple of beats of silence. "Oh! I didn't mean it like that! Oh my... Things come out of my mouth all wrong sometimes. I meant finding someone Jake can feel that connection with."

Adel knew exactly what her sister had meant, and she was meddling. She glared at Naomi, but her sister pointedly avoided looking at her.

"I just think that some mutual attraction is important," Naomi went on. "I've seen some women get married with all the hope their hearts could hold, but you'd never know they were married in public because their husbands treat them like strangers. When two people really care for each other, and really feel honest attraction, it's impossible to hide."

Adel's breath caught. Was it really that impossible? It had better be somewhat possible to hide, because she had a reputation to maintain! She licked her lips.

"There have been young people who relied solely on attraction, got married and lived to regret it, too," Adel said.

"Yah..." Jake said.

Adel glanced over at him. What did that mean? She turned front again.

"What do you think, Jake?" Naomi pressed.

"I think that attraction is incredibly important," Jake said. "But a man with half a brain in his head wants both attraction and a good woman. It's a combination."

"Very smart," Naomi said.

"Attraction can develop over time," Adel said. "It did for me."

"What if it doesn't?" Jake asked, his voice low.

"If you work hard, treat her like the most beautiful woman in the world, and—"

"But what if even after trying very, very hard and treating her with respect and consideration, I still don't feel any honest, spontaneous attraction with her?" he said, cutting her off. "It's a possibility. We've all seen couples like that. When you want to kiss a woman, it comes from a different part of you—it isn't about duty."

That kiss... The way he'd held her, the way his lips had moved over hers... She could have stopped him. She *should* have stopped him. How could she recommend him to another woman who'd trust her to guide them straight, all the time knowing she'd been kissing Jake out by the buggies!

"Anything is possible," Adel said. "It's true—it's possible to choose a woman you'd never develop those deeper feelings for. But so is a buggy accident, or a lightning strike, or a house fire, or a flood... We take a step forward in faith that *Gott* will protect us and smooth the path. That's all we can do."

"Is it?" Jake looked down at her meaningfully. "Is it really *all* we can do?"

Adel's breath caught in her chest, and this time she elbowed Jake in the side. This was not a conversation to have in front of Naomi, and she had a feeling he was about to open up.

"As your matchmaker, it's my best recommendation," she said.

But the warm, agonized look he gave her left no confusion about how he felt. She could only hope that her sister hadn't seen it.

When they turned into the drive, Jake straightened his back. "I should go back to my own farm tonight."

And she felt a sudden tug in her heart. She'd upset him. Something had happened tonight that never should have, and he was going to leave. They needed a little more time just to set their balance right again.

"If you have food there," Adel said.

He didn't answer. He seemed to be considering.

"Jake, have another night here," Adel said, softening her tone. "I'm sorry if I was arguing with you. The farmhouse is fumigated, but you don't have your kitchen stocked or anything. You don't need to make anything harder on yourself." She looked at her sister. "Don't you think, Naomi?"

"Of course," Naomi replied. "You can't go back without food in the cupboards."

"I appreciate that," he said, his voice low. "I'll take care of the horse and buggy tonight. You two can go inside."

Did he guess that Adel might offer to help? Because she would have.

"I still feel a little bad, considering you're our guest," she said. It was a token resistance.

"I'm a whole lot more than a guest, aren't I?" he asked, and irritation flashed in his eyes.

She looked up at him and felt her cheeks heat. "Thank you, all the same."

When he reined in in front of the house, Adel followed her sister out of the buggy and dropped down to the ground. Then he carried on toward the stable. Adel stood there for a moment, her heart pounding.

"I think he's a whole lot more than a guest at this

point, too," Naomi said, fishing the key out of her bag and heading toward the side door.

"Naomi, you need to stop that!" Adel followed her sister inside and shut the door firmly behind her. "He's my client! And I know that might be laughable to you, but I have a reputation to consider here!"

Naomi lit the kerosene lamp, and then turned toward her. "I saw you kiss him."

Adel's heart nearly stopped in her chest. "What?"

"I was coming to find you because I was tired and wanted to head home. I was hoping you were ready to go."

Adel swallowed. "I—" But she had no words. She couldn't defend herself.

"Adel," Naomi said quietly. "I'm not trying to shame you. I've been saying from the start that you're a good match for him."

"What kind of matchmaker would I be, taking him for myself?" Adel asked weakly.

"A terrible one," Naomi said bluntly. "But you'd also be married again, and happy."

"I am happy," Adel said curtly. "I know what I want, Naomi, and handsome as he is, he's a risk. He's asking what happens if the woman he marries doesn't end up sparking his romantic interest. Well, I have deeper concerns than that! What if I did allow myself to feel this, and the man I marry ends up being without any community respect? I'd go from the deacon's widow who everyone looked to for advice and wisdom, to being… married and nothing more."

"Married and nothing more? Marriage is a blessing all its own. If I could find the right man, I'd be honored to be married." Naomi glanced at her sister. "He's likeable, Adel. People are already accepting him back."

"*Yah*, but you know as well as I do that a woman's position in this life is reliant upon her husband's. I married a good and decent man in Mark. I loved him. I worked hard in our marriage, and I earned respect. I *earned* every ounce of that respect! It wasn't easy marrying a man so much older than me, but I did it, and I'm not giving up what I earned."

"Who's to say you'd give up respect? You might earn more of it. But let's say you are right. You wouldn't give up respect? Even for love?" Naomi asked softly.

Love... That was a heavy word that she didn't like to toss around lightly.

"He's a rebel at heart," Adel said. "I think that's all this is. I'm an inappropriate choice, so he sets his sights on me. And I don't need a rebel husband! I'd rather be a respected woman who can do some good around here than a married one whose time and effort are focused on maintaining a struggling relationship with someone who I only had one thing in common with—attraction."

Adel saw a bobbing lantern outside. Jake was coming back in.

"No more talk about this," Adel said. "Jake can't know what you saw, okay? And please, Naomi, don't breathe a word to anyone!"

"I won't," Naomi said. "But if you don't want him for yourself, you'd better be a whole lot more careful. Stop letting it get personal. Don't go for walks with him. He's feeling this—I can tell."

So could Adel, and she rubbed a hand over her eyes. "I'll do better."

* * *

Jake came out of the stable when his horse was settled into the stall for the night, and he sucked in a chest
full of fresh night air. He had been saying too much in
front of Naomi, and he was kicking himself for it now.
What he needed was some time alone with Adel to ham-
mer this out. Because that kiss hadn't been a mistake—
it had been honest—and he wasn't sorry for it. She'd
leaned into his arms, and she'd kissed him back, and
he'd felt a connection with her that he'd never felt before.

This was real—and she could reject him as was her
right, but she couldn't claim it hadn't been real.

When Jake came into the house, he found Adel and
Naomi in the kitchen. Naomi cast him a tired smile.

"I'm turning in," Naomi said. "Have a good night,
Jake. I hope I didn't offend you with taking too much
interest in finding you a match."

"It's fine," Jake said with a shrug. "I mean, I am
looking for a wife, right? Don't worry about it."

Naomi headed up the stairs, and Adel reached some
cereal boxes out of the cupboard and put them down on
the table in preparation for the next morning.

"Adel," he said quietly.

Adel turned toward him, her cheeks pink.

"You kissed me, too," he said.

The color in her cheeks darkened and she shot him
an annoyed look. "That's not what you should be telling me."

"I don't care what I should be telling you. I'm telling you the truth," he said. "If you hadn't been feeling
it, too, you would have smacked me."

She was silent.

"At least I think you would have…"

"*Yah*, I would have." She sighed. "That's why I'm embarrassed. I did feel it, too."

"Okay, well…good." Again, it was likely the wrong thing to say, but he was feeling frustrated. None of this was coming together the way it was supposed to. He was supposed to be courting another woman—*any* other woman!

"We need to be a whole lot more careful," Adel said. Overhead he heard the squeaking of floorboards. "But I meant what I said in the buggy. We have something honest and spontaneous between us, and that doesn't actually come around very often. I just wanted to say that."

"The spontaneous part is why we have to be so careful," she said. "I agree—we do feel something. It's my responsibility to keep this professional, and I've let you down there."

"I wouldn't blame you entirely," he said with a joking smile. "I have worked pretty hard to figure you out."

She smiled faintly. "You have." Then she sobered. "But for me, this isn't about attraction. This is about following the path I believe *Gott* has set me on."

Adel was serious, and he could feel her firm resolve. Jake's joking evaporated and he took a step closer. "I'm the man here. It's on me. I won't overstep with you again."

"Okay." She sucked in a wavering breath. "I'd better get to bed."

He longed to close that distance between them, even if only to hug her, but that wouldn't help either of them.

She turned toward the stairs. It was time for him to get to bed, too.

Jake closed the door behind him and headed into the little guest suite. He'd made his bed this morning, but it looked straighter than the way he'd left it, and there was a single chocolate left on his pillow like every other night. He picked it up and smiled faintly.

This was just a professional gesture, but he couldn't help but wonder if it was Adel who had left it there.

He unwrapped the foil, popped it into his mouth and sank onto the side of his bed.

I'm messing this up, Gott, he prayed silently. Were these the *Englisher* years coming back in his instincts, or had he always been this way? He liked to think that if he'd spent less time away from home and more time living Amish, he'd be a better man by now. Maybe he'd even be good enough to earn Adel's full respect and to have her take him seriously as a marriage candidate. The problem, in part, was the deadline. Maybe if he didn't have to act so quickly, he could make her see how right they were for each other.

Could he really marry another woman, feeling the way he did about Adel?

He opened his Bible at random, looking for some comfort. His eyes fell on a verse he hadn't seen in a very long time: *Keep thy heart with all diligence; for out of it are the issues of life.*

From *Gott*'s lips to his ears. Jake had to stop this now. Adel wasn't interested in a future with him, and he had a farm to consider. Maybe she was right and his self-control was more important than his emotion. Perhaps that was the making of a man, and he needed to grow before he would be husband material for a woman like her.

But time wasn't on his side.

"*Gott*, show me the right woman," he prayed aloud. "And help me to let Adel go."

The next morning, Adel stood at the kitchen sink drying the last of the breakfast dishes. She'd made a big breakfast—eggs, fried potatoes, sausage, cinnamon buns and some dry cereal, as well. Jake had eaten heartily before heading back to his farm to start chores, and now she stood in her quiet kitchen, listening to the soft ticking of the clock.

Today, there were no scheduled visits from tourist groups, and it would be a good time for Adel to sit down and balance the books. Yet, her mind kept going back to her current job of finding a wife for Jake. There had been some good options for him at the hymn sing last night, but he hadn't been able to think about them because he was blinded by what he felt for her.

If Adel truly cared about Jake's happiness, then she would step back and give him the chance to find a woman who wanted what he had to offer.

Like Sarai. She was almost everything he wanted, just a little younger than he'd hoped. But she was a grown woman, and no one else would worry about that age difference. While Adel had felt some jealousy at the thought of Jake with Sarai, that wasn't Sarai's fault. Adel would feel that with any woman he chose, and that put the responsibility squarely on Adel's own shoulders.

"I should go visit Sarai and talk to her a little bit about what she wants in a husband," Adel said.

"What's that?" Naomi popped her head in from the other room.

"I said, I should talk to Sarai...see if I can make that match for Jake," Adel said.

"He said he didn't want Sarai, though," Naomi said.

"Do you believe him?" Adel asked. "Sarai is sweet, bubbly, fun, full of personality...and of all the women he's met so far, she's the one he seemed to hit it off with the best."

"Maybe so," Naomi agreed, leaning against the doorjamb. "But if he isn't interested in her, then all you're doing is setting that poor girl up for disappointment. She really liked him."

"But him not being interested might be my fault," Adel said. "And if that's the case, I owe him a proper match, don't you think?"

"You do owe him a proper match," her sister agreed.

"And if we don't hurry up, he'll lose his farm."

"It's his farm to lose," her sister said quietly.

Adel pressed her lips together in frustration. Maybe it was his farm to lose, but he'd already been held away from home by gossip passed along by his cousin, and if he had lifelong regrets after losing the farm because his brain had been addled with thoughts of *her*, she'd never forgive herself.

"I'll talk to him about it tonight," Adel said. "He told me this morning before he left that he's coming back for one more dinner with us. But you're right. I can't plow ahead without his consent. It would be wrong, and I don't want Sarai hurt for nothing."

Outside, Adel heard hooves on the gravel and she leaned forward to look out the window. A buggy had turned into the drive, but Adel didn't recognize the driver. She was slim and pretty, and she held the reins with confidence.

"Who is it?" Naomi asked, coming up beside her. They both watched the woman drive past their line of sight, and then exchanged a look. "Do you know her?"

"I don't," Adel replied. "But we'd best go say hello."

Naomi went and opened the side door while Adel washed off the table and got a kettle started on the stove. A couple of minutes later, Adel heard Naomi's voice chatting cheerily, and then both came inside.

"It's a beautiful day," the visitor was saying. "Thank you so much for the offer of some tea. I'd love some."

"Hello," Adel said with a smile. "Come in. Sit down. You've met Naomi, but my name is Adel Draschel. You aren't from around here."

"No, I'm new here," she replied. "My name is Claire Glick."

She looked to be in her midthirties, and she had a pleasant smile and an easy way about her.

"Glick—any relation to our bishop?" Adel asked.

"*Yah.* Zedechiah is my second cousin. I've come to stay with his family for a few weeks while I get settled here in Redemption. He was the one who asked me to come see you—starting introductions, so to speak. He would have come along with me, but he said that he was busy and that you're so friendly, I shouldn't have any problems."

"That's kind of him," Naomi said. "And no, it's no problem at all. Are you moving here?"

"*Yah.* That's the plan. I'm not married yet, and it was time for a change of scenery, if you know what I mean."

Adel nodded. "We certainly do. You're very welcome here."

And it did explain why the bishop had sent this woman in their direction. She was single, looking to meet potential husbands, of the right age for Jake, and she seemed absolutely charming.

"So tell me about you," Adel said. "What are you looking for in a husband?"

She blushed. "No beating around the bush."

"Why waste the time?" Adel said, spreading her hands. "Besides, if the bishop sent you over, you already come well-recommended."

"Well, I'm thirty-two," Claire said. "Before I left Ohio, I had my own business making baskets."

"Just baskets?" Naomi asked.

"There was a surprising market for them," Claire said. "A lot of home decor stores were stocking what they called 'rustic baskets,' and having ones that were handmade by an Amish person drove up the demand for them. I was supplying several local home decor stores, as well as gift shops."

"You must have stayed busy, then," Naomi said.

"*Yah.* Very. I even taught a class on basket weaving for *Englisher* women in the area. It proved very popular."

"*Yah?* They wanted to learn?" Adel asked.

"I honestly think they were mostly curious about me," Claire said. "They made terrible baskets, but they loved chatting with me. They'd ask me all kinds of questions. And I made a decent income from it."

This woman was smart, a hard worker, willing to take a few risks to get her own business running...

"Good for you!" Adel was impressed. "You certainly find a way to make a living."

"Well… You have to, don't you?" Claire glanced around. "Zedechiah was telling me that you run this bed-and-breakfast, just the two of you. Some fellow women in business."

"*Yah*, we do," Adel said. "It's a labor of love. We've been in business five years now."

"And every year is busier than the last," Naomi added.

They chatted about everything from business to Claire's connections in Ohio. While hearing Bishop Glick called by his first name felt wrong on all sorts of levels, she seemed to be very happy to be getting to know his family better. Apparently, her invitation to come try out life in Pennsylvania had come from the bishop's wife, Trudy.

"Claire, why don't you stay for dinner?" Adel said. "We can talk more while we cook. There is someone—" she swallowed, tried to bring the earlier cheer back into her voice "—there is someone I want you to meet."

"Oh?" Claire's eyebrows rose.

"He's very nice. I think you'll like him. No pressure. Just…meet him."

Naomi met Adel's gaze, and Adel saw sympathy in her sister's green eyes. Adel was doing the right thing. From what she could see, the bishop had found the perfect match for Jacob Knussli. She had all of Sarai's charms, and she was a more appropriate age for him, too.

Maybe *Gott* was moving here, and all of this was

Gott's will. When *Gott*'s people were truly blessed, He used them to be the answer of someone else's prayer.

Gott's path was a selfless one. Perhaps Adel was getting a lesson in just that.

Chapter Twelve

Jake's stomach rumbled as he unhitched his horse from the buggy next to one he didn't readily recognize. Did they have another guest at the bed-and-breakfast? Whoever the owner, this buggy was well-cared for, which couldn't be said for his uncle's. He paused, his gaze moving over the battered, peeling paint. Uncle Johannes hadn't taken care of his things, and the first thing Jake would do when he got the land put into his name was to buy a new buggy of his own that he could be proud of. And then he'd take proper care of it.

There were too many things his family hadn't properly cared for—including the ties that bound them. He wasn't much better, he had to admit. He shouldn't have accepted secondhand gossip as gospel truth, even though it gave him the excuse to take the easy way out.

Jake opened the gate for his horse to enter the corral, locked him inside and then headed back toward the house. Adel waited at the door for him, and when he came up the steps, she gave him a nervous smile.

"Hi," he said quietly.

"Hi." She smiled, and some color touched her cheeks. "How was your day?"

"Busy. I tagged some new calves, and there's a mare that has hurt her leg, so that took some time to get her settled in the stable where she won't be bothered…" It was a day on the farm, and it wasn't really what he wanted to talk about. He lowered his voice further to make sure his words were private. "I missed you."

She dropped her gaze. "You shouldn't—"

"It's true, Adel. I thought about you all day. I tried not to. I *prayed* not to. I still did."

She looked up at him, her eyes full of agony. Was she going through the same thing?

"Did I cross your mind at all?" he whispered.

"Of course!" She sighed, and kept her voice low. "All day long. But I realized today that I'm in your way. I'm not much of a matchmaker if I'm stopping you from finding a wife. Luckily, the bishop hasn't forgotten you, and he sent someone over for you. Someone… rather perfect."

Her voice caught at the word *perfect*, and he wondered how hard this was for her.

"Who?" he asked.

"Bishop Glick's distant cousin who is staying with him for a little while. She's very nice." She swallowed. "She's in the kitchen."

Another setup. Of course—that was why he was here, wasn't it? It was supposed to be, at least. But his heart dropped all the same.

"Okay," he said.

Adel was silent a beat, as if she wanted to say more,

but then she seemed to steel herself as she stepped out of the way and gestured him inside.

"Claire," Adel said brightly, raising her voice to be heard. "This is Jacob Knussli. He's the one I was telling you about."

Claire was a pretty woman who looked close to his age. She had a ready smile that lit up her face in a rather nice way.

"This is Claire Glick. She's from Ohio."

Jake shook Claire's hand. She met his gaze easily, then gestured toward a coffeepot on the table.

"Did you want some coffee?" she asked. "I was about to get some cream."

"*Yah.* Thank you."

She was attractive, easygoing. They all chatted together as the final preparation was done on the meal, and when they all sat down, she was placed next to him, and Adel and Naomi seemed very engaged with each other.

He knew what Adel was doing—giving him a chance to talk to Claire. The more they chatted over a hearty meal, the more he liked her. She was a truly wonderful person. But every time he glanced over at Adel, his heart gave a little tug. Adel was special—there was no getting around it. But there was no opportunity to talk to Adel alone; she made sure of that.

Chatting with Claire didn't come with any of the nervous awkwardness he'd felt with meeting other women. If he wanted this match, he had a feeling it was falling into place rather nicely. Except no one had mentioned whether or not Claire knew about his need for a wife within a week. The time restriction was an important detail, but he was loath to bring it up for some reason he couldn't quite name.

Gott, is this the woman for me? he prayed. *Do I just have to ignore what I'm feeling for Adel and push past it?*

That was what he needed to know. Because he'd prayed all day that *Gott* would wipe his heart clean of Adel to allow him to move forward, and *Gott* hadn't answered. Was Claire the woman he'd been praying *Gott* would put in his path? Because next to Adel, all of Claire's wonderful qualities dimmed, just like with every other woman he'd met. Except he was able to admit that Claire did check off every single box on his list of wifely requirements better than any other...even if it didn't feel completely right.

After dinner, Claire helped to clean up, and between the three women, it took very little time. Then Claire thanked them for the meal and said she'd best get back, as she knew she'd be missed. He imagined that Bishop Glick and his wife could manage without her for a single evening, but maybe it was Claire's way of breaking free. What did he know?

"I'll help you hitch up," Jake said. It was the polite thing to do.

As he headed outside, Jake glanced over his shoulder and found both Naomi and Adel watching him go. Naomi looked thoughtful, and Adel was hiding whatever she was feeling behind a pasted-on smile.

Jake worked quickly to hitch up her horse, and Claire helped with the buckles on the other side of the animal.

"It was very nice to meet you," Jake said.

"Likewise." She smiled, then paused. "Perhaps I'll see you again."

"I'm sure you will," he replied. "I'm around." And if he could get past his own stubborn heart, maybe he'd go talk to her more earnestly later.

"You own a farm around here, you said?" Claire asked.

"I'm inheriting it. It's a bit of a process," he replied. She'd brought it up, and now was the time to tell her about his need for a wife, if any. But he couldn't quite bring himself to do it. The words stayed stuck inside him.

"I understand." Claire smiled again. "I'd better get going. I have someone waiting for me."

That was the second mention of someone waiting for her, and this time it didn't sound like she was referring to the bishop and his wife. Perhaps she wasn't quite so single as Adel thought.

"Of course." He offered her his hand, and she got up into the buggy. "Drive safely."

She waved, and flicked the reins as she expertly pulled the buggy around. He stood in the drive, watching her go. He heard the screen door slam, and he looked over to see Adel come outside.

She'd taken off her apron, and her teal-colored dress brought out the pink in her cheeks. She was the kind of beautiful that made it hard for him to look away.

"That was a delicious meal, Adel," he said.

"Thank you." She crossed the gravel and came to a stop beside him. "You're always welcome to come for dinner, you know."

"Yah?" He smiled faintly. "I feel like you don't offer that for all your bed-and-breakfast guests."

"You've become more," she said softly.

More. Yes, they'd both become a lot more to each other, but naming it was difficult.

"I intended to pick up a few groceries before heading home so I could fend for myself again," he said.

She nodded, then looked in the direction of Claire's buggy, turning on to the main road. "Did you like her?"

He could hear the pain in her voice she was trying to cover.

"She's nice," he said.

Adel met his gaze. "You know what I'm asking."

"I do know what you're asking," he said. "But I don't know her. She's very nice. She's cheerful, charming, sweet… And there is someone she's eager to get back to. I highly doubt it's our bishop."

Adel frowned. "I'm sure she's single. Bishop Glick wouldn't have sent her over otherwise."

"She mentioned getting back to someone twice," he said. "If she doesn't have someone else, then maybe she was just eager to get away… I might not be quite so charming as you think."

Adel rolled her eyes. "You're perfectly charming. You're handsome, hardworking, easy to talk to—" Her eyes misted and her voice caught.

"I don't think she's interested," he said. At least it would make things easier if she wasn't.

"I know Bishop Glick better than you do," Adel said. "And he knows his relative better than you do, too. I talked with her for a long time before you arrived, and she's confirmed that she's single. Very single. She's moved out here to get to know other available men."

"Maybe the bishop told her about my time away," he said. "It puts some women off."

"Did you tell her about the farm?" Adel asked.

"No."

"I think you should. It would explain the speed that you need to move in this. There isn't time to court her properly, or visit her weekly for a little while. There just isn't *time*!"

"I don't think she's for me," he said.

"She's—" Adel shook her head. "She's perfect, you woolen-headed man! She's perfect! Can't you see that? She's your age, she's smart, she's funny, she's talented, she's got a mind for business, and she's just as delightful as Sarai is! She's *perfect* for you!"

"She's—" Jake took off his hat and slapped it against his leg. "She's not you!"

"No woman will be!" she shot back. "And you don't have time to be picky. I've found you several appropriate women, and you've turned them all down, save Delia. And I have a feeling you would have turned her down if she hadn't done it first! You need a wife. I've given you good options. There aren't any other women to choose from unless you want to move to the widows in their sixties and seventies! I've done my best!"

"I know," he said.

"Then make a choice already!" Tears welled in her eyes. "Because this is killing me!"

She dashed the tears off her cheeks.

"It's killing you?" he whispered.

"What do you think?" she asked, shaking her head. "I have to find a woman for you and see you *marry* her. I have to see her fall in love with you, and you do the same. I have to watch you build a home with someone else. I hate every second of it!"

So she was feeling this, too. Just as strongly as he was. Because he didn't want to choose another woman.

He didn't want to build that home with a virtual stranger who would be ever so nice, but never quite fill his heart.

"Do you *really* want me to marry someone else?" he asked.

Adel stared at him, her heart hammering so hard in her chest that she could almost hear it. Jake stood so close to her that she had to tip her face up to look him in the eye, and a lump closed off her throat. She didn't trust herself to use words, so she shook her head.

"That's what I thought..." Jake gathered her up in his arms and his lips came down over hers. He pulled her in hard against him, and she instinctively grabbed handfuls of his shirt as she melted into his embrace. She didn't want him to marry someone else. She wanted him to stay like this—hers on some undeniable level. His kiss was slow, warm and heartbroken. It was like the evening just melted away around them, and nothing remained but the two of them and the soft whisper of breeze.

She'd been thinking about his kiss for a long time, and here in his arms, it was possible to forget about all her very good reasons to keep her heart walled off, how she needed to listen to *Gott*'s voice, not her own desires, and she believed He had given her a mission in life she shouldn't so easily discard.

With his strong hand splayed over her back, all she wanted were kisses like this one, and time alone where they were nestled away from everyone else with no questions to answer...

But this land of in-between could not last. If Jake wasted his time with her, he'd lose the land he longed to own, and eventually someone would come asking questions…

She pulled back, and Jake released her, but his gaze stayed locked on her face with a look of such longing that it nearly broke her heart.

"I don't want you to marry anyone else," she said helplessly, "but I can't marry you, either, so where does that leave us?"

"Why can't you?" he demanded. "We're both free and single! We'll run my farm. We'll figure it out."

He made it sound so simple, and it would be for the first few months. But she'd been married before. She knew how this worked. Ahead of them, beyond the wedding and the honeymoon period, real life was waiting for them.

"I'm not free!" She shook her head. "Not in the way you are. I'm tethered to a man's memory, and that's the only way I'll have the life I want."

"You can't change your mind about what you want," he said.

"I sacrificed for *years*!" Her voice shook. "I prayed and prayed while I was trying to have babies and I couldn't. I begged *Gott* to show me why He was denying me the one thing every other woman seemed to do so easily. And He did. He showed me a different kind of life where I was able to be so much more in my community because I had less to hold me back at home. And now, I have nothing to hold me back at home…and I can truly step into that role *Gott* showed me. I can't go against His will for me. I suffered for this, and if I give it up now, all that was for nothing!"

"Not for nothing," he said. "It would be a second chance at all those things you wanted."

"But it would be giving up the path *Gott* showed me," she said. "I saw what was possible... I just didn't know how much I'd have to give up. I can't bend at the first test put in my way. I have to stay true to the mission He's given me."

Jake looked at her miserably, silent. Adel looked over his shoulder toward the house, and there was no movement there.

"I've seen people rush ahead because of their feelings," she said. "And it doesn't always work out well! I've seen people get married and live to regret their choice. I've seen men choose a woman based on a pretty face or his physical attraction to her, but marriage isn't just about romance and whispering sweet things to each other. It's much harder than that. There comes a day when you have to *try* to do the romantic things that used to come so naturally. And when that day comes, you'll be stuck."

"I wouldn't be stuck..." he said. "I'd be grateful."

"And I'd be...a wife." She shrugged weakly. "That would be all. Just a wife. The bishop wouldn't come to ask my opinion. The other women wouldn't ask for my guidance. I wouldn't be free to spend my hours talking through a teenager's troubles, or helping a new wife adjust to the realities of marriage..."

"Why not?" he demanded. "I wouldn't stop you!"

"Because they wouldn't ask!" she shot back. "No one would ask anymore!" She swallowed against that rising lump in her throat. "I thought my future out. I had a plan that made me deeply satisfied with my life choices. It let me contribute to my community in a way I never could as a *mamm* with a houseful of her own *kinner. Gott* had bigger plans for me. I had embraced that. I can't just throw it aside now based on what I feel for you. Follow your heart, they say. But the Bible doesn't tell us to follow our hearts! It tells us to do what is right! Hearts can be disastrously wrong!"

"You don't trust that I love you?" he asked miserably.

Just like that, all her logical arguments blasted apart and her heart skipped a beat.

Her breath caught. "You love me?"

"*Yah*... I do love you. I know it's fast, but I can't get you out of my head. All I want is some time with you. Tonight, coming for dinner, I just wanted a quiet evening near you. Every woman I meet dims in comparison to you. I love you, Adel. And I might not be good enough for you, or stable enough, or respectable enough, but it's the truth."

He loved her...

"You are good enough..." she whispered. "But you need a wife in a matter of days, and if as your matchmaker I marry you myself, I will prove that I couldn't be trusted to help someone else, because I let those boundaries be blurred. I will prove that I can't be trusted with more."

"Do you love me?" he asked.

She looked into her own heart, at the tumultuous feelings inside her—her longing to be with him, her constant preoccupation with what he was feeling, what he might want...the way every part of her seemed to settle into bliss when he kissed her.

"I do," she breathed. "But I can't marry you in a

few days, even if I could give up the path I'm on. I'd
need more time, time to discern what *Gott* wants for
me. And you need a quick marriage. My love right now
isn't enough—don't you see? Your love isn't enough!
You need something more solid than romantic love.
You need your farm. So let go of your ideals of finding
love, and find a wife."

"Even if you have to watch me marry her, and build
a life with her?" he asked, tears misting his eyes.

"*Yah.* Even so. Get your farm, Jake. It's yours."

She'd made her choice a very long time ago, and
while she'd never known how hard it would be, she
would trust *Gott* to carry her through.

Her years of sacrifice could not just be heartbreak
that had no meaning. If they didn't lead to something
bigger, then all it was was pain…and she couldn't believe *Gott* would give her such heartbreak for nothing.

Jake nodded and took a step back. "I don't know if
I can do it, Adel."

"Go home," she whispered. "Sleep on it. Pray on it.
And choose the woman *Gott* shows you."

Claire, or Sarai…or even Lydia or Verna. Any of those
women would make loving and devoted wives. Given
time, he'd learn to love them dearly. They'd have *kinner*
together, and raise their family. Soon, he'd forget that
he felt anything more for Adel than simple friendship.

Jake needed a wife, and it could not be Adel.

Adel lay in her bed that night, her heart in pieces.
She'd thought she knew what heartbreak felt like. She'd
endured enough of it throughout her life. There had
been the nights she'd begged *Gott* for a baby—just

one—that would give her a little child in her home to love. She'd even looked around for an Amish child in need of a home, but somehow, *Gott* didn't open those doors, either. And there had been days that she'd sat in the silence of her own kitchen, wondering if she and Mark would ever feel that special connection that she longed to feel. Then, when Mark died, there had been entire years that she spent wishing she'd appreciated her time with Mark instead of longing for something more.

She knew what heartbreak felt like, and somehow none of it had prepared her for this.

Because she did love Jake. She loved him in spite of all her better instincts, but marrying him now would mean going back fifteen years. It would mean giving up all the growth in her community. It would mean giving up the respect that she longed for. She would just be a silly woman falling for a man and marrying him in a matter of days.

That wasn't who she was. If she ever did marry again, it would have to be done soberly, carefully and with lengthy prayer. Marriage was too precious and too difficult to enter into any other way. It would have to be done in a way her community could respect—not following her heart into a foolish leap.

Fifteen years ago, *Gott* had given her a greater calling. Jake needed a wife now. She couldn't do that. This couldn't be *Gott*'s will! So why did it hurt so badly to let Jake go?

Chapter Thirteen

The next day was laundry day, and Adel stripped down the guest room—Jake's room. His bag was gone, obviously, and the only remnant of him was the musky scent of his aftershave, and she stayed stock-still in that spot, inhaling it until she felt her heart would break.

"Stop it," she said aloud to herself, and she piled the sheets and towels into a hamper and carried it down to the basement where the gas-powered wringer washer was located. She did her best to focus on the work at hand, but alone with the laundry, she did stop and let the tears flow a few times. She loved him. That was the problem here. If she'd only kept her heart secure and been the professional matchmaker she was supposed to be, this would be fine. She could be happy for him.

But now, Adel had to stay true to her word and help the man she loved marry another woman, and that was going to be the worst punishment she'd ever experienced.

"*Gott*, it's my own fault," she wept. "But take away this pain! Give me the generosity to do my job!"

Jake deserved a loving wife…and she had to find a way to be the matchmaker for this marriage, because otherwise, she'd have to tell Bishop Glick exactly why she couldn't do this…and the bishop would never see her the same way again. Everything she'd worked for, the reputation she'd built and the bishop's faith in her would be forever shaken. All because she was silly enough to fall in love with her client.

Adel sniffled, wiped her eyes on the back of her hand and hauled the heavy laundry out of the washer and into a hamper. Overhead, she heard her sister's footsteps. Naomi was baking, and Adel didn't want her sister to know that she'd been crying. So she took an extra minute to dry her eyes on the edge of her apron, then started up the stairs with her heavy load.

"Oh, Adel…" Naomi said as Adel came up the stairs and into the kitchen. Her sister cast her a look of sympathy.

"What?" Adel asked, forcing some cheer into her voice.

"You've been crying."

"I haven't."

"And now, you've been lying," Naomi shot back.

Adel blinked back a fresh mist of tears. "I'm fine. I don't want to talk about it."

"What happened last night?" Naomi asked.

"Nothing—" She swallowed, hating to lie. "Okay, it's something, but it's private, and really, in the grand scheme, it's nothing that matters. It's fine. I'm just emotional."

"Private." Naomi cast her a hurt look. "It's not so private as you think. You're in love with Jake and you're too stubborn to marry him."

"I'm not stubborn!"

"But you are in love with him."

Adel rubbed her hands over her face. "*Yah... Gott* forgive me, I am."

"You don't need forgiveness for recognizing that the man *Gott* put into your path is perfect for you!" Naomi said.

Adel swallowed. "He's *not* perfect for me, but he will make another woman very happy."

"And you want that?" Naomi asked.

"No. I'm selfish. I'm in love with him. I want him to stay single and miserable right along with me, but I can't ask that of him. He'll marry someone, get his farm, and he'll be happy. I have to get over it."

"Easier said than done," Naomi murmured.

"I'll have to."

"Why is he not perfect for you?" Naomi prodded. "You love him. He loves you. When people are in that predicament, they get married. It's simpler than you think."

Adel shook her head. "I need more time. I can't marry him in a matter of days. I need to pray, to be sure that it's *Gott*'s will. I was so certain that He was showing me a different path, and now because of emotion that changes? I need time to be certain, and he doesn't have that. He needs a wife now."

Adel headed outside. She didn't want to discuss this anymore with Naomi. They were so different that her sister would never understand why her position in this community mattered so much and how she felt *Gott* had shown her a path she must faithfully follow.

The sheets were heavy, and it took a lot of muscle to get them up on the line and straightened out. She headed to the lawn, farther down the clothesline to take hold of the sheets and give them a good flap to get the wrinkles out when she heard a buggy on the drive. She turned and squinted into the morning sunlight, recognizing Claire from the day before.

Was she coming to see what Jake had said about her? Adel's stomach tightened. Claire was perfect, and it was very likely that *Gott* had worked on Jake's heart last night and he'd come with a similar request.

But when Claire pulled up at the house, Adel spotted a small boy on the seat next to her. He was all of three, wearing baby shorts and a pair of sandals. He had rumpled blond curls, and when Claire tied off the reins, he leaned into her arms as she gathered him up.

"Hello," Claire said.

"Hello!" Adel pushed back her own moodiness and forced a smile. "It's nice to see you again."

"Yah?" Claire lifted the boy toward her. "Would you grab him for me?"

Adel caught the little one in her arms and he looked at her in mild surprise. When Claire landed on the ground next to them, she took him back.

"This is Aaron," she said. "My son."

Adel blinked, and Claire's cheeks bloomed pink.

"Oh…" Adel swallowed. "Oh, you're widowed! I'd thought you'd said—"

"I'm not widowed," Claire interrupted. "I'm just a *mamm.*"

"Oh…" Adel nodded a couple of times as those details solidified into her mind. "Claire, I didn't realize. I'm sorry about that. Hi, Aaron. You're a sweet little fellow, aren't you?"

He leaned his face into his mother's shoulder, and Adel felt a flood of sympathy.

"I know it seemed like I was coming yesterday for your friend Jake," Claire said. "My cousin explained it to me when I got back. Then it all made sense… And Jake is very nice, but I didn't really come to see you for that."

"You came to start getting to know people," Adel guessed. "And you were right to come. I'm so happy I got to meet you."

"I know that me being a *mamm* might change things," Claire began.

"No!" Adel shook her head. "Not a bit. Claire, my late husband was a deacon, and I've seen people through the hardest times of their lives. I probably understand better than most. Don't think for a minute that I'd judge you."

Claire smiled mistily. "Thank you for that. But… I didn't just come to meet people. I wanted to ask for a job."

Adel stared at her. "A job?"

"I'm a hard worker," Claire went on, her voice shaking just a little. "Like I said yesterday, I've run my own business that was successful, and I could bring that to your bed-and-breakfast. I could make some baskets to sell, maybe even do some classes for some *Englishers*. That might bring in more customers, and spread the word about your place. I'm quite good with marketing that way... Or I was. When I knew people. But it worked really well in Ohio..." She seemed to run out of breath.

Claire needed a job. This wasn't what Adel had imagined at all!

"I don't really have a lot of extra income for the bed-and-breakfast," Adel said.

"But, I can cook, I can clean, I can scrub floors. I can garden!" Aaron wriggled on her hip and she put him down on the ground. "I could take care of the horses, too. If—" Claire swallowed. "I know it's a lot to ask, but if you'd let me live here, on-site. I wouldn't take up much space. But I have Aaron, and that makes getting married a little difficult for me. And getting a job where I have to pay someone else to take care of him... Well, I can't afford it. But if I could keep him with me, that would be my solution. I'd work hard. You could give me just a little extra for money in my pocket, and..."

"So...just to be clear...you don't want to marry Jake in a few days' time?" Adel asked.

"I don't *know* Jake." Claire shook her head. "I can't marry anyone that quickly. I have my son, and I can't risk his happiness being the unwanted child in the home of a man I leaped into a marriage with. I'd have to be more careful."

"I understand," Adel said, and she looked at the woman with a new understanding. Claire wasn't interested in just any man, and beautiful as she was, she was no match for Jake's needs right now.

"I know you aren't looking to hire someone right now, but Zedechiah seemed to think that you might make room for me."

"I honestly thought he was sending you to me as your

matchmaker," Adel admitted. "I'm just starting out as a matchmaker, and... I'm sorry. I jumped to conclusions."

Claire shook her head. "He actually told me about your late husband, and he said that you had the wisdom and perspective of a much older woman. He said that you'd been through so much that it softened your heart toward other people's pain, and of anyone in this community, he thought that you could understand my situation and...perhaps hire me."

Her pain had softened her heart... It was true! It had. Her loss, her struggles, her hardship had all worked together to show her just how reliant they all were on *Gott*'s grace and mercy. The bishop hadn't sent Claire to her because of her respected position here, or because of her matchmaking ambitions. He hadn't sent her because of Adel's experience with leadership among the women, or her late husband's position in Redemption. He'd sent Claire, a woman with a three-year-old boy born out of wedlock, to the Draschel Bed and Breakfast because of her ability to open her heart to a single *mamm*. Her previous marriage, her life experiences, had all factored into this, but it wasn't quite the way that Adel had anticipated. This wasn't about her husband's position, or her own... It was about her heart. The bishop was counting on her empathy...

Adel hadn't answered, and Claire plunged on. "I know it's a lot to ask. Maybe there isn't enough extra to pay someone, but with a place to stay and food to eat, and maybe I could find some extra customers for baskets, if you wouldn't mind me doing that on the side—"

"I'd pay you, Claire!" Adel burst out, breaking out of her reverie. "I wouldn't ask you to work for nothing. But if you'd be happy living here, that actually might work. Maybe what I could pay you would be enough that way."

"Oh." A smile touched her lips. "I'd be very happy to live here. I think I got along with your sister, as well."

"She likes you a lot," Adel said with a nod. "And so do I. I'll have to talk to her, of course, but I think we can sort something out."

Claire's face split into a smile. "Really?"

"*Yah.* I do." Adel nodded. "I love your idea of the basket-weaving classes, and you can definitely have your business on the side. We'll pay you for your work, and you can stay with us. We could use another pair of hands pretty much everywhere. And having your little one around will be a true joy. I promise."

Claire's gaze suddenly moved past Adel toward the garden and she startled. "Aaron! No!"

Claire rushed forward. The little boy had pulled leaves off a lettuce plant, and Claire scooped him up and turned back toward Adel, stricken.

"That happens when *kinner* are around," Adel said with a smile. "Would you mind picking that head of lettuce? We'll have salad tonight. No harm done."

But something new was sinking into Adel's mind. The bishop had come to her for advice because of her ability to understand others, and to sympathize. Mark had chosen her for that very reason, and Adel had assumed all this time that the community's respect for her had been because of her deacon husband. And maybe it had started that way, but somewhere along the line, the bishop had decided to send his single mother distant cousin *to her.* That showed just how much he trusted both her discretion and her sympathy. This was a member of the bishop's extended family who needed both.

He'd trusted her because of her heart.

And the bishop hadn't once suggested Jake for Claire, either, even though it might have solved Claire's problems... Adel's pulse sped up as she led the way up into the house.

She quickly explained Claire's situation to Naomi, and Naomi just nodded.

"I think we'd all work together very nicely," Naomi said. "Adel's the real owner, and she takes care of the finances, so if she says we can do it, we can do it."

Adel turned and looked out the window, her mind spinning.

Gott, is my reputation built on something deeper than my marriage to Mark? I've been so afraid to lose what I built, what I thought You wanted for me, but maybe it wasn't built so much as a gift from You. Maybe I've been trying to hold on to something with two fists that I wasn't in danger of losing...

"Adel?" Naomi said. "Are you okay?"

Adel turned and met her sister's worried gaze. "Who am I in Redemption? Am I the deacon's widow, or am I simply a trusted woman?"

"You're my sister," Naomi said with a confused shake of her head. "You're a business owner. You're certainly respected. You know that."

But that wasn't what Adel was looking for.

"My cousin said that you have a very unique and special ability to understand others' pain," Claire said quietly. "He called it a gift of the spirit."

Adel shot Claire a smile. "And *Gott*'s gifts don't just slip away, do they?"

"I don't believe they do," Claire replied.

Adel turned toward her sister. "That means it's not based on my marriage. At least not anymore." She nodded a couple of times.

Naomi seemed to connect everything in a heartbeat, because a smile suddenly spread over her face.

"You're going to marry him, aren't you?"

Adel felt her cheeks heat. "I don't know. We'll see. But I need to talk to him."

Claire looked at Naomi in confusion.

"I'll explain later," Naomi said. "Trust me, this is good. Now, is this little guy hungry? Because I have cookies!"

Adel let out a slow breath.

Gott, I love him. I do! I need to be certain if this is from You, though.

So if Jake is the man You mean for me to marry, then I'm sure he'll ask me again. And if he isn't for me, I'll let him ask for another woman—anyone. Claire even! That is how I'll know.

Jake had been meaning to go visit Alphie again for some time, and somehow, now that his fragile, unfounded hopes with Adel had been dashed, he felt like something needed to be properly sorted out in his life. And he couldn't face the thought of marrying another woman.

What do I do, Gott? he prayed. Because he'd felt hollowed out and empty ever since he'd left Adel's property. He loved her… It wasn't going to change, and *Gott* didn't seem to be giving him an easy way out. Was it that this farm wasn't meant to be his? After six months of working it alone, was *Gott* going to tell him to hand the land over to Alphie, after all he'd done to him?

Jake finished his morning chores, and he had a choice—clean out more of this old house and make it ready for a wife, or deal with the problem he'd been avoiding since his return. Somehow, Jake felt nudged in the direction of Alphie's hardwood flooring business in town. If nothing else, he could sort things out with his cousin, because family was family, and what were the Amish if they didn't have relationships?

An hour later, Jake parked his buggy behind the flooring shop, and he headed into the showroom. There were different styles of flooring, different types of wood, different polishes…all on display along the walls. For the moment, the store was quiet and empty of customers, and Alphie looked up from a book he was reading in mild surprise.

"Jake," he said. "Are you all right? You look awful."

Did he? If attraction was hard to hide, it seemed like heartbreak was even harder. He didn't have it in him to pretend everything was fine, either.

"I wanted to talk to you about the farm," Jake said.

"Your farm, you mean," Alphie replied with a good-natured smile. "How's it going? Do you need some extra muscle around there?"

"It's not mine yet. I'd have to get married in a few days to make that happen. I don't think I'll be able to do it."

Alphie closed his book, walked over to the front

door and flipped the sign to Closed. Then he turned to face Jake.

"I didn't think you'd have any trouble there, honestly," Alphie said. "You seem to charm the women easily enough."

"Marriage is long," Jake said. "It's a lifetime commitment. There is no room for error when choosing a wife…or a husband, for that matter. It takes more than charm."

For the right woman, at least.

"I know a few single women I could introduce you to," Alphie said. "I'll even put in a good word. One is named Delia—you know her, she lost her husband a couple of years ago. The other—"

"I've met them," he interrupted. "I've got a matchmaker, remember? And she's introduced me to every single available woman in Redemption she thinks is suitable for me."

"I see." Alphie blew out a breath.

"I have a matter of days before my time is up, and I don't have a woman lined up to marry me. I don't think I have it in me to keep trying, either."

"Are you telling me that the farm is mine?" Alphie eyed him uncertainly.

"Maybe."

"Don't give up yet," Alphie said. "I'm sure Johannes wanted you to have it. I'm sure of it. But he also wanted you married. And maybe this is the push you need to get you into a proper home with a wife of your own."

Maybe it was, but Johannes's plan had a flaw in it— Jake wanted more than a willing woman; he wanted a true, deep, abiding love he could count on.

"Why did Uncle Johannes set this up the way he did?" Jake asked, shaking his head. "Just get married. Was it to humble me? Was it a joke?"

"I have no idea," Alphie said. "But I was as surprised as you were at how he lined things up in that will. Jake, you know you deserve this land. It would have gone to your father, if he'd outlived Johannes."

"I know."

"If it falls to me, maybe we can work out a deal. Maybe you can rent it from me and carry on like you have. Maybe you could just keep running it and we'll forget about any rent."

"Maybe." Jake sighed. But it still wouldn't be his. It wouldn't be left to his children, either. It would be another man's land. Could Jake live there like that?

"Or just get married!" Alphie said.

"That takes more time than I have!" Jake shot back. "You can't just waltz back into a community after fifteen years away and have people trust you! An Amish life is about community, and that's something that's built over time. I'm still pretty freshly back. Six months— what is that? It's a blink for people around here!"

"Yah..." Alphie nodded.

"I should have come back sooner," Jake said with a shrug. "And I can't help but wonder why you never did suggest it."

"Because you didn't want to hear it," Alphie said, shaking his head. "You were full of stories about your *Englisher* life and plans, and you were so angry with your *daet* and your uncle—"

"Which you helped to fuel," Jake said curtly.

Alphie dropped his gaze. "It was stupid of me. I'm

sorry that I did that. I wasn't lying to you. I told you the truth about what was being said, but... My wife has since pointed out that just because it was true didn't mean it needed to be repeated. So I apologize for what I did."

"Were you hoping to keep me away?" Jake asked.

"No! I liked seeing you." Alphie looked around himself. "I'm not an important man, Jake. I... I thought you wouldn't want to keep having those coffee chats with me if I didn't come with information—some inside view of things. I admired you."

"A man who'd jumped the fence?" Jake asked, stunned.

"My older cousin, who was always better-looking, smarter and much more charming than I ever was," Alphie said. "I always had looked up to you. I didn't know I was holding you back. I feel terrible about it."

Jake heaved a sigh. "For all the good it's done me."

"Everything was harder for me than it was for you," Alphie said. "You charmed girls, and I had a tough time doing that. Even when you came back, women were looking at you, commenting on your good looks. Look at me! I'm short, balding and think of jokes ten minutes too late. I'm good old Alphie. No women ever looked at me like they look at you."

"Your wife does," Jake said.

"I had to put in time to get her, though," Alphie said, shaking his head. "I had to court my wife for two whole years before I could convince her to be mine. And before that, I had to build up a friendship with her, and wait while other boys took her home from singing. It was agony."

"But you got her," Jake said.

"With time. *Yah.*"

"Is that the secret?" Jake asked. "Time?"

Alphie shrugged. "Some of us don't have any other choice. But I have to tell you, you won't find a more grateful husband than me. I *worked* for her."

Time… That might be the only way. Alphie hadn't had any other choice, but it had been worth it in the end. He'd gotten the girl he loved and he had a family of his own now. If Jake wanted the same thing, he wasn't going to be able to count on charm or good looks. The woman he loved needed more than that.

"If you inherit the farm," Jake said, "would you give me the chance to buy it from you?"

"Do you have the money for a down payment?" Alphie asked, squinting.

"I might have just enough," Jake said. "I might not have done much else worth noting over the last fifteen years, but I did save."

"*Yah*, I'd be willing to sell it to you," Alphie said. "And I'd make it a good, low price, too."

"Thank you, Alphie," Jake said, giving his cousin's shoulder a squeeze. "I appreciate that."

"Don't give up quite yet," Alphie said seriously. "You have a few more days. Just…don't give up."

A few more days wouldn't count for much with winning over Adel, but Jake had come to a realization that needed prayer.

Sometimes, the things that mattered most in life took time: paying off a mortgage, saving up a nest egg, gaining wisdom…and most importantly, winning a wife. Maybe Alphie was right, and Jake hadn't ever built up the patience that men with fewer charms had to develop. But it didn't mean that patience wasn't the virtue that *Gott* was requiring of him.

Good things took time.

And so did prayer.

Chapter Fourteen

After chores that evening, Jake's muscles ached, but it was the kind of tired that felt good. He'd prayed just as hard as he'd worked that afternoon. The animals needed to be tended to, the barn and stables needed to be cleaned out. The bottle calf needed to be fed, and then fed again. And all that time, he prayed.

Because he was getting ready to give up on inheriting this farm. Maybe he'd buy it instead, if Alphie would stay true to his word on that.

Jake looked across the rolling hills, the familiar fence lines, and toward the house that held so many memories. But the foundation his Amish upbringing had given him wasn't just a house, land or memories. It was a faith in *Gott* to guide him through the unknown. A life of faith wasn't about clinging to what was rightfully his. It was about stepping forward into the future, and he wasn't going to marry some nice, hopeful but ultimately wrong woman. Not for a house, or a barn, or even all the memories this farm held.

Alphie had told him not to give up, but this wasn't

giving up—it was growing up. Jake knew what he was going to do tonight—he was taking a shower, and then heading back to the Draschel Bed and Breakfast. He was going to sit with Adel and have a cup of tea. That was it. But he was coming back every evening for a cup of tea for as long as it took for him to marry her. She needed time—he didn't blame her. There was no rush, but he'd prove himself. If it worked for Alphie, maybe it would work for him. Because she already loved him…

And if Alphie had other plans for this land when all was said and done, Jake was going to call that number for the dairy farm, and get himself a job. He wouldn't be a landowner, but he'd be an honest worker, and he'd have other hopes for his future that included Adel at the very heart of them.

As he walked toward the house, he spotted a black buggy parked in the drive, and a form standing next to the side door. She was dressed in pink, and he knew her immediately. What was Adel doing here?

His first thought was that she'd come because she missed him—because he sure missed her! But that thought dissolved as he realized that more realistically, she was probably here to get his decision on which woman he chose. He picked up his pace and she started toward him, too, so that when they met, there was a fence between them.

"Hi," he said, and he reached over the rail and caught her hand. She squeezed his fingers in return.

"I came with—" She held up a basket in one hand. "It isn't even my baking. My sister made the muffins. But they're very good and I thought you might like some."

Jake grinned. "Thank you. *Yah.* I wouldn't turn them

down." They were both silent for a moment, then he said, "I'm afraid I have to fire you."

"What?" She frowned.

"As my matchmaker. You're fired."

Her face paled. "You've met someone…"

"What?" That conclusion hadn't even occurred to him. He climbed over the fence and landed on the other side. "No, I didn't meet anyone. I'm giving this place up. I'm letting Alphie inherit it."

"Why?" she breathed.

"Because I know who I want to marry," he said, shaking his head. "And it isn't any of the women you've brought around. They're very nice. Very decent, and they all deserve someone who loves them dearly. In other words, not me."

"Where will you go?" she asked, and he saw tears mist her eyes.

"Alphie might let me run this farm for him for a while. He said he'd be willing to sell it to me, too, but I'd have to wait and see if he really meant that once all the paperwork puts it in his name. If I need to, I'll rent a room somewhere close by," he said. "I can apply for farming work around here. I have a lot of experience."

"So you're not leaving?" she asked quietly. "Not going back to the *Englishers*?"

"When I came back, I meant it. Adel, you can't get rid of me that easily," he said, dropping his voice so that she blushed. He liked the way he could make that happen. "I'm going to work hard. And I'm going to come visit you for a tea every evening I can manage it. I'm going to ask you for a piece of pie, too, so I do hope you'll make some."

"Jake, what are you talking about?" she asked, meeting his gaze.

"I'm talking about courting you," he said, "and doing it properly. You deserve a proper courting, and you deserve a man who can make you blush, and who will steal some kisses, and who'll wait for you, as long as it takes for you to be certain of me."

"But there wouldn't be a farm for you," she whispered.

"There'd be something better—a wife. Land doesn't make the home. A woman does. If I have to choose between a farm and your heart, there is no contest. I hope you'll be home tomorrow evening, because I'll be stopping by."

Adel laughed softly and shook her head. "You're saying you want to marry me that badly?"

"*Yah*, I am," He looked down at her soberly.

"And you think it'll take that long, do you?"

It was his turn to suddenly feel off-balance. What was she trying to say?

"It might… I'm willing to wait."

"And what if I'd come to a few realizations of my own?" she asked softly.

He held his breath as she continued.

"You see, I thought that I'd paid some sort of painful bill for the respect I had, and maybe I did at first. But I found out recently that the bishop wasn't sending people to me because of my late husband. He was sending them to me because I could understand hard times and broken hearts. So maybe *Gott* was using that time to grow me, to teach me to be a better woman, to love my neighbors better than I ever could have before. It wasn't wasted, Jake. That's what I needed to see—those years weren't a bill paid for blessings now. They were a character grown, a heart molded... Not a minute of them were wasted, because *Gott* was working on the inside of me. So maybe it's time to stop paying that bill and learn how to accept a gift from Above."

"Am I that gift?" he asked, almost afraid to say it.

"*Yah*, Jake. You are. I'm sorry I was so stubborn." She shrugged faintly, and his heart hammered hard, his mind spinning to catch up. He was fully prepared for months of effort, for a lengthy explanation...

"Are you saying you'd marry me?" he asked.

"Is that a proposal?" she asked, and she seemed to hold her breath.

"The first of a hundred proposals that you'll likely get from me," he said. "*Yah*. I want to marry you. I thought I was clear about that."

"Then yes." A smile broke over her face.

"Wait—" He put his hands on the side of her face, and looked down into her eyes. "Did you just say yes?"

She nodded. "Yes!"

He dipped his head down and caught her lips with his. He kissed her long and deep, and every bit of his heart went into it. He gathered her close, and the basket dug into the side of his leg, but he didn't care. When he finally pulled back, his mind had caught up.

"How much time do you need?" he asked. "You can have as much as you want. We can get married tomorrow, or we can get married next year. Whatever you need. Truly."

"Jake—" She smiled. "You need this farm, too. And I don't need any more time. But I'm afraid my matchmaking days are behind me, once I tell the bishop I'm going to marry you myself."

Jake barked out a laugh. "Adel, there are some very nice women in this community who deserve good husbands. I have a feeling you could do something about that."

Adel caught his eye and then she laughed. "I think I could."

"But as for you and me, we need to visit the bishop," Jake said. "We have a very quick wedding to throw together."

"Very quick," she whispered, and he couldn't think of anything better to say, so he pulled her back into his arms and kissed her all over again.

His heart filled with a bewildered, joyful swell. He was going to marry her... There wasn't a happier man on *Gott*'s green earth, he was sure of it.

Epilogue

Three days later, Bishop Glick stood with Adel and Jake in his sitting room, Adel in a new blue wedding dress, and Jake in his Sunday best. The banns hadn't been announced—there was no time. But the bishop and elders had agreed that his situation was a unique one, and they would announce the marriage instead of the banns, and it would be forgivable.

Naomi and Claire were present, as were Alphie, his wife and those three rambunctious *kinner* who kept trying to wander off into the kitchen, where Trudy had an array of food waiting.

But Adel didn't notice any of that. All she saw was Jake's warm gaze locked on her face as the bishop intoned the vows.

"Do you, Adel Draschel, accept Jacob Knussli as your husband, to love, support, respect and take care of all the days *Gott* gives you?"

"*Yah*, I do," she said.

Jake gave her a relieved smile.

"And do you, Jacob Knussli, accept Adel Draschel as

your wife, to love, protect, cherish and take care of for all the days Gott gives you?"

"Most certainly, I do," Jake said with an eager nod.

Adel felt a smile tickle her lips then, too.

"Then I give you the blessing of Abraham and Sarah, Isaac and Rebecca, Jacob and Rachel... May *Gott* richly bless your union."

Jake reached out and caught her hand and Adel smiled into her husband's eyes. Married... She was a wife again, and this time she was starting out with more than hopes for her future. She was starting out with a love so powerful that it left her weak in the knees. It didn't erase her past, or undo all the work and growth. It didn't take away from all that her marriage with Mark had given her. But it was a step forward with Jake at her side. Life was not over... Love was not a thing of the past.

Adel accepted the hugs and good wishes of the people present, and when they moved off toward the kitchen, Jake bent down and snuck in a kiss—the first kiss of their married life together.

"I love you," he whispered.

"I love you, too," she whispered back.

She may very well be the very worst matchmaker in all of Pennsylvania, but she'd make up for that in the coming months. Redemption would be bustling with weddings for the women who deserved the kind of love that she'd found.

Adel was already looking forward to going home that night, and sharing more kisses, more wedding cake and that quiet time at night when all they would hear would be their whispered hopes for the future...

* * * * *

THE AMISH TWINS
NEXT DOOR

Vannetta Chapman

This book is dedicated to Professor Audrey Wick.

Lo, children are an heritage of the Lord.
—*Psalm* 127:3

Chapter One

June 1

Deborah Mast stood on the front porch, worrying her thumbnail. How long had it been since she'd seen the boys? Ten minutes? Fifteen? What was worse, she couldn't hear them. As long as they were close enough to be within earshot, she didn't worry. But when silence descended upon the land, more often than not, that indicated trouble.

Double trouble.

No one had told her what raising twins would be like, and of course she hadn't expected to be a single parent. But there you had it. Life often did not turn out as you would expect.

She stepped off the porch.

Too quiet.

Something was up.

Circling the house, she checked the trampoline and swing set. They weren't at either of those places. Picking up her pace, she headed to the barn, but the door was firmly shut and latched.

Where else could they be?

Her *dat* was inside the house, so they weren't helping him.

Her *mamm* was cooking dinner, and they most certainly weren't helping her.

Then she heard it—a male shout, followed by Joseph's concerned voice and Jacob's peal of laughter. *Uh-oh.* She hurried toward the property line separating her parents' place from the new neighbor's.

Nicholas Stoltzfus had recently purchased the adjacent farm. Her father had spoken with the man several times, but Deborah hadn't yet met him. She knew he'd been raised in the area, had lived in Maine for ten years and had recently moved back. She also knew he was a bachelor, which meant he'd receive a lot of interest from the single girls in their community. At twenty-five, Deborah no longer considered herself a part of that particular group. True, she was single—as her *mamm* loved to point out—but she wasn't exactly on the prowl for a man. She had her hands full with Jacob and Joseph.

Breaking through the line of maple trees, she stopped in her tracks, hand pressing her side where a stitch had developed from running. The fingers of her other hand went to her lips in an attempt to hold in her laughter.

Jacob was standing on the fence rail, a fishing pole held in both his hands. Joseph had scrambled through to the other side and was attempting to catch the cattle dog that had apparently been hooked through his collar. And then there was the neighbor—tall, handsome and not amused.

She rushed over, admonishing Jacob to drop the fishing rod.

"But then he'll get away," her son protested.

"Drop it!"

The dog, realizing he was no longer being reeled in by a six-year-old, took off running toward his owner, dragging the rod behind him. Joseph threw himself at the dog and the reel and managed to get his arms around both.

"Hold on, boy. We'll set you free. Just hold on."

Even in her hurry to reach them, Deborah noticed how gentle Joseph was with the dog. He stopped to look in the dog's eyes and scratch behind his ears, then freed him from the fishing line.

"See. It's all okay. You're fine."

"It is *not* all okay." Nicholas Stoltzfus reached Joseph and the dog at the same time that Deborah did. "You could have hurt my dog. You could have taken out an eye with that fishing hook. What were you thinking?"

"Not possible." Jacob hopped off the fence and joined them, thumbs under his suspenders, straw hat pushed back on his head. "Wasn't using a hook. Just a small weight."

"The weight could have hit him in the eye."

"Oh." Jacob cocked his head to the side and studied the dog. "I didn't think of that. But how are we supposed to practice without a weight?"

"Practice on your own property."

"Technically, we were on our property…"

"Jacob, watch your tongue." Deborah stepped forward, though she was still on their side of the fence.

"But, *Mamm*…"

The look she gave him silenced his protests. He dropped to the ground and proceeded to smother the poor dog with affection—apologizing, assuring the beast that they meant no harm, complimenting him on his mottled coat and dark ears. Looking down at her sons, at their red heads touching as they played with the dog, Deborah couldn't hold back her smile. They were rambunctious and didn't always think things through, but what six-year-old did? They had compassionate hearts. That was what mattered most to her.

"I would think you'd take this more seriously."

"What?" She jerked her head up in surprise. "I'm sorry, we haven't met. I'm Deborah Mast. We live…"

"John's *doschder, ya*, I guessed. If you could keep your boys on your side of the fence…"

"Jacob and Joseph, stand up and say hello to our new neighbor. This is Nick."

"Nicholas," the man practically growled.

"Nicholas." Deborah attempted to smile her apology, but the man seemed intent on ignoring her. "Remember, your *daddi* mentioned him at dinner last night."

Both boys popped up and extended a small hand.

Nicholas shook them, then quickly stuck his hands in his pockets and took a step back. He was only a few inches taller than Deborah, maybe five foot eight, and slightly built. His hair was a light brown, and his face might be good-looking if he ever smiled. His dark brown eyes were set off by frown lines. This guy was a worrier, no doubt about that.

"Howdy." Joseph sent another longing look toward the dog. "What's his name?"

"Blue."

"But he's white and black and brown."

"He's a blue heeler. That's why I named him Blue."

Deborah barely resisted laughing at that. It seemed their neighbor was bad-tempered, inexperienced with children and wholly unimaginative. He named his blue heeler dog Blue? Did he name his chestnut mare Chestnut? Deborah only knew she was a chestnut mare because her *dat* had mentioned that he'd bought her from Old Tim and managed to talk him down on the price. Few people were successful negotiating Old Tim down. It usually wasn't worth the time involved.

Her neighbor was miserly, bad-tempered, inexperienced and unimaginative. Plus, he was older than she'd expected. Was that gray hair at his temples?

"Seems like a *gut* farm dog." Jacob kicked the toe of his shoe in the dirt, no doubt imitating what he'd seen the older boys do at their church gatherings. "Are you planning on more animals? I guess Blue would make a *gut* work dog, if you are planning to bring in cattle or goats. Me and Joseph, we want a dog, but *Mamm* says we're not responsible enough yet."

"As evidenced by the fishing line you managed to tangle around Blue." Nicholas crossed his arms and frowned at the boys.

"That was a *gut* cast, huh? I told Joseph I could do it, but he was worried we'd get in trouble. We're not in trouble, are we?"

Instead of answering that question, Nicholas addressed Deborah. "I'd appreciate it if you could keep your boys…"

"Jacob. My name's Jay—cob. And this is Jo—seph." Jacob spoke with slow exaggeration, but clamped his mouth shut when Deborah gave him *the look*.

She studied Nicholas a minute, then turned to her

boys. "Home, both of you, now. Wash up and set the table for *Mammi*."

"Race you," Jacob said.

And then he was gone. Joseph paused to give Blue one last hug and then trotted off in his *bruder*'s wake.

Deborah waited until they were out of earshot.

"You're not fond of children, I take it."

"I wouldn't say that."

Deborah held up both hands. "I get it. I wasn't terribly fond of them myself until I had two. Actually, I rather avoided children in general. Since I'm the youngest in my family, that was fairly easy to do. But now..."

Nicholas looked as if he wanted to ask what had changed, but to give him credit, he kept that rather intrusive question to himself.

"I'll certainly speak with my boys and remind them to respect our boundary line."

"Danki."

"But I have to warn you that they are boys, not yet seven, and they often forget what they're told."

"Maybe you should take a stronger hand with them."

"Is that so?" Deborah wished she could work up the energy to be offended, but she was too used to people telling her how to raise her sons. She was worn down to the point of simply ignoring and shrugging off such comments. "And you know that after spending ten minutes with them?"

"Well..." Nicholas nodded toward the dog, who was now lying with his head on his paws, staring after the boys. "If today was any indication, then yes."

"Your dog isn't hurt."

"But he could have been."

"They weren't even using a hook."

"If that sinker were to hit him in the eye, we'd be on the way to the vet's right now."

"I suspect Jacob did not cast that line with the strength of a major-league pitcher." Deborah wasn't exactly perturbed, but she wasn't pleased, either. Nicholas Stoltzfus seemed to be an irritating know-it-all. "I will remind Jacob and Joseph to stay on our side of the property."

"That's all I ask."

"But if they should forget…" She paused, waited for him to contradict her again and was profoundly glad when he didn't. "Simply send them back."

"Send them back?"

"Sure. Like a letter put in your mailbox that doesn't belong there. Return to sender."

"Fine."

"Fine." She plastered on an overly bright smile. "It was nice meeting you."

It wasn't, but she had to say something.

Nicholas, on the other hand, only nodded, though his scowl became more pronounced.

Deborah walked home slowly, enjoying the last of the day's light, savoring the moments of quiet. The first day of June brought with it a myriad of feelings for her. She enjoyed the longer days and warm sunshine. Summer would bring her sons' birthday, and in the fall they would begin school. How was she old enough to have children in school? June also brought with it a decision she needed to make—she'd promised her parents that she'd begin dating this summer. The boys were old enough to understand that it made sense for her to find someone and to marry. They were old enough to want a stepfather. Why did she find that thought so distasteful?

She loved her boys more than the air that she breathed, though she understood that they could be a handful. But children were a gift. They helped you see the world in a new light. They reminded you of *Gotte*'s love, of the joy in providing for others through a hard day's work. At least once a day, she would look at Jacob and Joseph and commit herself to leaving this world better than she'd found it.

An image of their new neighbor popped into her mind.

She was fairly certain that Nicholas Stoltzfus wouldn't agree with any of those things. He seemed quite intent on being left alone. She wished him good luck with that, but something told her that he hadn't seen the last of her twins.

Nick was sitting at the kitchen table eating an egg and toast for dinner when his younger *bruder* stopped by.

David dropped into a chair across from him and shook his head in mock consternation. "Why do you live this way, Nick?"

He grunted but didn't answer. He was thinking of the way he'd corrected Deborah when she'd called him Nick. He must have sounded like a real jerk, but he didn't care. He didn't want her to feel familiar, to feel casual around him. He had no intention of becoming friends with the neighbor's *doschder*, or any other woman, for that matter.

Once burned, twice shy, as his *mamm* liked to say.

"You really should come eat at our place."

"And miss my own excellent cooking?" He sopped up the last of the egg yolk, popped the bread into his mouth and then stood to refill his coffee mug. Waving the pot at his *bruder*, he asked, "Want some?"

"Caffeinated?"

"*Nein.* It's six in the evening. Who drinks caffeinated coffee in the evening?"

"Parents. We need it if we're going to outlast the young ones."

David had three children, though he'd only been married four years. He and Lydia seemed intent on setting some Amish record for having the most children in the least amount of time. Looking in the refrigerator, Nick retrieved a soda for his *bruder*, who then guzzled half of it.

"Speaking of kids..."

"Were we?"

"I met the neighbor's *doschder* and her twin boys today."

"Deborah. *Ya.* She and Lydia know each other, even visit occasionally."

Nick felt his eyebrow arch. "The boys, they're quite the handful."

"What children aren't? I can't imagine having twins and raising them alone. That can't be easy."

"What's the story there?"

"Story?"

"They're redheaded with freckles, so..."

"Ah. Right. I guess it's not gossiping since everyone knows, and Deborah doesn't attempt to hide it."

"Hide what?"

David shrugged. "Her past. Her sins or mistakes or whatever."

Nick told himself that he wasn't interested in either, but he waited for his *bruder* to continue.

"Nothing you haven't heard before. She dated an *Englischer* when she was eighteen or nineteen, I guess. She'd been living with an *aenti* over in Sugarcreek."

"Ohio?"

"That's the only Sugarcreek I'm aware of." David downed the rest of the soda, stood and dropped the can into the recycle bin under the sink.

"And then?"

"Then what?"

"What happened in Sugarcreek?"

"Oh. *Ya.* Well, I suppose they became engaged, she planned to switch over to the Mennonite faith, then became pregnant and the fella ditched her."

"Ditched her?"

"I'm not clear on that part. You could ask Lydia, though. Deborah doesn't make any bones about it. I think she views it as a cautionary tale for our *youngies*."

"The father has nothing to do with them?" Nick didn't want children. He didn't understand children. Honestly, they terrified him. But he couldn't imagine ignoring his responsibility to any that were his own. Not that he'd ever get caught in such a situation.

"I think Lydia mentioned he had signed over his parental rights, then joined a punk band and moved to Chicago."

Sounded like an *Englisch* soap opera to Nick, not that he'd ever watched one.

"When did all this happen?"

David laughed. "In the last seven years, obviously. Must have been when you were living in Maine."

That made sense. She had to be ten years younger than him, so it wasn't as if they would have been in school at the same time. Still, he was surprised that he didn't remember her at all.

"When she moved back, she spoke in front of our congregation—a confession of sorts, though the bishop didn't require that. She simply wanted to stop the gossip and set the record straight. She was baptized and formally joined the church. The boys were infants then."

"Those two boys are a handful. They need a father in their lives."

"You volunteering?" David grinned at him and leaned back in the chair, his arms crossed.

"I am not."

"Oh. Well, you know the saying…lead, follow or get out of the way."

"I have no intention of being in the way."

"Sounds like it won't be a problem, then."

But as David drove away, Nick found himself thinking not of the boys. No, he was thinking of Deborah Mast.

Her laughing brown eyes.

The way she looked at him with barely disguised amusement.

She was young, and he supposed some would find her good-looking—blond hair, a nice figure and a fabulous smile. Surely she could find a husband if she was willing to try. No one would hold her past against her— at least, he didn't think eligible men in their community would. A mistake made was just that—a mistake. She had come back and rejoined the fold.

So why was she single and living on her parents' place?

And how was he going to keep a healthy distance between himself and the family? He'd already agreed to raise goats with her *dat*. Though he wasn't quite old enough to retire and hand the farm over to a son, John Mast had suffered a stroke the previous year. His left side hadn't fully recovered. He'd offered to provide half the grazing land and pay for all the feed if Nicholas would handle the daily care of the goats.

He sank into his front porch rocker and groaned.

He'd gone to Maine to find adventure, had fallen in love there and had his heart broken by the woman he was certain would be his *fraa*. That had ended in disaster and hurt feelings. He simply wasn't good with women, and he certainly wasn't good with children.

But goats he knew.

Goats he could raise, and he could raise them well.

The only problem was how to do so in partnership with his neighbor—without getting involved with a spunky Amish mom and her two rowdy boys.

Because the one thing he knew for certain was that he wasn't going to risk having his heart broken again. He'd barely survived the last fiasco, and he had learned from his mistake. He was single and alone. He liked it that way. He'd do whatever needed to be done to keep a *gut* distance from the family next door—even if it meant that he came across as rude.

Chapter Two

Deborah kept a close eye on her boys the next two days. When they were outside, she took out her knitting and sat where she could see them. When they walked to the pond at the back of their property, she walked with them. They were old enough to do some things on their own, but they were also fascinated with the new neighbor and his dog, Blue. Hopefully that attention would transfer to something else soon. Until then, she planned to make sure they gave Nicholas Stoltzfus a wide berth.

The last thing she wanted was for her boys to show up on Nicholas's place only to be *sent back*, as if they were a letter delivered to the wrong address. That particular choice of words had been hers, but they had perfectly captured her neighbor's attitude toward her sons.

And her sons weren't the only ones interested in Nicholas Stoltzfus. Her *mamm* had come to the conclusion that *Gotte* had put him next door specifically to court Deborah.

"Where would you get that idea?" They were in the kitchen cleaning up breakfast dishes. The boys were sweeping the front porch. Deborah could hear the low murmur of their voices.

"I've prayed on it, Deborah."

She barely managed to stifle a groan—not this again. "*Mamm*, I know you mean well, but…"

"But what? We've spoken of this before. You can't hide out here forever."

"I'm not hiding."

"It's time for you to date."

"Our neighbor? He's barely moved in and you want me to ask him out on a date?"

"You're doing a *gut* job with Jacob and Joseph."

"Nice to hear." She scrubbed particularly hard on the skillet they'd cooked eggs in. "But…"

"But those boys deserve a *mamm* and *dat*."

Deborah dropped the steel wool into the soapy water, dried her hands on a towel and turned to her mother. Bethany Mast was a dear, wise and stubborn woman. Once she set her mind to something, she could resemble a dog with a bone. Blue popped into Deborah's mind, but she pushed the image away.

Putting a hand on each of her mother's shoulders, she waited until her *mamm* met her eyes. "He doesn't even like children."

"He doesn't know any."

"He's not interested."

"How do you know that?"

"And I'm not ready." She turned back to the dishes, searched in the sudsy water for the steel wool and resumed scrubbing.

"It's frightening, I know."

"How do you know? You've only ever been in love

with *Dat*. He's never hurt you in the way that Gavin hurt me."

"You're right, and you're also wrong." Her *mamm* reached for the skillet and dried it. "Your *dat* is the only man I've ever loved, but every marriage—every relationship—has its joys and also its hurts. I might not be able to understand exactly what you went through, but I understand what it feels like to have a bruised heart."

Her *mamm*'s response was so achingly honest that Deborah didn't know what to say. Her *mamm* took the pause as an opportunity to push on.

"You promised us that when the boys were older, you'd begin courting again, and we're going to hold you to that. It's time, Deborah. Stop looking as if I'm insisting you swallow castor oil. Courting is supposed to be a joyful time."

"Right."

"And if you don't want to step out with the neighbor, that's your choice."

"Danki." Relief flooded through Deborah. At least her *mamm* was willing to be reasonable.

"I have a list."

"A what?"

"A list of eligible men."

"Oh, *Mamm*…"

"We can go over it after dinner tonight."

Deborah suddenly needed to be outside. She muttered something about checking on the boys and darted out the door. Why were her parents pushing this? She was happy enough on her own, and the boys were flourishing on the farm.

Things were going quite well, other than their initial

fascination with Nicholas Stoltzfus, which seemed to have faded. She could almost believe they'd forgotten about the neighbor and the dog, but then later that afternoon, the goats arrived. Her *dat* went over to watch the unloading, and of course he invited Jacob and Joseph to go with him.

Deborah remembered her promise to keep the boys away from Nicholas's property. Then she blushed thinking of the conversation with her *mamm*.

But she was rather interested in seeing the new animals herself. Technically they half owned them, though how did you own half a goat? Still, she wanted to see. If that irritated Nicholas, it was his problem.

Besides, who could resist a baby goat? Possibly they were all grown, but even an adult goat could be fun to watch. She needed a break from weeding the garden, and it was a bright, warm, sunshiny kind of day.

She popped into the house to check on her *mamm*. "Want to go next door?"

"*Nein.* I believe I'll sit in this chair and enjoy a mug of tea." Bethany Mast was fifty-eight years old and thirty pounds over the weight the doctor insisted she aim for, with a pleasant personality. She also had the faith of a biblical warrior. Still, the last year, in particular the last three months, had worn her down. Since her husband's stroke, she'd seemed to bow under the weight of things. Now, she smiled at Deborah and said, "Go. The boys will love it."

"Promise me you won't start dinner. It's my turn to cook."

"Promise."

She'd barely stepped out of the room when her *mamm* called her back.

"Think about what I said."

Ugh. She was not going to let this courting idea go.

Deborah hurried out the door, practically running to catch up with her *dat* and the boys. Her *dat* was a big man—five foot ten and strong like an ox—but the stroke he'd suffered had affected his left side. His leg, his arm, even his smile was a bit crooked now. The stroke had slowed him down, though no one wanted to admit that. He now walked with a limp, which in turn caused his hip to ache. He never spoke about it, didn't complain at all, but Deborah could tell. When you grew up with someone, you knew them in ways that were hard to describe.

She knew her *dat* was not happy that the stroke had forced him to give up plans to raise goats, or plant the back field, or make a fort for the boys. Those plans had been put on hold—except for the goats, a venture he'd successfully roped Nicholas into sharing. She finally caught up with the little group, and they made their way toward the fence line, the boys dashing out in front of them.

"It'll be *gut* for Jacob and Joseph to help with the goats." Her *dat*'s voice was low, a true baritone that she could easily pick out during their Sunday morning hymn singings.

"Help?"

"Sure. If there's a weakness in a fence, a goat will find it."

"I don't think the boys are able to put up fence quite yet."

"But they can walk it, check for weak points—they only need to be shown what to look for." He waved toward Nicholas's property. "Three-sided, roofed housing is also important. Goats need a dry place to stay out of the weather. Jacob and Joseph could help with building shelters."

"I didn't realize you knew so much about goats." Deborah threaded her arm through her *dat*'s.

He patted her hand, then continued. "They also get bored easily, and a bored goat is a problem goat. The boys should be able to come up with some play equipment for them."

"*Dat*, they're only six years old."

"I'm aware. You were six when you started helping with your *mamm*'s chickens."

Deborah had forgotten about that. Those chickens had been more important to her than any baby doll. She'd fairly jumped out of bed every morning, needing to check on them herself before leaving for school. It was hard to believe her boys were now that same age.

She recognized the wisdom in what her *dat* was saying, but somehow, she didn't think that Nicholas would agree.

He'd stopped by the day before to speak with her father, but he found an excuse not to come inside. He didn't even step up on the porch, as if the boys might pop out of the house and launch themselves at him. That thought made her smile. Ha. It would serve Nicholas Stoltzfus right. Who didn't like six-year-olds? Her boys were adorable.

The day before, Nicholas had put a gate in the fence line between their property. It helped her *dat* not to have to walk around to the road, and it made sense because the goats would be grazing on both sides. She was a little surprised that he hadn't put up a Twins Keep Out sign as well.

As they hurried through the gate, a pickup truck pulling a trailer turned into the drive. The *Englischer* driving the vehicle backed up to a pen that looked as if it had been hastily put together.

Jacob and Joseph dashed ahead.

Hearing the boys' shouts of delight, Nicholas's head jerked up, and he met her gaze. Deborah was sure he was about to say something, to remind her of the promise to keep the boys on her side of the fence, but then his gaze shifted to her *dat*.

"John."

"Nick. It's *gut* to see you."

Deborah couldn't help shaking her head, remembering her neighbor's insistence that she use his full name. *Nicholas*, he had corrected her with a glare. Good grief. What was this guy's problem?

Still, it was a beautiful day, and the goats were here. She would focus on the fun of the moment.

"Brought my *grandkinner* to help with the goats."

"Oh, well, I don't think…"

"It's the least I can do, and it'll be *gut* for the boys. They're plenty old enough to learn the workings of a farm." Her *dat* waved Jacob and Joseph toward the trailer of goats. "Go on now. Do whatever Nick asks you to do."

The boys looked to Deborah, who echoed, "Yes, do what *Nick* asks you to do."

He looked ready to argue, but then the man driving

the truck stepped out, had Nick sign a receipt for the goats and began off-loading them.

Everything was going well, the goats stampeding down the ramp and into the small pen. The problem came when Nick closed the gate, then turned to wave a hand to the *Englischer* as he drove away. The gate must not have fastened, and of course Jacob was perched on it, leaning over the top. His weight caused the gate to swing open.

Jacob let out a "Yee-haw," as if he were a cowboy riding a bull.

Joseph's hands flew to cover his mouth as the goats stampeded toward him. He jumped out of their way and landed on his bottom in the dirt. Blue, who had been smelling the sides of the pen—dashing back and forth as if he could count the new arrivals—didn't even hesitate. He took off after the renegade goats, barking and circling them back toward the gate. Jacob hopped off the fence, waving his hands in an attempt to be helpful.

Unfortunately, that drove the goats back away from the pen.

Nick tried to intervene, as did Deborah. She didn't know what to do, but it couldn't be that much harder than chickens, and she'd dealt with those since she was six. She glanced back and saw her *dat* standing at the pen, ready to close the gate once the goats were back inside.

The goats were various sizes and colors. There were quite a few does and at least half a dozen kids. No billy goats that she could see, which was probably a *gut* thing. But the females must have been frightened and tired, and they also looked very thirsty. They headed straight toward a cattle trough, which was obviously too tall for them. That didn't slow down the lead doe, who proceeded to climb up on top of the pails sitting next to the trough, bleating loudly and calling the other goats toward her.

Blue circled around, barking with great enthusiasm.

The lead goat held her ground.

Blue cut right.

Another large doe cut left and ran into Deborah as she arrived on the scene.

"Oh…" She tried to lean forward, to regain her balance, but it was too late. She plopped into the stock tank, bottom first, with a splash. The water was cold, and the trough wasn't especially clean. She put her hands down, only to slip in slime that had accumulated on the bottom. She came up gasping for air and struggling to pull herself free.

Then two strong arms lifted her up and out and onto solid ground. She looked into Nicholas's eyes, hoping to see laughter there.

Not a chance.

As usual, his lips formed a straight line.

She was dripping wet and more than a little irritated, but as always, her thoughts immediately turned to Jacob and Joseph. They'd frozen in place—Jacob now on top of the pails where the goat had been, Joseph halfway between the pen and the trough. Both boys were silent, waiting, worried.

She could practically read their minds. Was this their fault? Were they in trouble?

And she couldn't stop herself.

Despite her wet clothes, her dripping hair and the look

of irritation on Nicholas's face, she started laughing—and once she started, she couldn't stop. She laughed until her sides hurt. The boys joined in, running up next to her.

"You looked like you were swimming, *Mamm*."

"You looked like you were searching for fish."

"Now you won't have to wash your dress."

"Just wring it out and put it on the line."

Taking in her two redheaded boys, smiles on their faces and laughter in their eyes, how could she be angry? This was a story they would tell until she was old and gray. Of course, at this rate, she might become old and gray much sooner than one would expect.

She glanced over at her *dat*, who also had a smile on his face.

And that, too, was worth her own misery. To see the worry fall away from her *dat*'s expression, if only for a moment, she would have slipped in a dozen watering troughs.

Blue, unencumbered by two energetic six-year-olds, had smoothly herded the goats into the pen, and her father slapped the gate shut, tapping down on the crossbar to be sure that it would stay closed.

Nick couldn't imagine a worse start to the Goat Venture. That's how he thought of it now—with capital letters. He'd hoped that the Mast family would head home after Deborah's dunking in the trough, but unfortunately, that didn't happen. John wanted to discuss housing for the goats as well as mineral supplements. He'd apparently done quite a bit of reading on the raising of goats, something that Nick had meant to do but hadn't quite found time for yet.

The boys proceeded to lean on the fence—thankfully not the gate—and call out names for the goats. Molly and Daisy and Ladybug. Buttons and Bobbins for two kids. Rose and Lola. Jethro for a particularly large doe—that name would have to be changed, since it was a female. Who named goats, anyway? Maybe the boys would forget or, better yet, be distracted by the next great thing, which hopefully would not be on his property.

A doe with a lightly tanned coat became Butter.

And the lead goat, the one that had drawn the others over to the water trough, they named Bertha.

Deborah even joined in the game. When the boys couldn't decide on names for the last two, she stood between them—dress drying in the summer sun—and suggested Ginger and Nutmeg.

The boys high-fived, then raced off after their *daddi*, who'd waved goodbye, calling out that he'd be back the next day.

John and his grandsons would be back tomorrow.

Good grief.

Nick needed to do something before this venture spiraled completely out of control.

He hurried over to speak with Deborah, but she'd turned toward her family. He reached out, snagged her arm, then jumped back when she turned to look at him.

"Sorry."

"For?"

"I'm not sure." He shuffled his feet, stared off at the

retreating boys and summoned his courage. "Listen, can we talk for a moment?"

"Sure, Nicholas…" She smiled and leaned a little closer. "Or is it Nick?"

He felt hot around the collar of his shirt and resisted the urge to tug on it. "Nick, actually." He started to add, "My friends call me Nick," but that seemed rather petty, since he'd specifically corrected her when she'd used the shortened version. He swallowed the explanation, ignored her knowing smile and focused on what he wanted to say.

"We didn't get off to a very *gut* start," he began.

"True enough."

"And since we are going to be neighbors—"

"Apparently…"

"I thought it best if I was just honest with you."

"More honest than before? When you told me I should take a stronger hand with my boys?"

"You should. They're out of control."

Her look of surprise quickly changed into exasperation. Closing her eyes, she pulled in a deep breath, probably counted to five, then opened them again and offered a smile—a colder, less sincere smile. "What advice did you want to offer today, Nick?"

"It's not advice so much as…as a plea." He took off his hat, slapped it against his pants leg, then turned back toward the penned goats, who were now huddled on the far side of the enclosure. "Look, you don't know me, and I don't know you. But I came back to Indiana and bought this place because things didn't go well up north. Now all I want is to be left alone, to farm and do my part in the community, and to…"

When he couldn't find the words, she suggested, "Not be bothered?"

"Yes. Exactly." He turned to her now, studied her in her mud-covered dress. As usual, her *kapp* was pushed back, revealing her blond hair. She didn't seem to care about how she appeared or what others thought. Perhaps they had that one thing in common. "I have a five-year plan, and I can't afford to be distracted."

"A five-year plan?" Now she looked at him with undisguised curiosity, as if he'd said something incomprehensible.

"To get this place up and running. Actually, I have one-, three-and five-year plans." He could practically see the neatly written-out business goals, the timeline, the projected costs and income.

Deborah crossed her arms, then pressed her fingers to her lips.

"It's not funny. Why would you think that's funny?"

"Oh, I don't know. Because no one else has such a thing. You don't plan a farm. You work a farm."

"You can still plan."

"Why would you?"

"Why wouldn't I?"

They stood only a foot apart, hands at their sides, scowls on their faces, ready to do battle. Nick took a step back. "Your *dat* seems intent on involving the boys with the goat-raising venture."

"He is. He reminded me on the walk over that I was their age when I was given the chore of caring for our chickens." Now she leaned back against the fence and crossed her arms, staring toward her parents' place, toward her boys. "He's right. It's time they learned responsibility."

"Can't they do that on your place and stay out of my way?"

She sent him a pointed look.

He held up his hands and muttered, "No offense."

"And yet offense is taken." She didn't look peeved, but neither did she back down. "Look, as you pointed out, this was my *dat*'s idea, not mine. I've kept my part of the bargain we made two days ago. I've kept the boys away from you."

"And I appreciate that. It's been a blessedly quiet two days, until…"

"Until what? Your goats had a free run before going in their pen? What is your problem? Why are you so… so stiff?"

"Stiff?"

"Formal."

"I'm formal?"

"You're incorrigible, but I was trying to use small words." Now she laughed.

Her words indicated she'd lost her patience with him, but she laughed.

He did not understand women, and he most certainly did not understand Deborah Mast—nor did he want to. He'd learned his lesson in Maine. He was done with women.

Perhaps he should try a different approach.

"Goats are inexpensive to purchase." He waved the receipt at her. "It seemed like a *gut* idea when your *dat* suggested working together. I'm not ready for all that is involved with caring for a milk cow, but the goats will provide what I need plus some. I should be able to sell the extra milk to a bigger place—"

"Yoder's will take all you can sell them."

"Exactly, but still it's probably not a *gut* idea for your sons to get attached. Goats come and go. Sometimes they have to be sold. Sometimes they die of natural causes..." His words trailed off, sounding pathetic even to his own ears.

"You're worried about Jacob and Joseph? About their feelings?"

"I'm simply pointing out that maybe you'd rather they not be involved."

Deborah took her time straightening her dress, brushing a hand over the mud stains and choosing her words. She stepped closer to him—closer than he was comfortable with, but he wasn't about to back up standing in his own front yard.

"They are involved, though, because you made a deal with my *dat*. If you want out of that deal, speak with him. Now, if you'll excuse me, I have a dress to wash."

He watched her walk away—head held high, *kapp* strings bouncing. He was at a complete loss as to what to do next. Anyone could see that Jacob and Joseph weren't ready to help with goats. Some six-year-olds might be, but those two weren't. They were a menace!

The old cartoon *Dennis the Menace* popped into his mind, but he brushed it away. This was no laughing matter. This was his farm, and he had the right to run it as he saw fit.

If Deborah couldn't see the logic in that, he'd have to talk to someone else. He didn't want to bother John— the man obviously had enough to deal with just recovering from his stroke. He walked with such a pronounced limp that Nick had noticed it right away.

Which left one person that he could think of.

One person who could and would intercede on his behalf.

One person that Deborah might actually listen to.

He'd speak to the bishop on Sunday.

Chapter Three

Nicholas barely heard a word of the Sunday sermons—either one of them. When he'd arrived at the bishop's house, where Sunday service was being held that week, he'd walked straight to the first open seat he'd seen on the men's side and sat next to his younger *bruder* David. Unfortunately, John Mast took the seat on his left, which meant that Jacob and Joseph crowded in the row as well.

The boys squirmed, giggled, left for a drink of water, returned, then left again for a bathroom visit. The last time, they came back with a suspicious lump in Jacob's coat pocket. At least, Nick thought it was Jacob. The boys were identical in every way—same height, same build, same red hair and freckles. But he was learning that Jacob was the instigator. It made sense, when he thought of the old biblical story of Jacob fighting with the angel. Yes, that name seemed to fit.

Whereas Joseph was quieter, more thoughtful, more like a carpenter, as Jesus's father, Joseph, was.

The lump in Jacob's pocket made an occasional *ribbit* sound. If John Mast noticed, he ignored it.

The man sang with gusto.

Bowed his head during the prayers.

Offered *amen*s during the sermons.

He seemed oblivious to what was going on to his left.

Maybe he couldn't see what was going on to his left. Had the stroke affected his vision? Or perhaps the stroke had taught him what was important and what wasn't.

Nicholas pushed that thought away, because it wasn't his problem. His problem was the two boys with their heads bowed, pretending to pray but in fact studying a toad.

When the service was done, Nick made his way to the serving line. Wouldn't you know it, pretty Deborah Mast was helping at the main dish table, wearing a clean pale blue dress and starched white *kapp*. In that moment, he almost let go of whatever animosity had built up between them. But then she said, "*Gut* morning, *Nicholas*."

She wasn't going to allow him to forget their first meeting. That was fine with him, because he hadn't forgotten how much trouble her boys were. Nick was going to talk to the bishop as soon as the meal was over, and perhaps he could put a stop to this situation before it spiraled further out of control.

"Would you like chicken or ham? Or both?"

"Either is fine."

She plopped two large pieces on his plate, then turned to the person behind him. He'd basically been dismissed. He finished filling his plate, then sat beside his *bruder* David, with his wife and three kids crowded in beside them. On the other side of the table sat David's neighbor Silas, with his family. Silas's wife, Freida, had tried to set Nick up with her younger *schweschder*. He'd adamantly refused, and she'd been cool to him since—turning away every time she saw him. Why couldn't people just leave his private life alone?

He focused on eating, attempted to be polite and waited for the bishop to go for a stroll. Bishop Ezekiel always stood and went for a walk after eating. It was basically an open invitation for anyone who would like a private word to approach. Nick fairly catapulted out of his seat when he saw Ezekiel go to the front tables to scrape his plate clean. Before he'd stepped away from the table, Nick was at his side.

"Could I have a word, Bishop?"

"Of course, Nick. Let's walk to the pasture fence and look at the new foal."

Ezekiel's farm wasn't particularly large, but it was well cared for. His youngest son, Paul, had taken over the main job of handling the place. Nick gazed around him in approval. Everything looked to be shipshape. He hoped that by the end of the first year, his place would look the same.

Ezekiel was old for a bishop. Though the job of bishop was for life, many gave additional responsibilities to their deacons as they aged. Ezekiel was at least eighty, and he didn't seem to be slowing down much. His skin was wrinkled, his eyes kind and he used a cane—his only concession to an old knee injury. "A foal is an amazing thing. Don't you think?"

Nick did not want to talk about horses, but he nodded his head in agreement. The foal they were watching was still a bit uncoordinated—its gait changing from slow and careful to fast and speedy in a split second.

The mare kept a watchful eye on the foal while she grazed nearby.

"When a foal is born, its legs are eighty to ninety percent of their adult length, and they can stand and walk within two hours of birth." Ezekiel nodded at the black foal with white socks. "Most are born at night, as this one was, and they weigh approximately ten percent of the mother's weight. Nature is amazing. *Gotte* is amazing."

"*Ya.* Indeed." Nick tried to refocus the conversation. "Ezekiel, I was wondering if perhaps I could speak to you about my neighbors."

"The Mast family? *Wunderbaar* people."

"I'm sure, but the thing is that the boys…"

"Are growing at the speed of this colt." The bishop laughed. "I remember when Deborah first had them—two little redheaded bundles. Those boys are a real blessing to Deborah, her parents and our community."

"*Ya.*" The conversation wasn't going the way he wanted it to go at all.

"Have you considered courting Deborah? I think her parents would approve."

"*Nein!*" The word came out more sharply than he intended, and Nick could feel his face blush with embarrassment.

"Deborah is a *gut* woman, a *gut* Christian. You're single and live next door. Sounds like a match made in—"

Nick held up his hand before he could say *heaven*. "I'm not in a place where I'm ready to begin courting."

"Financially?"

"Emotionally."

"Ah." Ezekiel nodded as if he understood what Nick was trying to say.

"What I wanted to speak to you about is Jacob and Joseph. Those two boys are quite the handful..."

"All the more reason for the Mast family to be glad you're next door."

"Oh, I don't think Deborah feels that way at all."

"A neighbor can have a large influence on a child, Nick."

"Yes, but that's not what I'm trying to say."

Ezekiel looked fully at him now, and waited.

"What I'm trying to say is that I'd like you to speak to them—the boys. Or maybe just to Deborah." Sweat trickled down his back. "To the family, I mean."

"About?"

"About respecting boundaries."

"Boundaries?"

"Property lines, fences, another man's property." The words landed like sharp stones on the ground between them.

Ezekiel didn't interrupt. He didn't say anything at all, as if he needed to be sure Nick was done.

Then he smiled, tapped his cane against the ground and began walking toward the play area, where the children had congregated. They didn't speak as they walked, but when they came to the shade of a maple tree, Ezekiel sat at a picnic table, and Nick joined him. They were close enough to the children for their laughter to reach them, but far enough away that they could still easily talk over the noise.

There had to be two or three dozen of them—different sizes and shapes, girls and boys, all full of energy. They tumbled down the slide, chased one another through the green grass, pushed one another on the swings. Jacob, Joseph and several other boys were in the corner of the play area where a birdbath sat, filled with water. Nick could practically see in his mind's eye the toad they were releasing back into nature.

Ezekiel drummed his fingers against the top of his cane. "Do you know what Paul wrote in the fifth chapter of Galatians?"

"Can't say as I do."

"That all of the law can be fulfilled in one word—in one idea, so to speak. Isn't that marvelous?" Ezekiel combed his fingers through his white beard, then raised and lowered his eyebrows. "Think of it, Nick. To follow His way, we don't have to remember a list of rules or follow certain traditions. We don't have to offer specific types of sacrifices on certain days. *Nein*—Paul made it clear that those things are not what make you a true believer."

In spite of himself, Nick was caught up in what the man was saying, what he was describing. He was thinking of his business plan and of Deborah's laughing at him about having such a thing. He was the kind of person who liked a plan, and he did believe they were necessary. But what Ezekiel was saying… Could anything really be that simple? Could anything of real importance be simplified down to a single idea?

"Love thy neighbor as thyself." Ezekiel met his gaze and smiled. "That's it. Easy to remember, *ya*?"

"But maybe not so easy to do."

"You've hit on the very thing I was going to point out—not so easy to do."

"You're saying…" He stopped, unable or unwilling to follow Ezekiel's line of thought.

"I'm saying that you're not merely struggling with the antics of two energetic boys, or even with having neighbors who will—by both proximity and necessity—be involved with your life. And mark my words, your neighbors *will* be involved with your life. You can either embrace that or fight it, but it's the way of the world. No man is an island unto himself."

"Proverb?"

"John Donne—British poet, seventeenth century."

Nick sat forward, elbows on knees, head in his hands.

"I take it I haven't been much help."

"Well, you didn't give me the answer I wanted."

"Sleep on it. Pray on it. Your heart will tell you what to do."

But Nick wasn't thinking of his heart. He was thinking of the pages of carefully detailed business plans and how two six-year-old boys could make every single line on those pages more difficult.

Ezekiel was called away by another congregant needing a private word, and Nick was left alone. He watched the children—energetic, happy, growing. He glanced back over his shoulder at the colt that was now galloping about the pasture—awkward still, all legs, growing.

Nick was a farmer. He understood what it took for something to grow into what it should be. A plant needed sun, water, nutrients. A crop was nothing more than a collection of plants. The goats he'd purchased needed the same, but they also needed structure and training. Leave a gate open and a goat could be hurt or injured. Fail to care for them and they could become sick.

Untrimmed hooves would cause a goat to limp.

A lack of iron could cause weak muscles.

Insufficient copper supplements would result in weight loss and a low milk supply.

And Jacob and Joseph? He supposed that their needs were simple, too. It was obvious that Deborah provided for their home and food and clothing, but structure was what they were missing. They had a lot of energy, like his goats, and that energy needed to be funneled.

Nick didn't want the job. It would take time and attention to be done right, and he had other things to do. But ignoring what needed to be done would result in trouble—double trouble, in this case.

He'd go home, work out a plan and then he'd present it to Deborah. Surely she would see the logic of what he proposed. No, he wasn't an expert on raising children, but he could see things a bit more objectively than she could. Maybe she'd even thank him for offering to help.

Monday afternoon found Deborah outside, beating the living room rug with surprising gusto. She was frustrated, and she fully intended to take it out on the rug. Sunday hadn't been the day of rest that she'd hoped it might be. The fact that she was beginning the week tired and out of sorts irritated her even more.

After they'd arrived home from church, her parents had brought up courting again. Why couldn't they let things be? She was happy—or rather, she was happy enough. Were her boys really suffering from not having a father? They had her *dat*. A man couldn't possibly add anything to her life but additional laundry, unreasonable expectations and heartache.

Holding the broom like a baseball bat, she whopped it against the old rug that she'd draped over the porch railing.

She wanted to enjoy Sundays, to rest, to learn spiritual truths and spend time with her friends.

Whop.

She did not want to have to fend off unwelcome advances from old widowers.

Whop. Whop.

And she did not want to even think about what Nick had said to Bishop Ezekiel. He'd definitely looked over his shoulder at her as they'd walked away.

Another solid whop.

Dust rose from the old rug, and she peered through it. Nick Stoltzfus was making his daily trip to speak to her *dat*. He was early. Usually he waited until she was inside cooking.

Blue walked by his side, which was an instant attraction for her boys. They surrounded Nick and the dog, laughing and waving their arms back and forth, explaining something that Nick was obviously not listening to. His eyes were locked on hers. She knew that look. He was coming back for round two, or was it three?

Instead of putting up the broom, she whacked the rug again, but this time with less focus. Barely any dust rose at all. Nick looked as if he was about to give her advice on how to clean a rug. Fortunately for him, Jacob interrupted whatever he might have said.

"I have a ball in the backyard...an old tennis ball. Do you think Blue would chase that?"

"I suspect he would." Nick never looked away from her, so Deborah set down the broom and crossed her arms.

Best to get this over with.

Jacob ran to fetch the ball for the dog.

Joseph dropped to his knees and proceeded to lavish affection on the blue heeler—rubbing his belly and stroking his ears.

Nick stepped closer to the porch. "Can I speak with you?"

"Of course."

But then he didn't seem to know how to proceed, which struck Deborah as funny. The one thing she knew about the man standing in front of her was that he had no problem speaking his mind. So why the hesitation?

Nick sank onto the front porch step, as if he no longer had the energy to continue standing. Deborah was not falling for that. She refused to feel sympathy for Nicholas Stoltzfus.

On the other hand, she was tired from a long day of cleaning house. She sank down on the step next to him.

"I spoke with Bishop Ezekiel yesterday."

"*Ya*, I saw you two walking off together."

"To be honest…"

Deborah felt herself tense.

"I was wanting him to resolve…this." He waved at the boys.

"Resolve?"

"Clear up our differences, make a useful suggestion, determine our next step." Nick rubbed his hands over his face. "Honestly, I don't know what I expected him to do."

He glanced her way, and Deborah saw that the exhaustion lines around his eyes matched her own. What was keeping him up nights? Problems with his five-year plan?

"I wasn't expecting *this*, Deborah. I wasn't prepared."

"What is *this*?"

Instead of answering, he pushed on. "I thought I could buy a little place and make up for the Lost Years in Maine—that's how I think of them, like a book title with capital letters. But it's not working out as simply as I had hoped."

"And that's Jacob's fault? That's Joseph's doing?"

"I never said either of those things." He gave her a sideways look. "You're quite defensive when it comes to your boys."

"Comes with the job description."

"You remind me of a mama bear."

"And you've met one of those?"

He laughed, though it came out sounding more like a bark. "*Nein*, but I can imagine one well enough."

Jacob had returned from the backyard. He tossed the ball in the air, and Blue went scurrying after it, retrieved it and returned it to Jacob.

"I want to try." Joseph repeated the throw, with the same result.

The boys were beside themselves with amazement.

"Did you see that?"

"Did you see Blue?"

"He's so smart."

"Smarter than a circus dog."

They continued playing with Blue, and Deborah braced herself for whatever Nick was about to throw at her. She guessed she wouldn't like it, but suddenly she was too tired to fight. Perhaps she was sick. Maybe she was catching a cold. Or possibly raising twin boys took more energy than she had some days.

"I'd like to help you raise the boys."

Deborah almost fell off the step. She opened her mouth to speak, but nothing came out. What could she even say? How was she supposed to respond to such a completely unexpected and ludicrous suggestion?

"It can't be easy, doing it alone. Also, it's plain that your *dat* has his hands full with this place and his health concerns."

"You want to help *raise* Jacob and Joseph?"

The shock in her voice must have surprised him, because he turned to look at her quizzically.

"What? Why are you looking at me that way?" He rubbed the back of his neck, glanced at her again, then clasped his hands together.

And then the laughter did win, spilling out of her like water from a faucet. The boys turned to look at her, shrugged their small shoulders and resumed running back and forth with the dog. Nick shook his head as if she made no sense at all—as if she was the one who had said something incomprehensible.

Nick cleared his throat. "I don't mean to be too familiar, but we are neighbors, as the bishop pointed out. We have a duty to one another as members of the same church community, and—" He took off his hat, reshaped it with his fingers, then plopped it back on his head.

He wasn't a bad-looking man. It was just that he so rarely smiled. What had happened to give him such a sour disposition? Or was he born with it? She'd had an *aenti* who could point out the flaw in any handmade quilt, knitted shawl or baked cake. She wasn't even aware when she did it. She seemed to have no idea why the rest of the family avoided being alone with her.

But Nick knew what he was doing, because a blush was creeping up his neck. He was embarrassed but not backing down. He honestly thought he could do a better job of raising her own sons than she could. The arrogance of the man amazed her.

And yet, she was curious.

Or perhaps she simply wanted the satisfaction of hearing him concede he was wrong—which she suspected wouldn't take very long. A week? A day? Possibly even a couple of hours, and then he'd be apologizing and admitting that he had grossly underestimated how much time and energy and wisdom it took to raise two boys.

She patted her cheeks to cool them, then cleared her throat. "You're making a couple of assumptions that I probably don't agree with."

"Such as?"

"You think I need help."

"Don't you?"

"Some days I could use a hand—I'll admit that. But I'm not sure you're it." When he looked at her in surprise, she added, "It's not as if you've had a lot of experience. You've not been married and have no children of your own."

"I've never raised goats before, either, but they're doing quite well."

"Children are not goats."

"I didn't say they were, but honestly…can it be that much harder?"

This time Deborah literally prayed for patience before answering. "What exactly did you have in mind?"

"I was thinking that they could come over for an hour in the morning…" He swallowed visibly, as if the words were difficult to spit out. "And an hour in the afternoon. I'll show them how to properly care for the goats, maybe a few other everyday chores."

"So basically, you want my boys to be your farm hands, for free."

Nick pulled at his left ear, now refusing to meet her gaze. "It's not as if I expect them to be that much help. Why would I pay them? Perhaps we could think of it more as a free apprenticeship."

"They are six years old." She emphasized the last three words, because she still didn't think he understood that they were *kinner*. They weren't *youngies* looking for their life work. They were boys waiting for the school term to begin. "They turn seven in July and start school in the fall."

"Great. Only a few months, then." Nick grinned, then schooled his expression. He must have realized that he sounded overly relieved to know his apprentices wouldn't be around forever. "Sorry. What I meant to say is that for the summer, I think it could be a *gut* arrangement, and then during the school year I expect they'll be too busy."

She didn't answer. She didn't know what to say.

"And the things they learn at my place, they'll be able to use here…to help your *dat*."

Why did he have to add that particular point? If there was one chink in her motherly armor, it was that she felt guilty for piling more work on her parents' plate. If the boys could learn to be helpful rather than exhausting…well, she supposed it might be worth considering Nick's idea.

"You won't have them do anything too difficult?"

"Of course not."

"I wouldn't want them to get hurt."

"And I wouldn't let that happen."

She stood, walked down the steps of the porch and stared at her sons. They had a lot of energy. Truthfully, she wouldn't mind having a couple of hours free of her parenting responsibilities, though she'd probably spend the time beating rugs and gardening. What else did she have to do? The boys were her life. They were what she planned her day around. She could no longer remember who she'd been or what she'd done before having them. Surely she'd had hobbies and interests.

She'd forgotten all about those things, left them behind when she'd picked up her first diaper. There'd been no point—no time. It seemed she rarely had even a moment for herself anymore. She'd almost forgotten what it felt like.

"Okay. We'll give it a try."

Nick actually smiled. "You won't be sorry."

"But you might. Twins aren't as easy as you apparently think."

"Oh, that. Well, I have four *bruders* and three *schweschdern*, all younger than I am."

So, he was the oldest. Somehow that wasn't a surprise. The oldest sibling tended to be the bossiest—at least that was true in Deborah's family, and her oldest *schweschder*, Molly, would readily admit to it.

"Twins can't be harder than seven younger siblings," he added. He was once again confident.

It made her want to roll her eyes or laugh or shake him good and hard. She glanced toward the house in time to see her *mamm* peeking out the window. She actually gave Deborah a thumbs-up sign, then darted out of sight.

"What just happened?" Nick turned to look behind him, then faced her again. "You were all for it, and now I can see you're hesitating."

"*Nein.* It's just—I have a problem of my own." She studied him, then added, "A problem you might be able to help me with."

"I'm already helping you with the boys."

"Uh-uh. That's me doing you a favor, though I won't pretend to understand why you came up with this idea to begin with. Still, maybe we can help each other."

"What do you need help with?"

She pulled in her bottom lip. Was she actually going to suggest this? Then the curtain over the kitchen window moved again, and she knew she was going to have to do something soon or her *mamm* would have all the eligible men in the county lining up down the lane. That list! She did not want to think about it. Instead, she tugged on Nick's arm and pulled him away from the front porch, out of the hearing of her well-intentioned *mamm*.

"My parents want me to begin courting."

"I'm not interested." Nick's ears turned a rosy red when she stared at him. "Not that you're not..."

"What?"

"I just mean that you're nice-looking enough."

"Compliments like that will surely go straight to my head."

"I'm not interested in courting in general, is what I mean. I want to focus on my—"

"Five-year plan. I'm aware. Here's the thing, Nick. I'm not interested, either, but my *mamm* is pretty determined. She's not going to back down unless she thinks that I'm courting."

"Oh."

"It doesn't have to be real."

"'Course not."

"I'm no more interested in you than you are in me."

He looked slightly offended, but she pushed on. "My boys will apprentice with you, for free, and in return you and I pretend to court."

"For how long?"

She tapped a finger against her lips. Yes, she could do this. Her *mamm* volunteered at the school in the fall, so she'd be too busy to worry about matchmaking. "Through the summer. That should calm my parents down a bit. At the end of the summer, we'll make up some excuse as to why it wouldn't work."

"That shouldn't be hard, since we're complete opposites."

"I noticed." She smiled up at him, then held out her hand. "Deal?"

"What is it with you people and shaking hands? It's a very *Englisch* thing to do."

"Is it a deal or not?"

"Ya." He shook and mumbled, "I suppose."

"Gut." They walked back toward the porch. "Now about the boys…"

"They can start tomorrow."

"Why not now?"

"What?" He'd been looking quite pleased with himself, but that look vanished. "Now…today now? Bad idea. I'm not ready."

"Not ready?"

"I was going to make some lists—of daily chores. Maybe tack it above a cubby in the barn, where the boys can keep their tools and check off each item."

"They're *gut* readers for their age, but I'm not sure that will work. Remember, they're six."

"Have you tried it?"

"*Nein.* I talk to them. I don't have to leave them a note."

Nick's eyes darted to the boys and back to her. "I mean, I'll tack it there and we'll see how it works. But I'll follow up—verbally."

Deborah only wished she could be a fly on the wall in that barn when he set this plan into motion.

Nick looked across the yard and called Blue to his side. The boys followed as if they were invisibly tied to the dog.

"Jacob and Joseph, I have some *gut* news for you." Deborah nodded toward their neighbor. "Nick has offered to teach you how to raise goats."

The boys' eyes widened in surprise, then they high-fived one another and attempted to high-five Nick, who simply looked at them as if he didn't know what they wanted.

"You'll spend an hour at his place in the morning and an hour in the afternoon."

"We could spend all day," Jacob offered.

"*Ya*, there's nothing to do around here. All day would work for me." Joseph glanced at Deborah, suddenly worried about her feelings. "Not that we don't like being here around you. It's just…"

"We'd enjoy doing some guy stuff." Jacob clapped his *bruder* on the back.

"Exactly."

Nick was now standing behind the boys, making very obvious *no* gestures to the idea of all-day helpers.

"Let's start with the two hours and see how that goes. Now fetch the rug that's on the railing and carry it back inside for me, then see if your *mammi* needs any help with dinner."

They ran up the porch steps with the same enthusiasm they'd shown with the dog, struggled to pull the rug off the porch railing and managed to knock over two pots of flowers as they dragged it into the house.

Deborah righted the pots, swept off the dirt and looked up—surprised to see that Nick was still standing there.

"Having second thoughts?"

"*Nein.* Of course not."

"Then the boys will see you tomorrow—9:00 a.m."

"Perfect."

"And we can go on our first…date on Saturday. If that works for you."

"I guess."

She leaned forward and whispered, "I won't expect you to buy me dinner. We can go Dutch."

He nodded, looking as if he wanted to say something else, as if he had more questions or possibly more words of wisdom to impart, but he wisely kept them to himself.

Deborah stood there, watching him walk back across the field to his place. After a moment, she realized that he hadn't spoken with her *dat*. Was he that distracted at the thought of teaching her boys? Then why had he offered?

Or did the thought of dating make him so uncomfortable that he had to tuck tail and run home?

She almost laughed out loud. She'd found the one person who wanted to date less than she did, and she'd coerced him into a fake relationship. Well, he deserved it. And by the end of the summer, she suspected he would have his eye on someone more his type.

In truth, she didn't understand men at all.

Nick spoke with her *dat* every day, updating him on the shelters he was building and how the goats were doing. They were partners, in the full sense of the word—except Nick provided the manpower and her *dat* provided the funds.

Only now her boys would provide part of the manpower.

It gave her a funny feeling, the same mild nausea as when she thought of them attending school. She wanted to see them have these firsts, for them to grow independent and confident. But each step they took was a step away from her, and they were her only children. It was very doubtful she'd marry again and have more. She didn't see that happening.

How could she be sure that a prospective husband would care for her boys as much as she did? How could she trust someone with such a precious part of her life, even more precious than her own heart? Because she could guard her heart. She could stand up for herself if someone was unkind. Her boys were still young, still vulnerable.

Nein. She wouldn't be remarrying anytime soon, or seriously dating, for that matter.

She didn't need to.

She was perfectly happy with her life exactly as it was. Only as she walked into the house, she knew that wasn't precisely true. One part of her was happy enough, but another part was still a young girl expecting to have her own special happily-ever-after.

Chapter Four

H e noticed that Deborah had walked over with the boys and was standing by the fence, her hand shielding her eyes from the morning sun. Why did she feel she had to accompany them? The boys knew the way to his place. She really did coddle them, but then Nick supposed that was normal with first-time parents.

She spotted him and waved. He did the same, and she turned and headed back toward her place. She didn't seem any more keen on his plan than she had the day before. He wondered if she'd take to their fake dating with the same lack of enthusiasm. Why had he agreed to that?

He shook the thought from his head, then greeted the boys, who had broken into a trot as soon as they saw Blue.

"Gudemariye."

"Morning, Nick," they replied in unison, somewhat out of breath from their jog.

"We're here to work," one said.

"We waited until nine, like you told us," said the other. "But we could come much earlier."

"I need to know how to tell you apart," he admitted. When they were getting in trouble, he knew it was Jacob leading the charge. But when they were standing there patiently, red hair neatly combed, hats pushed back and smiles on their faces, he hadn't the slightest idea which was Jacob and which was Joseph. "Any clues?"

The boys laughed, and then Jacob pointed to his left eyebrow. "I have a scar, from the time that we tried to ride one of the old buggy wheels down the hill."

"Didn't work," Joseph explained. "He crashed."

"Got it. *Danki.*"

"Gem gschehne," they again replied in unison.

"So, do you want us to come earlier?" Jacob asked.

"Nine is fine. I have other things to do before you get here."

"Oh. Maybe we could help with those things."

"Let's see how you do with the goats before we add to your chores."

"Got it," Jacob said.

"Let me show you where your cubby is."

"We have a cubby?" Joseph's voice rose a notch.

The boys shared an incredulous look, then high-fived one another. They had plenty of enthusiasm, that was for certain.

He took them to the barn and showed them the cubbies he had designated for their use.

"They have our names." Joseph traced the letters.

Jacob hopped from one foot to another. "And it's in permanent marker."

Nick realized he hadn't quite thought that through, but a permanent marker was all that had been handy. Did he consider the boys as permanent farm hands? He did not. Still, the permanent ink was a minor problem for another day.

He had explained to them that they were responsible for returning their tools at the end of their work time. "Your chore list will be here every day. I want you to check it, first thing."

"Only has one item on it." Joseph squinted at the sheet of paper in puzzlement.

"'Build goat playground.'" Jacob took off his hat and tossed it in the air, missed catching it, lurched forward, crashed to the ground and landed on top of the hat. "This is going to be awesome."

"I'll give you a longer list when I'm sure you can properly finish one thing, and we'll need to get you some work gloves."

"*Daddi* sent some." Joseph pulled his gloves from his back pocket, as did Jacob.

Jacob frowned at the single glove in his hand. "I had two when I left the house."

"Trace your way back and find the other, then meet Joseph and me in the goat pen." Jacob was almost to the barn door when Nick called him back. "Don't let any of the goats out when you come into the pen. And maybe... walk instead of run, so that you don't frighten them."

"*Gut* idea." Jacob flashed a smile and took off at a run.

Blue looked confused as to whether he should follow Jacob or stay with Joseph. Perhaps his dog needed the energy of young boys, because Nick seemed to have lost the mutt's allegiance in a very short amount of time. Plainly the dog preferred the boys' company to his.

Well, what dog wouldn't? Nick rarely took the time to toss a ball or give the mutt a tummy rub.

"With us, Blue."

Nick planned to spend the next hour introducing the boys to the goats and showing them what he wanted them to build. He didn't expect them to accomplish much, but perhaps they could start building the structure when they came back in the afternoon.

Things didn't go exactly as he'd planned.

Jacob returned, taking giant, deliberate steps as if he was playing a game of Mother May I. The goats immediately ran to the opposite side of the pen.

"Why are you walking that way?"

Jacob froze midstride. "Because you told me not to run."

"Just walk, normal like."

"Oh." He cocked his head, raised a foot, then set it back down. "I normally run."

"Hurry up, will you?" Joseph sounded as impatient as Nick felt. "I mean, hurry up, but slowly. Nick was just about to tell us some interesting goat stuff."

"It's important that you learn to use the correct words. A female goat is a nanny or a doe."

"What about the males?" Jacob peered under the closest goat, trying to get a closer look.

"We don't have any males, but if we did, they would be called a billy or a buck."

"Why don't we have any males?" Joseph asked.

"Because we don't want any pregnant does yet."

Jacob scratched his head. "I don't really understand how that happens."

"Ask your *daddi* or your *mamm*." Nick did not plan on

explaining the birds and the bees to these two. "Younger goats are called kids."

Which sent the boys into peals of laughter.

"And remember, a bored goat is a problem goat."

"Same thing *Mamm* says about us," Joseph noted.

"I've brought over some old tires and crates, and there's a cluster of rocks over there. Today, your job is to—"

"Build a goat playground. Just like it said on our chore list." Joseph looked up with a smile, as if he was expecting a gold star.

"Right. First of all, stack the tires and crates around the rocks so that it resembles a climbing area. You want it to be nice and solid—no wobbly crates. As you work, let the goats get comfortable around you. No running or shouting. That stirs them up."

Jacob had been about to shout. Now he buttoned his lips closed.

"What are you going to do?" Joseph asked.

He'd planned on staying in the goat pen with them, but how hard could it be to stack up crates and tires? They needed to learn how to work without supervision. Now was as good a time as any to see how they'd do.

"I'll be in that field, checking the crop." He pointed to the west. "Do you both know how to whistle?"

In response, both boys stuck their fingers in their mouths. Jacob emitted an earsplitting whistle. Joseph pulled his fingers out and stared at them, as if the problem could be found there.

"*Gut*. Do that if you need me, but only if you need me. No fooling around. Taking care of goats—and crops—is serious work."

Both boys attempted grave expressions and stuck their hands in their pockets. Nick had never spent much time around twins. It was amazing how much their mannerisms mirrored one another, and yet in so many ways they seemed to be polar opposites.

Jacob and Joseph assured him that they understood what he wanted them to do.

Nick told Blue to stay, then walked out of the pen, securely fastened the gate and headed toward the west field. He'd planted corn three weeks before. He was happy to see it was coming in nicely. He spent the next thirty minutes walking up and down the rows. It was a perfect June morning—the day had started off cool and was already growing warmer. The sun shone brightly, and a slight breeze stirred from the east.

Things were going well. He congratulated himself on having an organized, well-planned morning. Having defined steps toward his goal always helped to ease his worries. He'd spent two hours the night before reworking the plan for his farm, for his life. The boys wouldn't really slow anything down, not if he could teach them to be *gut* workers.

Twins weren't so difficult.

No doubt, Deborah was a good *mamm*. He suspected she simply wasn't methodical enough. Often people didn't realize how important it was to think through a thing. Maybe he would be a good influence on her. Stranger things had happened. As for their dating—he rather wished he hadn't agreed to that, but backing out now didn't feel right, either.

He was puzzling over that and walking toward the far end of the field when he heard someone running and shouting. He turned to see Joseph racing toward him, arms waving, looking as if something was on fire.

"What's wrong?"

"It's Jacob." He bent over, hands on knees. "He fell, and he's…"

He took in another gulp of air, then finished with the last word Nick wanted to hear. "…bleeding."

Deborah pulled two cherry Popsicles out of the freezer and handed them to both boys.

"Danki, Mamm." Joseph smiled up at her as she ruffled his hair. "But I didn't even lose a tooth."

Jacob mumbled something unintelligible as he tried to hold the cold rag to his mouth and stick the Popsicle in at the same time.

"You're both *gut* boys. Now take those out back to the swing set."

Her parents had gone to town for her *dat*'s monthly checkup at the doctor, and Nick was sitting on the front porch—his head in his hands.

She poured him a glass of iced tea, grabbed the container of peanut butter bars and pushed through the front door. "Drink this. It'll help."

He took the tea and downed it in one swallow, but waved away the peanut butter bars. "I have to say…that looked like a lot of blood to me."

Deborah laughed. "Jacob has always been a bleeder when he loses teeth. It doesn't last long."

"And the bump on his head?"

"The swelling is already going down."

He finally looked up and met her gaze. "Took a year off my life at least."

"You get used to it."

"I don't want to get used to it, and I don't understand what happened. Or how it happened so quickly. Or why I didn't anticipate that it might happen."

"You can't plan for everything." Deborah didn't feel nearly as upset as Nick appeared to be. If she panicked every time there was a bruise or scratch or lost tooth, she'd spend a lot of time in a state of fright.

She had only been mildly alarmed to see him hurrying toward the front porch with the boys. She'd rather suspected he'd had his fill of them and was there to *return them to sender*. Nick had arrived at the front porch looking quite shaken and out of breath. One look at the spots of blood on Jacob's shirt and his grin revealing a nice gap between his teeth, and she'd figured out what had happened. She'd whisked them inside.

"I left them there alone. Was that the wrong thing to do?"

"They won't be very *gut* helpers if you have to watch over their shoulders every moment."

Nick nodded as if that made sense. "They understood what I wanted them to do. Why would Jacob decide to climb on top of the stacked crates and jump?" He glanced up at her with a look of such puzzlement that she took mercy on him.

"He's six. That's what I've been trying to tell you. Six-year-olds do things that don't make sense to you or me." She scooted back in her seat and pushed the chair into a gentle rocking rhythm. "When he was only four, he came in crying because he'd climbed to the top of the swing set and jumped off. I asked him why he'd do such a thing, and do you know what he told me?"

"I have no idea." Nick reached for the container of peanut butter bars, selected one and ate it in two bites.

"He told me that it didn't hurt the first time he jumped and only hurt a little the second time, but the third time he was pretty sure he broke something."

Nick shook his head in amazement.

"Turned out it was just a sprain, but who knows why he thought he could do such a thing. Joseph apparently stayed on the ground, marking his distance with a stick in the dirt each time."

"Maybe I should supervise them more closely. Wouldn't want him to knock out all his front teeth."

"I thought you said they did a *gut* job."

"Yeah. They stacked everything so that it's solid and steady. The goats are very happy."

"Then we'll consider today a success."

"But the tooth…"

"Was going to come out anyway. Joseph's shouldn't be far behind."

Nick pulled in a deep breath, then stood. "Well, I'm behind my day's schedule, so I should go. *Danki* for the tea and snack."

"Thank you for walking the boys back."

"Couldn't very well send them home alone, bleeding." He snapped his fingers. "Which reminds me, though, you don't have to walk them over every morning. Plainly, they know the way. Seems a bit…overprotective."

She resisted the urge to sigh. "Maybe I enjoy taking a stroll in the morning."

"Or maybe you're afraid to let them walk from your place to mine alone."

That stung. She wasn't exactly afraid, though she was cautious about letting them out of her sight for too long. Still, she didn't think it was his place to point that out.

"It certainly didn't take you long to fall back into lecture mode."

"I'm not lecturing."

"If you say so."

"Just…a suggestion." He shrugged and walked down the porch steps. Turning and walking backward, he said, "I guess the boys will want the afternoon off."

"Oh, no. They'll be over at four o'clock sharp."

Was that disappointment on his face? Well, this entire plan had been his idea. She wasn't about to let him squirm out of it on the first day, especially because of a little mishap like a tooth popping out.

Nick nodded, as if he'd expected as much. She watched him as he walked toward his place. One minute he could be so normal, and the next he fell into a parental role, or worse than that a big *bruder* role. She didn't need a big *bruder*. She had two older *bruders* and two older *schweschdern*. She'd been bossed around her entire life, but she wasn't going to be bossed around by her neighbor. She drew the line there.

That evening, she sat knitting while her *mamm* worked on the binding of a baby quilt. The boys had gone to bed without any argument, probably owing to the fact that they were worn out. They'd spent their afternoon at Nick's brushing goats. Apparently, that took more energy than one would think, since they spent much of the time chasing the goat that was to be brushed.

Her *dat* had also retired early.

"What did the doctor say?"

"That your *dat* is doing *gut*. That it will take time before he regains the ground he lost with the stroke."

"But he will?"

"There's every reason to believe so." Bethany glanced up and smiled, then added, "*Gotte* willing."

"How could *Gotte* not be willing?" Deborah considered herself to be a person of faith, but that didn't mean that she understood why things happened. Maybe no one did.

"*Gotte*'s ways are not our ways—Isaiah 55, if I remember correctly."

"I guess." Deborah was too tired for a religious discussion. Perhaps she should have rested while the boys were working at Nick's, but instead she'd decided to scrub the oven. What had possessed her to do that?

Unfortunately, her *mamm* wasn't as willing to drop the discussion.

"Your *dat* and I won't live forever. I'm sure you realize that."

"But he's getting better, and you're—you're fine. Aren't you?"

Her *mamm* paused in her sewing and waited for Deborah to meet her gaze. "I'm fine."

"Gut."

"But, Deborah, we must all prepare for the future as best we can."

"Okay."

"It's one of the reasons we want you to date. We won't always be here for you and Jacob and Joseph. It hurts my heart to think about you raising those boys alone."

Every conversation seemed to circle back to this.

Deborah wanted to groan in frustration, but instead, she tried reasoning with her *mamm*. "I have four siblings, and they all live relatively close."

Her *bruder* Simon and his family lived down the road. Her older *schweschder* Belinda lived on the far side of Shipshewana with her husband and six *kinner*. Stephen lived in Elkhart with his family, which required hiring an *Englisch* driver to visit. Molly lived in Goshen, which was also too far for a buggy ride. They were all somewhat scattered across northern Indiana, but they didn't live far. It wasn't as if she would be left alone when her parents passed.

"Simon has put an offer on a farm in Middlebury."

"What? Mary didn't tell me that."

"I spoke with them at church."

"And you're just telling me now?"

"It's only an offer. The owners might have received a better offer. It's nothing to get excited about."

"I'm not excited." Why did everything have to change? Why couldn't the world just slow down for a moment?

"Middlebury isn't so far from us, but my point is the same—we want you to have some stability. Yes, your *bruders* and *schweschdern* will always be there for you, but, sweetheart, I'm not just talking financially or practically. I'm talking emotionally, too."

"I think you worry too much." Seeing that her *mamm* wasn't going to let the topic drop, she added, "I forgot to tell you that I have a date for this weekend."

Her *mamm* let out a yelp, dropped the quilt she was working on and stuck her finger in her mouth.

"You don't have to be that surprised."

"Who says I'm surprised?"

"Your eyebrows say you're surprised."

"Who are you going out with? Simon Lapp?"

Ugh. Widower Lapp was twenty years older than her and had six children. Plus, he had a very unkempt beard. How could she look at that every morning? She'd constantly be reminding him to comb it or pluck the food out of it.

"Nick."

"Nick…" Her *mamm* stared up at the ceiling.

"Nick Stoltzfus. Our neighbor!"

"Oh." Her *mamm* plucked a tissue from the box on the coffee table and spent an inordinate amount of time wrapping it around her finger.

"What?"

"Nothing."

"I thought you'd be happy."

"Oh, I am. Of course. *Wunderbaar* news."

"But…"

"It's just that I thought the two of you were at cross-winds with one another."

"What's that supposed to mean?"

"I've never heard you say anything complimentary about him."

"That's not true."

"You said he's bossy."

"He is."

"And that he pretends to know how to raise children when he's never had any."

"Also true."

"And didn't you tell me that he talked to the bishop about the boys?"

"We've worked all that out, *Mamm*. And we're going on a date Saturday evening. I was hoping you could… you know…babysit the boys for me."

"You don't have to ask me to babysit. They're my *grandkinner*, and they live here."

"I'll take that as a yes. *Danki*."

"Your *dat* will be so happy to hear this." Her *mamm* smiled.

"It's just a date, *Mamm*."

"Now it is, but it could turn into more."

"I suppose." Deborah gathered up her knitting. "Today wore me out. I think I'll head to bed early."

"Parenting can be an exhausting thing."

Deborah was afraid her *mamm* would add something to that statement. Like *that's why you need a husband*. Fortunately, she didn't.

Instead, she raised her face when Deborah stopped by her chair, so that Deborah leaned down and kissed her on the cheek. She wasn't quite sure when she'd started doing that, but now it felt as natural and normal as brushing her hair in the morning. Kissing her *mamm*'s weathered cheek reminded her of how very important this woman was to her.

"We love you, Deborah. You're a *gut* girl—a *gut mamm* and a *gut doschder*."

Deborah nodded and hurried from the room, tears stinging her eyes. For some reason those words pricked her heart more than any criticism could have.

As she readied for bed, she tried to push the conversation with her mother from her mind. Yes, she understood that her parents would not live forever, but they were only in their late fifties. Many people in their community often lived to their eighties. She knew she shouldn't count on that, but there was also no reason to borrow trouble.

She punched her pillow and rolled onto her side.

Simon and Mary were moving?

Middlebury wasn't far, but they would definitely see each other less. Deborah was closer to Simon than any of her siblings. And Mary was like her best friend. Why hadn't they told her? Probably they didn't want to worry her until it was a sure thing.

Was everyone concerned about worrying her?

Did they consider her so very fragile?

She sat up, fluffed the pillow and tried lying on her other side. Sleep continued to elude her. She felt more wide-awake than she had downstairs. Probably she should get up and do some knitting. She didn't, though. Instead, she stared out the window at the night sky, wondering why things always had to change and why she always felt like the one being left behind.

Chapter Five

Deborah stood in front of the pegs where she kept her five dresses, trying to decide which one to wear. *Englischers* were sometimes surprised that they didn't have closets, but who needed one? The pegs and shelf located across from her bed worked fine. She reached out for the church dress, but Mary stopped her.

"Too formal."

"None of my dresses are formal."

"You know what I mean. It screams *church*." Mary was three years older than Deborah. She was tall and thin and one of the nicest people that Deborah knew.

"In case you haven't noticed, all of our clothes look the same."

"The style, yes. But the color, no. The dark blue screams church. The lavender whispers fun."

Deborah turned to give her sister-in-law a pointed look, but Mary didn't back down. "The lavender one looks nice on you. Try it."

"Honestly, I'm a little afraid it won't fit." She pulled

the dress over her head. The waistline was snug, but not too tight.

"Very flattering. You have a *gut* figure, Deborah."

"I have a *mamm*'s figure."

"Nothing wrong with that." They shared a smile. Mary had wed Deborah's *bruder* Simon nine years ago. Sadly, they'd only been able to have one child. Christopher was a year older than Deborah's twins, and the younger boys idolized him.

"Are you sure you don't mind taking the boys home with you?"

"I know you're kidding. Christopher has been asking for weeks—since school let out in May."

Deborah had been staring into the mirror as she combed out her hair in order to rebraid it. She met Mary's eyes in the mirror. "I'm going to miss you."

"Middlebury is only eight miles away."

"But it won't be the same."

Mary stood and walked behind her. Taking the comb, she ran it through the back of Deborah's hair. "It reaches past your waist now."

"Remember when the boys hid chewing gum in my chair and I sat back and got it stuck in my hair?"

"Had to cut a *gut* three inches off. You've grown that back and more." Mary finished the braid, twisted it into a bun and secured it with a few hairpins. "Life is always changing, *ya*?"

"I suppose." Deborah picked up her freshly laundered *kapp*, pinned it in place and tried not to frown at her image. She looked older. When had that happened? She plopped down on the bed next to Mary.

"You're no longer the young woman who came home

from Ohio all tears and worries. It was snowing and cold when you came to the house and told Simon and me that you were pregnant."

"I was scared and more than a little embarrassed."

"We cried together."

"I had no idea what to do."

"And then we prayed."

Deborah ran a finger across the stitching of her quilt—a friendship quilt that Mary had hand-sewn and given to her. "You and Simon even came over for support when I told *Mamm* and *Dat.*"

"We've been through much together."

"It's been a *gut* seven years. I feel safe and protected here. I feel as if the world can't get in. Do you know what I mean?"

Mary nodded and reached for her hands. "But even Plain families have their challenges and troubles, as we both know. Life is always changing, Deborah—even for Plain folk, and I've heard we really like for things to stay the same."

"I wouldn't change what happened to me for anything in the world. I was frightened and worried, and coming back to Shipshe—coming back to our family and our church—was difficult. I didn't want to admit to the mistakes I'd made, and yet doing so opened up a whole new path for me."

"Coming home was the right thing to do."

"As for Jacob and Joseph—they're my heart walking around in work pants, button-up shirts, suspenders and straw hats." Deborah smiled at that, then sobered.

"I know what you're thinking, but we won't grow apart."

"We won't?"

"I won't allow it." Mary stood and pulled Deborah to her feet. "Now, do we need to go over the rules of dating?"

"I think I got it."

"It's okay to mention the boys, but don't talk about them all night."

"What else do I have to talk about?"

"Don't pick a fight, either."

"Why would I do that?"

"Find something to compliment him on."

"Nick is confident enough. He doesn't need my compliments to make him feel better."

Mary cocked her head to the side. "I think you intimidate him."

"What?" It came out as a squeal. Deborah fought to lower her voice and asked again, "What?"

"You're intimidating."

"I am not."

"You're an independent woman, a *gut mamm*, and you know your own mind. Plus, you're not afraid to voice your opinions."

"Those things don't make me intimidating."

"They might." Mary stepped forward and embraced Deborah in a hug, then she whispered, "Just have fun."

"It's not even a real date."

"So you've mentioned."

"I'm having second thoughts."

"Too late, because I believe Nick just drove up."

They both moved to the window and looked down. Nick exited the buggy at the same moment Jacob, Joseph and Christopher came running around the corner of the house. Deborah and Mary couldn't make out what was being said, but the boys laughed, high-fived Nick, then ran off.

"He's *gut* with the boys."

"Maybe." They locked gazes once more, then both hurried downstairs and out the front door. Deborah was mortally embarrassed to find her parents on the front porch, as if they needed to check out her date before they were allowed to leave.

Nick looked up, saw her and did a double take. He raised his eyes to hers and smiled appreciatively. Deborah could have easily melted into the porch floor. This wasn't a real date! Surely he remembered that.

The boys returned with something in their hands, making a big show of needing to talk to Nick in private. He turned his back, and apparently items were exchanged. A quarter for each of the boys, if she wasn't mistaken. When Nick turned to face her, he was holding a bouquet of wildflowers.

"Every woman deserves flowers, right?"

"So nice of you to...bring them?"

The boys shouted, "We picked them."

"I never would have guessed."

"My *dat* gives my *mamm* flowers sometimes," Christopher piped up. "And then they kiss."

Jacob made kissing noises, and Joseph shook his head as if to dislodge the thought. Deborah could hear her *dat* ask her *mamm* if she'd like a bouquet of wildflowers, but she didn't turn around. She kept her attention on her sons, who were still watching her quizzically.

"Why can't we go with you, *Mamm*?" Jacob hopped onto the porch step, then cocked his head to the side. "You look—different."

"*Gut* different or bad different?"

Jacob shrugged, but Joseph jumped to his rescue. "*Gut*. Of course. You always look *gut*, *Mamm*. Even that time you fell in Nick's trough."

Hoping to avoid the retelling of that story, Deborah pulled her purse strap over her shoulder and squatted down in front of Jacob and Joseph. "Be sure and take your toothbrushes and a change of clothes to your cousin's house."

"We don't need clean clothes," Jacob reasoned. "We'll just get them dirty again, and that's more work for you."

"We already have everything set out in our packs, by the front door." Joseph put his arms around her neck, then kissed her cheek, reminding Deborah of the night before, of kissing her own *mamm*.

Jacob tugged on his *bruder*'s arm. "Come on. We gotta show Christopher our frogs."

"Be back in fifteen minutes," Mary called after them.

Nick had been talking to her parents about the goats. Great. They had two topics of conversation to cover on this supposed date—goats and children. He nodded toward the buggy, and she walked in that direction, suddenly feeling clumsy and self-conscious and as if she were sixteen again.

But she looked up and saw her *mamm* and *dat* and Mary, and that helped to settle her nerves. She waved and they waved back and smiled, as if this was a good idea. As if it wasn't a farce. Which was okay. Her parents looked pleased. Even Mary looked happy with the turn of events.

It didn't really matter what Nick thought of her—

whether he liked her more or less after their first date. Her family knew her best. They'd been through the very worst with her, and still they loved her. What more did a woman need?

She pushed her fears and insecurities behind her and turned to face the man driving the buggy. With a resolve she didn't quite feel, she shook away the thought that this was her first date in seven years. She pushed down the memory of the terrible feeling of rejection she'd experienced when Gavin had told her he was leaving for Chicago. It didn't matter. None of that mattered.

It was time to step out of the past and live in the here and now.

Even if that meant going on a fake date with a man who could push her buttons better than a six-year-old. Her expectations for the evening were low enough that she didn't think she'd be disappointed—unless she had to wash the dinner dishes. That would be a disappointment for sure and certain.

Nick tugged at the collar of his shirt and tried to focus on directing his mare. "Get on, Big Girl."

"That's her name? Big Girl?"

"What's wrong with it?"

"Nothing. I didn't say anything was wrong with it."

He glanced her way, but he did not need to look at pretty Deborah Mast while he was driving. He might drive into the ditch. That would be a fine story to tell his siblings. Somehow they'd caught on to the fact that he had a date, and he was pretty sure there would be a thorough interrogation the next time they were all together.

"She's big for a mare, and—"

"She's a girl." Deborah's laughter spilled out. He liked the sound of it, though he'd never tell her that. She spent enough time laughing at him. No need to encourage her.

"What is so funny?"

"It's just that, well, you named your blue heeler Blue."

"And?"

"I just figured you might have named your chestnut mare Chestnut." She pressed her fingers to her lips, but it didn't stop her laughter.

"I get it." He sat back, resettled his hat and tried to pretend he was hurt. "You're making fun of the guy who doesn't have an imagination."

"Now, I did not say that." She hesitated, then added, "But it sounds like maybe you've heard it before."

"Indeed."

"Tell me."

"Let's see…" He ran his fingers along his jawline. He'd shaved for the date because it seemed like the polite thing to do. He shaved every other day, and always in the morning, but he'd made a special effort for Deborah. It might be a fake date, but she was still a woman who deserved to be treated as if she was on a real date.

"I once named a tabby cat Tabby."

"You did not."

"Yup. There was another calico barn cat that I named—"

"Calico."

"You got it."

"I think you're making that up."

"I'm not." He shrugged. "Seemed to make sense to me."

"When you do marry, you might want to let your *fraa* name the children."

"*Boy* would be a fine name for a son."

She was laughing again and laid a hand on his arm. "Stop. You're giving me a stitch in my side."

"*Girl* for a *doschder.*"

Her laughter seemed to lift the tension from the buggy and drop it on the side of the road. They spent the next ten minutes talking about childhood pets.

When they entered Shipshewana proper, he said, "Thought we'd eat at Blue Gate—enjoy some *gut* Amish food."

"Oh." She blinked several times. "Okay."

But he drove past it, laughed when she pointed out that he'd done so and parked in front of the pizza parlor. "My *bruder* David reminded me that you eat Amish food all the time. He suggested—"

"Pizza. Sounds *wunderbaar.*"

By the time he'd set the brake on the buggy and thrown Big Girl's reins over the hitching post, Deborah was out of the buggy and standing beside him. "Have you eaten here since you've been back?"

"A couple times with my *bruder*'s family." He cupped her elbow, walked her to the entrance and then opened the door before she could. It was all coming back to him now—though it had been a long time since he'd been on a date. Still, it wasn't that hard.

1. Arrive on time.
2. Look your best.
3. Be a gentleman.
4. Make conversation the other person will be interested in.
5. Don't talk about previous relationships.

They walked to the front counter, studied the menu board and settled on a pizza that was half meat supreme, half veggie. With two glasses of iced tea, the total came to just a tad over twenty dollars. He was pulling the money from his wallet when Deborah slipped a ten-dollar bill onto the counter.

He didn't say anything in front of the cashier. But when they were seated with their drinks, he said, "Let me give you your ten dollars back."

"No way."

"I know we said this isn't real…"

"It isn't." She sipped her tea and smiled broadly at him. When he didn't respond, she leaned forward and said, "Takes the pressure off. Don't you think?"

"*Ya.* I guess so." Nick stared across the room, trying to remember what else was on his list of dating etiquette. He had actually written one out, in the back of his five-year-plan journal. He couldn't have explained why he did it, but lists made him feel better. They made him feel more in control. He'd even written out a list of topics to talk about. Unfortunately, he couldn't remember a single one.

The silence was quickly growing awkward when Deborah jumped in with, "Tell me about the goats."

"Oh, well. Let's see." He took a sip of his iced tea. "They're Nubian goats. But I guess you knew that."

"Not really. Why did you pick Nubians?"

"High fat content in their milk, which is a good thing."

Deborah smiled and rubbed the condensation off the side of her glass. "*Ya,* I bought skim milk by mistake once. My boys wouldn't have a thing to do with it."

"I'd like to add some Alpine goats, maybe next year. Top goats can produce two gallons a day."

"That much?"

"*Ya*. I wouldn't kid you."

Surprisingly, she seemed interested. She propped her elbow on the table and rested her chin in her hand. She looked pretty that way, and if he'd been an *Englischer* who carried a phone around twenty-four hours a day, he'd ask to take her picture.

"If I had the money and time to raise goats, I'd raise Angoras."

"Because of the mohair?"

"Yes!" She spread her hands out flat on the table. "I like to knit. It's just…you know, something I do. But if money and time weren't a problem, I'd love to raise my own goats for the hair, then learn to spin it."

"You could do that."

"I guess."

Her expression turned suddenly melancholy. He searched his mind for a way to bring back her earlier, lighter mood. Finally he settled on telling her how his lead doe, Bertha, would stand on the very top of the play area Jacob and Joseph had built, bleating loudly. "The others crowd around her until it looks as if they're posing for an *Englisch* photographer."

He described the work the boys had done and how they'd improved throughout the week. "No more blood," he murmured as the waitress dropped the large pizza pie between them.

His diet of leftovers and sandwiches must be affecting him more than he realized—the pizza looked like a gourmet meal, and the smell was *wunderbaar*. "I'm tempted to sit here a minute and just savor the smell."

"You go ahead." Deborah reached for a piece from the veggie side and slipped it on her plate. "I'm starved."

He liked that she seemed to enjoy the meal.

"What are you thinking about?"

"Nothing."

"Go ahead. Say it."

"Just that I like how you eat."

"How I eat?" She snagged a napkin and wiped at her face.

"I like that you're enjoying the meal."

"Is that unusual?"

"Some women don't. Some are so worried about their figure and such that they can't relax around food."

"It sounds like you speak from experience."

He nodded, but he didn't explain. Rule No. 5—*Don't talk about previous relationships*—had popped into his mind like a blinking neon light.

"I had a cousin who had an eating disorder." Deborah chose another piece, studied it and then took a good-sized bite. Reaching for her tea, she added, "We all knew Tabitha was thin, but we didn't realize that she *couldn't* eat, that she was struggling so. Later, after she'd been to a treatment place over in Middlebury, she told me that when she looks in the mirror, she actually sees a large person. She was probably ninety pounds at that point. Isn't that odd? How your thoughts about a thing can change the way you perceive that thing?"

And there it was—another quality he really liked about Deborah. She didn't shy away from serious topics. She didn't mind discussing the hard stuff, like when she'd taken him to task for thinking he knew how to raise twins.

"Why are you smiling?"

"I was just thinking how you speak your mind."

"My *bruder*'s wife, Mary—she's probably my closest friend—she told me that I can be intimidating."

"I'm not intimidated."

"Gut."

Nick sighed. "Better to say what you're thinking than keep it inside. That only leads to trouble."

Deborah waited patiently, but he changed the subject.

They spoke of summer and crops and festivals. Finally, Nick realized he couldn't eat another bite. "Want to go and walk down the Pumpkinvine Trail a bit?"

"I'd love to."

The sun was just beginning to lower as he pulled the buggy into the small parking area at County Road 850. Deborah stood in front of Big Girl and pulled a carrot from her apron pocket.

"Have you been carrying that around all night?"

"Nein. I asked the cashier if I could snag a couple from the salad bar." She dropped another piece of carrot into his hand. "Go ahead. Spoil your mare. Everyone does."

He laughed and fed the carrot to Big Girl, then assured the mare they'd be back soon.

They walked down the trail, passed other couples and families, even stopped to try and identify a few plants. Together, they enjoyed the summer day coming to an end. Nick almost reached for her hand. He almost let himself forget that this wasn't real.

It was when they were driving back toward home

that she brought up their dating arrangement. "So, your family knows, about us, I mean?"

"That we're fake dating? *Nein*. They think it's real. It's not that I lied, but I didn't correct their assumptions."

"And why is that?"

"Honestly? I was worried if I let on that this is some convoluted plan of yours—"

"Thank you very much."

"Then someone might mention it to someone else, who might mention it to your folks, and then you'd be right back in the same place you were."

"Danki." Her voice was soft, sincere.

"You don't have to thank me, Deborah. When I took the time to consider your plan, it made sense for me, too. My family hassles me probably as much as yours hassles you."

"I doubt that very much."

He laughed. "Okay, well, maybe half as much."

"That's possible." She hesitated, then asked, "So why don't you date—for real date, I mean?"

He sighed deeply. Somehow, he'd known this was going to come up, but he was hoping it wouldn't be on their first fake date. Still, probably better to get it out of the way.

"I'm sure you've heard that I was to be married when I was living in Maine."

"I did hear that. Someone mentioned it at a church social. What happened?"

He was glad he was driving, that he had an excuse to not look directly at her. "Olivia changed her mind… sort of a runaway Amish bride."

"Did she actually run away?"

"She did." He glanced at her, then back at the road. "Don't look so horrified. It's a little funny now that I think about it."

"Seriously? It doesn't still…sting?"

"Well, yes. It does. But I can also see the humor in it. Rather than speak to me, she caught a bus to Tennessee. That's a little desperate, don't you think?"

"I'm so sorry, Nick. You didn't deserve to have that happen to you."

Many people had tried to cheer him up about what happened, but he wasn't sure he'd ever had someone commiserate with him so sincerely. Perhaps that was because Deborah knew a little about being rejected.

He cleared his throat. "My *bruder* told me a little about your situation."

"I was quite the topic of conversation my first year back." She drummed her fingers against the purse in her lap. "I suppose I deserved it. I was a living cautionary tale for every Amish girl who stepped out with an *Englischer.*"

"You cared for him, this *Englischer*?"

"I did. I thought he was the one." She stared out the window.

"And now? Do you still think that?"

"Nein." She turned to face him. "Anyone who could turn their back on Jacob and Joseph… They aren't the kind of person that I could love and make a life with."

"Sounds like you're over him."

"Oh, *ya*. Most definitely. I don't pine for Gavin anymore. When I think back to those days, it's almost as if it all happened to someone else."

"It's his loss, Deborah. Your boys—they're a handful, but they're *gut* boys. I can't imagine walking away from my own children."

"To be fair, he never met them. As soon as he learned I was pregnant, he legally terminated his parental rights."

"Wow."

"Yup. And then he left the area. Sort of like your runaway bride."

"I don't understand people sometimes."

A quiet settled around them, but it wasn't an uncomfortable silence. He was thinking about what strength it took to walk away from that type of rejection and what courage it took to go home.

To admit your mistakes and ask forgiveness.

To raise two boys on your own in the manner you believed they needed to be raised.

Nick directed Big Girl down her parents' lane. He pulled to a stop in front of the house but made no move to get out of the buggy. How did one end a fake date? Was he supposed to kiss her?

Before he could decide, she opened the door and hopped out of the buggy. Leaning in, she said, "Best fake date I've ever had."

"Only fake date I've ever had."

"Me, too. Thanks, Nick."

"Thank you, Deborah." It all sounded rather formal in his ears. He just was not good at this sort of thing.

She waved, smiled, shut the door and hurried up the steps.

Driving home didn't take long, since he lived next door. But it was long enough for him to sink into a very familiar gloom. Their fake date had awakened him in some way. He realized that he didn't like being alone, not all the time.

Blue met him at the barn door. Nick unharnessed Big Girl, stabled her and then headed into his house. It was pitch-dark inside, and he had to fumble around for the battery-powered lantern he kept on the kitchen counter. Its light seemed to mock him, accentuating just how bad his kitchen looked. In truth, the house was barely habitable and in desperate need of remodeling.

The house was lonely. *He* was lonely.

He couldn't consider seriously dating. Who would date him? Who would be willing to wait until he had the fields cultivated, the barn restored and the herd built up? He stood there, in the light of the single lantern with Blue at his feet, and wondered if his five-year plan might be wrong.

Because at that moment, five years—one thousand, eight hundred and twenty-five days—seemed like a very long time to wait to date. He was an idiot. He'd thought he could keep his heart wrapped up and tucked away, like the set of good dishes packed away in the barn.

Walking over to the sink, he filled a glass with tap water and stood at the window drinking it. He could just make out a light in the upstairs room of the Mast farm. Was it Deborah's room? Had she enjoyed the night? He hadn't even asked her.

She'd seemed to enjoy herself.

He readied for bed, his thoughts filled with her laughter and smile and direct way of looking at him. Deborah would make someone a fine *fraa*. Someone who was ready to marry. But she wouldn't want to wait five years. The boys would be eleven years old by then. They deserved to have a father now.

They deserved someone who would make them a priority.

He was very certain of one thing—that someone wasn't him. He'd make a terrible father. Maybe if he could start when they were babies, he could learn as they grew. The last week with Jacob and Joseph had proven that he didn't know a thing about raising young boys. He'd thought it would be easy!

Nick shook his head, climbed into bed and tried to put thoughts of the woman next door out of his mind.

He didn't succeed. Instead, he came up with a *wunderbaar* idea for their second fake date. She'd love it. Maybe he could be a good influence on her. Just because he was waiting five years didn't mean she should. Maybe she'd realize dating wasn't so horrible, and then she could find a real romantic interest and date that person.

That was the ticket.

It was a solid plan, and plans were what made things work. A smile on his face, Nick fell into a deep sleep. Unfortunately, his dreams were peppered with images of Deborah and the boys and a future that wasn't his to claim.

Chapter Six

For Deborah, the next week went too well, if that was possible. It wasn't that the boys didn't seek and find trouble. They most certainly did. It was more that Nick seemed to be handling things on his own.

When Jacob and Joseph managed to get into a mud fight after Monday's rain, Nick had them take off their shirts, scrub them clean in his sink and then hang them on the line. By the time they arrived back home, they were cleaner than when they left. Even more surprising, Nick did not show up on her doorstep when Jacob managed to cut his hand attempting to leap over a barbed-wire fence. Instead, Nick cleaned and bandaged the wound as well as Deborah could have, pinned a note to Jacob's shirt outlining what he'd done, and insisted the boy explain to her how it had happened.

Jacob did, in fine dramatic detail, ending with, "I'm supposed to tell you how it won't happen again."

"Is that so?"

"I can't tell the future, *Mamm*."

"Do you think that's what Nick meant?"

They were sitting on the back porch. She'd sent Joseph out to look for eggs in the chicken house so she could have a word with Jacob privately. The boys exchanged a look that said they'd tell each other everything once they were together again.

"Do you think Nick was expecting you to see into the future?"

"I guess not."

"So, what do you think he meant?"

Jacob pulled a piece of grass growing near the porch steps and stuck it in his mouth, something he'd probably seen the older boys do. He chewed on it a minute, then passed it from the right side to the left. "Nick seems to think that I get hurt a lot because I go too fast."

"Mmm-hmm."

"But isn't fast a good thing?"

"Sometimes it can be."

"He also said that I don't stop and consider what might happen."

Deborah felt an old flare of defensiveness rise up in her. The boy was six. True, he was about to turn seven. Also true, he did go too fast, and he most certainly did not think things through. Still, was it Nick's place to tell her son those things?

Jacob stood, brushed off his pants and tossed the piece of grass onto the ground. Moving to a lower step, he faced Deborah and put his small hands on her shoulders. "He could be right. I'm going to test out this theory."

"Test out this theory…" When had he started talking like an adult?

"For one week, I'll try to go slower and more carefully—which I have to tell you doesn't sound like much fun."

Deborah tried to hold back a grin.

"But the medicine he poured in my cut wasn't fun, either, so maybe it'll even out."

"That sounds like a mature decision."

"Only one week," he reminded her. "If I still get hurt, then I might as well go as fast and recklessly as I want."

He kissed her cheek, then took off in search of his *bruder.*

Deborah was left feeling proud of her son and more than a little discombobulated. Later that night, as she pulled out her knitting, she replayed the conversation in her mind. What about it had bothered her so much?

"You're frowning at that baby yarn as if you don't like it very much."

"Oh, I like it." She fingered the variegated yarn—pink, yellow, blue and green. What was there not to like? She remembered when she'd made something similar for her own boys. Now she knitted for new babies born into their church family, but not so much for Jacob and Joseph. Maybe a hat or scarf, but other than that, they had insisted that they'd rather stick to regular guy clothes.

"They're not babies anymore."

"Indeed. Jacob and Joseph are turning into fine boys."

"I rather miss the baby days." She ran her fingers over the yarn, sighed and finally picked up her knitting needles. This blanket wasn't going to knit itself.

"You'll have children again, Deborah. I suspect Jacob and Joseph will have many siblings. Don't be worrying about that."

Deborah threw a skeptical look at her *mamm* but managed to keep her opinions on that subject to herself.

"Are you and Nick going out again this Saturday?"

A subject she was even less eager to talk about. "Um... I think so. Say, I think I'll have a cup of tea. Can I bring you one?"

"That would be *wunderbaar*."

Her *dat* had retired early, as he often did these days. Upstairs she heard a thump, followed by laughter. The boys were supposed to be reading, but Deborah suspected they usually spent the twenty minutes before bed having a pillow fight. She missed cuddling them, reading to them. Now when they sat together with a book, the boys insisted on sounding out the words themselves.

She made the cups of tea and added the tin of oatmeal cookies to the tray. When her *mamm* had set aside her quilting and chosen a cookie, she sat back, looked at Deborah and said, "You might as well tell me. It's plain as the apron over your dress that something is bothering you."

"The boys are doing well over at Nick's."

"He's been a real blessing to this family, for sure and certain."

"Sure. I guess."

"But..."

"I don't know. When the boys were younger, I longed for an hour to myself. Now I have no idea what to do with it...let alone an entire morning." She sipped her tea and scowled at the tin of cookies. She used to do the baking for her *mamm*, but she wasn't needed in the kitchen any more than she was needed with the boys.

"It's normal to feel a little at loose ends when you're in between *bopplin.*"

"And what if I don't have other children?" She held up her hand to stop her mother's protest. "I know you believe I will, but what if I don't? What am I supposed to do every day?"

It sounded ridiculous even to her ears.

Instead of arguing, her *mamm* nodded in understanding. "Your situation is a bit unique for an Amish woman."

"Exactly. Most women my age, women I know, have their hands so full that they're overwhelmed. Even Mary is busy, what with the move and helping with Simon's business."

Her *bruder* Simon was a farmer, like most Amish men, but he also offered tours of his farm. Mary handled most of those details. They hoped that the move to Middlebury would increase the number of tours they could do. Mary had shared with Deborah that they made more from the tours than they did from the crops. Since Mary wasn't able to have any more children, she'd become a real partner to Simon.

"No one is useless in this world who lightens the burden of someone else, and you have lightened my burden for sure and certain this last year."

"But…"

"But now that your father's health has stabilized…"

"You don't need me like you did."

"Extra hands make lighter work, Deborah. You're a *gut* cook and a *gut* cleaner, too."

"I learned from the best." Deborah meant it as a compliment, but it was followed by such a heavy sigh that even she heard the despair in her voice. "I honestly don't know what's wrong with me."

"*Gotte* made us each with unique abilities and talents. I love to quilt, but you're one of the best knitters that I know."

Deborah glanced down at the yarn in her hands and then shrugged. "I like knitting. I always have."

"You know, I hear the yarn shop in town is looking for part-time help."

Deborah nearly choked on the piece of cookie she'd popped in her mouth.

"It's only an idea."

"That I get a job? That's absurd, *Mamm*. I need to be here, with the boys."

"Maybe. But summer will be over before we know it, and then they'll be in school all day. If you don't think you'll be married by then…"

Now Deborah spilled her tea. "*Mamm*, why would you even say a thing like that?"

"Because I'm a bit mischievous." She leaned forward and handed Deborah a napkin to soak up the spilled tea. "It's okay if you don't feel that way about Nick yet. Sometimes love comes on slowly."

Deborah didn't know how to answer her mother. She had the sudden urge to confess that Nick wasn't really interested in her, but she wasn't ready for that conversation yet. So instead, she said, "I guess. But working in a shop… I don't know even one *mamm* with young children who does that."

"As we said, your situation is unique. You're in an in-between place right now, Deborah. It doesn't mean that *Gotte*'s done with you, only that you can't see His path for you yet."

That was the understatement of the year. "You think I should apply for the job?"

"I think you should consider it. Or maybe you'd rather serve pie at the Blue Gate."

"I would *not* rather do that."

Her *mamm* laughed. "Plain and Simple Yarns sounds like a better fit."

Did it? Another thud sounded from upstairs. Deborah stuck her knitting back in her bag. Jacob and Joseph might be growing up before her eyes, but they still needed tucking into bed. "On that note, I'm off to check on the boys. Perhaps an early night for myself will set things right."

But sleep didn't come so easily.

Should she apply for the job?

Could she work and still be a *gut mamm*?

Nick would probably make a list of pros and cons. Actually, that wasn't a bad idea. She tossed off the covers, found her journal, a pen and her night-light. Her *dat* had given her the battery-operated lamp when he'd caught her reading beneath the covers with a flashlight. "Better on your eyes," he'd explained, patting her shoulder.

She made a list. It didn't take long. There wasn't much to put on the con side. After all, if she found that working at the shop was too much or that the boys were suffering because she wasn't there, she could quit. And the truth was that the boys probably wouldn't notice. They loved spending mornings over at Nick's—the single hour having expanded to lunch. Soon she'd need to pay him for babysitting.

Only they weren't babies.

And he wasn't "sitting" with them. He was working with them. He was doing the things a father would do. Things that Deborah was ill-equipped to do.

Nick might not be genuinely interested in her, but he was a *gut* neighbor, a *gut* friend to her boys. She should be grateful for that.

And she should apply for the job at the knit shop, even if the very thought of doing so set her stomach to churning. She tossed from side to side, knowing she needed to sleep. Finally, she flipped onto her back and stared up at the ceiling. And there she found her answer, something her *mammi* used to say.

Her *dat*'s *mamm* had lived with them for several years when Deborah was a young teen. She was fond of proverbs—biblical and otherwise.

A merry heart doeth good like a medicine, but a broken spirit drieth the bones…from Proverbs.

The last cow closes the door…from her grandfather.

Oiled machinery runs smooth…just something people used to say.

That was often her answer when they questioned her. "Oh, it's just something people used to say." Deborah and her *schweschdern* had often rolled their eyes at *Mammi*'s sayings. Her *schweschder* Belinda had threatened to stitch them into pillowcases. *Mammi*'s pillowcases. They'd been sure *Englischers* would snap them up at The Mercantile. Unfortunately, hand-stitching letters onto cotton had been a monotonous task for teenage girls. They'd given up before they'd finished the second example.

But the sayings had worked their way into Deborah's heart. Now she thought of one that her *mammi* often repeated to Deborah's *bruders*.

Common sense is often wisdom clothed in work clothes.

Just maybe, it was time for Deborah to put on her work clothes.

The next day passed quickly, and Saturday morning seemed to arrive in a blink.

Her boys had planned to spend the day with Deborah's *schweschder*. Since Belinda lived on the far side of Shipshe—a good eight miles away—they only saw each other once or twice a month. Belinda and her husband had six girls. Jacob and Joseph enjoyed pretending that they didn't want to spend a day with six girls.

"They play the stupidest games, *Mamm*." Jacob extended his arms and pretended to swing a bat. "Why don't girls like normal games, like baseball?"

"Some girls do."

"Janie tried to braid my hair." Joseph shook his head in confusion as he finger-combed his bangs.

"She is only four. Perhaps next time you could distract her with—"

"Oh, look. They're here!" Both boys dashed off toward Belinda's buggy, any reservations about spending the day with six girls forgotten.

Belinda leaned out and hollered, "I need to get back to make lunch. Tell *Mamm* I'll visit when I bring them home this afternoon."

Deborah stood there, waving after them, and then

hurried inside to prepare for her date. Nick had stopped by the day before and suggested that Deborah wear something she didn't mind getting dirty for their Saturday outing. He'd also asked if they could move the time to late morning. When she'd raised an eyebrow at the question, he'd only said, "Trust me," and walked off whistling.

He was whistling a lot these days.

She had no idea what that was about.

"I've never seen that dress before." Nick smiled at her as he held open the buggy door.

"Because I only wear it for cleaning." She gave him a pointed look. "Someone told me to dress down."

"Regardless, the blue fabric is causing your eyes to sparkle."

"I think that's my wariness shining through."

Nick laughed. He was feeling *gut* about this plan. If he was attracted to Deborah, then certainly other Amish men would be, too. It was only a matter of them getting to know her, of coaxing her off that farm. She'd find a proper beau, be in an authentic relationship, and he could go back to his five-year plan.

"What's the surprise?" she asked as Big Girl trotted down the lane and out onto the main road.

"Wouldn't be much of a surprise if I told you."

"Uh-huh." She sat up straight, peering out the window. "Seems like the same road we drove down last time. Taking me back to the pizza place?"

"Nope."

"You wouldn't have told me to wear an old dress for that."

"Nope."

"You're being quite mysterious, Nicholas Stoltzfus."

"Yup. Trust me. If you don't enjoy the outing, you can pick next week's destination." Only if things went well, there wouldn't be another fake date. "Tell me about your week."

She worried her thumbnail for a moment and finally shrugged. "I applied for a job yesterday."

"Seriously?"

"Yes. It was my *mamm*'s idea. I've been a bit out of sorts lately."

"Why is that?" He'd thought he'd done a *gut* job with Jacob and Joseph. He hadn't even panicked when Jacob had cut his finger. "Am I doing something wrong with the boys? Because you're right… Twins aren't as easy as one might think."

She laughed at that. He liked that he could make her laugh. He relaxed when the worry lines between her eyes faded.

"Quite the opposite. It's strange having an entire morning to myself. I feel like I should be doing more…"

"My *mamm* says that keeping a neat house is like threading beads on a string with no knot."

"Your *mamm* sounds like a wise woman."

"No doubt."

"But the thing is that I don't have a house to keep neat. My *mamm* does that. I help, of course. But there isn't enough work for the both of us. She shoos me away most days, or makes up something that doesn't really need to be done, like painting the fence around the garden."

"I noticed that. I thought maybe the boys had done it."

"Can you imagine my boys with paint?"

Nick gave a mock shudder, and she laughed again.

"Tell me about this job."

"My *mamm* encouraged me to apply at the knit shop in town. I'll find out next week if I've been chosen for the position."

He could see she was conflicted about working outside the home. "You're a *gut mamm*, Deborah. You're doing an admirable job raising boys that will grow into fine young men."

He thought she might tease him for saying that, since he'd given her such a hard time when they'd first met. She didn't. Instead, she stared out the window and returned to worrying her thumbnail.

"We're here."

He pulled into the Shipshewana Outdoor Market parking area and directed Big Girl to the back of the lot, where several other buggies were parked. The horses had been unharnessed and released into an adjacent field.

"Why are we here? Are we going in that van?"

"Trust me. Remember?"

"Uh-huh."

But she suddenly looked very wary. Other Amish couples were climbing into the van—all chattering and wearing older clothes. It seemed everyone knew where they were going except Deborah.

"It's definitely not an old folks' tour," she whispered as they neared the van.

Nick was pleased to see that the couples were probably close to her age. And some didn't seem to be couples at all, but rather friends.

She turned on Nick before they were within earshot of the others.

"What's this about? And don't give me that *trust me* line again. I hate surprises."

"Seriously?"

"Sort of. Today I do."

"We're going kayaking."

"Kayaking?"

"I heard from my *bruder* that a group meets here every Saturday at noon. They travel over to Bristol, rent kayaks and spend a few hours going down the river." Unable to resist, he reached out and tucked a wayward lock of hair into her *kapp*. "Come on. What's the worst that could happen?"

"I could fall in."

"Water won't hurt you."

"I could drown."

"Can't you swim?"

"Yes. I can swim." She rolled her eyes, then marched toward the van.

He'd found something Deborah Mast was afraid of, and it wasn't kayaking. She avoided social situations. Had she always been that way, or only since her return from Ohio? Was she afraid that people were judging her, or was it simply a matter of being out of practice?

Nick paid the driver ten dollars and followed Deborah to the back of the bus. Bristol was only a fifteen-minute ride away, but most people preferred not to take their horse and buggy that far. Also, there wasn't a good place at the park to leave a horse for several hours. With each person paying five dollars, the driver certainly made enough for it to be worth their trouble, and the man who ran the outdoor market—which wasn't open on Saturdays—had given his permission for them to leave the horses and buggies in his field.

As they drove toward Bristol, everyone introduced themselves. Nick didn't think he'd remember all the names, but it didn't matter. He'd brought Deborah here so she could meet more people her age, and so she could learn to be comfortable in a group of singles again.

Sitting beside her on the van seat, he had to remind himself that he'd brought her here so she could find a proper beau. He didn't think sharing that with Deborah was a good idea, though. Instead, he struck up a conversation with two brothers sitting across the aisle, who looked to be Deborah's age. By the time they pulled into the parking lot of Fluid Fun Paddlesports, it felt as if they all knew each other.

The kayaks were a rainbow of colors—orange and blue and yellow and red. Deborah seemed to relax once they were paired off again, choosing their kayaks and paddles and vests.

"I'm supposed to wear this?" She held up the life preserver.

"*Ya.* Keeps you from drowning if you fall in."

"I was kidding before. I can swim."

"But it's required...see?" He pointed toward the sign near the rental kiosk, then helped her into the orange vest, adjusting the straps and laughing when Deborah pretended she couldn't breathe. Standing that close to her, breathing in the smell of lilac and soap, he felt momentarily light-headed. It was probably just that he hadn't had a proper breakfast. There were several snack bars positioned along the river, so he'd remedy that soon enough.

Fifteen minutes later, they were in a two-person kayak, and a teenage *Englisch* kid was showing them how to use the paddles, how to turn the kayak and how to back up. After a brief tutorial, he told them to be careful and that lifeguards would be patrolling the river if they needed help.

Deborah was tentative at first, but it didn't take her long to learn the paddling motion. They practiced in the middle of the river, and then when they were more confident, Deborah directed the kayak to a cluster of reeds, where they paused to watch turtles climb up onto a log. Twice they nearly collided with other kayakers, which resulted in everyone laughing and attempting to back up.

When she splashed him with water, he knew that she was truly enjoying herself. They paddled around the bend in the St. Joseph River and pulled up to a snack bar nestled on the bank of the river.

"Hungry?"

"Starving."

He hopped out of the kayak and pulled it to the edge of the water, then reached for her hand. And in an instant, the moment went from light and carefree to something different. Deborah's eyes met his. Nick felt disoriented, off balance, even. Then she smiled, lifted her dress so that it wouldn't get any wetter than it already was and sashayed up to the snack bar.

Was she flirting with him?

Good grief. He was an idiot. He was going about this all wrong. He needed to remind her that this wasn't a real relationship. He needed to remind himself of the very same thing. Nick crammed his hat down on his head, hoping it might change the direction of his thoughts, and hurried to catch up.

They both ordered hot dogs and chips and bottles of water and sat on the grass, looking out over the river.

"This was a *gut* idea."

"It was?"

Deborah had taken a large bite of the hot dog, and now she started laughing and nearly choked on the food.

"What's so funny? Do I have moss in my hair? Water stains on my shirt?"

She caught her breath and took a drink from the bottle of water she'd purchased. This time she'd insisted on paying for his lunch, though he had no idea how she managed to have any extra money.

"What was funny was the look on your face when I complimented you."

"Oh, *ya*. That was a big surprise."

He bumped her shoulder with his and bit into his own chili dog. How could a chili dog taste so good? It was probably the same cheese, chili, bun and meat that he'd tried to make at home last week. His had tasted like cardboard. Now, sitting on the banks of the St. Joseph River, sitting next to Deborah in the summer sunshine, the food tasted like a gourmet meal.

When she leaned toward him to point out a family of ducks paddling across the river, Nick had an urge to put his arm around her. Then she looked up at him, eyes wide, lips slightly parted. All he had to do was lean forward an inch, maybe two. All he had to do was put his fears and insecurity behind him and kiss her.

Instead, he jumped up, knocking his water bottle over and dropping his paper plate and napkins.

"What's wrong?"

"Nothing."

"Nothing?"

"Just…um…decided I'd like some ice cream." He started walking away from her, walking backward so he could keep talking to her. "Can I get you some?"

"You want to buy me ice cream?"

"Sure. I'll just…"

"Surprise me." The words were soft, and she was looking at him as if he'd lost his mind.

He had lost his mind. He was supposed to be scoping out a new beau for her, a real beau. He was not supposed to be falling for Deborah Mast.

He ordered two double dips of ice cream, getting a variety of flavors since he had no idea what she liked. Passing the money to the teen working the cash register, he noticed his hand shaking slightly.

Get a grip, man.

Pulling in a deep breath, he accepted the change, tossed it into the tip jar and carried the ice cream to Deborah.

"Mint chocolate chip with strawberry? Interesting combination…"

"Uh, *ya.* Or you could have this one…" He thrust the second cone toward her.

"What is that?"

"I have no idea."

She stepped closer to him, accepted the mystery ice cream and took a bite. "Butter pecan on top, and I'm pretty sure that's chocolate chip on bottom. Pretty *gut,* too." Smiling and looking intently into his eyes, she wagged the cone back and forth. "Let me know if you want to trade."

Then she made her way back to the water, balancing easily as she stepped into the kayak and walked to the back seat. Turning, she plopped down and took another bite of her ice cream.

Nick practically groaned.

He could not be falling for this woman. She was all wrong for him. She was independent and strong-willed and the *mamm* of two boys.

She was beautiful and made him laugh.

But most importantly, she was everything that his five-year plan did not allow for. He pushed the kayak back into the water, hopped in and sat facing Deborah. The kayak slowly drifted to the middle of the river as they enjoyed their ice cream.

The silence wasn't awkward or strained.

It was peaceful, except for the thoughts zipping around in his mind. How attached was he to that five-year plan? Nick knew that plan was a crutch. He'd developed it when Olivia had first run away, when he'd decided to leave Maine behind and return home. He'd made the decision to throw his life into work and to leave relationships to other people. In that way, he was no better than Deborah. He was avoiding getting hurt, and he had a feeling that she was, too.

The important question was whether he was willing to take a chance. The woman eating ice cream in the sunshine of a near-perfect June afternoon wasn't what he needed, but she might be everything that was missing in his life.

Chapter Seven

Deborah checked the messages on the machine in the phone shack Monday afternoon. Her stomach flipped when she heard the voice of the manager of Plain and Simple Yarns asking her to return the call. Pulling in a steadying breath, she did, and Maggie Jennings offered her the job. She would start out working mornings, three days a week, and they'd add more hours as needed if she wanted them.

Her first day of work was Wednesday.

She was a wreck.

What if the boys needed her? What if her *mamm* needed her? What if her *dat* had another heart episode?

"Your parents will ring the bell if they need anything," Nick had assured her when he met her buggy as she'd pulled down his lane. "And you don't have to worry about the boys. They're helping me in the vegetable garden today, plus doing their regular chores with the goats."

Jacob and Joseph looked up from the garden and waved at her. Not so long ago, they would have run to see her, but with Blue watching them with adoring eyes—and given the dirt fight that seemed to be going on—they didn't have time for such childish things. The thought depressed her even more.

"You said you wanted this." Nick stepped closer to the buggy, putting his hands on the open window.

She looked down at those hands—a farmer's hands, complete with calluses, a scratch or two and, of course, a suntan. She looked at his hands and wondered what they'd feel like touching her face.

"Hey. Are you okay?"

She jerked as if a bee had stung her. "Of course. I'm just having an emotional morning. It happens when you're a parent."

"I would know nothing about that."

"Lucky you."

"I would say 'break a leg,' but that doesn't sound appropriate for working in a yarn shop."

"Please don't wish that on me." Her laughter was weak, but the kindness in Nick's eyes did a lot to calm her heaving stomach.

"You can do this, Deborah. You'll be *gut* at it. And your family will be fine."

"Right. I know that."

"Try to enjoy the time off the farm."

"Uh-huh. Okay." She plastered on a smile, then called out to Rhapsody and turned the buggy toward town. In spite of her completely unnecessary side trip to Nick's, she made it to the shop ten minutes early. She tied her mare to a hitching post in a shady spot. Rhapsody was a five-year-old red roan with a white marking running from her forelock to her muzzle. Stopping to rub her on the white spot, Deborah whispered, "Back in a few hours. You're a *gut* horse."

The mare nodded in agreement.

Maggie Jennings was every bit as nice as she'd seemed during the interview. She insisted that Deborah call her Maggie instead of Mrs. Jennings, was super patient when she had to explain the cash register procedure three times and didn't even get perturbed when Deborah tripped and spilled several baskets of wool yarn.

"I've been meaning to move those." Maggie cocked her head. She was probably only ten years older than Deborah. Her hair was brown streaked with blond. She was dressed in jeans and a button-down shirt that had the store's logo on the pocket. "Want to try your hand at creating a new display?"

"Me?"

"Sure. Let's see what you come up with. If we don't like it, we'll change it."

Deborah liked the *we* in that statement. She spent the next hour playing with the display until she came up with something that she thought looked appealing. Clearing off the top of a bookcase that held knitting books, she turned the round baskets on their sides and stacked them in a pyramid fashion. She secured the right and left sides with heavy ceramic bowls that she'd seen in the storeroom. The red wools went in one ceramic bowl, the purples in the other. The rest of the yarn went into the baskets, making a delightful palette of colors from light to dark.

"Wow."

"Do you like it?"

"Nope." Maggie shook her head, causing her long earrings to bounce back and forth. "I love it."

The last hour of her first day was busy. It seemed that lunch hour was a prime time for shopping. She only messed up two of the eight transactions.

"It gets easier every day, Deborah. I think you're a good fit for my shop."

"*Danki*... I mean, thank you."

"Honey, I'll take a thank-you in Amish or English. Now, I know you're anxious to get home and check on those boys, so off you go."

By the time Deborah walked out to Rhapsody, she was exhausted but also feeling more confident. She could do this. Knitting came naturally to her. She understood the different weights and could put together what kind of fiber worked best for each type of project. But more importantly, she had a pleasant boss.

Unfortunately, the satisfied feeling didn't last. She came home to find Jacob sitting at the kitchen table, holding an ice pack to the top of his head.

"What happened?"

"You know that thing we talked about?"

"Going slow and being careful?"

"Yeah. I sort of forgot."

Joseph was sitting at the table, watching his *bruder* with worried eyes. "Are you still seeing double?"

"What? You were seeing double? Do we need to go to the—"

"*Nein.*" Her *mamm* walked in holding a dust rag. "I checked the chart the doctor gave us last time."

"I can walk a straight line."

"He remembers his birthday," Joseph offered.

Jacob immediately perked up. "Speaking of birth-days—"

"Let's not. Why don't you tell me what happened?"

Jacob studied the ceiling as if what Deborah wanted or needed to hear was written there. "We were playing Frisbee with Blue. You remember that old Frisbee that *Onkel* Simon gave me? It's a bright orange with—"

Deborah sank into a chair opposite her sons. She motioned for Jacob to hurry along his story.

"Well, the Frisbee went up on the roof, and Blue was barking…"

"It went up on the roof? All by itself?"

"Maybe?" Jacob glanced to Joseph for help.

"Actually, no," Joseph clarified. "Remember? You said something like 'watch how high I can throw this.'"

"You're not helping, *bruder*."

Deborah closed her eyes and prayed for patience.

Jacob cleared his throat and tried again. "Turns out I'm *gut* with a Frisbee. I can throw it quite high. After it went on the roof, we needed to get it down, and we didn't want to bother Nick. He was out in the field."

"You climbed on the roof?"

"Shimmied up the rain gutter, which would have been fine, except when I got up there, after I'd thrown the Frisbee down to Blue…"

"He caught it, too," Joseph piped in. "Blue is a *gut* catcher."

"My foot slipped, and down I went. Next thing I knew, Joseph was standing over me and Blue was licking my face."

"I made sure he could open his eyes and then ran to fetch Nick. He was not too happy."

"Nope. I'd say he would have grounded me if he could, so I guess it's a *gut* thing he's not our *dat*."

Deborah winced at that. The boys seemed to be waiting to see whether she'd give them a Popsicle or a lecture. She stood, removed the ice pack and studied the red lump. At least it wasn't bleeding. He didn't seem to have a concussion. She supposed she should be grateful that he wasn't hurt any more seriously.

"You're lucky you didn't break anything."

"*Ya*, for sure, I am."

"And you should be ashamed for breaking your word to Nick. You promised him that you'd be careful."

"I wouldn't say I broke my word—"

"Stop talking."

Both boys sat up straighter, their eyes wider, their attention now focused completely on her.

In that moment, Deborah wondered if she'd somehow overcompensated for their not having a father. Had she been too lenient with them? Was this her fault?

"I want you to write an apology note."

Jacob groaned. "You know my writing is terrible. Couldn't I just clean out the horse stall or something gross like that?"

"It will be neatly written, even if you have to copy it down more than once."

"I'll do one, too," Joseph offered. "We'll do it together."

"Nope. This is Jacob's problem, and Jacob is going to handle it." She squatted in front of Jacob's chair. "I'm disappointed in you, son. You broke your promise, you probably scared a year off Nick's life, not to mention your *mammi*'s, and most importantly, you could have been seriously hurt."

He stared at the floor, no doubt unaccustomed to being lectured. For once, his confident, cocky smile was missing. That was a good start. Perhaps he'd feel real remorse and be more careful in the future.

But somehow, she didn't think it was going to be that easy.

It took great resolve, but Nick managed to wait until late afternoon before going over to Deborah's. Ostensibly, he still stopped by a couple times a week to update John on how the goats were doing. He felt that excuse was wearing a bit thin. There was little to report on the goat front.

But Deborah's *dat* seemed to enjoy his visits.

He'd managed to avoid Bethany's offers of dinner. Somehow it felt like an invisible line he shouldn't cross. Deborah's mother meant well, but eating together felt too much like being one of the family. Since their outing on Saturday, he'd been arguing with himself as to whether his feelings toward Deborah were real or simply a product of his loneliness. At least he'd come to terms with the fact that he was lonely. He could have gone years—five years, to be exact—pretending that he was perfectly happy living alone on the farm. Now he accepted that simply wasn't the case.

His resolve to keep at least some amount of distance between himself and Deborah's family crumbled when he walked into the house and smelled dinner cooking. When Bethany once again invited him to stay for the meal, his mind went blank and he couldn't come up with an excuse that he would believe, let alone anyone else. Instead, he said he'd love to and then sat in the living room, discussing summer crops with John. "Say, it's awfully quiet around here. Where are the boys?"

John smiled and drummed his fingers against the rocking chair. "Jacob's in his room, writing an apology letter."

"An apology letter?"

"For this morning's incident."

"Ah." He couldn't think of anything else to say to that piece of news. When he'd seen Jacob lying on the ground, his first thought had been that Deborah would kill him—he was supposed to be watching the boys while she was at work. His second thought was that Jacob apparently only learned by experience. "And Joseph?"

"Out spoiling my horses with carrots, mainly because Deborah said he couldn't help with the letter."

This time Nick simply nodded.

None of this was making sense to him, though. He hadn't asked for an apology letter.

"And Deborah's on the back porch, cleaning it as if spring had just arrived." He looked at Nick and winked. "She could probably use some help."

"Oh, *ya*. Sure. I'll go and see if there's anything I can do."

John waved him toward the kitchen. He walked into the room and stopped as the smells from what Bethany was cooking caused his stomach to grumble loudly.

Deborah's *mamm* looked at him and smiled. "Dinner will be ready in fifteen minutes."

"Fifteen minutes. Got it." He'd been to the Mast place many times in the last month. But he hadn't ever been on the back porch. No doubt he looked as confused as he felt.

"Through the mudroom," Bethany said as she checked the dish in the oven.

"Smells *gut*."

"Should taste even better."

A thump sounded from the back of the house.

Nick paused and breathed in deeply. "My house doesn't smell like this."

Bethany turned and studied him. "I suspect that being a bachelor has its advantages, but eating well isn't one of them."

"Probably you're right. Guess I'll just…" He headed toward the mudroom and walked through it and out onto the porch.

The porch stretched across the back of the house and was screened in all around. It looked like something out of a magazine—rocking chairs, bright-colored cushions, potted plants, even an old barrel turned over and made into a spot to play checkers.

Deborah was standing on a chair, whacking a broom against the ceiling, determined to knock down something Nick couldn't see.

"Need help with that…whatever that is you're doing?"

"Dusting cobwebs. Seems new ones pop up every day." She whacked the ceiling again, scowled at it, then hopped off the chair.

"Your *mamm* said dinner would be ready soon."

"Don't tell me you're finally going to try my *mamm*'s cooking?"

"She wore me down."

"I know that feeling."

"Plus, who can say no to chicken casserole and fresh bread?"

"I wouldn't." Deborah looked somewhat upset. Her eyes kept darting left and right, and she was still clutching the broom.

"Want to tell me what's troubling you?"

She didn't bother denying that something was bothering her. Instead, she sank onto a swing that looked out over the garden area. Nick could have sat in the chair next to her, probably should have, but she looked so forlorn. He sat beside her on the swing, pushed his foot against the porch floor and set the swing to rocking. He didn't rush her. Didn't question her. Just waited. He didn't know a lot about women, but his *schweschdern* had taught him to be patient and quiet when they were in a mood.

"I clean when I'm upset."

"*Ya?* I tend to work in the barn. There's always some unpleasant job there that needs doing."

"We have more in common than I would have thought." Deborah shook her head. "I do not know what I'm going to do with my son."

"Which one?"

"The one that's in trouble."

"Heard he's upstairs working on a letter."

"Yes, and when I told him he would write one, he suggested that he clean out the barn instead—so maybe your good work ethic is rubbing off on him."

"Ah."

"How was your day?" She turned and looked at him fully, as if she was quite interested.

Nick wasn't used to that type of scrutiny. He stared out at the garden, a smile forming on his lips. "Oh, just a normal Wednesday. Tended to the goats, cared for my horses, then worked in the fields. I had two *gut* helpers, so the morning passed quickly."

"Except one of your helpers happens to be quite accident-prone."

She began worrying her thumbnail with her forefinger. He put his hand on top of hers, intertwined his fingers with her fingers. It was a stupid thing to do, but Deborah looked as if she needed a bit of comfort. It wasn't like he'd reached over and kissed her, though suddenly that sounded like a fine idea, too.

"Jacob may be intent on learning things the hard way," he admitted, "but he is learning."

"Are you sure?"

And now she had tears in her eyes. One slipped out, and he reached up and thumbed it away. For the briefest moment, Deborah leaned into the palm of his hand, then she jumped up off the swing and began pacing back and forth in front of him.

"I don't know why I'm so emotional."

"It was a big day for you—new job and all. You probably didn't sleep well last night thinking about it."

"True."

"How did it go?"

"Well."

"*Ya?* That's *wunderbaar.*"

"Is it? While I was gone, my son fell off a roof. He could have…could have broken something." She turned away from him, faced the view of the garden and beyond that the fields and finally his place.

Nick stood and walked over to her, reached for her hand and pushed open the screen door. "Let's take a walk."

She rolled her eyes, but she didn't resist. Now that he was holding her hand, it seemed strange to drop it, so instead he again intertwined his fingers with hers. They walked up and down the rows of the garden, between the green beans and tomatoes and squash plants, breathing in the smell of summer. The garden was bordered with bright flowers that appeared to be nodding at them.

When she seemed to have control of her emotions, he cleared his throat and said, "It didn't happen because you were at work."

"I know that."

"Would have happened even if you'd been here."

Now she simply nodded.

"Doesn't make you a bad *mamm*."

"But maybe I am a bad *mamm*. I enjoyed my morning away. I liked being away from my children." She pulled her hand from his and pinched off a few dead pansy blooms. "I don't think that's normal."

"Hmm…"

"You disagree? Because you know so much about raising children and what is and isn't normal."

He held up a hand to stop her argument. "Wasn't going to say either of those things. But I love my farm—love the fields, the animals, even the old house I live in."

"Okay."

"I still enjoyed our day on the river. Doesn't mean I love my farm any less."

"You're comparing my sons to a piece of land."

"I suppose I am."

She shook her head, but a smile was forming on her lips. "Maybe you're a bad farmer and I'm a bad *mamm*."

"Maybe."

"But you don't think so."

"I don't." He smiled broadly. "Tell me about your first day in the yarn shop."

As they walked back toward the house, she described her boss, the customers and the display she'd created.

"What was your favorite part of being there?"

"The smell."

"Ya?"

"Yarn has a smell about it that is earthy, clean… Why are you laughing?"

"Because that's what I like best about my barn."

Dinner was the best he could remember having in a very long time. The boys kept the conversation going, the food was delicious and Deborah's parents were a pleasant couple to be around. But Nick's attention kept drifting back to what Deborah had said on their walk.

Why did she put so much pressure on herself?

What was it like to raise children without a spouse to help?

Why had the boys' father walked out on her?

What kind of fool was the guy?

One man's loss is another man's gain… The saying popped into his mind, and he pushed it away. He was Deborah's friend, nothing more.

When the boys had cleared the table, placing all the dishes next to the sink, they stood next to their *mamm*.

"Can we go now?" Jacob asked. "It's the best time to catch frogs."

Joseph nodded in agreement. "We promise to go slow."

"And careful." Jacob shifted restlessly from one foot to the other.

"Not yet." Deborah stared at Jacob. When he only crossed and uncrossed his arms, she prompted him with, "You have something to give Nick."

"Oh. Right." He dashed out of the room, then called from the stairs, "I'm going slow."

He returned with a single sheet of paper that had been folded into a triangular football—the kind that Nick used to make when he was sitting through a math lesson and was bored.

Jacob stopped in front of Nick's chair, his expression now quite solemn. "I wrote this for you."

"Should I read it now?"

"*Ya*. Of course."

Nick unfolded the piece of paper, aware that everyone's eyes were on him. With a strength he didn't realize he had, he held in his laughter and kept his voice quite serious. "*Danki*, Jacob. That's a very nice apology letter."

Jacob's worried expression transformed into a grin, and he threw his arms around Nick. "I'm glad you liked it," he whispered, and then with a nod from their *mamm*, both boys were out the back door, across the porch and into the yard.

"Lots of energy there," John said.

"Oh, *ya*." Bethany laughed. "They remind me of your *bruders*, Deborah."

Deborah's parents tried to do the dishes, but Deborah and Nick insisted they leave the kitchen cleanup to them. Nick ran the tap water until it turned hot, then plugged the sink and squirted in dish soap. Deborah had gone to the mudroom, and he wondered if she needed help with something. He turned off the water and went in search of her. She was standing at the door to the porch, watching her parents, who now sat in the same place that she and Nick had occupied an hour earlier.

But John's arm was around his wife's shoulders, and her head rested against him.

Deborah glanced up at Nick, smiled weakly, and they both went back to the kitchen. They spoke of summer and the boys' upcoming birthday and the goats and how quickly the days were passing until they began school. Nick told her that he was considering adding a few pigs to his menagerie, and Deborah tried to describe a new sweater pattern that she was going to knit for a fall display at the yarn shop. In other words, they shared their day.

For the first time in a very long time, Nick didn't think about the work still to be done at his place, or the progression toward his five-year plan, or how long they should continue their fake relationship. For the first time in a very long time, he didn't look forward or back. He simply enjoyed the moment, the setting sun on a June day and the presence of the beautiful woman standing beside him.

When it was time to go back to his place, he said good-night and turned away, but Deborah pulled him back. "The note from Jacob, do you mind if I read it?"

"Not at all. He did a *gut* job." Pulling the note from his pocket, he handed it to her.

She unfolded the single sheet of paper, and he stepped behind her so that he could read it—again— over her shoulder.

Nick,
Mamm *said I must rite this note.*
  Bcuz I brok my promise.
  I 4got to go slo.
  Sorry I climbed on your ruf and fell off.
  Blue is a gut *dog.*
  I'll try to do better.
Jacob

Deborah sighed heavily, refolded the note and handed it back to Nick.

"It's a *gut* note," he assured her.

"His spelling is terrible."

"*Ya.* I noticed that. But someone reminded me not that long ago that he's only six."

She rolled her eyes, but a smile replaced the worried lines on her face.

And that was enough to ease the ache in Nick's heart. He needed to know that Deborah was okay, that she wasn't worrying or sad. It didn't mean that he cared about her more than any other friend. It simply meant that they were important to one another, as they should be, as *gut* neighbors were.

Yup. That explained his relief and the fact that he whistled all the way home.

But once again he was confronted with a house that was empty, in need of fresh paint, lonely. His mind insisted on comparing his kitchen to the one next door—no good smells, no lively discussions, no family. Then he glanced out the window at his porch, if it could even be described as that. There wasn't a chair or a plant or a pillow cushion in sight—just Blue, head on his paws, fast asleep.

He could remodel the house, adjust his plans to do it earlier than he'd scheduled. He could make it more hospitable. But he was honest enough with himself to know that new paint wouldn't ease the ache in his heart. Which left him wondering—what, exactly, would?

Chapter Eight

Jacob and Joseph turned seven on the fifth of July. Fortunately, it was a Tuesday, which meant that Deborah's work hours at the yarn shop didn't interfere with the birthday celebration.

Deborah had spoken to her *schweschder*-in-law twice to confirm plans. They'd all meet at Howie's Ice Cream at four in the afternoon. The treat might ruin the boys' appetite for dinner, but as Jacob pointed out, "Never hurts to eat dessert first. That way you have plenty of room for the important stuff."

She worried whether she should invite Nick, but that turned out to be a waste of worrying time. The boys had taken the liberty of inviting him.

"You should have asked me first." She licked her thumb and attempted to settle Jacob's cowlick.

He ducked away with a drawn-out *"Mamm..."* and a smile.

"Nick loves ice cream," Joseph explained. "It would have been rude to not invite him. Especially after Jacob let the pigs loose."

"Nick doesn't get mad anymore, but he gives us this look and somehow you just know you did the wrong thing." Jacob shrugged. "The pigs seemed to enjoy a run through the field."

True to his word, Nick had purchased a sow and three piglets. They'd arrived the week before. The boys were fascinated with them, which might explain why they came home every day in damp clothes. Apparently Nick insisted they wash the mud off themselves so that Deborah wouldn't have extra laundry. She suspected these washings turned into water fights, but she couldn't get very worked up about boys playing in the water on a hot summer day.

Nick arrived with his horse and buggy promptly at three thirty. After knocking on the front door, he called out, "Anyone want to ride with me?"

The boys dashed through the door with a shout and darted for his buggy.

Deborah followed the boys, then stopped halfway between Nick's buggy and her *dat*'s, uncertain which buggy to get into.

Nick stepped closer and lowered his voice. "We're still supposed to be fake dating, so you might want to…" He nodded toward his buggy.

"Oh, *ya*." She smiled up at him sweetly. "I almost forgot."

"Somehow, I don't think you did forget. After all, it was your idea to show me your yarn store last Saturday."

"I thought you wanted to buy yarn."

"And the week before that, you nearly killed me."

"Bicycling the Pumpkinvine Trail?"

"A lot of the Pumpkinvine Trail. What did we do... five miles?"

"Something like that."

"My legs are still sore." He winced with each step as they walked toward his buggy. She liked this side of Nick—the casual, fun Nick. Why had she ever thought he was a grumpy old bachelor? He was actually a good-natured old bachelor.

Stopping at the back of his buggy, he lowered his voice and nodded toward the house. "Your parents are standing at the front door watching us. Should I kiss you?"

"You should not!" Heat blossomed in her face, but she was rather enjoying his teasing. Turning back to her parents, she called out, "Looks like you two are going to have a nice quiet ride."

Her *mamm* and *dat* stepped out onto the porch.

"It'll be like when we were courting, John."

"You can remember that?"

"Of course I remember." She swatted his arm. "And for suggesting that you don't, you can buy me a double scoop."

John winked at Deborah. "Your *mamm* knows how to keep me in line."

"Your parents have this marriage thing figured out."

Deborah looked at her parents again—now they were walking arm in arm.

When they were in the buggy, trundling down the lane and following her *dat*'s buggy, Nick returned to the subject of her parents. "You're lucky to have them living so close."

"Like in the next room?"

He laughed. "My parents moved to Tennessee, to help my *bruder* with his farm."

"What about your siblings?" She couldn't believe she hadn't asked him this. She'd been so focused on her own life, her own problems, that she realized she knew very little about him.

"You know David and Lydia."

"Sure."

"They're the only ones that stayed in the area."

"So why did you move back here?"

Nick shrugged. "Felt right to come back to where I'd been raised. I don't know anything about Tennessee, and I'd already tried living in a completely different place."

"What was Maine like?"

"Cold. Lots of snow. We had to shovel it off the roofs each year."

The boys, who had been uncharacteristically quiet, popped up and stuck their heads in between them.

"Did you ever try sliding off the roof?" Jacob asked.

"What did your animals do?" Joseph ran his fingers over the top of the seat. "I mean, were they okay in the cold?"

"We did not slide off the roof, as someone could have been hurt." Nick directed that comment to Jacob, who scratched his head, as if he'd never considered such a thing. "The animals are used to the cold for the most part, but Blue—well, that's why he lives inside with me. In Maine, it didn't feel right leaving him on the porch or in the barn."

"I'd like to have a dog that slept in my bed," Joseph declared.

"Oh, he's not in my bed." Nick laughed at the thought. "He sleeps on the floor beside my bed."

"That would work for me," Jacob said. "Can we get a dog, *Mamm*? For our birthday?"

Deborah put them off with "Maybe next year."

The boys sat back, resuming a game of I Spy, which included "something green and slimy," "a very old person" and "an *Englischer* wearing a funny hat."

Nick directed his mare into Howie's parking area, which was really just a grassy spot under some trees, and the boys shot out of the buggy, greeting their grandparents as if they hadn't seen them in years. Simon pulled his buggy in right after theirs. In a blink, Christopher had joined the boys, Simon began talking to Nick about summer crops, and Mary joined Deborah at the back of the group.

"You and Nick were looking quite snuggly."

"Snuggly?"

"Well, you were standing close."

"Because he helped me out of the buggy—that's all. There's nothing to it."

Mary wiggled her eyebrows. "Didn't know you needed help out of a buggy these days." Then she slipped her arm through the crook of Deborah's and guided her toward the group.

They stood in a line in front of the small trailer that was Howie's Ice Cream, studying the board of flavors. Deborah glanced at Nick, thinking of the strange way he'd acted when they'd gone kayaking, of the ice cream he'd bought her, of the way he'd held her hand.

He hadn't done anything like that since.

She supposed he was simply trying to give the impression that they were really dating to the others. Somehow, at the time, it had felt different, but perhaps she'd made that up. Her feelings regarding Nick were quite confused. She was getting what she deserved for coming up with a dating scheme to start with. She should have simply told her parents the truth—that she wasn't ready to date.

But she'd tried that.

And in a moment of weakness, she'd agreed that she would date by that summer. It was Nick or the list of widowers her mother had compiled.

Nick slipped back beside her, lowered his voice and asked, "Having a hard time deciding?"

"Yes, something like that." And then she started laughing, because he had no idea that she was referring to men and not flavors of ice cream.

She supposed there was a comparison there, though. You might enjoy a scoop of pistachio, but did you want it for the rest of your life? Probably not. At the same time, vanilla would be rather boring if that was all you could have. She stepped up to the window, ordered a double dip of chocolate chip and strawberry, and smiled back at Nick. Strawberry reminded her of Jacob and Joseph and their red hair. And chocolate chip? Well, it seemed to perfectly represent this man who could make her angry or make her laugh—often at the same time.

Ten minutes later they were gathered around the picnic table.

"I love birthdays," Joseph confessed.

"I love ice cream." Jacob managed to get a spot of chocolate on his nose and then couldn't figure out what everyone was laughing about.

When it came time to give the boys their gifts, Deborah felt somewhat self-conscious. On the one hand, they both needed new hats, but on the other hand, it seemed rather boring.

Jacob and Joseph were thrilled. Both hats were straw with a black band. She'd marked their initials on the inside, though she suspected Joseph's would stay pristine much longer than Jacob's.

"Use your old hat when you're working at Nick's," she reminded them.

"*Ya*. That way if I slip in the hog pen again, my hat won't get dirty."

She closed her eyes and tried not to envision that scene.

Her parents gave the boys a new deck of Dutch Blitz cards and a new checkers set. Their old set was missing several pieces, and they'd taken to using buttons for markers.

Simon, Mary and Christopher gave them small coolers for carrying their lunch to school—red for Jacob and blue for Joseph.

But it was the gift from Nick that brought tears to Deborah's eyes.

Jacob received a new baseball mitt. Joseph's gift was a book on raising animals—written on a level he could understand and with plenty of pictures. What pierced Deborah's heart was how well Nick knew her boys. Jacob would rather play catch than any other thing she could think of. He was constantly throwing the ball for Blue, and on Sundays the baseball game after church was the highlight of his weekend.

Joseph did those things with his *bruder*, but he was

fascinated by animals—their mares, Nick's pigs and goats, even Nick's dog. He had more questions than Deborah had answers, and often her *dat* was already retired for the evening.

Nick had understood what both boys would treasure most.

She mouthed *"danki,"* and Nick nodded in response.

Jacob declared it the best birthday ever, and Joseph beamed at everyone and thanked them again and again.

Simon, Mary and Christopher said they needed to get home—their move day was coming faster than anyone was ready to accept.

It was her *mamm*'s idea that the boys ride home with them, declaring they were lonely in the big old buggy all by themselves. Then she winked at Deborah, causing her to wish that the ground would swallow her there and then.

She should have enjoyed the ride home alone with Nick. Mothers had precious few moments that were quiet and undisturbed, but her heart felt tender—sore, almost. It was a familiar feeling, one that sometimes threatened to overwhelm her.

"It was a *gut* day, *ya*?" Nick waited for her answer, glancing her way and then back toward the road. "What's wrong?"

"Nothing, I guess." She sighed. "They're growing up so fast."

"Oh, *ya*. Seven to seventeen will happen quick." He snapped his fingers so she could fully understand what quick meant. Growing serious, he said, "Let me guess— baby blues."

Now she did laugh. "What do you know about baby blues?"

"Lydia goes through it when every baby learns to walk. It's as if she's lost something once they're able to ambulate on their own."

"Ambulate?"

"To walk from place to place."

"I know what it means." She shook her head but appreciated his effort to lighten her mood. "It could be that, I suppose. Most Amish *kinner* have a baby *schweschder* or *bruder* by the time they're seven."

"Most have several."

"That's my point." Now she angled in the seat so that she could study him. "Jacob and Joseph aren't living a normal Amish life."

"Because you haven't had another baby?"

"And they don't have a father." The words popped out of her mouth before she could stop them.

Nick didn't answer immediately. He didn't brush away her concerns or assure her that she was making mountains out of molehills. "I think we want to believe that everyone in an Amish community has the same life, but it's not true."

"What do you mean?"

"Everyone doesn't have the perfect family."

"I never said they did."

"Take Lydia, for example, my *schweschder*-in-law. Her *dat* died right after she was born, and her *mamm* didn't remarry for many years. She grew up thinking of her older *bruders* as her father figure."

"Okay."

Now he grinned. "She turned out just fine. Jacob and Joseph will turn out just fine, too."

"But how do you know that?"

"I think the Scripture tells us as much."

"It does?"

"I can't say as I know all of the Bible, but I know enough of it to understand the basics."

"Such as?"

"*Gotte* has a plan for each of us, and He loves us."

"I guess."

"Nope—you know I'm right. You just don't want to admit it." He reached over and tugged on one of her *kapp* strings, and she slapped his hand away.

They both laughed at the absurdity of it—acting like *kinner* when they were grown adults. Next, he'd be sneaking a frog into her school desk.

As they pulled into her parents' place, Deborah found herself wishing the drive had lasted longer. She hadn't realized until that very moment how much her talks with Nick helped. She needed someone her age to share her worries and emotions and dreams with each day.

She shouldn't get used to Nick, though. She shouldn't depend on him. They'd stop their fake relationship by the end of the summer, he'd find a nice girl to settle down with and Deborah would once again be on her own.

He set the brake on the buggy, hopped out and was at her door when she opened it. He reached for her hand, helped her down, then intertwined his fingers with hers. How could such a simple thing calm her so? They walked slowly, shoulder to shoulder, covering the space from the buggy to the front porch all too quickly.

Their relationship most certainly was make-believe. She reminded herself of that fact often, but maybe she could pretend that it was real for a little longer.

July passed in a rush of days spent tending goats, pigs, crops and two energetic boys.

Nick thought it might be the best summer of his life, other than his tendency to wrestle over his relationship with Deborah—or rather, his lack of a relationship. The plan he'd had to introduce her to one of the men at the kayaking trip hadn't panned out. He had no doubt one or two might be interested. He'd even met up with two of the guys once to go fishing, but he'd lost his nerve at the last second. He didn't want to give them the number for the phone shack closest to Deborah. He didn't want them to even think that she was available.

He wasn't the right man for Deborah, but who was?

Nick tried to put it out of his mind, which was impossible to do. Especially since they continued to go out on a "date" once a week. It didn't help that he'd invariably hold her hand or touch her shoulder or sit closer than was strictly necessary. It was as if his mind understood the absurdity of it. He wasn't ready to court anyone, and he knew it. But his heart? That was proving a bit harder to convince.

Instead of attempting to deal with the situation, he worked longer hours, checked out more library books to read up on farming and goats and pigs, even planted an extra field that he hadn't planned on cultivating until the following year—anything to keep busy and help him fall asleep at night.

The one bright spot of the summer was Deborah's twins.

The boys continued to create nearly as much work as they completed, but somehow it bothered Nick less. There was a lot to do to help the pigs settle in—a pigpen to build and fencing to put up. They'd done that the first week. Giving the animal book to Joseph might not have been a good idea.

"They need a mud wallow, Nick. I read about it again last night. I can show you the page, if you'd like."

"Yes! I am all about making mud." Jacob dropped the brush he'd been using to care for the goats. One look from Nick, and he picked it back up. "I'll just go put this on the shelf in the barn."

"*Gut* idea."

By the time he was back, Joseph had convinced Nick that a mud wallow was indeed a good and necessary thing for pigs. According to the book, it would help the pigs keep their body temperature down and also served to promote good skin condition. Nick wasn't one to argue with the written word, so they set about creating a mud bath positioned across the end of the pig enclosure.

This required that he dig down two feet and line the bottom with bricks. Fortunately, there was a big stack of old bricks behind the barn. Jacob and Joseph loaded them in the wheelbarrow, pushed it to the pigpen and then helped him to place them along the bottom of the enclosure. Next, they put the soil he'd dug out back in and added some red soil, which had to be carted from the west field. The boys returned wearing nearly as much dirt as they'd managed to put in the wheelbarrow. Their clothes were almost as red as their hair.

"Where will we get the water?" Joseph asked.

Jacob hopped from one foot to the other. "Carting it over here in a bucket will be a lot of extra work every day."

Nick sat back on his heels, scanning his farm. Snapping his fingers, he said, "There's an old lawn hose in the barn, next to the feed sacks."

The boys took off without being asked.

"They certainly save me some steps," Nick muttered to himself—or he thought he was talking to himself until Deborah responded.

"You might gain weight if the boys do all of your fetching." She stepped up on the bottom board of the fence, draped her arms over the top and smiled down at him.

He was suddenly aware of how sweaty, dirty and grimy he was. "When did you get here?"

"Just now. Building a pig wallow?"

"What was your first clue?"

"My son read those pages to us at breakfast. I sort of figured he might talk you into it."

"Joseph can be persuasive, and Jacob is always so eager to run anywhere." He stood and stretched, popping his back and feeling every day of his thirty-five years. He might have let out a small groan to go with the popping.

Deborah's eyebrows arched and she started laughing, but she didn't have time to tease him. The boys arrived with the hose, Nick connected it to the faucet next to the horse trough and Deborah held the end—pointed toward the new mud-and-brick enclosure.

"How did that three little pigs story go?" Joseph asked.

"The first pig made his house of straw." Jacob shook his head, as if he couldn't fathom such silliness. He pulled off his hat and scratched his head. "And the second—"

"The second built his house of sticks." Deborah was now directing a steady drip of water toward the mud.

The sow and piglets Nick had purchased stood at the far end, grunting and studying them but not moving any closer.

"The old wolf blew down both houses, if I remember correctly." Nick had climbed out of the pen, and now he stood next to Deborah, his shoulder touching hers. She glanced at him and then away, as if suddenly quite interested in her job of creating mud.

"But the third pig's house was made of bricks," Jacob said, laughing. "The wolf couldn't blow it down."

"Maybe that's why we make mud wallows out of bricks." Joseph jogged over to where the pigs were huddled in the corner of their pen.

Nick lowered his voice so that only Deborah could hear him. "Joseph has a way with those animals. Watch this."

As she watched, he dropped to his knees and scratched the large sow behind the ears. The piglets, who at first were huddled behind the sow, poked their heads out and were soon nuzzling around Joseph.

Jacob was sitting on the opposite side of the fence. "Come on, Momma Pig. Show those babies what to do."

It didn't take a lot of encouragement.

Joseph walked toward the mud wallow. The sow followed Joseph, and the piglets followed the sow. She sniffed suspiciously at the mud, then squealed and flopped over, rubbing her back against the muddy bricks, feet in the air, a contented look on her face—if a pig could have a contented look. The piglets crowded in beside her. She flopped back over to her stomach, snout down, and let out a contented *oink*.

Jacob and Joseph high-fived one another.

Deborah laughed and proclaimed them to be "*gut* pigs."

They spent the next fifteen minutes putting away tools. Nick suspected that Deborah hadn't come over just to see him. No doubt she was ready for the boys to return home. They often stayed past lunch and into the afternoon. Most days, Nick found himself taking on a project that had not been on his weekly to-do list. Usually it was something—like the mud wallow—that he thought the boys would enjoy.

He probably needed to focus more on his list.

Deborah walked over to the goats, cooing and calling to the younger ones. Jacob and Joseph dashed back and forth in a game of impromptu tag.

Soon the boys would be in school all day, Deborah would be at her parents' place or her job, and then he could resume following his schedule. He told himself that he'd be mighty glad when that happened, but a small part of him wondered if he'd get lonely.

He glanced at Deborah again and wondered what it would be like to kiss her.

Would he be lonely when they were all busy with their own lives?

He'd purposely purchased his own farm a few miles

from his *bruder* so that he'd have plenty of time alone. He enjoyed the solitary life. Family was *gut*, and of course he liked spending time with his nieces and nephew, but he thought of himself as what the *Englisch* would call an introvert. *Ha.* Put a picture of an Amish farmer beside the definition of introvert. It would be spot-on.

Deborah was still calling out to the goats, leaning over the top of the fence and trying to tempt them with a carrot. Jacob and Joseph were standing next to the pump, trying to swipe the dirt off their pants, which only succeeded in spreading it around.

"Boys, there are food scraps in the bucket under my sink. Want to fetch them for me?"

He was rather surprised that they hadn't fallen in the mud, or flung it at one another, or even traipsed it into his house. Of course, it was the first day with the wallow. He suspected they'd manage all those things before the end of the week.

He waited until they were out of sight, and then Nick did what he'd wanted to do since he'd looked up from the mud and seen Deborah staring down at him.

He made his way over to the goat fence, careful not to make too much noise, and stopped when his shoulder was brushing up against Deborah's. She pulled back in surprise, but he shook his head—once, definitively. She studied him, the look on her face one of curiosity and uncertainty. He didn't wait. He didn't weigh the pros and cons. He gently turned her shoulders so that she was facing him, leaned forward, and he kissed her—at first lightly, then again, properly this time. Thoroughly.

Her cheeks turned a rosy pink, and he figured that he'd done the thing correctly, though he was no expert at kissing. It had been a while. Still, he supposed some things you didn't forget. The boys clambered out of his house, carrying the scraps bucket and singing a made-up song about pigs.

In that moment, Nick thought that everything was right with his world. It was as it should be. And the look on Deborah's face gave him hope that she felt the same.

Seeing the boys, she turned toward them, straightened the apron over her dress and checked her *kapp*.

"You look perfect," he said in a low voice, which caused her to blush even more dramatically.

She began walking toward her parents' farm, then turned and walked backward. "Dinner in thirty minutes, boys." And without another word, she practically sprinted back home.

He'd rattled her.

Why had he done that?

Why had he kissed her?

He'd just had a conversation with himself about how satisfied he was being alone.

But he'd definitely flustered her, and that was fine by him, because it meant that she felt as confused and lovelorn as he did. At least, he thought that was what it meant.

The next question was, what was he going to do about it?

Perhaps it was time to ask her.

Maybe it was time to end this fake dating and begin their relationship in earnest.

Yes, it was the opposite of what he'd decided not

twenty minutes earlier. Good grief, he was a mess. Possibly it was time to get some advice, and he knew just the person he should speak to.

Chapter Nine

Deborah felt as if she spent the next few weeks in something of a dream state. Whole days seemed to pass without her being aware of them. She was actually surprised when her *mamm* changed the wall calendar to August.

How could it already be August?

What had happened to the summer?

Everything was going well—perhaps too well. She felt as if she was waiting for the other shoe to drop.

Jacob and Joseph were thriving. They clearly loved their time spent with Nick, and Deborah couldn't remember the last time Nick had complained about the boys. They still managed to find trouble when they were at home. Like the time they were going to help her pick the produce from the family garden, and they ended up finding a garden snake, which they then sneaked into their bedroom. Deborah found it and nearly had a heart attack when she was picking up their dirty laundry—something Nick would probably insist they should do themselves.

They *should* do it themselves.

But each step of independence and maturity was a step away from her, and it already felt as if her heart was breaking.

Maybe she did have baby blues.

It didn't help that her emotions regarding Nick were all over the place. Her parents were plainly hopeful that they'd be making an announcement soon. Deborah felt terrible about that. She was going to have to correct their assumptions eventually—and sooner rather than later, or they'd be planning her wedding.

She and Nick had continued to go on a date once a week. But he hadn't kissed her again. In fact, he'd pulled away. Why had he pulled away? Had she done something wrong? Had he realized that a ready-made family was more than he cared to take on? Had she misread the whole thing? Was their relationship fake, or was it real?

The one bright spot was that her job was going well, and she was finally overcoming her guilt about enjoying it. She was *gut* with yarn, had even created several original patterns, and now she was teaching a class at the yarn shop. They'd had to cap the attendance at a dozen because that was all the chairs they could rustle up. She loved that group of women. Loved being with them, hearing their laughter and watching their skill grow. The group was comprised of Amish and *Englisch*, young and old. What they shared was a love for knitting, for creating something both beautiful and useful for their family members.

Working at the yarn shop had opened Deborah up to the person she'd been before her life had gone off track. And perhaps it had shown her that having her own dreams and being a *gut mamm* were both possible.

But, oh, how she mourned the way summer seemed to fly.

Her two little boys would be going to school. They'd become older boys, then young men. They weren't her babies anymore.

Finally, the day for the school cleaning arrived. Deborah had been dreading it, though the boys had written it on the calendar and even circled it with a blue crayon.

Saturday, August 27, was a fine summer day. The terrible heat of the week before had eased, and a light north wind stirred the leaves on the trees. Deborah's *mamm* said she'd be along later. The older women tended to put out a lunch spread while the parents of the schoolchildren worked to ready the single classroom, bathrooms and playground.

She was surprised when she drove up to the little one-room schoolhouse and saw so many buggies. There were nearly a dozen, and she very quickly picked out Nick's.

Nick?

Why was Nick here?

She supposed it wasn't so unusual for him to come. Sometimes bachelors did lend a hand, or so she told herself as the boys jogged off to join their friends, who were painting the long board fence that surrounded the schoolyard.

"Good thing you put them in their old clothes."

She nearly jumped out of her apron, spinning around to find Nick standing right behind her. "I noticed your buggy," she murmured, trying to look anywhere but directly at him. Why did her heart race so when he stood next to her? Maybe she was coming down with something. Or maybe she had a crush on Nicholas Stoltzfus. She was definitely acting like a lovesick schoolgirl.

"My buggy looks like all the others."

"All right. I suppose I noticed Big Girl, then."

"Sure you weren't looking for me?"

Her face felt suddenly hot, but she ignored the insinuation and walked toward the schoolhouse. "Since you have no children, I was surprised. That's all."

"Oh, I heard that they could use an extra hand. Turns out the roof needs a bit of repair."

It was then that she noticed the ladders and the men hoisting up shingles to other men, who were standing on the schoolhouse roof.

"Want to come up and help us?"

"I do not."

"It's a beautiful view up there."

Why was he intent on teasing her? She hurried up the porch steps, flung a "be careful and don't fall off" over her shoulder, and escaped into the single large room.

Women were already cleaning chalkboards, washing windows and moving desks. Deborah spent the next two hours scrubbing floors and using soapy water on cubbies. The teacher was the same they'd had the year before, though of course Deborah hadn't formally met her.

The woman's name was Nancy. She was a Mennonite who lived in Shipshewana proper, and she had a husband and four grown children of her own. She was short with gray hair that was covered with a traditional Mennonite veiling. She wore a long dress and smiled readily, which did much to set Deborah's mind at ease.

Nancy offered a greeting and thank-you to the group as they settled down for lunch.

"I hope that if you have any concerns, you will come and speak to me about them. No need to lie awake worrying over a thing. Also, those of you who had me last year know that I like to send notes home in lunch boxes, so look for at least one note a week from me. It doesn't mean your little one is in trouble, only that I like to keep you up-to-date."

The boys and girls collectively dropped their heads into their hands, which caused laughter to spread around the table.

"For my new moms and dads, I want you to rest easy. Your children will learn, not only from me, but also from the older children in the schoolhouse. We have a fine group of scholars here, and I'm proud to be their teacher."

Deborah sincerely hoped that the teacher still felt that way after trying to corral Jacob and Joseph into a desk every school day. Nancy sat down at an adjacent table, Bishop Ezekiel offered a blessing over the meal and the school year, and conversations around each table resumed. Deborah tried to pay attention, but her thoughts were all over the place.

She must have eaten her lunch, because she looked down and the plate was empty. She didn't even remember chewing. Smiling at the women sitting next to her, she stood and excused herself. Perhaps she needed a little comfort food. Sugar surely would help her mood, which was plummeting faster than the thermometer after the first cold front.

Nick sidled up beside her at the dessert table as she

was trying to decide between a brownie and a piece of pie. "Take one of each. You look worried."

"I am worried."

Nick leaned closer and lowered his voice. "She seems perfectly capable to me. No doubt she's dealt with twins before."

"Yes, but we're talking about Jacob and Joseph. Jacob tried building a frog house in the mudroom last week—without telling me—so when I fetched the bucket and mop, several frogs jumped out at once, and then off they went, hopping through the house."

"Didn't she say she's been teaching for twenty years? Certainly those classes included plenty of energetic young boys."

"Maybe." She turned to study him and thought back to that first day when she'd met him. She'd thought that he looked tall, handsome and overly serious. He still looked tall and handsome, but now she understood that his seriousness was a shell he wore to keep people at arm's length. When he relaxed, he laughed and teased and his eyes squinted in a way that made her want to slide her fingers from his temple to his jawline.

She grabbed the pie and turned away from him, heading toward the playground so that she could put some space between them. Nick didn't take the hint. He picked up two brownies and followed her to the swings.

Plopping down in one, she stabbed her fork into the lemon meringue and put a nice-sized bite into her mouth.

Sweet, tart, creamy.

That should fix any mood.

Nick dropped into the swing beside her and was

making a swipe for the rest of her lemon pie when someone called his name from across the playground.

"Are you ready?" Stephen Lapp called.

"Sure. *Ya.* Coming." But before he left, he leaned closer to Deborah. "You owe me a bite of pie."

"I do not. Get your own."

"What fun would that be?" And with a wink he was gone, jogging to catch up with Stephen.

"They're going to get firewood," Anna explained, taking the swing that Nick had been occupying.

Anna had been in the same grade as Deborah. They'd been friends long ago, but they'd grown apart once they were both out of school. Deborah had left to live with her *aenti* in Sugarcreek, had met Gavin, fallen in love and found herself pregnant. She realized that was a watershed moment in her life. Not the move or Gavin or even finding herself handling the situation alone. No, deciding to have her boys had been the moment in her life that separated all others. There was before the boys and after the boys. It seemed that her life had become what it was destined to be on the day they were born.

Now, watching them play a game of baseball with the older kids, her eyes stung with tears. She'd been so busy focusing on getting through each day that she hadn't appreciated how quickly time with them would pass.

"My *schweschder* tells me it's normal to feel emotional when our oldest starts school. Seems I was just bringing Suzie home from the birthing center, and now she's playing school at the kitchen table—practicing, as she calls it. I've been blubbering all week."

"I thought I'd be happy to have a few hours to my-

self. Now I have no idea what I'll do with all that time."
Deborah smiled and swiped at her eyes.

Anna laughed and switched her baby boy from her
left shoulder to her right. "Baby Aaron and the four
in between keep me plenty busy, but it's still a bitter-
sweet moment."

"Aaron is beautiful." Deborah would have asked to
hold him, but she didn't think her heart could handle
any more ache at the moment. "How old is he?"

"Three months and still not sleeping all night. All
of my others did, but Aaron here is intent on being a
stinker." She held him up, kissed his forehead, then
settled him across her knees. "Your boys seem to have
grown quite fond of Nick."

Deborah's mind went blank. How was she supposed
to answer that?

"Which must be...you know, a weight off your mind."

"Because..."

"Because you two are dating."

Deborah looked at her, wide-eyed and waiting.

What was she waiting for?

Anna lowered her voice. "He seems quite smitten
with you."

"Nick?" The word came out two octaves higher than
she intended. "Oh, I don't know about that."

"Sometimes it's hard to see when you're in the middle of a thing." Aaron started fussing, and Anna stood,
jostling him over her left shoulder. "I best go and feed
him, but if you need any help, you know, with plans..."

"Plans?"

"Wedding plans, silly. If you need help, let me know."
And then she was gone, walking toward the school-

house, where she could nurse the baby. As for Aaron, he stared over his *mamm*'s shoulder at Deborah, then shoved his thumb into his mouth. Life was apparently pretty simple if you were three months old.

Wedding plans...

Deborah glanced around the group that was now breaking up to finish the last few chores. Were they expecting her and Nick to announce their intention to marry? What had she been thinking? How had she let this fake dating get out of hand?

Nick had no intention of marrying her. He had a five-year plan. She'd seen it, and her name was nowhere on the list.

She stood and brushed off her skirt, then marched back into the schoolhouse. The floor under the teacher's desk could use a good scrubbing, and Deborah had enough frustration to tackle the project enthusiastically.

But somehow, it didn't stop Anna's words from echoing in her mind. *If you need help, let me know.*

Nick had told himself he'd be thrilled to have his mornings to himself, but the first day of school seemed to crawl at a snail's pace. He finished twice as much as he would have with the boys there. Not that it improved his mood.

By the time he sat down to eat lunch on the front porch—a lunch that he ate alone, because the boys were at school—he admitted to himself that he'd become used to having Jacob and Joseph around. Jacob was barely able to sit through lunch, often bouncing up to tell a story, using both of his hands and hopping around for effect. Joseph always shared at least one tidbit he'd recently read about pigs or goats or sheep.

Are you sure you don't want sheep, Nick? My book says they're gut animals to raise.

Sheep were not in his business plan.

Neither were two little boys, but they'd managed to wriggle their way into his heart.

Their beautiful mother was not someone he should be preoccupied with, but how could he help it? He had wanted to kiss her while she was sitting on the swing. He'd wanted to hold her hand and walk her to her buggy. He wanted everyone to know how he felt about Deborah Mast. He'd spoken to his *bruder*, who had told him to *plant something or get out of the field.* He was pretty sure David had made that up. It certainly wasn't a proverb he'd ever heard before.

By the time three o'clock rolled around, he'd decided he really needed to cut the grass out by the mailbox. "Want to go with me, boy?" Blue grabbed his favorite ball and trotted down the lane in front of him. Nick wasn't too surprised that Deborah was already there, arms crossed, foot tapping, watching for Jacob and Joseph.

"Wouldn't let you pick them up, huh?"

"Nope. Insisted they could walk to and from school alone, just like any other young scholar." She worried her thumbnail.

"Sounds like something Joseph would have said."

Blue dropped to the ground, his ball beside him, his head on his paws, watching in the same direction they were. Did the dog actually know where the boys had gone and that they were both standing there waiting for their return? Could a dog sense that?

"How did getting them off to school this morning go?"

"Jacob simply ducked away from my kiss and headed out the door. Joseph paused long enough to give me a two-second hug." She turned toward him and cocked her head. "Wait a minute. What are you doing here?"

"Me? I'm just cutting grass around this mailbox." He dropped to his knees and began using the hand cutters that he'd had to go back and grab because he'd forgotten them the first time he'd started down the lane.

Deborah propped her elbows on the mailbox and gave him a quizzical look. "You want me to believe you just happened to be out here working?"

"Part of being a farmer. Our work is never done." He sighed heavily. "Plus, I just lost my two best workers, so there's more for me to do."

"And that's why trimming grass around the mailbox rose to the top of your list?"

Before he could answer, they heard laughter, and both turned in the direction of the schoolhouse. Jacob and Joseph were walking down the middle of the road, apparently kicking a rock all the way home. Blue sent a beseeching look to Nick.

"Sure, go ahead."

Which was all the permission the dog needed. Jacob and Joseph broke into a run when they spied Blue. Both boys exclaimed over him as if they hadn't seen him in weeks. When they looked up and saw Deborah and Nick, they again broke into a sprint.

Nick had thought they might be tired after a full day

of school, but apparently that wasn't the case. They had as much energy as usual, possibly more.

"How was school?" Deborah asked even before they'd arrived.

"Gut." Both boys skidded to a stop.

"Our teacher has an entire shelf of books, *Mamm.*" Joseph smiled broadly. "We can check one out each weekend."

Jacob dropped his lunch box down on the ground and opened it. "We're supposed to call her Nancy. Boy, she can really give you the *be still* look."

"Yup. Even Jacob was still when she did that."

"Everyone was."

"We got to sit by each other."

"And the older boys let us play baseball at lunch."

Jacob pulled out a single sheet of paper and thrust it in her hands. "Our first assignment was about our family. Look, I got a star. See that, Nick? A star, right there by my name."

Nick glanced over Deborah's shoulder, saw Jacob's name and the gold star. The drawing was of a stick family whose heads were extraordinarily large compared to the rest of their bodies.

"I got a star, too." Joseph pulled his sheet from his pocket and carefully unfolded it. "We could write or draw, so I decided to write."

"And I decided to draw."

Nick looked from the drawing to the page of writing. Both were titled *My Family.* Deborah had gone suddenly still. Her eyes widened, and he detected a sharp intake of breath. He looked at the drawing closer. "Hey. You included Blue."

Jacob's page was filled—left to right—with stick figures. Each figure had round eyes and a huge smile. Bethany and John, Deborah, Jacob, Joseph and Nick. They stood between a tree and a pond with their stick-figure hands connected to one another. The adults were nearly as tall as the tree, which, if Nick wasn't mistaken, was the maple tree by the pond at the back of John's property. A stick dog, colored blue, stuck his head out between the two boys.

Nick reached out to read what Joseph had written, but Deborah snatched the papers away, folded them neatly and handed them back to the boys. "Go show these to *Mammi*. She'll want to put them in the homework box, and I think she has cookies and milk ready for you both."

That was all Jacob and Joseph needed to hear. Giving Blue one last pat, their mother a hug and Nick a high five, they raced toward the house.

It was nice to have the boys home, and Nick was pleased they'd had a *gut* first day. He didn't realize that he'd been worried about that. It was important to enjoy your schoolmates, your teacher and the entire school environment. Otherwise, it would be a long year for everyone. Perhaps Deborah could stop worrying now. Perhaps he could stop worrying.

"See? There was nothing to be concerned about. They both had a *wunderbaar* day."

"We need to talk."

"Talk?"

"About us." Her arms were crossed tightly around her middle—as if she had a stomachache—and her lips formed a straight line.

He glanced around in surprise. Something had changed in the last few minutes, but he had no idea what it was. "I'm not…" He swallowed and then tried again. "I'm not sure what you're referring to, exactly."

Deborah raised her chin a fraction of an inch, but she didn't quite meet his eyes. Instead, she stared at a spot over his right shoulder, then down at the dog, then back at her house.

"Of course you don't know what I'm talking about. This has all been some sort of game to you."

"This—"

"Our dating."

"Wait a minute, Deborah. That was your idea."

"I know it was. I came up with this ridiculous plan, and so I suppose it's my job to end it."

"End it?"

"Our fake dating." Now she looked directly at him, and Nick had a sudden moment of clarity that he was messing this up. What was he supposed to do? What should he say? He was suddenly aware that Deborah was fighting to show an expression of disinterest, but underneath, he sensed that she was feeling vulnerable.

"About that…" He reached for her hand, but she snatched it away. "What I was about to say was that it wasn't fake for me."

"It must have been. It was for both of us." She forced a smile.

"Don't say that." His voice was low now. He didn't fully understand what was happening, but he didn't like the direction this conversation was going. "Deborah, I care about you."

"*Nein*, you don't."

"Why would you say that?" Now his temper was piercing his confusion.

"You've never misled me, Nick." She dropped her arms and stood even straighter. "You've never once said you had feelings for me, so don't expect me to believe you do now."

"I know I haven't *said* it, but—"

"And people are talking." The pretense fell away, and the confusion, fear and sadness in her expression caused an actual ache in his heart. "People at church, at the school, probably even my parents. And my boys?"

She stared toward her house, then again crossed her arms as if she needed to protect herself, as if she needed to guard her heart. "Jacob is drawing you in his family picture, and Joseph is writing about you. I won't have it. I will not have them getting their hopes up. I won't have them thinking that something is real when it isn't."

"But—"

"Unless I'm wrong. Unless you do care for us, all three of us…"

He hesitated, because he knew this was an important moment. He wanted to get it right.

Unfortunately, Deborah took his hesitation to mean something else entirely. "You were correct when you said this was my idea, and now it's time for me to do the right thing and be honest with those I love."

And with those words, she strode away, leaving him standing by the mailbox, grass cutters in his hand, Blue at his side and a world of questions and regrets weighing him down.

Chapter Ten

Deborah was tempted to stick with her original plan—tell her parents that she and Nick had tried dating, but things hadn't worked. They were simply too different. She could probably tell that story convincingly, since it seemed they were too different. In the end, she couldn't go through with the lie. They deserved to know the truth.

After dinner that evening, while the boys were upstairs getting ready for bed, she told her *mamm* and *dat* everything. She explained about her idea to fake date Nick, how they'd become friends but nothing more, and that now she was worried Jacob and Joseph were becoming attached to Nick. She was sorry that she'd tried to deceive them, all because she was embarrassed. She'd chosen to be less than honest rather than have the difficult conversation that she knew was coming.

"We've had this conversation about your dating before." Her *dat* seemed to be choosing his words carefully. "Our reason for wanting you to… It's not because we don't want you here."

He paused, waited, made certain he had her complete attention. When Deborah nodded, he continued.

"Having Jacob and Joseph around, having you home again, has been one of the greatest blessings of my older years. But what I want isn't enough in this case. You deserve more, Deborah. And those boys deserve a *dat*, should *Gotte* have one for them."

"Which you can't know unless you actually come out of your shell." Her *mamm* reached for her hand, then, upon seeing her tears, she turned to snag the box of Kleenex and pushed it into Deborah's lap. "I understand that you were hurt before, that Gavin did not cherish and honor you as you should be. That's his loss, Deborah."

"But I made..." She hiccupped and pressed the Kleenex to her eyes. Why were her tears like water from a faucet? Would the day never come when she'd cried herself dry? "I made that mistake. My boys shouldn't have to pay for it."

"Your boys are lucky to have you as their *mamm*. You're a *gut mamm*, Deborah." Her *dat* waited until she looked up. "Your *mamm* and I have prayed over this many a night. We want you to have a complete family. We want you to know the kind of love that we share."

"But what if I never do? What if that isn't in *Gotte*'s plan for me?"

"He gives *gut* things to His children, but let's for a moment say you're right. Let's consider that possibly *Gotte* intends for you to raise those two boys upstairs by yourself." At that exact moment, there was a thud from above, followed by boyish laughter. Her *dat* smiled and reached out to pat her hand. "Then you will do that, and your family and neighbors and church will help you. But how can you know such a thing for certain if you don't at least open up your heart to the possibility of love?"

"We're happy to have you here with us, Deborah. We would be happy for you to stay for the rest of our days." Her *mamm* shook her head and sat back on the couch. "But that's a selfish thing on our part when it's possible that you could have a husband, a home of your own and more *kinner*. To think that you would miss out on all of that because you're comfortable here, because you're hurt or shy or afraid..."

"That's not what we want."

Deborah nodded and pulled in a deep breath. "You're right. You're both right. At first, I think it was because I was still hurting from Gavin's rejection..."

"Eight years ago, Deborah...or very nearly eight."

"Right." She sat up straighter, smoothed out the fabric of her dress. "After that, I guess it was just easier to live here and believe no one wanted me. Much easier than putting my heart on the line, or my boys..."

She thought of Nick, thought of the boys' *My Family* assignment and fought to swallow more tears. But she was tired of crying. She was tired of being afraid.

"Your boys will mirror your attitude. If you're heartbroken and bitter and afraid, they will be, too." Her *dat* tapped the arm of his rocker. "I know you don't want that for them. Show them how to be courageous, how to love courageously. Be the type of person that you hope they will grow into."

"I'll try." She closed her eyes, then opened them and looked around the room. This house—the place she'd grown up in, the place she'd fled to when life became too much to handle alone—it had been a true haven of peace for her. Had she become too content here? Was she too eager to pretend this was her only option? What happened to the young girl who envisioned her own home, a loving husband, a roomful of *kinner*? When had she given up on her own dreams?

"I'll try," she repeated. "*Mamm*, let's get out your bachelor list tomorrow and decide how to proceed."

"We'll start with the younger men. I know all too well how you feel about older widowers." Everyone laughed, though even that felt as if it hurt Deborah's heart.

She'd thought the conversation with her parents would be the worst part of the night, but as she made her way upstairs, she knew that she owed it to her boys to be honest with them as well.

She explained to them that she'd made a mistake, that she and Nick were only friends, that they wouldn't be going on dates any longer.

Jacob was lying on his bed, tossing a tennis ball against the ceiling. "Does this mean we can't go over to see Nick anymore?"

"Of course not. He'll still be our friend and our neighbor." She hoped that was true. She wasn't particularly proud of how she'd treated him earlier that day.

"Works for me."

Joseph was sitting up on the side of his bed, a closed book in his lap. "So, you're saying that he won't be our *dat*."

"I'm sorry, honey, but *nein*—I don't think so."

"You don't think so, which means he could be."

The hope in that last statement caused tears to sting Deborah's eyes, but she blinked them away. "I'm going to quit pretending I know the answers or what the future holds, but I wouldn't get your hopes up about that."

Joseph finally looked up at her, and the vulnerability she saw on his face pierced her heart. "Did we do something wrong?"

"You most certainly did not. It's just marriage requires a stronger bond than friendship. Nick and I are friends, but nothing more."

Even as she uttered those words, she wondered if she was lying again, so she added, "At least I don't think we are."

Both boys hugged her, assured her that they were a *gut* family, just the three of them, and Jacob offered to erase Nick from his picture.

"*Nein.* One day we'll all laugh about that, so let's not erase him."

"*Gut.* It would have left a big hole." He resumed tossing his ball at the ceiling.

"Time for bed. You are scholars now, and you have school tomorrow."

That reminder earned her some groans, but both boys were smiling as she bent to kiss them. They didn't even plead for five more minutes when she turned out the battery-powered table lamp. No doubt they were as exhausted from the day as she was.

She was at the door when Joseph called her back. "Nick sure seemed to like you. I guess you could be wrong about how he feels. Right?"

"I could be, but I don't think so."

"Good night, *Mamm.*"

"Good night, Joseph."

"'Night, *Mamm.*"

"Good night, Jacob."

She realized as she went to her room that they hadn't talked about how she felt about Nick. She wasn't even sure. As she prepared for bed, she forced herself to look directly at that question.

Did she care for him?

Did she love him?

She might. It could be that he'd worked his way under her protective shell. Or perhaps seeing him with her boys, seeing him teaching and caring for them, had caused her to drop her guard.

But she had asked him, point-blank, if he cared for her in that way. He'd stood there stumbling over his words and glancing around for the nearest exit.

She sighed, pulled back her quilt and slipped between the sheets. She shouldn't have been so upset with him, and she'd need to apologize for that. After all, it wasn't his fault that her boys had included him in the family drawing and essay.

Nick wasn't to blame, but she'd done the right thing. She was done with fake dating, with pretense and artifice. It was time to start living her life authentically. Even if it meant that, once again, she had to start over alone. She wasn't really alone, though. There were plenty of people who loved her—the two boys down the hall, her parents downstairs, her siblings and even her friends. Perhaps one day she would laugh with Anna about this. She definitely did not need help planning a wedding.

But perhaps one day she would.

Until then, she'd have to grin, bear it and start giving the men on her *mamm*'s list a chance.

* * *

"Explain it to me again." David was looking at Nick like he had pie on his face.

Lydia merely shook her head and reached for her coffee mug, fascinated by his story. *Ya*, it was entertaining all right. The story of how he'd managed to mess up the best thing in his life. The story of how he'd become tongue-tied when asked the most important question in the universe.

"Why didn't you just correct her, Nick? It's plain you do care for her."

"*Ya*, I do, and I was going to correct her, but then before I could find the words, she walked off."

David sat back with a huff and crossed his arms. "Didn't you listen when we talked before? I told you to make your intentions plain."

"You told me to plant or get out of the field. What does that even mean?"

Lydia rolled her eyes, but she did nudge the dish of peach pie toward him. Normally he could eat several pieces of Lydia's desserts, but tonight he was pretty sure that it wouldn't settle well. Nothing was settling well. His stomach had been in turmoil for days. After seeing Deborah pass him on the road in Widower Schrock's buggy, he'd headed to his *bruder*'s. He couldn't face another moment on his farm alone.

He pushed away the pie, stood and paced the length of the kitchen several times. Finally, he sat back down, determined to be completely honest with his family.

"I thought I could wait. After my experience in Maine, with Olivia, I wasn't eager to jump back into the dating scene."

When they both nodded in understanding, he pushed on. "I made a plan—a five-year plan for turning my land into a profitable farm and my house into a home." He stopped there, unsure how to proceed.

Gently, Lydia asked, "How is that working out for you?"

He laughed, covered his face with his hands and finally sighed. "Just fine until I met two little redheaded boys and their beautiful *mamm*. I didn't expect to fall in love."

"But you do love her?" Lydia pressed.

"For sure and certain, I do. Mind you, I wasn't looking for a relationship, and I definitely had never considered an instant family, but now they are all I can think about. And my plan... Well, it seems rather pointless if I'm the only person in it."

David and Lydia shared a look, and then they both smiled.

"Sounds to me as if you've grown up, *bruder*."

"It also sounds as if your heart has healed."

"But what do I do now? How do I...straighten this out?"

They spent the next half hour talking about courting, how to be honest with someone about your feelings, how to begin a genuine relationship and enjoy time with one another. They spoke about the importance of establishing a firm foundation, one built on honesty and hope and the future—not the past.

By the time he left their home, he was feeling better about his prospects. On the one hand, he had seen Deborah going down the road in Widower Schrock's buggy, which meant that she was allowing her *mamm* to set up dates for her. On the other hand, he already had Jacob and Joseph on his side, and he lived close to her. It would be easy to stop by with a bouquet of wildflowers or vegetables from his garden. Plus, they had a history together. He knew what she liked and what she didn't.

All he needed was for her to give him a chance.

The next day was a Saturday. He waited until he was sure that everyone would be up and about, then checked his hair in the mirror, combed it down with his fingers and called out to Blue. He'd spied purple asters growing next to the fence. He cut a few sprigs of prairie grass as well, tied them together with a ribbon that Lydia had given him and headed next door.

Deborah was in the back garden, harvesting the last of the tomatoes and green beans and peppers.

"Where are your helpers?"

She glanced up in surprise, looked at the flowers in his hand and then resumed harvesting. "Jacob and Joseph have gone to their cousin's for the day. You know Mary and Simon moved to Middlebury, and my boys have decided it's the very best place to spend their Saturday."

Nick set the flowers on the bench at the end of the garden and joined her in plucking vegetables from the plants. "How has your week been?"

Deborah reached out and scratched Blue between the ears. "My week? Okay, I suppose."

Hmm. She wasn't making this easy, and she was still tossing him quizzical looks, as if wondering what he was up to.

"Did your knitting class folks like the new pattern you shared with them?" When she raised her eyebrows in surprise, he defended himself with, "What? I listen. I even know you were going to use variegated thread."

"Yarn."

"Whatever."

The laughter seemed to set them both back on solid ground. As they finished gathering vegetables from the garden, Deborah told him about her class of knitters, which included one woman who was a beginner and couldn't quite learn how to cast on. Nick hadn't the faintest idea what that meant. It sounded like something you'd do with a rope and a boat, but then again, he'd always taken for granted that hats and scarves and sweaters simply appeared in his dresser drawers. He'd never before appreciated how much thought and work went into them.

"The shop and the class are lucky to have you there, Deborah."

"Danki." She met his gaze, smiled slightly, then stood and brushed the dirt from her apron.

He picked up the bounty of their labor, walked closer to her until there was only the basket of vegetables between them, both of their hands holding it for a moment before he passed it to her.

"I suppose I should get these things inside."

Blue lay in the dirt, staring from Deborah to Nick and giving him a look that said *what are you waiting for?*

"Could we talk for a minute?"

Deborah pulled in her bottom lip, something he'd noticed she did when unsure about a thing, but she eventually decided in his favor and nodded.

They walked to the bench, both sat and he offered her the flowers. "I thought you might enjoy these."

"I appreciate that, Nick. I really do…"

"But?"

"But…why are you doing this? We're not dating anymore."

"We're not fake dating." He reached out, tucked a stray lock of hair into her *kapp*, let his fingers linger on her cheek. When she didn't pull away, he leaned forward and kissed her softly. But he knew, from his talk with Lydia and David, that kissing wouldn't solve this. He needed to use words to tell her how he felt.

"I'm in love with you, Deborah."

Her eyes widened in astonishment. "What?"

Why was she surprised? Had he been that negligent in letting her know how he felt? He'd thought it was so obvious.

"I don't know when it happened. It might have been when we ate pizza together on our first date—"

"Fake date."

"Or it might have been when we were kayaking."

"You nearly tipped our kayak over into the St. Joseph River."

"I can't tell you when it happened, but I can tell you that I care about you."

She looked as if she wanted to believe him. Glancing down, she ran her fingers up and down the piece of ribbon. Finally, she looked up, met his gaze. "But the other day…when I asked you…"

"I was trying to find the right words, and I'll be honest. You deserve nothing short of complete honesty from me. I was afraid. I didn't know if you felt the same."

He waited, a lump forming in his throat as she hesitated, started to speak, then stared out across the garden. When she looked up at him, his heart felt like it sank to his shoes. Was she going to turn him down? Had he imagined that she felt as he did when, in fact, she didn't?

"I care about you, too, Nick."

He wanted to jump up, grab her in his arms and twirl her around.

"But…"

There was that word again.

"I've done some serious thinking about myself, my life, even my fears of moving forward. I've spoken about all of this with my parents. I've agreed to date again…to date properly."

Widower Schrock!

"My boys deserve to have a mother who isn't afraid. I want to be courageous and bold. I also want to be careful, for their sake as well as my own."

"You and Widower Schrock…"

She shrugged. "I barely know Nathaniel." She stared up at him. "I barely know you."

"I want to remedy that." He reached for her hand. "Would you allow me to court you…properly?"

His mouth grew dry, and the muscles in his left arm began to twitch. Was she going to say no? Had he waited too long? Was he about to pay the price for his own cowardice?

Then she looked up, smiled and said three words that caused his heart to sing. "I'd like that."

Nick knew he could do this. Deborah was worth doing it and doing it correctly. How long it took wasn't important. So what if courting Deborah pushed his five-year plan to six or seven? None of that mattered when considering a life without Deborah and Jacob and Joseph. And in that moment, he understood that Deborah wouldn't only be looking for a man who would be good to her and love and cherish her. She was also looking for a man who would be a father to her children.

Nick was determined to prove to her that he was the man for both jobs.

Chapter Eleven

Nick took Deborah to dinner that evening. They drove by her yarn shop and stopped to see the window displays she'd created. There were hats of various sizes pinned to what looked like a clothesline. Below them were sweaters that matched the hats—some on teddy bears, some on hangers, some tossed over a rocking chair. Everything was done with fall colors.

"Makes me want to buy some thread and take up knitting myself. Plus, I heard this shop has a *gut* teacher."

Deborah laughed, slipped her arm through his and explained the difference between thread and yarn. Nick noticed how her eyes lit up when she talked about her customers.

They ate at the pizza place, laughed about their first time there, then took a leisurely drive home. It was the best date of his life, and they really hadn't done anything. But they had spent time together. It was all he wanted—time with Deborah.

Sunday was a church day, and although he noticed Nathaniel Schrock talking to Deborah before the service, she didn't sit with him at lunch. She sat with Nick and his *bruder* and their *kinner*. Deborah knew David and Lydia, but they hadn't spent much time together. The women were soon talking about children, fall activities and even the upcoming Christmas season. When they'd finished the meal, Nick asked Deborah if she'd like to take a walk down by the creek. When she said yes, David gave Nick a covert thumbs-up sign.

Their courtship seemed to fall into a very natural rhythm. He looked forward to seeing her, thought about little else, and he spent time listening. Lydia had emphasized how important that was. *Don't try to solve her problems for her, Nick. Just listen.*

When Deborah described the latest antics of Jacob and Joseph, he'd only sympathized. She'd seemed surprised when he didn't tell her what she was doing wrong. She'd even called him on it. "You once told me that raising twins couldn't possibly be harder than growing up with seven younger siblings."

"I might have been seeing that from the viewpoint of a *bruder*, not a parent."

"Meaning?"

"Meaning things like raising children aren't as easy as it looks from the outside."

She'd laughed and reached for his hand. It was progress. She hadn't decided she could trust him completely, but she was giving him a chance. That was all he could or would ask for.

On school days, he made sure he was busy in the afternoons. He didn't stand by the mailbox waiting for Jacob and Joseph. He wanted to, but he also understood that he hadn't earned that spot in their lives yet.

On Tuesday, he stopped over to see her *dat* before dinner—to update him on the goats, the pigs and how they might expand their collection of animals in the spring. Bethany invited him to stay for dinner.

"I'd love to, if it's okay with Deborah." He didn't want to crowd in on her family. She needed space and time to decide what she wanted in her life and whether or not that included him.

Deborah laughed and said, "It's chicken stew— you're in for a treat."

He played ball with Jacob and Joseph as they waited for dinner, and he knew—with all his heart, he was certain—that this was what he wanted. He wanted a family. He was ready to be a *dat* and a husband.

On Wednesday there was a fairly intense storm that blew through rather quickly. Lots of wind, a little rain, and then the sun was out again. He checked the goats, worked on a portion of fence that had fallen over and brushed down Big Girl.

Late Thursday afternoon, he was adding fresh water to the pigs' mud wallow, thinking of the day the boys had helped him create it, when he looked up and saw Deborah running down his lane.

He dropped the hose, turned off the water, then met her as she stopped near the goat pen. She bent over, holding her side and pulling in deep breaths.

"What's wrong?"

"It's Jacob and Joseph…"

With those four words, it seemed as if time stopped. He didn't breathe, couldn't move, couldn't think. *It's Jacob and Joseph…*

"They didn't come home from school. I can't find

them. I... I traced their route back to the schoolhouse, but everyone was gone already."

"Okay. Is there anywhere they stop along the way?"

"Nein. It's all fields. There are a few houses, pretty far off the road...but the way they come home there are no other children."

"Okay." He put a hand on both of her shoulders and waited for her to look up. "We'll find them—together. Let's go back. Walk me through it, and we'll find them. They're boys. They probably got to playing somewhere and lost track of time."

She nodded. He understood that she wanted to believe him, but fear was nipping at her heels. The sun was going down, and it would be easier to find them if they could do so before dark. He glanced at the horizon, judged that they had an hour at the most, and then he pulled her into his arms.

Deborah's body trembled, and he held her tighter. "We will find them, Deborah. It's going to be all right."

He called to Blue, who joined them as they started down the lane and turned in the direction of the schoolhouse. They walked slowly, looking for any sign of two seven-year-old boys.

"Did you tell your parents?"

"Nein." She stepped around a puddle. *"Dat's* been feeling poorly. I didn't want to worry them, and then when I couldn't find Jacob or Joseph, when I'd gone all the way to the school and back...all I could think of was coming to you."

"I'm glad you did." He hoped his smile held more confidence than he felt. Where could they have gone? Fields stretched in every direction. Farmhouses were set a good distance back from the road. There was no sign of other children. No animals that could have tempted them away from the route home.

Blue trotted along beside them. The dog didn't show any indication that he understood they were looking for the boys. Blue was an Australian cattle dog. He was bred to be energetic and work hard, and he was by nature loyal. He wasn't necessarily a tracker, though, and that was what they could use right now.

If they didn't find the boys by dark, he'd take Deborah back, tell her parents and phone the bishop. They'd call the police. Children had wandered off before. It didn't happen often, but it did happen. Their entire community would insist on being part of the search party. They would find Jacob and Joseph. He had to believe they would. His heart cried out to *Gotte*, praying that they were okay, that they weren't frightened or hurt.

And then he saw it...to the east and set back a good quarter mile. "There," he said.

Deborah stopped, frozen in place.

They stared at the dilapidated barn—old, half-fallen and close enough to the road that the boys might have seen something. Jacob might have chased something into it. A dog, maybe? If they'd glimpsed an injured animal, Joseph would have insisted on seeing if they could help it. They only had a few minutes until dark, but this felt right—it felt like the place they should search.

Deborah had been walking up and down the fence line. Blue put his nose to the ground and walked slowly in the other direction. Suddenly he began to bark, and when they looked toward him, the dog spun in a circle—then barked. Again. Deborah and Nick both ran and knelt by a T-post that held up the barbed wire. The wire had obviously been pulled apart, and sitting next to the T-post were two lunch boxes.

"Are they theirs?"

"Yes."

He held the wire apart as she ducked through, then she did the same for him. Blue had already pushed under the bottom two wires and was trotting toward the barn. Even as Nick tried not to picture what might have happened, they were running toward the structure, calling out the boys' names.

The side of the barn that was still standing was the side that offered no doors, no windows. He led the way around to the other side, to what should have been the front, but it was merely a heap of old boards and shattered windows. They continued following Blue and picking their way over the scattered debris.

"The wind did this?" Deborah's voice was a strangled whisper.

"It's been ready to go for some time. The wind simply did in ten minutes what might have taken another six months."

"If the wind caused this to happen yesterday, then it couldn't have fallen on the boys today."

"I don't know. Let's keep looking."

"They can't be here, Nick. Surely they wouldn't have…"

And then Blue barked—once and with authority. Both Nick and Deborah froze and strained to listen. A tiny meow pierced the gathering dusk.

"This way." Together they rounded the corner. If anything, this side was even worse. Nick looked down, looked at the mud and saw Joseph's footprint. Or was it Jacob's? Blue was scrambling on top of the wreckage, whining and pawing at the debris.

"Jacob. Joseph. If you can hear us, call out."

"Jacob! Joseph!" Deborah had also seen the footprint. She began pulling at boards, tearing them away, completely unaware of the abuse to her hands, frantically calling out to her children.

Nick put a hand on her arm. "Listen."

It was a cough—small, under the rubble, but unmistakable. Blue barked twice and bounded over to Nick, then took off around the corner.

"We're coming." Deborah darted around to the other side of the rubble and resumed clawing at the boards.

"Jacob, Joseph." Nick cleared his throat, his voice gravelly with unshed tears. "Can you holler out? Let us know where you are, but don't try to move."

"Over here." The voice was followed by more coughing.

Nick was certain it was beyond the initial pile of rubble. Blue had disappeared in that direction.

"Give me your hand," he whispered to Deborah. "Try to step where I step. We go slow and carefully."

She seemed to understand the risk they were taking. Should they unsettle the pile, cause it to shift, it could hurt the boys even more. But Nick didn't think it would. He thought they were past that. He hoped, he prayed fervently, that he was right.

They climbed over the top and looked down to where Blue was lying on his belly, whimpering joyfully and licking Jacob's face.

"Jacob!" The scream that tore from Deborah nearly broke Nick's heart.

"Mamm?"

They scrambled down the pile of debris. Jacob was pinned beneath a piece of roofing. His face was covered with dirt. Tears had left paths down his cheeks. He also had blood running down his face from a cut on his forehead, but otherwise he seemed unhurt.

Nick lifted up a corner of the roofing and saw that there was maybe a three-inch clearing between it and a fallen roof brace. "Do your legs hurt, Jacob?"

"Nein." He wiggled his feet. "I'm just… I'm stuck."

"Okay. On three, I'm going to lift, and your *mamm* is going to tug on your legs and pull you free. If anything feels like it's broken, if you feel any sudden pain, you holler out, Jacob, and we'll stop. We'll think of something else. Got it?"

"Ya."

Blue took three steps back and sat. Nick pulled in a very deep breath and planted his feet. "One, two, three…" Sweat bathed his forehead as he fought to lift and hold the section of roofing.

"He's free," Deborah called. "Jacob, oh, Jacob."

Blue bathed the boy with kisses, and Jacob slung one arm around the dog's neck and the other around his mother's.

"Where's Joseph?" she asked.

"That way." Jacob inclined his head to the south side of the structure. "He was talking to me, but then…" Tears caught in his throat, but he pushed on. "Then he stopped."

"I'll look," Nick said. "Stay with Jacob."

Deborah remained kneeling beside Jacob, touching him, kissing his face, telling him everything was going to be all right now that they'd found him. "We'll get Joseph out. We'll be home before you know it."

He glanced back in time to see her pull the boy into her arms. Nick closed his eyes, and tears cascaded down his cheeks. His heart was filled with joy that they'd found Jacob and fear that Joseph was badly hurt—possibly even unconscious.

He turned his attention to the direction that Jacob had indicated. Blue, apparently understanding that his work wasn't done, joined the search for Joseph. Nick was reminded of the childhood game of pick-up sticks, only this time there was more to lose than a game. This time Joseph's life might depend on their actions.

He walked slowly around the large pile and spotted the boy at the same moment that Blue did. Joseph lay near the edge of the debris, under a portion of wall that had collapsed. Next to him was a small kitten, tucked under the boy's arm, looking frightened and thin. Nick scrambled around the debris until he was kneeling beside him. Blue commenced licking Joseph's face and whined softly whenever the kitten glanced in his direction. Joseph wasn't aware of any of it. His eyes were closed, and he lay perfectly still. Nick reached over, laid his fingers against the artery in the boy's neck and felt a pulse. Hope rose in his heart like a bird taking flight.

"I've got him, Deborah. Stay where you are. I'm going to try to…" But she was already at his side, exclaiming over her son, who still didn't stir.

"He's going to be okay."

"I know. I know he will be." She swiped at her tears. "Should I run for help?"

How long would it take? Thirty minutes? An hour? Did Joseph have that long? Nick had no idea what was wrong with the boy. He stared at the wall that had pinned him to the ground. There was only the one piece. It wasn't a pile like Jacob had been pinned under.

"Let's try first. If we can't do it, then I'll run for help while you stay with them."

She nodded in agreement.

"I'm going out the way we came and in through…" He pointed to where the last ray of sunlight was piercing the other side of the rubble. "I'll lift from there, and you lift from here."

"And I'll pull out Joseph."

Nick hadn't heard Jacob walk up. He looked small, exhausted and scared, but his expression was one of pure determination. "I want to help."

"Okay. Wait for my signal."

To Deborah, it seemed as if freeing her son took a lifetime, and it also happened more quickly than a heartbeat. Nick was standing on the opposite side, again planting his feet and squatting to grab the portion of fallen wall.

"With me… One, two, three."

She tried to lift when he said *three*, tried with all her might to pull up on the section pinning her son. It looked as if it didn't move at all, and then there was a slight change. Deborah dug in, prayed for the strength of a thousand warriors and pulled up on the section of wall.

Her voice came out a ragged whisper. It seemed to rise up from deep in her soul. "Now, Jacob."

She looked across at Nick. His face had turned a dark red, and she knew they had a few seconds, no more.

"He's free. I got him."

She dropped the section at the same time that Nick did. Dust rose up from the pile, and Blue jumped back. The kitten scooted farther into Joseph's jacket. Joseph didn't so much as blink.

"Is he okay?" Jacob asked.

Deborah was afraid to move him, afraid something was broken. She touched his face, ran her hands down his arms, checked his legs. Everything seemed okay, so why didn't he open his eyes? What was wrong?

"He's unconscious." Nick's voice was soft in her ear. "I don't think we'll make matters worse by lifting him."

"Okay." She turned to Jacob and noticed the gash on his forehead. Had she seen it before? How could she have missed it?

She reached for the hem of her apron, tried to rip off a piece, but she couldn't make the fabric tear. Nick pulled a pocketknife out of his pocket and poked a hole in the fabric. She tore it free, then wrapped it around Jacob's head, at least temporarily stanching the flow of blood.

"Okay," she said. "Let's get out of here."

Jacob picked up the kitten.

Deborah reached out for Jacob, who slid his small hand into hers. Nick picked up Joseph, who still hadn't stirred. Blue stood just outside the shadow of the structure. The last of the day's light had fled, and darkness was coming.

They would get Joseph home.

He would wake up. He had to wake up.

They crossed the field to the portion of fence where

they'd climbed through only a few minutes earlier. Jacob ducked in between the wires and knelt by their lunch boxes, settling the kitten inside his before snapping the lid shut. "Just for a few minutes," he whispered.

"Hold the wire for your *mamm*, Jacob."

He did, Deborah crept through and then Nick handed Joseph over to her. In that moment when both of their hands were supporting the weight of her son, Nick's eyes met hers, and she knew, she truly believed, that some good would come of this. She silently promised herself, promised *Gotte* and her boys, that she would never again take another moment with them for granted.

Nick ducked through the fence, took Joseph back into his arms and gave her a weak smile. Blue was already on the road, waiting for them, leading the way home.

They hurried into a darkness that had now completely cloaked the fields. They practically sprinted down the road, back to the lane and to her parents' house. She was barely aware of collapsing on the porch, of her *mamm* and *dat* running out to see what was wrong, of Nick harnessing Rhapsody to the buggy. One minute she was standing in front of their porch, so very grateful to be home. The next moment Rhapsody was headed down the road at a quick trot—all six of them, plus one dog and one kitten, crammed into the buggy.

The next several hours passed in a blur, and yet Deborah understood that it was a night that would remain in her memory if she lived to be one hundred. Jacob needed four stitches in his forehead, but otherwise he was fine. Joseph's situation was more complicated. A nurse had started an IV in his arm.

"I ordered the IV because Joseph seems somewhat

dehydrated," Dr. Cramer explained. She was about Deborah's height, with short black hair. Her manner was patient, understanding, even.

"When will he wake up?"

"In approximately ten percent of concussions, the person is rendered unconscious for a time. I'd like to do a CT scan to make sure there's no bleeding in his brain. We'll have those results back pretty quickly, and then we'll talk again."

Deborah nodded as if she understood what the doctor had said. CT scan? Bleeding in his brain? She reached for her *mamm*'s hand, clung to it. Her parents had both been amazingly calm throughout the entire ordeal. Concerned, but also certain that Joseph would be fine.

Once they wheeled Joseph out of the room, her *mamm* stood. "I'll take Jacob to sit with your *dat*. No doubt, he'd like a *gut*, rousing game of checkers."

"Think we could eat first?" Jacob asked. "Or…"

He turned to look at where his *bruder* had been, then at his *mamm*. "Maybe I should wait until Joseph can eat?"

Deborah squatted in front of him. "Joseph is going to be fine, and he'd want you to go ahead and have some supper. You need to keep up your strength."

"Ya?"

"Sure and certain. Joseph may need help at first, so he'll be depending on you."

"Okay."

He flung his arms around her neck, and she felt his hot tears against her skin. A surge of love pierced Deborah's heart, reminding her of the day they were born, when the midwife had first placed both boys in her arms and she had wondered at the miracle of their birth.

Jacob pulled back and swiped the sleeve of his shirt across his eyes. The nurse had cleaned up around the cut on his forehead, but the rest of his face still held layers of dirt and sweat and tears.

"Go with your *mammi*. I'll send word as soon as we know anything else."

Deborah's *mamm* was at the door when Deborah called out to her, "Could you ask Nick to come back?"

"Of course."

She couldn't have said if two minutes had passed or twenty. Suddenly Nick was standing in front of her, and she could no longer hold back the tears that had been building since she'd first realized that her boys were missing. She lurched out of the chair and into his arms. She wept until her emotions were spent.

Nick didn't tell her to stop crying.

He didn't pretend to know what was going to happen next.

He simply held her.

Finally, she collapsed into the chair and dried her face with the torn hem of her apron. He walked over to the sink, found a washcloth in the cabinet next to it and soaked it in warm water. Wringing it out, he snagged a hand towel and brought them both back to her.

"Danki."

"Gem gschehne."

She pressed the warm cloth to her eyes, then scrubbed at her face. Handing the cloth back to Nick, she patted everything dry. Then she reached for Nick's hand. He interlaced his fingers with hers and they sat there, waiting and praying, hoping. Believing.

An hour later, an orderly rolled Joseph's bed back into the room. She heard his voice even before she saw his red hair. She heard his voice, and suddenly she could breathe again. Hopping to her feet, she tried to scoot around the bed as they pushed it into the room.

Joseph smiled at her, and Deborah didn't know if there'd ever been a more beautiful sight. "You're awake."

He waved a small hand at her.

"Oh, Joseph. You're awake. How do you feel?"

"Okay. That machine they put me in was pretty cool, *Mamm.*"

The orderly repositioned his IV bag on the pole and told them the doctor would be in soon.

Deborah looked at Nick and understood that he was waiting, not wanting to intrude. She nodded at him—just a short, brief gesture, but it was all he needed. He popped out of his chair and stood on the other side of the hospital bed.

"Hey, Nick."

"Hey, Joseph."

"Is Blue here? I had a dream about him. He was licking my face."

"He is here, but we had to leave him in the buggy."

"And the kitten?"

"Also in the buggy, but lying on the blanket under the seat."

"So the kitten is safe?"

"Very. Blue learned his lesson with cats long ago. He won't bother your kitten."

All this talk about a stray cat! Her son had been returned to her. Her son was going to be okay. Deborah straightened his cover, patted his hand and again kissed his forehead. "How do you feel? Does your head hurt?"

"*Ya*, and the lights seem awfully bright in here."

"We can fix that." Dr. Cramer stood in the door to the room. She reached over and switched off the light directly over Joseph's bed. "How's that?"

"Better."

The doctor remained in the doorway, staring down at her tablet. Finally, she looked up, smiled and said, "Good to meet you, Joseph."

Joseph looked at Deborah.

"This is your doctor—Dr. Cramer. She's helping you get well."

Dr. Cramer walked next to the bed, pulled up a chair and sat. "Can you tell me what happened, Joseph?"

"I woke up, right as they were putting me in the brain machine."

"And before that?"

He shook his head, stared at the ceiling a minute, then closed his eyes. "Jacob and I were walking home, and I saw a little kitten—sitting by the side of the road and crying. We tried to catch it, to bring it home..." He stopped, looked at Deborah. "We were going to ask first, of course, but we couldn't just leave it there and go back. We might never find it again."

She nodded once, and he resumed his story.

"The kitten ran into an old barn, under some boards. Jacob was on one side, and I was on the other. We thought we could tease her out, but then...then there was a rumble, like thunder, and...and I don't remember anything else until I woke up a few minutes ago."

"The barn fell down, Joseph." Deborah shook her head in wonder.

Nick was now standing behind Deborah. He let out a long sigh—an expression of wonder and gratitude and disbelief all combined together. "I suspect it was leaning anyway from the storm that came through the day before. When you were searching for the cat, you must have bumped into the one thing that was keeping it propped up."

Joseph shrugged. "Maybe I'm glad I don't remember that part."

"Cat, huh?" The doctor smiled and set down her tablet. "Next time maybe fetch a can of tuna and wait for the cat to come to you."

Dr. Cramer spent the next fifteen minutes checking Joseph's vision, balance and cognitive functions. She pronounced him a healthy seven-year-old with a big bump on his head and most certainly a concussion. "He's passed all of my tests, the CT scan looks good and he's keeping down the juice we gave him. Let's give it two more hours, make sure he can eat, and then we'll send him home."

Everyone smiled at that. The doctor said she'd be back in a couple hours and to call the nurse if they needed anything.

Nick had sunk into the chair the doctor had vacated. Deborah tapped him on the shoulder. "Would you mind staying here a few minutes?"

"Nowhere I'd rather be." And something in his voice convinced Deborah that he meant it.

That and the tender look he gave her sent shivers down her arms. She wanted to explore that, to consider what Nick's words and his actions of this evening meant. But she was too tired. She would be lucky to make it through the next few hours without falling asleep.

"I'll be quick. I want to tell *Mamm* and *Dat* the *gut* news."

"And Jacob. Don't forget to tell him." Joseph yawned. "I think he worries about me."

"I'll be sure to tell Jacob, too."

When she reached the door to the room, she glanced back. Nick was sitting by the hospital bed, right foot propped over his left knee. She could tell by the words she caught here and there that he was describing Blue's help in the search and rescue.

Deborah glanced down at her hands—torn and bruised from trying to dig her sons out from beneath a pile of rubble. Her apron was tattered, and she didn't want to think about what her *kapp*, hair and face looked like. Nick glanced up and smiled. He had dirt smudged across his face, and she knew that if she looked, his hands would be as dirty and bruised as hers.

It had been a long day, an eternity if measured in fears and hopes, but something told Deborah that it was also the day she would always look back on as the beginning of the rest of her life.

Chapter Twelve

Nick realized he was not the person he used to be. That Nick—the old Nick—might have been scared off by the incident with Jacob and Joseph and the Old Leaning Barn. That was the way the boys referred to the incident, always emphasized as if they'd used capital letters and written a story about it. Actually, Joseph did write a story about it once they returned to school, and Jacob once again drew the picture.

In the drawing, Blue and the kitten peeked out from a leaning stick barn. Deborah stood next to the barn, her stick arms reaching out to gather the boys to her. And beside the barn was Nick, larger than the barn itself, a smile on his face as his stick arms reached out to lift the barn.

This time, Deborah didn't become upset that he was included in the picture. She handed it to him and said, "Put it on your refrigerator. I'm not likely to forget that day."

Both Jacob and Joseph seemed to have recovered quite quickly from the incident.

Deborah was another matter. She was quieter, a bit more pensive, and Nick wasn't exactly sure what she was thinking. He tried to give her space while at the same time assuring her that he was there for her. It was a fine line to walk, but she was worth the effort.

The last weekend in September, he offered to take the boys to town to see the Six Horse Hitch Classic Series World Finals.

"You wouldn't mind?"

"Of course not. I'd enjoy it, and I think they would, too." He hesitated, and then asked, "Would you like to go with us?"

"I would, but…"

He didn't even attempt to finish that sentence for her, didn't push, simply waited.

"*Dat* doesn't seem quite himself," she admitted. "I think I'd like to stay here and help around the house, maybe give *Mamm* a few hours to run errands or visit a friend."

They were sitting on the steps of the front porch. Nick was thinking about the time he'd stormed over and offered to show her how to raise twins. What an arrogant thing to suggest.

"I'm sorry," he said.

"For what?"

"For thinking I knew how to do things better than you." He shook his head at what a fool he'd been. "You're doing a *gut* job, you know."

"I am? With what?" She raised her eyebrows and dared him to go on.

"With your life, your parents and most especially the boys."

Deborah laughed and leaned her head against his shoulder.

They sat that way awhile, just enjoying a beautiful Saturday morning and the company of one another. The quiet scene was broken when Oliver, the new kitten, tore around the corner of the house, paused and hissed at Blue, then scampered under the porch. Blue plopped into the dirt at their feet, head on his paws, one eye on the kitten, the other drifting shut so that it looked as if he was winking at the feline.

The boys arrived seconds later, trying to tempt the kitten out with a piece of yarn. Blue attacked the yarn, and the cat scampered out and ran up Jacob's pant leg, causing him to yelp and laugh at the same time. Joseph lavished attention on Blue, throwing his arms around the dog and knocking over a flowerpot in the process.

Deborah sat up and said with a laugh, "They're all yours. Bring them back before Christmas."

The afternoon was quite nearly perfect. As Nick and the boys drove into Shipshe, he noticed the brightness of the day, the falling leaves, even the pumpkin displays in the Amish and *Englisch* yards they passed. Parking took a few minutes, but they were able to find a seat where they could see the finish line. The boys were amazed at the size and power of the horses.

Joseph stared at them in fascination. "Why are they so much bigger than Rhapsody, Nick?"

"They're work horses, what we call draft horses. Surely you've seen them during the harvest."

"I guess we have," Jacob said.

"Maybe last year, but we were just kids then."

Jacob tossed his ball in the air, the baseball that was

always in his pocket, then smiled. "Kids don't notice things like the size of horses."

They cheered mightily for all the teams and laughed when the older Amish gentleman who won stood and took a bow. The crowd dispersed, but it seemed no one was in a hurry to go home. Nick thought that perhaps Deborah could use another hour alone, so he bought them cotton candy. They walked through the crowd, greeting church members and smiling knowingly at one another when *Englisch* tourists attempted to snap a covert picture. Nick realized that Shipshe was a *gut* place to grow up—always had been. Yes, the larger world occasionally crowded in, but that wasn't always a bad thing. The boys would learn how to live a plain and simple life in the middle of the twenty-first century. He hoped he would be there to help them with that.

As they were headed toward home, the boys put their heads together and whispered for a moment. Apparently, Joseph was deemed the one to ask the question. He sat up straighter, cleared his throat and said, "We'd like to know your intentions toward our *mamm*."

Nick almost choked on the soda he'd taken a drink from. "My intentions?"

"We'll be honest with you, Nick." Jacob tossed the ball from his right hand to his left—back and forth, back and forth. "My *bruder* and I don't actually know what the word *intentions* means, but we've heard it plenty."

"We happened to be, uh, listening in the last time Nathaniel Schrock came to pick up *Mamm*. He told her that his intentions were honorable." Joseph pulled off his straw hat, scratched his head, causing his red hair to stand on end, then replaced the hat. "What does that mean exactly?"

Wow.

Nick couldn't think of a more uncomfortable conversation to have with two seven-year-old boys, other than the birds and the bees. Though if his relationship with Deborah progressed as he hoped it would, that might be his job one day. Not today, though. Not when they were only seven. Suddenly he was grateful that this conversation wasn't that one.

"Okay. Well. Intentions refer to our goals or purpose."

The boys looked at each other and then shook their heads.

Nick tried to think of a way to bring the topic down to their level. "Jacob, why do you toss that ball constantly?"

"Missed one in the outfield last week. I want to get better."

"Okay, so your intention is to improve your ball-playing skills."

"Sure."

Joseph sat up straighter. "And when I practice my letters on an assignment, my intention is to write better."

"Exactly." Nick felt rather proud of himself. He'd handled that well.

He reached for his soda cup, took another sip through the straw and spewed it when Joseph asked, "So what is your intention? What are you trying to get better at? And what is Nathaniel's intention?"

Was Deborah still seeing Nathaniel Schrock? They hadn't talked about courting exclusively, but he'd assumed…

Nick felt sweat break out on his forehead. This was like being grilled by a boss when applying for a job. "I suppose I'm trying to learn how to be a better friend to your *mamm*. I can't speak for Nathaniel. You'd have to check with him."

"Fair enough. I guess you have to ask a person a thing if you want to know. Otherwise, you can't really be sure of what another person is thinking..." Jacob bumped his shoulder into Joseph's. "Unless you're a twin."

Which started both boys laughing, and like a sudden shift in the wind, their attention turned to Blue and Oliver the kitten and schoolmates.

Leaving Nick with their question circling in his mind. He knew his intention, had known it since Deborah had broken off their fake dating. He'd been trying to give her time and space. Although that had only been a few weeks ago, it seemed much longer. So many things had happened. So much had changed between them. They'd grown closer, given what they'd been through together.

Perhaps he'd waited long enough.

Maybe it was time to broach the subject with Deborah. Maybe it was time to make his intentions known.

The next day was an off-Sunday, meaning the community didn't meet for a church service. Instead, families and neighbors gathered for a meal and to catch up on recent events. Deborah was relieved to have a day off to spend at home. She felt as if she could lie down and take a nap for hours upon hours. Of course, she didn't.

They'd prepared for the meal the day before. The

boys were quite excited about showing Oliver off to their cousin Christopher. Her parents had invited Nick to join them as well. It made for a nice, medium-sized group—six adults and three children. They ate lunch on the front porch, since it was a stormy day. The soft patter of rain on the roof soothed Deborah's soul and calmed her spirit. The boys were playing in the barn—their solid, safe barn. They'd taken off with Blue and Oliver, promising to be careful.

Deborah's brother Simon and Nick were discussing the upcoming harvest, plans for the next spring and the merits of buying versus borrowing draft horses. Her *dat* listened and nodded occasionally.

"Where did your *mamm* go?" Mary asked. They were standing at the kitchen sink, washing and rinsing the lunch dishes.

"Said she wanted to lie down for a few minutes."

"Is she okay?"

"I guess." Deborah's hands stilled in the water. She leaned forward to peer out the kitchen window, to better see the men where they sat on the porch. Watching her *dat*, she sensed that something had changed, but she couldn't put her finger on exactly what was different. He looked the same, though he wasn't as involved as he usually was. It was almost as if he was only partly with them.

Mary crowded in to see what she was staring at. "And your *dat*?"

"I don't know," Deborah answered honestly. "He hasn't been himself these last few days."

"Should he go to the doctor?"

"*Mamm* suggested it last night. He said that if he ran

to the doctor every time he felt tired, he'd never get a thing done."

"Oh, dear."

"She'll wear him down. *Mamm* usually wins in health matters. She's like a slow, solid drip of water on a rock, leaving its impression until the rock has no idea what happened to it."

Mary laughed. "We all need someone like that in our lives. I suppose in my home it was my oldest *schweschder*. She'd pop us into the buggy at the first sign of fever."

They finished cleaning the dishes, then wiped down the counters. They spoke of their boys, school days, the coming harvest, even Christmas plans. Since many of their gifts were homemade, it was something best started on in October. Deborah realized with a shock that October was right around the corner. Where had the month gone?

She and Mary walked to the barn, carrying a tin full of cookies, a thermos of milk and a stack of five plastic cups. The boys paused in their game of tag long enough to swig down the milk and stuff extra cookies into their pockets, then they were off again.

Mary nodded toward the hayloft and raised her eyebrows. Deborah laughed. "Sure. Why not?"

It was while they were sitting there, their feet hanging over the edge and swinging back and forth, that Mary asked about her courting.

"Still seeing Nathaniel?"

"Nein." Deborah smiled. "He's a nice person, but there's no spark between us."

"Spark, huh?"

"You know what I mean."

"I do indeed." They could just see out the barn doors to the porch, where the men were sitting. "I still feel that spark with your *bruder*."

"You don't say? Even after all these years?"

"Even so." Mary flopped onto her back.

Deborah did the same, staring up at cobwebs in the corners of the ceiling. "Nick told me he loves me."

"What?" Mary popped up and stared at her in surprise. "When did this happen? When were you going to tell me? What did you say?"

"I said that I cared about him, too."

"Ouch. That's it?"

"Some days I'm not sure I believe in love anymore— romantic love, I mean. Then I watch you and Simon, and I realize that a part of my heart still does."

"And do you love Nick?"

"Maybe. I think I could, but it's…well, it's scary to admit."

"It can be."

"After the talk with my parents—remember, I told you about that…"

Mary nodded.

"I promised myself I would live courageously. That I wouldn't hide any longer inside my parents' house. That I'd put my heart out there, if for no other reason than so my boys might have a normal home."

"Oh, Deborah."

Deborah looked over in surprise at Mary. "You sound so melancholy. What did I say?"

Mary sat up, staring down at the floor now. It seemed that she was determined to choose her words very carefully. Deborah sat up, too—interested, needing to know what her sister-in-law thought. They were the closest of friends. Deborah really did look up to her, and she admired the relationship that Mary had with Simon. She wanted that sort of relationship, that kind of home.

Clearing her throat, Mary said, "It's only that I don't think you can decide to fall in love for the sake of your boys. We can do a lot of things for our children, but I'm not sure that's one."

"Then what do I do?"

"Listen to your heart…and whatever you decide, decide it based on your needs and feelings. It's okay to do what is right and true for you. Of course, you always consider your children in your decisions, but your feelings for Nick? Well, that's something between the two of you. For a moment, I think, you have to stop being a *mamm* and simply be a woman."

"What if I don't know how to do that?"

Mary reached for her hand and plopped back down on her back. "It's rather like riding a bike. You might be wobbly at first, but eventually it will come back to you."

Did she believe that? Could she become the young girl she had been before Gavin had rejected her? She had no desire to be that young, naive girl again, but maybe she could take that girl's dreams—her dreams—and embrace them in a new way.

The rest of the afternoon passed pleasantly.

The rain stopped, the sun came out and everyone except her parents went for a walk to the back pond. Deborah watched Simon and Mary together. She watched Nick with her boys, and she wondered if she had the courage to simply be a woman, even for a little while.

The timing seemed all wrong.

Her *dat* needed to see the doctor. Her *mamm* was looking exhausted. The boys, as always, were a handful.

But perhaps love didn't wait for the perfect moment.

Maybe, just maybe, the perfect moment was the one when you decided to step out in faith.

Chapter Thirteen

Nick walked through a field, parting the tall stalks of corn as he searched. He could hear Jacob and Joseph laughing, but he couldn't see them. Occasionally a stalk would move, followed by the sound of small feet running. He wanted to call out to them, to tell them to be careful. He wanted to find them to assure himself they were all right. He parted two of the stalks, but instead of the boys, he found Deborah. She was sitting cross-legged, her head down, hands covering her face, crying.

"The boys are okay."

She shook her head and continued to weep.

He knelt in front of her. "I just heard them. They're only playing a game. They're fine."

Now she looked up, and his heart began to pound in his chest as if he'd been the one running. Something was wrong. Something was very wrong, and he needed to help her.

But then he was in the barn, alone, brushing Big Girl.

The mare was restless, more nervous than he'd ever seen her.

"Whoa, girl. Easy."

The mare looked at him, terror in her eyes, then tossed her head back, straining against the lead rope.

Nick needed to do something, but what?

He heard a high-pitched sound. His heart rate accelerated again, sweat dripped down his back and he felt real fear. There was something he needed to do. Somewhere he needed to be. Big Girl neighed loudly and then nudged him, putting her muzzle in his hand, licking his hand.

And that was what woke him. Only it wasn't Big Girl. It was Blue—sitting beside the bed and licking Nick's hand, whining and waiting.

He sat up, trying to push away the dream, the fear, and that was when he realized the ringing in his ears was actually the sound of an *Englisch* ambulance. He lurched to his feet, and Blue ran from the bed down the hall and to the front door, barking loudly.

"*Ya.* I understand." He pulled on a pair of pants, yanked the suspenders over the nightshirt he slept in, stuffed his feet into his shoes and ran out the door.

The ambulance had stopped at the Mast place. Its siren continued to blare, and Nick could see the red emergency lights piercing the darkness.

Blue kept pace with him as he dashed to the fence and through the gate. He silently thanked the Lord that they had put the pass-through there. By the time he made it to the front of the Mast home, Deborah was standing on the porch. Both boys held tight to her hands. The paramedics were loading John into the back of the ambulance. Nick had one glimpse inside, just long enough to see Bethany sitting beside her husband and an oxygen mask over his face. One paramedic climbed up into the back of the vehicle and beside the gurney, and the other slapped the door shut and jumped into the driver's seat. They headed back down the lane and to the main road, turning toward town.

Nick pivoted back toward the house in time to see Deborah sink onto the top porch step.

Blue had dropped to the ground, head resting on his paws, his gaze firmly locked on the boys.

Jacob and Joseph were uncharacteristically silent.

Nick walked closer to the small family huddled on the porch. "What happened?"

"I don't know." Deborah's voice trembled, and she pulled the boys tight against her side. "I woke to *Mamm* hollering. She told me to run to the phone shack, to call 911. By the time I got back, *Dat* was clearly in distress, clutching his arm and struggling to pull in a deep breath."

"Okay." He stepped in front of her and squatted so that they would be eye to eye.

The boys were watching him now, tears streaking their faces. He thought the fear reflected there might be the saddest thing he'd ever seen. It reminded him of his dream—of looking for the boys and for Deborah, of trying to calm his mare. The boys' expression reminded him of the very real fear he'd felt, and the way his heart had beat so hard in his chest it had actually hurt.

He put out a hand for each boy, and they grabbed it as if they were drowning. He didn't even ask if they wanted to pray, he simply closed his eyes and voiced what they had to all be thinking.

"*Gotte*, please be with John at this moment. Keep

his heart beating strong. Guide their path to the hospital. May Your hand be upon him, upon Bethany, and may You guide the paramedics and nurses and doctors. *Danki* that Deborah was here to run for the phone, that the boys were here to support their *mamm*. Grant us wisdom and peace and guidance in the coming days."

The boys swiped at their eyes.

Deborah whispered, *"Danki."*

And then she told Jacob and Joseph to go inside, to put on school clothes and grab their books.

"We're going to school?" Jacob's eyes widened in surprise.

Joseph put a hand on his *mamm*'s shoulder. "We want to go to the hospital."

"We will. All of us will…" She hesitated and then looked up at Nick.

He nodded. Of course he'd go with them.

Deborah stood, smoothing down her nightgown and pulling her sweater more closely around her. "You may go to school, but you'll be going late, if at all. First, you'll go to the hospital with me and Nick."

The boys nodded solemnly, paused to shower Blue with attention, then hurried off to their rooms. The screen door had barely slammed behind them when Deborah walked into Nick's arms, and that was when his heart rate finally slowed. Deborah in his arms. The boys upstairs dressing. They were the most important people in the world to him, and he would do anything to protect their family and their home.

"It's going to be okay."

"You don't know that."

"True, but I believe it."

She pulled back enough to look up into his face, then snuggled in against him. "I'm glad you're here. I'm glad I don't have to face this alone."

He wanted to say several things.

I'll always be here.

I love you, and I love your boys.

Marry me.

He didn't. Instead, he kissed the top of her head and whispered, "I'll hitch Rhapsody up and meet you back here."

"They won't let us in until they get *Dat* settled. You have time to go home and finish dressing." There was a hint of amusement in her voice even as she pulled in a shaky breath.

"Oh, yeah. A proper shirt would probably be *gut*."

"And socks."

"That, too." He cradled her face in his hands, kissed her lips softly and thumbed away the tears still leaking from her eyes. "If I'm going home, I might as well hitch up Big Girl. She enjoys a nighttime drive."

"It's nearly morning."

He glanced east and saw she was right. On the horizon the sky was lightening ever so gently, the sun's rays sending out the barest of pink and lavender streaks. He kissed her again, then hurried home, thinking that the coming sunrise would splash across the first day of the rest of his life—the rest of his life with Deborah and Jacob and Joseph, with Bethany and John.

The dream and the emergency and the look on their faces—it had all combined to banish any last question. It didn't really matter if he could provide a perfect home.

He no longer cared if his five-year plan urged caution. What mattered was the love he felt in his heart.

They made it to the hospital in record time—Big Girl tossing her head the entire way.

"Your mare is fast, Nick." Jacob sat back against the seat. "*Gut* thing you were here to drive us."

Deborah turned and scowled at her boys, who were sitting in the back seats. "I can drive a mare."

"*Ya.* You can, but it takes you a lot longer to hitch one up," Jacob pointed out.

"And we're still too short." Joseph sounded as if it was a crime that they hadn't grown to their full height yet.

Deborah reached out and tousled their red hair, then turned back around in the seat. Nick could sense that everyone was feeling better, definitely less shaky, but they were all still worried.

By the time they reached the hospital, Bishop Ezekiel was already in the waiting room. Nick didn't ask how he'd managed to beat them there. When had anyone had time to call him? All moot points. The man was here, and Nick was glad he was.

"I just spoke with Bethany." He motioned toward a sitting area. A few other people were waiting in the chairs, but they walked to a far corner where they'd have a bit of privacy.

"As you can guess, it looks like your *dat* had a heart attack. The *gut* news is that you and your *mamm* acted quickly. The doctors are stabilizing him now, and his heart doctor will be out to update us as soon as possible."

It was Jacob who voiced the question they were all wondering. "Can we see him?"

"Not yet. For now, let's sit, wait and pray."

Which was exactly what they did. Within an hour, the waiting room was full with Deborah's *bruders* and *schweschdern*, nieces and nephews. They'd brought thermoses of coffee, containers of milk and several types of baked goods—homemade cookies and brownies and granola bars. Mary, Deborah's *schweschder*-in-law, herded the children off to another part of the waiting room so the adults could talk without little ears craning to hear every word. The children sat in a circle as if they were about to play Duck, Duck, Goose. But instead of games, they quietly accepted the light breakfast.

Everyone was in shock, though this wasn't completely unexpected. It was only that they'd hoped that her *dat* was growing stronger. No one had dared to express any concern about a setback.

Had there been symptoms?

Nick didn't remember John seeming more tired or weaker.

He was thinking of that, wondering if he should have paid closer attention, when a middle-aged woman wearing a doctor's lab coat walked out and headed straight toward the family. The name stitched on her coat was Dr. Green.

"Your father has suffered a myocardial infarction."

"A heart attack?" Simon rubbed a hand up and down his face. "I knew he needed to slow down. He won't listen."

"How's he doing?" Deborah crossed her arms, then uncrossed them. "And what's next?"

"I ordered some blood work. We also performed a noninvasive echocardiogram and a cardiac cath. We were able to determine the severity and location of arterial blockage. Fortunately, it doesn't require open-heart surgery. Instead, I'd like to put in a stent to open the affected arteries."

"What exactly does that involve?" Simon asked.

"Think of the artery as a straw. Sometimes the blockage becomes so advanced that it keeps the blood from flowing through. We put in a stent to prop the artery open."

Simon looked around the circle, which included Ezekiel. Each person nodded in agreement. Nick felt a surge of relief. They wouldn't need to do open-heart surgery. He knew that was a good sign.

"Okay," Simon said. "*Ya.* Let's do the stent."

"Excellent."

Deborah sighed in relief. "When can he come home?"

"As long as his condition remains stable? He should be home tomorrow."

There were shouts of *hallelujah* and *amen* at that.

"But he is going to need to take it easy," Dr. Green cautioned. "Exercise is important, but he needs to start slowly and build his strength. What he eats is also important—less red meat and salt, more fruits and vegetables. But what's most critical at this point is that he not overdo it. And I want him in my office for a checkup at regular intervals. We may need to adjust his medicine, depending on how he's responding."

They all nodded gravely.

One way or another, they would see that John followed the doctor's orders. As they resettled in the waiting room chairs, Nick felt proud that the Masts had included him as if he were part of the family. None of Deborah's siblings lived as close as Nick did. He could be there every morning and every night. He would be there. He'd be a *gut* neighbor, and hopefully—once things were settled and Deborah had recovered from this latest blow—he'd be more than a neighbor. If she would have him, if she felt as he did, Nick was ready to officially be a part of this family.

The next week passed in something of a blur for Deborah. Her *dat*'s condition was addressed with two stents. He was able to go home three days after his attack, on the following Saturday. Deborah went to church with the boys on Sunday, but her parents stayed home. She was astonished when every single person in their congregation stopped by to speak with her.

They offered meals.

They volunteered to care for the fields and the animals.

They vowed to pray for her and the boys and her parents.

Deborah had always felt at home in her church, even after she'd left for Ohio, considered becoming Mennonite and returned as a single mom. She believed that most people accepted her back into the fold, though no doubt a few privately judged her. She was okay with that. She still occasionally judged herself for her missteps, but then she'd watch Jacob catching a frog or Joseph playing with Blue and she'd thank *Gotte* for the blessings He'd brought from those very same missteps.

On the Sunday after her *dat*'s heart attack, something

in Deborah shifted. She no longer felt as if she was on the outer fringe of her community. She realized she was an important member of it—every man, woman and child was. She understood, maybe for the first time, that a church was a family of people—complete with their talents, their weaknesses and, yes, their missteps.

"You're having very serious thoughts over there." Nick nudged her foot with his under the picnic table.

They were sitting at a table with other young couples—most married and a few others who had made known their intention to marry. She and Nick hadn't done that. They hadn't really talked about where their relationship was going.

Were they a couple?

She thought of the way he'd kissed her as they'd stood in front of her parents' home, the sun just peeking over the horizon and her *dat* on the way to the hospital. She remembered the comfort of his arms around her. She considered the way he'd been there for them, almost as if he was a part of the family.

Deborah glanced up and smiled. "I suppose I was."

"Care to share?"

She shook her head, then tacked on a "Maybe later."

And she did, later, when the boys were playing with the other *kinner* and she and Nick were walking along the creek. October had arrived in a flurry of color—crops to be harvested, trees losing their leaves, the sky a bright blue. Soon it would be winter, then Christmas and then another year passed. She pulled in a deep breath, and bared the burdens of her soul to this man that she was falling in love with.

She told him how her father's health scare had helped

her to appreciate her community, her neighbors, her family and him.

"Ya?" He entwined his fingers with hers.

She liked that about Nick. He enjoyed holding hands, or nudging shoulders or sitting side by side. He liked being close to her, and he seemed to draw some strength from her, as she did from him.

"More serious thoughts? I can practically hear your brain churning."

She almost held back, almost pushed the questions down to wrestle with later that night. But what was the point of doing that? Life was short—her *dat*'s illness had brought that fact home quite clearly. What was she waiting for?

"I was thinking that our *freinden*, they're all either married or planning to marry."

"Hmm." Nick rubbed his chin thoughtfully. "Can't say as I've noticed." He easily sidestepped her playful swipe. "That means you're saying…"

"I'm not saying anything," Deborah protested. "I've never been quite in step with everyone else."

"Ya, I get that. But I guess the question is—do you want to be?"

"Do I *want* to be in step with everyone else?" She should have been aggravated at his teasing, but the way he was looking at her caused her emotions to tumble here and there. They continued walking beside the creek, and she finally said, "Well, I'm not sure. What are you suggesting?"

Instead of continuing to tease her, Nick stopped. Since they were still holding hands, she bounced back like a yoyo connected by a string. Nick smiled, put his arms around her, then ducked his head and kissed her lips.

Wow! She felt chill bumps all the way to her toes.

"You're blushing."

"Well, *ya.* Kiss a girl like that and she's likely to blush."

Instead of letting her go, he waited for her to meet his gaze. "Do you want our relationship to become more permanent?"

"Our fake relationship?"

"*Nein.* You know very well that we're done with that. I'm speaking of our real relationship."

She heard Jacob and Joseph laughing and running toward them, but she didn't look away. She also didn't pretend, even to herself, that this moment wasn't very important. It was what she'd wanted, probably since he'd scolded her boys for catching Blue on the end of a hookless fishing line. It was what she'd dreamed of since the first time he'd kissed her. In that moment, she accepted the truth of how much Nick cared for her and how much she cared for him. And when she did that, the fears that she had so tightly clung to slipped away.

She wasn't unlovable.

She could trust her instincts—especially in regard to Nick.

She could allow herself to be happy.

"I'd like that very much."

"Me, too." He kissed her again, clasped her hand and they walked back toward the boys.

Chapter Fourteen

The next few weeks did not go as Nick hoped. John's health improved, then worsened, then improved again. The entire family pitched in to help with the work on the farm, but the bulk of it fell to Nick—mainly because he wanted to do it. He wanted to be there. He needed to be there.

But running two farms was no easy thing.

It was a Saturday, three weeks after John had the stents inserted, when Simon confronted him. Simon had come over from Middlebury on Friday to help with the harvest, as had the other siblings in the family. But it was Simon and Nick there at the end of the day, in the barn, doing the daily chores after a full day of harvest.

"How long do you think you can do this?"

"Do what?" Nick paused, pitchfork in hand, standing in the middle of Rhapsody's stall.

Simon was leaning against the opposite wall, arms crossed, hat tipped back. "How long do you think you can run two farms?"

"I'm not—"

"You are. Don't think we haven't noticed. Don't think it's not appreciated, either, because it is. The truth of the matter is that *Dat*'s never going to be able to do these things again. We need to come up with a more permanent solution."

Nick swiped at the sweat dribbling down his face. He always did work up a sweat when he mucked out a stall, even when it was a cool October evening.

"About that..."

"*Ya?*"

But then he didn't know how to say it. He hadn't looked at his five-year plan in weeks. He couldn't envision how this was going to work out, but maybe he didn't need to depend on his five-year plan. He knew that asking Deborah to marry him was the right thing to do. He knew it was what he wanted to do. *Gotte* had placed him in this place at this time to care for Deborah and her family.

"The thing is that I'd like to ask Deborah to marry me."

"So, what are you waiting for?" The question held no condemnation, only amusement.

"I guess the perfect moment. The timing just feels— wrong."

"Ah, *ya*. I've heard of those perfect moments—the sun is dipping over a pristine field, your gal is by your side, maybe a redbird lands on a tree branch just at the edge of your vision. You hear a melodic song, and you know it's the perfect moment. You turn to the love of your life and ask her to be your *fraa*, and she says yes."

"Now you're making fun of me." He pointed the pitchfork at Simon, but he laughed with him. "Was that how it was with you and Mary? Sunsets and redbirds and all?"

"Hardly. Mary and I had been to an outing over in Middlebury. I guess the place we ate, the food must have been bad or something, because she was terribly sick for the next twenty-four hours. I went to her parents' home to check on her…" He shook his head at the memory. "I saw her in bed, all exhausted and sweating, and I knew…it was the perfect moment."

"Seriously?"

"Oh, *ya*. She puked before and after I asked her to be my *fraa*."

Nick laughed so hard that he had to press a hand to ease the stitch in his side. "You're making that up."

"I'm not." Simon joined him in the stall, and they quickly finished mucking it out and laying fresh hay. As they hung the tools on their hooks on the wall, he clasped Nick on the shoulder. "The important thing was that she said yes. That's what makes a perfect proposal, my friend. When both parties say yes."

Nick went to bed at his normal time, and he should have fallen right asleep. He didn't. Instead, he crossed his arms behind his head and stared up at the ceiling. Blue lay snoring softly on the rug. A slight breeze whispered through the open window.

He was an idiot.

Simon was right.

He didn't have to wait until he had the answer to every question about their future. They'd find those answers together. But Nick might be wrong about the proposal. Deborah deserved more than food poisoning and a puke bucket.

By the time he fell asleep, he had the perfect plan— or at least he thought it was the perfect plan.

The next day Nick and Deborah's *bruders* spent another four hours in the field, but then the harvest was done. John watched from a chair set out under the shade tree. Bethany sat beside him, shelling peas. Deborah helped with the harvest, as did her *schweschdern*. Her hair was covered with an old *kapp*, and she was wearing the same work dress she'd worn the day they'd gone kayaking. Was that the day he had well and truly fallen in love with her? He suspected it had happened even before that. Maybe it had even been the first day he'd met her.

He'd spent too much time struggling with those feelings. He was ready to accept them, to own them and to see where they led. He wanted Deborah and the twins in his life, for the rest of his life.

Jacob and Joseph were growing as fast as the corn they'd just harvested, though Joseph was beating Jacob by a fraction of an inch. Nick could now tell the two apart. He wondered that he'd ever had trouble with that. They might be twins, but they were two very different people. Joseph was quiet, thoughtful, a bit shy. Jacob was more impulsive, but he also had a commendable amount of energy.

A lump formed in his throat as he realized that both boys would probably have families of their own in fifteen years. Fifteen years. They would pass in the blink of an eye.

Everyone trooped back to the house for a late lunch. After they'd finished the meal, Nick motioned the boys outside and shared with them what he had in mind. He didn't tell them everything—he didn't tell them why he wanted to be alone with Deborah or what he was going to ask her, but he had a feeling that maybe they knew.

High-fiving his brother, Joseph declared, "I'll grab the picnic quilt and the sheets from the homework box."

"I know where the mason jars are." Jacob bounced from foot to foot. "I hope we can find the right kind of flowers."

"Anything will do. And boys…" Nick waited until they turned to look at him. *"Danki."*

They grinned again, then, instead of running to the house, they stepped closer and both gave him a tight hug. It brought tears to his eyes, but Nick wasn't embarrassed. Happiness that overflowed from your soul wasn't something to be self-conscious about. It was something to be grateful for, and he was.

The boys took off on their errands. Nick gave them thirty minutes, and then he went in search of Deborah.

He found her in the mudroom, rinsing out the dishcloths. "Care to go for a walk?"

"Sounds lovely, though sitting on the porch sounds even better."

"Oh, but—"

He didn't know how to finish that sentence. Deborah turned to study him. She laughed and wagged her finger at him. "Sounds like someone would like to go for a walk, though, so I'm all for it."

"Gut. Real *gut.* Well, I'll just…um… I need to go and speak with your *dat* first, and then I'll be ready."

"Okay. He's on the back porch." She nodded toward the double swing that they'd sat on together so many times. "I'll go with you."

"Nein!"

Now she looked at him as if he was wearing his suspenders backward.

"What I mean is, I have a hankering for some of those oatmeal cookies you made."

"After all the lunch you ate?"

"And maybe a thermos of coffee. That would hit the spot." He needed to buy himself five minutes, maybe ten. "I'll come and get you after I'm finished speaking with John."

"That sounds like a *wunderbaar* plan." She shook her head in amusement. "I'll go and make a pot of coffee."

Excellent. Coffee took a *gut* ten minutes to percolate.

He waited until she'd walked back into the kitchen, then he pushed through the screen door.

John smiled up at him when he sat down. "We appreciate your help, Nick."

"*Ya*, of course. No problem."

"We recognize all you've done around here these past few weeks. You've been a real blessing to me and to my family. *Gotte* knew what our needs would be when He prompted you to buy the farm next door."

Nick swallowed past the lump in his throat. He could hear Deborah and Mary talking in the kitchen. He was aware of a slight breeze stirring the bare tree limbs. He could smell coffee and cooking and autumn. It was as if every one of his senses was on hyperalert.

"Something on your mind, son?"

And that last word helped him over the hurdle of his insecurities. "I'd like to ask Deborah to marry me, but before I do… I'd like your blessing. That means a lot to me, John. It's important that you know how I feel about her, about the boys, about the entire family."

John smiled, but he didn't interrupt. He let Nick have the space to speak what was on his heart.

"Jacob and Joseph, they're amazing. And though they aren't my children in one sense, they will be in all the ways that matter. I care for them. I will pray for them every day. I already do, and I'll do my best to guide them—as you've guided your *kinner*."

Nick ran out of words there. He didn't know what else to say, how best to present his case. His house was too small, too old, and then there was the matter of the two farms.

But those were details that could be worked out.

What mattered was John's response and Deborah's answer.

John tapped his fingertips against the arm of the swing. "I believe you have loved this entire family since the day that you bought the goats..."

"And Jacob let them loose."

"And Deborah fell in the trough." John smiled, nodding his head at the memory. "You were aggravated at them, but I believe you were more aggravated at yourself because my family didn't fit into your future plans."

"My five-year plan."

"*Ya.* A family can mess with plans. Sometimes things take a turn in unexpected directions, but that's not what matters. What matters is that you can count on the fact that the people you love will be there for you and *Gotte* will provide."

"As far as the two farms—"

"Don't worry about that, Nick. We'll work it out."

"We will?"

"Together—after you ask Deborah, that is. And if she says yes."

"Do you think she will?" His plans for the future skidded to an abrupt stop. "Do you think she won't?"

"There's only one way to find out." But John's smile indicated his confidence that things would turn out the way that Nick hoped they would.

Deborah called from the door of the mudroom, "I have coffee and cookies. Anything else you need for this walk?"

"*Nein.* That sounds perfect."

At that point Jacob and Joseph appeared in front of the porch, waving wildly and giving him a thumbs-up sign. When Nick waved his thanks, they jogged off toward the front of the house. Blue dashed after them, hot on their heels.

John patted him on the back, and Nick stood and walked toward Deborah, toward the single person who mattered the most to him, and hopefully—toward his future.

Deborah was tired from the harvest. Traditionally, women did help in the fields—harvesttime was an all-hands-on-deck sort of activity. In addition, there was the usual cooking and cleaning to go along with the work in the fields. Her siblings had all shown up to help for the last two days, and of course Nick had been there.

She darted a peek in Nick's direction.

They were once again holding hands as they walked away from the house. He was up to something. She could tell it by the way he kept looking at her and then glancing away.

"Did you have a specific destination in mind?"

"*Ya*. I thought we'd sit by the pond for a spell."

"We should have invited Jacob and Joseph. In fact, where are the boys?"

"Oh, I think they...uh...had other things to do."

"Other things?"

"You know how they're always trying to teach Blue new tricks."

"They do love that dog. They're still pestering me about getting them one of their own."

Nick opened and closed his mouth.

"Do you think I should?"

"Oh, I don't know. They spend a lot of time with Blue. Just last week, Joseph taught him to sink onto his belly and then crawl backward. And Jacob is still convinced he can outrun the dog, though I've told him that blue heelers are cattle dogs. They're basically bred for speed and endurance. Some days it seems as if Blue is more their dog than mine."

He paused, and Deborah had that sense again that Nick was up to something. He glanced at her and then quickly looked away. And was he blushing?

She hoped something wasn't wrong. Dealing with her *dat*'s recuperation was enough pressure, not to mention the shenanigans Jacob and Joseph fell into on a daily basis. Deborah squeezed his hand. "You know you can tell me anything, right?"

"Oh, sure. *Ya*. You're a *gut* listener."

Hmm. That didn't work. There was definitely something on his mind, but he wasn't ready to spill it yet.

She supposed she'd find out soon enough, so she focused on breathing in the crisp fall air, enjoying the colors of the leaves they were walking through, listening to the birdsong. It was a *gut* day—a perfect day.

Then they rounded the corner toward the pond, and instead of sitting on the closest side, he led her around to the back.

As they walked toward it, she looked, stopped walking, looked again and shook her head in disbelief. She covered her mouth with her hand, but the laughter spilled through her fingers. "When did you have time to do this? A real picnic…"

He didn't answer. He pulled her toward the quilt Jacob and Joseph had placed under the bare limbs of a maple tree. As they drew closer, she saw half a dozen mason jars filled with clusters of wildflowers. Red, yellow and brown fall leaves had been sprinkled around the mason jars. Under one of the jars, someone had tucked two pieces of paper.

Nick set the thermos and container of cookies down on the quilt, then tugged on her hand until they were standing in the middle of it. The quilt was an old, tattered one—something they often used for picnics. But how did Nick know about that?

"Let's sit."

"Okay."

When they were settled, he reached for the sheets of paper that were tucked under one of the mason jars. It was only then that she realized what they were—Jacob's drawing. Joseph's story. She took them from his hands, staring first at the drawing. She ran her finger across each person—her *mamm*, *dat*, herself, Jacob, Joseph and Nick. They were all stick figures, their stick-figure hands connected to one another. They all had huge smiles on their faces, and a stick dog—Blue, no doubt—stuck his head out between the two boys. They stood in a line, a tree next to them and the pond off to the right.

She looked at Nick, who had been silent, studying her, waiting. "It's the same spot."

"It is."

"Did you do this? The flowers and the quilt and… this?" She held up the sheets of paper.

"*Nein.* Jacob and Joseph did."

She looked at the second sheet. Joseph's title at the top in bold, heavy letters read *My Family*. A few lines jumped out at her.

Our neighbor Nick…
Blue is the best.
We're like a family.

Nick scooted closer, so that they were sitting knee to knee, like two teenagers with their legs crossed and their faces mere inches apart. His voice, when he spoke, was soft and low and choked with emotion. "I wanted a private moment with you, Deborah, but I also wanted the boys to be a part of it."

Now her thoughts were swimming. She heard his words, saw the tender look on his face, but she couldn't quite make sense of what was happening. She put down the sheets of paper, carefully setting them back under the mason jar so they wouldn't blow away, and she noticed that her arms were shaking.

Then Nick reached for both of her hands, held them tenderly in his, and her shaking stopped.

"I love you very much, Deborah."

"You love me?"

"I do."

"I love you, too." She didn't even have to think about it. The words felt like a natural extension of everything she carried in her heart.

"I brought you out here because I wanted a special place to ask you to marry me."

"Marry you?"

"I wanted you to know that I'm not just asking you. I'm asking Jacob and Joseph, too, if they're willing to be a family. It seems to me, though…" He nodded at the papers. "It seems that they've already answered that question. Maybe they understood what was happening before I did."

"You're asking me to marry you?"

"*Ya.* I am." He looked as if he wanted to say more, but he didn't. Instead, he stopped and waited. He gave her a moment to gather her thoughts.

But Deborah didn't need any more time to think. She'd been thinking about this—dreaming about it— for some time now.

"Yes."

"Yes?" He looked surprised.

She laughed. "Did you expect me to say no?"

"Yes!" He jumped up, let out a whoop, turned in a circle, then dropped back down beside her. "We're going to be married."

"Yes, we are."

It was then that he cradled her face in his hands, moved toward her and kissed her lips.

In that kiss, Deborah felt his love for her. She felt his confidence in their future together, and his promise to be by her side. Could a single kiss hold that much? She thought maybe it could. She thought this kiss did.

They sat there another hour, talking about their future, enjoying the cookies and coffee. Finally, the boys, unable to contain their curiosity any longer, jogged toward them, Blue loping at their side.

Deborah had recovered from her surprise.

The world was no longer tilting.

In fact, she'd never felt on more solid ground.

"Nick has a question for you two."

Both boys dropped onto the quilt. Their red heads and freckles and earnest expressions tugged on Deborah's heartstrings as they always did. And this man sitting with them, he seemed part of a painting of their life—like Jacob's drawing and Joseph's story.

"Did we do *gut* with the flowers?" Joseph asked.

"Were you two kissing?" Jacob made a horrified look, and everyone laughed.

"You both did a *wunderbaar* job. I picked this special place…"

"It's the place in my picture!" Jacob had been staring down at the sheet, and now he looked around in surprise. "I draw pretty *gut.*"

"And I write pretty *gut.*" Joseph looked up from rereading his story. In the traditional Joseph way, he looked more serious than his *bruder*, as if he was waiting for something important.

"I picked this place because I wanted somewhere special to ask your *mamm* to marry me."

Jacob and Joseph exchanged a look, then turned their attention to Deborah.

"What did you say?" Jacob asked.

Joseph tightened his grip on the sheet of paper. "Did you say yes?"

"I did." Deborah felt tears prick her eyes for the first time. Why would she cry now? Her heart, her dreams, were one thing, but oh, how she loved these two boys. Their dreams were even more important than her own. "I did, and that means we'll be a family—like in your drawing, Jacob. And in your writing, Joseph."

"We want you to know that you're an important part of this decision," Nick clarified. "I guess what I'm saying is... I'd like to be your *dat*, if that's okay."

For their answer, both boys launched themselves into Nick's arms. And it was when Deborah saw that, when she saw the man she loved holding the boys who meant so much to her, that tears slipped down Deborah's face.

"Don't cry, *Mamm*." Joseph shifted to sit beside her. "This is a *gut* thing."

"*Ya*, it is." Jacob turned his attention to Blue, who had dropped down onto the quilt beside them. "Hear that, Blue? You're going to be our dog."

And then both boys were on their feet. Jacob pulled a ball from his pocket. He threw it, and Joseph and Blue took off running, Jacob only a few steps behind.

Deborah and Nick stood, then moved off the old quilt. She reached for the blanket, began to fold it, but Nick took it from her and set it down on the ground, next to the mason jars. He turned her to face the pond and beyond that the boys and the house. He stood behind her, his arms around her, and pulled her close.

"I love you, Deborah."

"I love you, Nick." She tilted her head back to look

at him. "This is going to throw a lot of kinks into your five-year plan."

"Indeed, it is."

Now she spun in his arms, touched his face and softly kissed his lips. Foreheads touching, she whispered, "And to think it all started with fake dating."

"Best idea you ever had."

"My boys can be a lot of trouble," she admitted.

"Double trouble."

Then he laughed, and she did, too. As the fall sun tilted toward the western horizon, covering the land with golden rays, they walked back toward home, following the dog and the two boys. It seemed to Deborah that together—as a family—they were walking into their future.

Epilogue

A workday was scheduled in March, and Nick's home was gutted, then rebuilt. It was done ahead of his five-year plan. It was done for his family.

The wedding took place on a beautiful April afternoon. The weather allowed for an outdoor celebration that was held at Deborah's parents' farm, back by the pond—the very same place that Nick had asked her to marry him. The same place that Jacob and Joseph had described in their schoolwork.

Deborah wore a pale green dress.

Nick wore black pants and a new white shirt.

Jacob and Joseph sported new hats as well as their Sunday best clothes. Jacob had a spot of mud on his pants that Deborah pretended not to notice. Joseph kept straightening his suspenders.

Someone had even thought to bathe Blue.

Bishop Ezekiel smiled at the boys and the dog, who sat in the front row. Then he turned his attention to Deborah and Nick.

"Do you, Nick Stoltzfus, and you, Deborah Mast, vow to remain together until death?"

"We do," they said in unison.

"And will you both be loyal and care for each other... even during, especially during, times of adversity?"

"We will."

"And during affliction?"

"Yes."

"And during sickness?"

"We've already done all that," Jacob muttered to Joseph, who hushed him.

Nick's smile grew even wider, and Deborah felt as if her heart literally hurt from the joy and importance of the moment.

"We will," they both said.

Ezekiel carefully shut his Bible, running a weathered hand over the well-worn cover. Then he tucked it under his arm, and reached out for Deborah and Nick. He placed his hand over theirs.

"All of your neighbors, *freinden* and family gathered here today will pray for you and your marriage and your family. As your bishop and friend, I will pray for you. We all wish you the blessing and mercy of *Gotte*."

He turned them gently to face the crowd.

Deborah looked out through tear-filled eyes. The day had been perfect.

And then Blue caught sight of Oliver. The cat hissed. The dog barked. Joseph threw himself at the dog, but Blue was too fast. Joseph landed on the ground, Jacob helped his *bruder* up, and after looking for permission from their *mamm*, they chased after the dog. Oliver sat primly, cleaning his face.

Nick stepped closer and whispered, "I suspect we will have few boring moments in this family."

"And you're okay with that?"

"I am. In fact, boring is overrated." He intertwined his fingers with hers, and together they walked into the embrace of their friends and family.

* * * * *

Get 3 FREE REWARDS!

We'll send you 2 FREE Books plus a FREE Mystery Gift.

FREE Value Over **$20**

Both the **Love Inspired**® and **Love Inspired**® **Suspense** series feature compelling novels filled with inspirational romance, faith, forgiveness and hope.

YES! Please send me 2 FREE novels from the Love Inspired or Love Inspired Suspense series and my FREE gift (gift is worth about $10 retail). After receiving them, if I don't wish to receive any more books, I can return the shipping statement marked "cancel." If I don't cancel, I will receive 6 brand-new Love Inspired Larger-Print books or Love Inspired Suspense Larger-Print books every month and be billed just $6.49 each in the U.S. or $6.74 each in Canada. That is a savings of at least 16% off the cover price. It's quite a bargain! Shipping and handling is just 50¢ per book in the U.S. and $1.25 per book in Canada.* I understand that accepting the 2 free books and gift places me under no obligation to buy anything. I can always return a shipment and cancel at any time by calling the number below. The free books and gift are mine to keep no matter what I decide.

Choose one: ☐ **Love Inspired Larger-Print** (122/322 BPA GRPA) ☐ **Love Inspired Suspense Larger-Print** (107/307 BPA GRPA) ☐ **Or Try Both!** (122/322 & 107/307 BPA GRRP)

Name (please print)

Address   Apt. #

City   State/Province   Zip/Postal Code

Email: Please check this box ☐ if you would like to receive newsletters and promotional emails from Harlequin Enterprises ULC and its affiliates. You can unsubscribe anytime.

Mail to the **Harlequin Reader Service:**
IN U.S.A.: P.O. Box 1341, Buffalo, NY 14240-8531
IN CANADA: P.O. Box 603, Fort Erie, Ontario L2A 5X3

*Want to try 2 free books from another series? Call 1-800-873-8635 or visit www.ReaderService.com.

HARLEQUIN
PLUS

Try the best multimedia
subscription service for romance
readers like you!

Read, Watch and Play.

Experience the easiest way to get
the romance content you crave.

Start your **FREE TRIAL** at
<u>www.harlequinplus.com/freetrial</u>.